Frank Zappa
FAQ

Frank Zappa FAQ

All That's Left to Know About the Father of Invention

John Corcelli

Backbeat
Books

An Imprint of Hal Leonard Corporation

Published in 2016 by Backbeat Books
An Imprint of Hal Leonard Corporation
7777 West Bluemound Road
Milwaukee, WI 53213

Trade Book Division Editorial Offices
33 Plymouth St., Montclair, NJ 07042

All images are from the author's collection, unless otherwise noted.

Excerpts from *The Real Frank Zappa Book*: Reprinted with the permission of Simon & Schuster, Inc., from THE REAL FRANK ZAPPA BOOK by Frank Zappa with Peter Occhiogrosso. Copyright © 1989 Frank Zappa. All rights reserved.

The FAQ series was conceived by Robert Rodriguez and developed with Stuart Shea.

Printed in the United States of America

Book design by Snow Creative

Library of Congress Cataloging-in-Publication Data

Names: Corcelli, John, author.
Title: Frank Zappa FAQ : all that's left to know about the father of invention / John Corcelli.
Description: Montclair, NJ : Backbeat Books, 2016. | Series: FAQS series | Includes bibliographical references, discography, and index.
Identifiers: LCCN 2015043396 | ISBN 9781617136030 (pbk.)
Subjects: LCSH: Zappa, Frank—Miscellanea.
Classification: LCC ML410.Z285 C67 2016 | DDC 782.42166092—dc23
LC record available at http://lccn.loc.gov/2015043396

www.backbeatbooks.com

"A genius is the one most like himself."
—*Thelonious Monk*

Contents

Foreword ix

Acknowledgments xi

Introduction xiii

1 "Who I Am Not": Frank Zappa's Origins 1
2 All Good Music: Zappa's Musical Influences 11
3 A Day That Will Live in Infamy: Mother's Day 1965 25
4 Unemployable: The Mothers of Invention 32
5 Noodling: Zappa and the Jazz Influence 39
6 Beefheart vs. Zappa: A Clash of Icons 44
7 Mr. Dad, Frank Zappa: The Artist as Parent 51
8 No Dope-Heads: Zappa's Drug-Free Zone 57
9 Welcome to the Machine: Zappa and the Record Business 61
10 Liking the Sound of His Own Voice: Choice Quotations 72
11 Zappa and His Fans: A Cultivated Audience 78
12 Send-Ups: Zappa Lampoons the Beatles, Bob Dylan, and Michael Jackson 83
13 Today's Lesson: Does Humor Belong in Music? 90
14 The Recordings: A Curated Look at the Zappa Collection 106
15 Bootlegs: Zappa and the Power of Ownership 133
16 The Gift That Keeps On Giving: Zappa's Archives and the UMRK 137
17 Modern Sounds: Zappa Goes Digital 143
18 A Man's Man: What Women Think About Zappa's Music 153
19 A Guitarist's Guitar Player: Zappa as Instrumentalist 161
20 We'll Fix It in Post: Overdubs Galore 169
21 On the Road: Opening Acts Get a Shot 174
22 The Woodstock Festival Without Zappa: The Mothers Make Other Plans 178
23 Best to Prepare: Auditioning for Frank Zappa 181
24 Playing Zappa's Music: Insights from His Musicians 186
25 Annus Horribillis: 1988 190
26 Music Theories: Zappa's "Conceptual Continuity" 198

27 Not a Place to Stay: *200 Motels*   203
28 Steal This Video: Frank Zappa's Visual Productions   211
29 A Medium with His Message: Selected TV Appearances   218
30 User Discretion Advised: Zappa and the Politics of Censorship   223
31 Yearbook Signing: Zappa Alumni   229
32 Father and Son: Zappa's Legacy, Part 1   260
33 Cover Bands: Zappa's Legacy, Part 2   266

Recommended Reading: The Real Frank Zappa Books   273
Complete Discography   277
Selected Bibliography   285
Index   289

Foreword

I've been a rabid Frank Zappa fan since I first saw his band the Mothers of Invention in a small club in Philadelphia called the Electric Factory in February of 1969. I was fourteen years old.

Prior to that event, I had gone to that very club to see the coolest "underground music" bands of the day: the Flock, the Byrds, Jethro Tull, and many more. This was before Woodstock, so you could see these incredible acts in a small club. I saw the Who do "Tommy" in this tiny club!

Standing out above all the others was the Mothers of Invention. As soon as Zappa stepped onto the stage, I thought this had to be the coolest fucking rock star I had ever seen. He was as witty and sardonic as anyone can imagine. The band opened with "Uncle Meat," the title track of the album that hadn't been released yet. The show ended with "King Kong," also from that album.

"Uncle Meat" was stunning. I had never heard music like that before. And "King Kong" started my love affair with modal jazz.

After decades of learning how to play and arrange jazz and all sorts of other music, I came back to Zappa after attending an event called Zappa's Universe. Frank was supposed to be there, but it had just been disclosed that he was seriously ill.

Mike Keneally, the guitarist and musical director of Zappa's Universe was beyond belief. I was so inspired, I dropped everything I was doing and started arranging a bunch of my favorite Zappa tunes for my big band.

Frank died soon after. It was then I started playing my arrangements of Frank's music live, and I haven't stopped in twenty-two years!

Frank is my biggest inspiration. I believe his genius is of such otherworldly depth that he belongs in the same category as the greatest composers. I have learned so much by transcribing his music.

John Corcelli's book is an invaluable addition to the tomes written about Zappa. It's very well researched and insightful. I'm a total Zappa-phile, so if John was wrong about any of it, I'd know!

Ed Palermo, musician, arranger and leader
of the Ed Palermo Big Band
April 2016

Acknowledgments

Like the proverbial child being raised by a village, I enjoyed the help, inspiration, and support of a few people during the writing of this book. Be it a lead to a Zappa fan, an obscure album or video, or a small discovery that I would have missed during the course of my research, it all mattered, and I am grateful.

My sincere gratitude goes to my wife, Helena, for her sharp eye in tracking the images in this book. You are my favorite. To my family, whose love and support made a real difference, and to Kevin Courrier, a true "Zappa Scholar," who recommended me for this prestigious gig. Special thanks to my agent, Mr. Robert Lecker, and my resilient colleagues at the Canadian Broadcasting Corporation in Toronto. Special thanks to Bernadette Malavarca, Tom Seabrook, and the rest of the Backbeat Books team.

And now the honor roll: Roman Garcia Albertos, Michael Alexic, Tobi Baumhard, Arthur Barrow, John Bell, Marlene Black, Nicole Blain, Laura Boyd-Clowes, CJRT-FM, CKLN-FM, Donald Brackett, Rebecca Bruton, David Churchill, Peggy Corcelli, Mark Clamen and the Critics At Large, Howard Cramer, Mick Ekers, Havoc Franklin, Tina Grohowski, Greg Heard, Bärbel Hoppe, Bob and Ken Jones, Tim Keele, Dan Kopilovich, Maureen and Martin, Tom Metuzals, Allan Morris, Ed Palermo, Tony Palmer, Dean Ples, Grace Quinn, Avo Raup, Dan Reynish, Mark Rheaume, Shlomo Schwartzberg, Adrian Shuman, Kimberly Silk, Ashley Margaret Slack, Thomas Stewart, Hitesh Tailor, Julian Tuck, United Mutations, Hannah Webb, Barrie Zwicker, Patrice "Candy" Zappa, and Frank Vincent Zappa.

Introduction

On the outside of a refurbished two-story building at the corner of Hastings Ave. and Queen Street E. in Toronto, Ontario, Canada, hangs a large, color illustration of a man's face with long black hair and a moustache. He has a sly expression, with one eyebrow raised and the hint of smirk around the mouth. Beneath it is a caption: "Stupidity has a certain charm. Ignorance does not. Frank Zappa."

In a small park in Vilnius, Lithuania, can be found a tall steel pedestal with a bust of Frank Zappa on top of it. It was created by Konstantinas Bogdanas and erected in 1995, even though Zappa never played there and has no ties to the city or the country.

On September 19, 2010, at the Pratt Library in Baltimore, Maryland—the birthplace of Frank Zappa—it was officially declared "Frank Zappa Day" by municipal officials. A bronze bust of Zappa was unveiled, with members of his family in attendance among a crowd of 3,000 people.

On July 20, 2014, Adrian Belew, a former member of Zappa's band, posted a Facebook selfie beside a bust of Frank Zappa while touring in Bad Doberan, Germany. Forged by the Czech sculptor Vaclav Cesak, it sits permanently in a small park, about waist-high above the ground.

Enter the words "Frank Zappa" into Google and you get over eleven million results.

So what's all the fuss about?

During his lifetime, Frank Zappa released sixty-two albums, produced several films and videos, wrote a couple of books, and toured extensively, yet his music is widely considered too difficult to play or just too complicated for mainstream audiences to hear. Despite the challenges of the music business and limited airplay from commercial radio, Zappa's recordings have never gone out of print for very long. In fact, since his death in 1993, another thirty-eight albums have been released from his archives. His son Dweezil now leads a band called Zappa Plays Zappa, which has taken up the mantle of Frank's music, bringing it to new audiences around the world.

To define the man easily reduces us to a list: composer, musician, charismatic bandleader, movie producer, singer, political activist, father, husband, and occasional talk show guest. But a list is superficial. The monuments are permanent: physical reminders of the man and his contributions to art and politics. Yet the name "Frank Zappa" remains a bit of a mystery to many people.

I first heard the song "Dirty Love" (on Toronto radio station CHUM-FM, believe it or not) when I was about sixteen years of age. It was my musical gateway into the world of Frank Zappa I loved its lyrical wit and its tightly arranged musical hooks. That led to my first Zappa album, *Over-Nite Sensation* (1973), and I've been a fan ever since.

As a musician, I really appreciate the depth and breadth of his compositions and now, at age fifty-seven, I'm inspired by Zappa's music even more. But I'm still trying to keep up with him. He was an artist who created his own niche and cultivated it until he died. Consider the fact that his albums continue to sell, and how the popularity of his works is such that they are now part of fake books for jazz bands and scored for classical orchestras around the world. A large constituency of people would agree that Frank Zappa remains one of the most important artists of the twentieth century, and his legacy continues to evolve. In January 2016, the Sundance Film Festival premiered a documentary by Thorsten Schütte called *Eat That Question: Frank Zappa in His Own Words*. In March, American director Alex Winter launched a Kickstarter campaign that raised over a million dollars to preserve and restore Zappa's archives. Winter's documentary called *Who The F*@% Is Frank Zappa?* is expected by 2017. In April, Dweezil Zappa made the *New York Times* in a story about the Zappa Family Trust that said he was in violation of copyright if he toured under the name "Zappa Plays Zappa." The story created a rift between Dweezil and his younger brother Ahmet. (In a 1,500-word open letter on Facebook, Ahmet responded by dismissing many of the accusations Dweezil made and offering reconciliation.)

This is an un-complex book aimed at telling the complex story of Frank Zappa. It's set up in three sections: "biography" (the origins of Zappa; where he was born, where he went to school, etc.), "music" (a survey of his recordings, his playing style, and his use of humor in his songs), and "odds and ends" (which gathers miscellaneous information about Zappa's former bandmates, his gear, and other subjects). Within these sections I offer up interesting facts about the man's history and the evolution of his work. Consider it a guide or gateway into Zappa's unique approach to satire, composing, and politics. To paraphrase the man himself: just what the world needs . . . another book about Frank Zappa.

Frank Zappa
FAQ

"Who I Am Not"

Frank Zappa's Origins

In a 1979 interview with *Musician* magazine, when asked by writer Dan Forte about his ethnic origins, Zappa replied, "I'm a Mediterranean mongrel. I'm Italian, Greek, Arab, and French." Born in Baltimore, Maryland, on December 21, 1940, Frank Vincent Zappa was the first child to parents Francis and Rose Marie ("Rosie") Zappa. His paternal grandparents had immigrated to Baltimore from Sicily in 1908, to escape poverty and start a new life. Zappa's father, who was born in Partinico, Sicily, was three years old at the time. Zappa's mother, Rose Marie Colimore, was born in Baltimore in 1912 to a large, eleven-member family. Her family was part Sicilian and part French, and she was now a part of the great melting pot known as the United States.

In America in the early part of the twentieth century, the sooner you assimilated into the culture, the better chance you had of getting an education, finding a job, and having the ability to support your family. This was particularly important to Frank's father, who was able to complete high school and go on to college. Frank's mother finished high school in 1931, just as the Depression was taking hold of the economy, but two years later she got a job at the French Tobacco Company as a typist, at $20 a week. Francis and Rose Marie met socially in 1935 and dated for four years, eventually getting married in 1939. According to Candy Zappa, Frank's sister, their aunt Fifi had introduced them to each other at a soiree at the Italian consulate in Baltimore.

Frank's dad had an aptitude for mathematics and chemistry. When the United States declared war on Italy in 1941, Francis Zappa, like many Italian-Americans at the time, didn't enjoy the resentment he felt from non-Italians. Italians were ostracized and considered traitors if they sided with Italy against the United States—at least by the paranoid minds of the Federal Bureau of Investigation, which occasionally arrested the so-called treasonous supporters of Fascism on the home front. Italians quickly put their patriotism to the test by joining the armed forces or working in the defense industry.

Like many of his generation, Francis Zappa exhibited his patriotism by getting a job with the navy, which took him to the city of Opa-Locka, Florida, south of Miami. It was a move that benefited his eldest son, who suffered from asthma. Young Frank's condition was virtually cured in the short time he lived in the Southern climate of Florida. The family—which now included Frank's brother, Robert—remained there for a few years until their mother got homesick and wanted to return to Baltimore. (In his autobiography, Frank lists ten memories of his time there. "Number 10: we went back to Baltimore and I got sick again.") According to Candy Zappa, in her short memoir *My Brother Was a Mother*, the return to Maryland came about after her mother developed an abscessed tooth and wanted it treated by her dentist in Baltimore. Her father packed up the whole family, because it wouldn't have looked good for Rose Marie to return by herself. As Candy puts it, "If Mom went back there alone, her mother and sister would try to keep her there, so he [Francis] figured that if he was there too, that wouldn't happen. He was right."

The Zappa family moved to a house in Edgewood, Maryland, home of a US Navy chemical factory that produced mustard gas. Francis took a job here as a chemist and often brought his work home, literally, for his eldest son to play with. Beakers, flasks, and petri dishes found their way into the house, along with liquid mercury, making Frank's bedroom a chemistry lab all its own. As he admits in his autobiography, *The Real Frank Zappa Book*, "By the time I was six years old I knew how to make gunpowder; I knew what the ingredients were and I couldn't wait to get them all together and make some."

This fascination with chemistry made a deep impression on his health as well as his attitude regarding the power of chemicals. During his childhood, Zappa spent a lot of time in bed, sick with either flu or some respiratory infection, so he passed the time reading comics and magazines and making experiments. It was suggested by author Barry Miles, in his biography of Zappa, that the cause of Frank's illnesses was probably environmental, considering where he was living at the time.

California, Here We Come

Due to his son's poor health, Zappa's father took a job as a teacher of metallurgy at the US Naval Postgraduate School in the much warmer location of Monterey, California, in 1951. The family later moved to the nearby quiet community of Pacific Grove. Frank was eleven years of age and now the eldest of four children, following the arrival of brother Carl (born in September 1947) and sister Patrice, nicknamed Candy, who was born in March 1951.

It was a big move, and one that shaped Frank Zappa socially. In an interview with Kurt Loder, cited by Neil Slaven in his book *Electric Don Quixote*, Zappa said that there was little time to form friendships in the anonymous housing projects in which the family lived: "I was moving around all the time and living in mixed company, so I never had that real strong meatball sandwich identity." School held little interest for him in those formative years, but he did like music, and he jumped at the chance to play the drums when teacher Keith McKillop introduced him to the instrument at summer school. Zappa learned to play rudiments in percussion on a single snare drum and even composed his first piece of music, which he called "Mice," at the age of twelve, performing it solo at a season-ending concert.

In 1954, the family moved to Claremont, California, located between Los Angeles and San Bernardino, after Zappa's father once again had to take a job on the government's terms as a metallurgist. One year later, they moved to El Cajon, east of San Diego, where Zappa's dad took an assignment at the Atlas missile project manufacturer Convair. Entering his teen years, Frank went to three different high schools, getting into trouble for not attending class or being caught smoking while wearing his high-school band uniform (the latter infraction coming at Mission Bay High School in San Diego). By 1957, the family had moved, once again, to the hybrid community known as Lancaster, located in the Antelope Valley of the Mojave Desert. It was the home of alfalfa farmers and military families who worked at the Muroc Air Force Base (later known as Edwards).

Frank attended Antelope Valley Union High School, home to over 2,500 students at the time, which he found wanting because most of the courses didn't engage him. He developed a reputation for telling jokes in class and taking up a radical, anti-authoritarian manner. As he told Dan Forte in the August 1979 issue of *Musician*, "I would refuse to sing the school song; I would refuse to salute the flag; I would wear weird things to school; I would get in trouble all the time, and get thrown out of school." But not all was lost, because in those days, radical or troublesome students ended up in art class, where they could learn how to paint or make 8mm films. For Zappa, it was an early opportunity to find his voice and learn how to do things on his own: a combination of independent thought and artistic expression. It was also a chance for him to work without too many academic restrictions. Like the bedroom that had been his practice lab, high school gave him the chance to develop his own experiments using different media.

Frank Zappa, Painter

In 1957, Zappa entered a state art competition and won first prize for a painting called "Family Room." It was an abstract work reflecting the theme of that year's award, "Symphony of Living." He was interviewed and photographed by the Antelope Valley High School (AVHS) newspaper, by which he was asked if he intended to pursue a career in art. He replied that he preferred composing music to painting (or writing for that matter), thus setting his own path at the age of seventeen. By this time, Zappa was playing drums in an eight-piece R&B band known as the Blackouts. He was also taking music classes and composing his own "classical" works. Nearing graduation in 1958, albeit short a few credits, Zappa was given the chance to conduct the AVHS orchestra, which performed two of his own works, "Sleeping in a Jar" and "A Pound for a Brown on a Bus."

In 1959, Zappa took a course in harmony at the Antelope Valley Junior College in Lancaster. That same year, he was given the chance to write the score for writer Don Cerveris's low-budget western film *Run Home Slow*. Cerveris had been Zappa's English teacher in high school; he was unable to release his film until 1965 due to financial struggles. You can see and hear the music from the opening credits on YouTube; selections from it also appear on the *Mystery Disc* (1985) and *The Lost Episodes* (1993).

Life in Lancaster, California, was as desolate as the geography. In an interview with Bobby Marquis on CKCU-FM, first broadcast August 12, 2015, his brother, Bobby Zappa, said that he "didn't like living there, I don't think Frank did either. It was the kind of town where the kids that we went to school with were the sons and daughters of people who owned alfalfa farms and cattle ranches . . . and people who worked in the aircraft industry. We were pretty much outsiders."

For the restless Frank Zappa, music was an important diversion that not only prevented him from getting bored but also tapped something in his heart that never left him. So, if the chance to listen to a jukebox in a local restaurant presented itself, Zappa filled the device with every quarter he had. Today, young people have Pandora or YouTube or iTunes as a means to hear new music, but after World War II into the sixties, jukeboxes were, besides radio, the most popular devices used to hear new recordings. They were found in pool halls, bars, restaurants, barber shops, bowling alleys, and high-school gymnasiums. Using his initiative, Zappa got to know the people who serviced the jukebox at a local restaurant and promised to feed the machine with coins if they filled it with some of his requests. The owner agreed, and, for a couple of years, Zappa used it to listen to different types of music, including jazz innovator Charlie Parker and blues musician Johnny "Guitar" Watson. At sixteen he got a job as a buyer at a record store, stocking R&B singles by the Dells, Little Richard, and blues great Clarence "Gatemouth" Brown. He was also getting into contemporary classical music by Edgard Varèse and Igor Stravinsky. He would continue to pursue a self-directed education throughout his life.

Zappa Meets Van Vliet

In 1957, Zappa met Don Vliet in high school. They shared an interest in R&B music and immediately connected. Vliet (born in 1941) was an only child who dropped out of high school in order to take care of the family bread-truck business after his father suffered a heart attack that left him unable to work. Vliet's non-conformist attitude and love of R&B helped create a friendship that lasted for years. A skilled harmonica player and painter, he later changed his surname to Van Vliet to mark his Dutch heritage. But it was Frank Zappa who came up with his most popular nickname, Captain Beefheart, when his art career stalled and he decided to go into music in 1963.

In these formative years, Vliet's friendship with Zappa was key to their mutual artistic growth. It was a fruitful experience for the pair who, as white working-class kids, opted for the subversive sounds of blues and R&B—which to them were non-conformist styles of music—instead of pop. Zappa's parents often admonished him for tuning the car radio to R&B stations. As Little Richard once said of white kids who were trying to hide their interest in rock 'n' roll in the fifties, "They may have had Pat Boone on top of the dresser, but they had Little Richard *in* the dresser." (Boone covered several songs by Little Richard and made them palatable to conservative parents and radio stations.) For Zappa and Vliet, the black music they collected as teens was the artistic gasoline that fueled their lives. (For more on their complicated relationship as artists, see the "Beefheart vs. Zappa" chapter later in the book.)

In 1959, the Zappa family moved back to Claremont, California, about thirty miles (or fifty kilometers) east of Los Angeles. Francis Zappa got another job, while his eldest son, who was now in closer proximity to L.A. and Hollywood, moved out of the house. He found a small apartment in Echo Park but lasted barely a year there due to having little money and a poor diet. He suffered from stomach ulcers and eventually moved back home, much to the delight of his mother. Zappa spent the next couple of years following his muse and getting more music education at the Antelope Valley Junior College. He took courses in harmony and fundamental piano while continuing to play guitar at home.

One of Zappa's instructors, Joyce Shannon, told him she felt he had the aptitude and work ethic necessary to learn how to compose music. Encouraged by this, Zappa enrolled in 1960 at Chaffee Junior College in Alta Loma, California, where he studied music and met girls his own age. One of them was fellow student Kathryn (Kay) Sherman. By the summer of that year they had moved in together, much to the annoyance of Zappa's parents. In fact, his father didn't speak to him for months as a way of punishing his son for his "anti-Catholic" behavior.

All that changed at the end of December when Zappa married Sherman just after his twentieth birthday. Sherman was twenty-one, with a full-time job in a bank, and her steady income provided the young guitarist with the chance to branch out as a musician. Zappa took part-time jobs as a way of making ends meet, including a gig at the Nile Running Greeting Card studio in Claremont. By all accounts, it was a happy marriage for the first few months, but Zappa's overriding interest in music and recording eventually put a strain on his relationship with Kay.

Paul Buff and Studio Z

In 1963, Zappa used the money he earned from scoring *Run Home Slow* to take over a failing operation known as the PAL Studio, located in Cucamonga, California, and previously owned by Paul Buff, a retired navy technician who built most of its equipment by hand. (Buff died on March 14, 2015, at age seventy-eight.) Zappa had spent the previous three years there under Buff's tutelage, learning the fine art of editing tape, recording techniques, and studio management.

Considering Zappa's appetite for all things musical, he probably spent more time in the studio than he did at home, which no doubt contributed to the fracturing of his marriage to Kay. By the end of that year, they had separated. Frank moved into the studio, renaming it Studio Z, and Kay filed for divorce. At that point, Zappa focused most of his time on learning how to write, record, and play his own music in his own studio. It was another lab for his musical experiments—one that brought him limited financial success but created a number of important connections with musicians and singers, including vocalist Ray Collins. Collins invited Zappa to play with his R&B group, the Soul Giants, later to become the Mothers of Invention.

Zappa's studio work in 1964 laid the groundwork for his methodical approach to recording and, more importantly, his desire to archive everything he did. Some of the early recordings can be heard on *Mystery Disc* (1998), which includes a short segment featuring Don Van Vliet called "Opening Night at Studio Z." Several other ditties from those early years capture his musical and spoken-word experiments. He was also equipped to produce his own films and film scores, continuing an interest in moviemaking that had begun in high school. One of these early projects was *Captain Beefheart vs. The Grunt People*, a sci-fi movie treatment. Zappa was running his own business, full-time, at the age of twenty-four, which gave him a hands-on business acumen that never left him. He worked hard to build a clientele by taking a steady flow of projects from paying customers. His studio was available for any kind of recording project, from demo tapes to soundtracks. But as word spread, so too did the rumors of illegal activities in Studio Z.

Zappa Gets Arrested

On March 26, 1965, in an effort to bust an apparent porn operation, Sgt. Jim Willis of the San Bernardino County Sheriff's office's vice squad arrested Zappa for making an audio sex tape. Six months earlier, in a classic case of entrapment, Willis, who suspected criminal activity at Studio Z, had offered Zappa $100 to make a sex tape featuring the sounds of a man and woman on a squeaky bed. Zappa took the job but never heard from him again. Meanwhile, Willis put Zappa's place of business under surveillance, on the assumption that it was a pornography studio. Eventually, Zappa and his girlfriend at the time, Lorraine Belcher, were charged with conspiracy to commit pornography, for which the maximum penalty was twenty years in jail.

The story made the front page of the local newspaper the day after the arrest: "Vice Squad Raids Local Film Studio" was the headline of the *Daily Report* dated March 27, 1965. Police confiscated eighty hours of tape, and Zappa was arraigned a week later. Fortunately, support came from Paul Buff, the studio's former owner, and Zappa's father, who put up $1,500 to cover the cost of a lawyer, who in turn advised Frank to plead "no contest" to the charges. During the short trial, the judge called the prosecution and defense lawyers into his office, along with Frank, to hear the tape in question. According to Barry Miles, in his biography of Zappa, the judge found the tape hilarious and not worthy of a serious penalty. The charges against Lorraine Belcher were dropped completely, while Zappa's charge was reduced to a misdemeanor (instead of the higher crime of a felony). His sentence was reduced to six months in jail, with all but ten days suspended.

Zappa served the ten days, which changed his life forever. The jail he was placed in was an overcrowded, filthy, and highly repressive place known as Tank C. Ten days in this dreadful place was all it took to fundamentally change Zappa's outlook on life and liberty. In his autobiography, Zappa offers up his version of the starkness of the place and softens his disgust by describing a few of the characters he came across. These included a pair of guys known as the "chow hounds," who ate everything they could, including the repulsive food other inmates failed to finish. He concludes that jail had given him a "good whiff" of the state laws in California and the failure of the legal system in general.

To his biographers, including Barry Miles and Ben Watson, Zappa's time in Tank C was transformative. When he got out, Zappa no longer trusted authority, he questioned the education system, and he made it a point to challenge the very basis of the American way of life: the US Constitution. He also wrote two songs about his experience there: "San Ber'dino," from *One Size Fits All* (1975), and a more frightening track originally featured on *Zoot Allures* (1976) called "The Torture Never Stops," on which Zappa holds nothing back in his description of a "dungeon of despair."

Shortly after his release in the spring of 1965, Zappa closed his studio and became the new guitarist with the Soul Giants.

The Zappa Family

In his autobiography, Zappa reveals little about his family life outside of his disdain for moving frequently during his childhood and the volatile relationship he had with his parents. In "Chapter for My Dad," he writes that although he found his father "interesting," they didn't get along very well. About the only things they had in common were smoking and an agreement to disagree. Once Frank had achieved some success in the music business, he bought his parents a house. This gift probably eased their relationship, as revealed in a *Life* magazine portrait in 1971 featuring rock stars and their parents at home. Ironically, the picture of the Zappas was taken in Frank's house in Los Angeles, not at his parents' place where the other images in the magazine were shot. But for the most part, Zappa's lifestyle was completely different from that of his conservative parents, with whom he maintained a relationship that could best be defined as "civil." The elder Zappa died of heart failure in 1973, at the age of sixty-eight; Rose Marie Zappa died on January 30, 2004, at the age of ninety-two.

Frank's siblings—brothers Robert (aka Bobby) and Carl and sister Patrice, better known as Candy—didn't necessarily fall under the shadow of their older brother in the way that his children would. Bobby played guitar on some of Frank's early recordings, which can be heard on *The Lost Episodes* (1993). He joined the US Marines in 1961 and served during the famous blockade of Cuba in October 1962. After that crisis was averted, Bobby began a tour of duty in Vietnam. When he was discharged, he went into publishing, initially as an editor with McGraw-Hill in New York, which led to management positions at MacMillan, Prentice-Hall, and Simon & Schuster, before he entered semi-retirement in 2002. At that time, he joined the New York City Teaching Fellows program, which hires older, more experienced individuals to teaching positions in "hard to staff" schools. Zappa was posted at a school in the South Bronx. He retired fully in 2014 and decided to write a memoir about his famous brother called *Frankie and Bobby: Growing Up Zappa*, which chronicles his life with Frank from the late forties to 1967. In the aforementioned interview with Bobby Marquis, Bob Zappa said his focus was "building the case for how [Frank] became who he was. What made him be the clear thinker; the musical genius that he was." In other words, describing the formative years in Frank's life, of which Bob was a part.

Carl Zappa appeared in his brother's movie *Uncle Meat* but has generally kept a low profile over the years. He did, however, agree to an online interview with a Russian fan by the name of Vladimir Sovetov, who offered up trivial questions regarding Carl's relationship with his famous sibling. All we learn from the interview is that Carl's favorite album is *Cruising with Ruben & the Jets*. He also once loaned his brother a pair of white gym socks before a concert in the Garrick Theater in New York, as Frank acknowledges on the live album *Roxy & Elsewhere* (1974).

In 2003, Frank's sister Candy published her book *My Brother Was a Mother* about growing up in the Zappa household and being constantly on the move in her early years. It features some insightful personal photographs and memories of her older brother. A second volume was released in 2011, covering her career as a vocalist in the years following Frank's death. Candy was also a huge part of the Zappanale 13, the popular Zappa music festival in Germany, where she remarked, "If I'd known that as a little girl living with him that I would grow up and come to a foreign city and see posters of my brother sitting on a toilet, I wouldn't have believed it." She currently lives in Van Nuys, California, pursuing a part-time career in music that includes performing songs written by Frank.

2

All Good Music

Zappa's Musical Influences

Frank Zappa loved a wide variety of music. His interests ranged from doo-wop to blues, jazz, and the avant-garde. His favorite musicians and composers were equally varied. To imagine his record collection is to see albums by Johnny "Guitar" Watson and Edgard Varèse, Igor Stravinsky and Spike Jones, Charles Ives and the Jewels, Johnny Otis and Charles Mingus, all side by side. Zappa had a facility for music and he was open to hearing new and unusual sounds, no matter where they occurred, regardless of form and genre. He also loved the human voice and heard melody in a conversation.

Zappa knew what he liked and he dismissed the rest, often poking fun at "cowboy music" (country) and pop forms such as disco, which to him was nothing more than the soundtrack to a certain type of fashion and lifestyle. Frank Zappa had a diverse musical personality that distinguished him from everybody else. His ability to incorporate, mix, and occasionally parody all of his influences in his own compositions was one of his greatest talents.

Classical Music

In his youth, Frank Zappa was an avid record collector. He bought singles at first because they were affordable and easy to store. But in 1952 he came upon an article in a worn-out issue of *Look* magazine, dated November 7, 1950, that changed his life. It was a short review of the *Complete Works of Edgard Varèse, Volume 1* by columnist Joseph Roddy. The review was positive and encouraging: "Varèse is unlike anything else in music and well worth knowing."

For the twelve-year-old Zappa, that was a strong recommendation. He went looking for the LP in local record stores, but to no surprise, nobody had it. About a year later, while visiting a friend in La Mesa, California, he checked out a store that had a sale on 45s. To his amazement, there was a copy of the very same LP, albeit a used copy. Zappa negotiated the $5.95 price tag down to $3.75 and walked out of the store with his very first album. He absorbed the liner notes and played the record over and over, not only for himself but also for his friends from high school, who probably didn't appreciate it the same way he did.

For his fifteenth birthday, Zappa was granted the chance to telephone Varèse in New York after asking his mother to pick up the cost of the long-distance call from California in lieu of a gift of five dollars. Louise Varèse answered and said that her husband was in France completing a new work. Varèse never met Zappa, but he did communicate with him by letter. Fortunately, that album is still available today as a digital download on iTunes, and it's worth a listen.

Edgard Varèse

Edgard Varèse was born in France on December 22, 1883. (Zappa was born almost exactly fifty-seven years later, on December 21, 1940.) At the age of ten he was enrolled in a music school in Turin, Italy, and he composed his first opera two years later. Around 1903, after his mother died, Varèse moved to Paris and settled into the French music scene by getting to know composers Erik Satie and Claude Debussy. Debussy once told him to break the rules of music or composition and to forge his own unconventional ideas.

In 1915, having been excused from service in the French army, Varèse moved to New York City, where he found work as a teacher while continuing to compose music. In 1927, he became an American citizen; he remained primarily in New York but enjoyed extended stays in San Francisco, California; Santa Fe, New Mexico; and Paris, France. During this time Varèse was soaking up the industrial sounds of the economically prosperous city and incorporating them into his music. While in New York, Varèse was considered a leader in presenting, directing, and conducting concerts of new music by composers from Europe and the United States. His music was heavy on percussion and evoked the sounds of a modern technological environment, yet it was well received by American audiences at the time.

When Frank Zappa brought home the *Complete Works of Edgard Varèse, Volume 1* (EMS 401), he listened to "Intégrales," written in 1924; "Density 21.5," from 1936; "Ionisation," from 1931; "Octandre," from 1924; and

segments of *Desérts*, completed in 1954. The album is an excellent introduction to Varèse's works, which are full of the dramatic and often dense
sounds Zappa absorbed and later put into his own music. "Ionisation"
was written for percussion instruments, with no discernable melody or
harmonic structure. The only musical tones in the piece are from bells
and clusters of piano chords. The sound that links the piece together is
that of a siren winding up and down at predetermined points in the score.
Much like the work of Spike Jones, whose tightly scripted musical madness
encouraged in Zappa the idea of adding humor to his music, "Ionisation"

Varèse in New York City, c.1915   *Library of Congress*

offered a true alternative to conventional music by creating a wider, more varied palette of sounds.

Igor Stravinsky

Zappa's record collection expanded again when he bought an RCA Camden recording of *The Rite of Spring* by Igor Stravinsky. This, Zappa's second LP, was performed by the World-Wide Symphony Orchestra, which was a pseudonym for the Boston Symphony Orchestra, conducted by Pierre Monteux. Anyone familiar with this work knows that it is Stravinsky's *tour de force*, an orchestral celebration of life written for the 1913 season of *Ballets Russes* in Paris. The choreographer was the Russian great Vaslav Nijinsky, who also starred in the ballet.

To put it simply, Zappa was amazed by Stravinsky's *Rite of Spring*, just as audiences today are amazed by its earthy, percussive rhythms and sharply contrasting moods. It has a sense of the mysterious about it, too. As with so many great works that are highly revered today, however, the critics at the time quickly dismissed the music, while the incensed audience actually started arguing over it in the hall as they poured into the streets of Paris.

Anton Webern

It was Zappa's high school music teacher, Mr. Kavelman, who introduced him to the music of Anton Webern. The LP was on Dial Records and featured the Pro Arte Quartet on side one and the Paris Chamber Orchestra on side two. Zappa soon picked up his own copy. The album features Webern's Five Movements for String Quartet, Op. 5, Six Bagatelles for String Quartet, Op. 9, and his Symphony, Op. 21, from 1928.

Webern was born in Vienna, Austria, on December 3, 1883. His mother was a singer and pianist and his father a civil servant, so he had the means and encouragement to study music. He attended Vienna University in 1902 to study composing. While he was there, he was introduced to fellow Austrians Arnold Schoenberg and Alban Berg, two of the leading composers of a revolutionary new form of music called the "twelve-tone technique"—essentially a method of composing music without a key signature, using all twelve tones of the chromatic scale. No emphasis is given to any one note in the scale as it relates to the others, but they all have to be sounded equally in number, without repetition.

Stravinsky around the time of the premiere of *The Rite of Spring*.   *Library of Congress*

The sound of this music isn't atonal, like Varèse's, but it is unusual to hear. Webern used this technique in all of his music, but it was his string quartets and Symphony, Op. 21 that were the most interesting to Zappa. In an interview with Mike Douglas in 1976, Zappa said he listened to Webern's quartets when he wanted to relax.

Charles Ives

Charles Ives wasn't the first but was probably the best example of an artist who didn't "quit his day job" to pursue his muse. He sold insurance on the advice of his father, George, who he respected. George Ives had served as a bandleader in the US Army during the American Civil War. When the war ended in 1865, he returned home to Danbury, Connecticut, to raise a family and scratch out a living as a music teacher, bandleader, and composer. Charles was born in 1874 and grew up in a musical house that took its weekly inspiration from church hymns and its daily inspiration from the folk songs of Stephen Foster.

George encouraged Charles to learn piano and the rudiments of harmony based on European music theory, but he also had an ear for sounds beyond the written page. He taught Charles how to listen to his environment and to use those sounds to compose his own music. For this reason, Charles Ives has often been called "the pioneer of American music." His bold compositional skills went against the standard theories of harmony and composition as had been established in European schools during the nineteenth century.

Ives got his first job in music as the organist at his local church. He was fourteen years of age, and he was encouraged to write music for church services by his father. The earliest among these works is a piece for organ called "Variations on America" that was premiered for the Fourth of July celebrations of 1891. Going forward, Ives finished high school and attended Yale University, where he mixed his academic studies with varsity sports and music composition. Between 1897 and 1906, Ives completed or worked on his first three symphonies, a string quartet, and two works for chamber orchestra called "Central Park in the Dark" and "The Unanswered Question." These latter compositions expressed Ives's interest in the dissonant sounds he heard growing up in New England. His gift was for translating the sounds in his head into musical notes on the page to be played by musicians. His work is structured but it doesn't *sound* that way, which is part of his inventiveness and genius as a composer.

"Central Park in the Dark" is an impressionistic work with a certain amount of emotional tension created by the steady whole notes played by the strings. Ives was recreating the experience of sitting on a bench on a hot summer night. This theme never stops as outbursts of bassoon, clarinet, and piano shake up the listener to the randomness of sound. In the middle of the work we hear two bands crossing paths by playing two different songs popular at the time: "Hello, My Baby" and Sousa's "Washington Post" march. It literally sounds as if the bands run into each other in the middle of the park. It's as funny as it is dissonant. The piece ends as carefully and quietly as it began, leaving the listener a little uneasy.

Even by today's standards, Ives's work stands out as something modern, new, and unromantic. For Zappa, this meant that he too could layer his works and mix tempos, throw in different sounds, and shake the foundations of an audience's expectations. One of the best examples of this is Zappa's instrumental "Charles Ives," as played by the Mothers of Invention in 1969. It's definitely modeled after "Central Park in the Dark," with the horns gracing the main theme punctuated by grunts or wordless vocals from the band and dashes of percussion courtesy of Jimmy Carl Black and Art Tripp III. (It was released on *Vol. 5* of *You Can't Do That on Stage Anymore*.)

In his *Essays Before a Sonata*, Ives goes to considerable and highly rhetorical lengths to explain his music. The notes, which you can read at www.gutenberg.org/ebooks/3673, often read like Zappa's autobiography, as published in 1989, because the two share the same kind of irreverent attitude toward Western conventions of composing music and society's expectations of them. Zappa could easily have written this statement from Charles Ives: "Beauty in music is too often confused with something that lets the ears lie back in an easy chair. Many sounds that we are used to, do not bother us, and for that reason, we are inclined to call them beautiful."

In Chapter 8 of his autobiography, Zappa reproduces a hilarious speech he delivered to the American Society of University Composers (ASUC) in 1984, which he titled "Is New Music Relevant in an Industrial Society?" But for the use of the "F" word, it could have been written by Charles Ives. Zappa was simpatico with Ives because they pushed the boundaries of conventional music while expressing their own personalities, knowing full well that the risk was greater than the reward. Ives composed music in relative obscurity during his own lifetime; during the day, he sold insurance. Zappa didn't have a day job to fall back on during his career, so he had to persevere and work with the "star-maker machinery," as Joni Mitchell called the music business.

When Charles Ives died of heart failure in 1954, most Americans had never heard of him. His music was essentially "discovered" and performed by students of American contemporary music such as Leonard Bernstein and Bernard Herrmann, who composed scores to Hitchcock's films. Herrmann actually promoted Ives's music when he was music director of the CBS Symphony Orchestra in the forties. He conducted a radio broadcast performance of Ives's Symphony No. 3 in 1946. In 1947, in a slightly belated tribute, Ives was awarded the Pulitzer Prize for that symphony, which was written and published in 1910. By the mid-sixties, most of Ives's orchestral music was recorded and available on LP.

For Frank Zappa, Anton Webern, Edgard Varèse, Charles Ives, and Igor Stravinsky wrote music that filled his mind with wonder. Their work informed his work. Among the best examples are Zappa's compositions "The Little House I Used to Live In" from *Burnt Weeny Sandwich* (1970), and "Amnesia Vivace" from *Absolutely Free* (1967) that blends doo-wop vocals with Stravinsky-like precision. Another instrumental worth hearing is the fourteen-minute "When Yuppies Go to Hell" from *Make a Jazz Noise Here*, featuring the 1988 big band. This piece is extraordinary because it showcases Zappa's compositional skills and the freedom he gained by listening to the classical masters he loved and respected. It's music that foreshadows Zappa's late works for the Ensemble Modern on *The Yellow Shark* and his Synclavier music on *Dance Me This*, which was issued in 2015. By now, Zappa was taking musical risks far removed from anything he had written for the Mothers of Invention.

Nicolas Slonimsky

One of the least-known composers in Zappa's sphere of influence was Nicolas Slonimsky. Born in St. Petersburg, Russia, in 1894, he grew up in a working-class family with a strong interest in music. His mother's sister, Isabelle Vengerova, was his piano teacher as a child. She later helped in the funding of the Curtis Institute of Music in Philadelphia in 1924. (Robert Martin, who played with Zappa in the eighties, graduated from that school in 1971.)

Slonimsky immigrated to Paris after the 1917 revolution in Russia and sought work as an accompanist and music teacher. His first important gig was playing piano for the Russian tenor Vladimir Rosing, who toured Europe in recital in the early twenties. That association proved fruitful for the young Slonimsky when Rosing asked him to teach at the newly established Eastman School of Music in Rochester, New York, in 1924. At the time, Rosing was head of the opera curriculum. For the next two years, Slonimsky developed his skills as a composer under the tutelage of fellow Russian Albert Coates and conductor Eugene Goossens, who led the Rochester Philharmonic Orchestra from 1923 to 1931.

Slonimsky moved to Boston in 1926 and got a job as a translator for the Russian composer and conductor Serge Koussevitzky. Koussevitzky was the music director of the Boston Symphony Orchestra from 1924 to 1949. The timing was perfect for Slonimsky, whose interest in contemporary American music offered him the chance to meet and work with composers Henry Cowell and Charles Ives, whose passion for breaking the conventions of European music in America inspired Frank Zappa. Slonimsky founded the Boston Chamber Orchestra in 1927 with a mandate to perform new works by Ives, Cowell, and Varèse. In fact, Slonimsky conducted the world premieres of Ives's "Three Places in New England" in 1931, and, two years later, Varèse's work for thirteen percussionists, "Ionisation"—one of Zappa's favorite pieces of music. Slonimsky recorded the work for Columbia Records, with the results taking up both sides of a 78 when released in March 1933.

For the next thirty years, Slonimsky developed his skills as a musical philosopher or interpolator by writing and publishing a steady diet of critical essays about music and composers. Many of his favorite essays rocked the establishment with their unconventional criticism of some of the most revered composers of our time. They were included in a book called *Lexicon of Musical Invective: Critical Assaults on Composers Since Beethoven's Time*, published in 1953, which Slonimsky compiled. It included music reviews from George Bernard Shaw, Oscar Wilde, and Friedrich Nietzsche (to name but three), all of whom could certainly turn a phrase in their day. W. W. Norton reprinted the book in 2000, with a new introduction by Peter Schickele, aka P.D.Q. Bach, who called it "a supermarket tabloid of classical music criticism." Schickele, an accomplished musician and composer, made a career poking fun at the stiff manner in which classical music was presented in society.

Frank Zappa could easily relate to the radical thinker and his uncompromising point of view since he had one himself, but Slonimsky also provided him with a practical guide to thinking about composition in a different way. His book *Thesaurus of Scales and Melodic Patterns*, first published in 1947, often circulated among musicians such as John Coltrane because it suggested new ways of thinking about improvisation—the quintessential element in jazz—and the kinds of unconventional chord structures that were useful to composers. Zappa once called it "the bible of improvisation."

Zappa was motivated to reach out to Slonimsky after reading the book and learning that the composer lived in Los Angeles (having done a similar thing when he first heard the music of Edgard Varèse years earlier). Zappa invited Slonimsky, who was eighty-seven years of age at the time, to his home to play a couple of his piano pieces. The very next night, December 11, 1981, at a concert in Santa Monica, California, Zappa invited Slonimsky to play his composition "Orion" on electric piano. Slonimsky fondly remembered the performance in 1992, in an interview with Don Menn for the periodical *Zappa!*: "Usually I have just a hundred or two hundred people, but this was a huge audience, and they shouted and everything!" According to the composer, the two became fast friends after the show. They often shared musical ideas and listened to recordings of Zappa's orchestral works together. Slonimsky named his cat Grody-to-the-Max after hearing the phrase from Zappa's daughter Moon.

Slonimsky thought highly of Zappa's orchestral scores, considering them "beautiful ideas," as he puts it in the *Zappa!* article. "It has been my luck to have lived to see the emergence of this totally new type of music which a hundred years ago didn't exist. Zappa sticks to twelve different notes and eleven different intervals. What he does with them in terms of organization is what is so far, far from traditional approaches. That's the secret of his greatness . . . [he] puts musical sounds together and creates something new but not destructive of scales or intervals."

Zappa described what he learned from Slonimsky in an interview with Don Menn at *Guitar Player* magazine in 1992. "I asked him to explain the theory behind the chords in that book [*Thesaurus of Scales and Melodic Patterns*] . . . it's based on the simple idea that if you take an octave or groups of octaves and divide them into proportions other than the way in which normal music is divided, [root, third, fifth, seventh, et cetera] then you wind up with different types of harmony. It never occurred to me that that was the simple logic that was generating all those scales." Most of what Slonimsky and Zappa had in mind can be heard on *Civilization Phaze III* and *Dance Me This*, Zappa's final albums (as covered in chapter 14).

Nicolas Slonimsky died on December 25, 1995, at the age of 101.

Rhythm and Blues, Doo-Wop, and Blues

While the influence of classical music on Zappa loomed large, it was balanced by his love for R&B, blues, and especially the doo-wop groups of the fifties. One of the most prized singles in Zappa's collection was a 45 by the Jewels called "Angel in My Life," released in 1955 on the Imperial label. Imperial was the home to blues great T-Bone Walker, among others. The Jewels were an R&B group from Los Angeles (not to be confused with the sixties girl group from Washington, D.C.).

One day, Zappa took the 45 into music class and asked his music teacher why the song was so good. "Parallel fourths" came the reply from Mr. Kavelman. But Zappa also liked the fact that the band was having a lot of fun playing the music. He also collected singles by the Coasters, Johnny Otis, Hank Ballard and the Midnighters, Don and Dewey, and Jesse Belvin. Zappa loved his R&B singles for their emotional appeal on a shoestring budget. In an interview with Keith Altham in the February 5, 1972, issue of the *NME*, Zappa stated, "The feel of those performances; everything they have is cheap. But the sound that comes out of it is just great, it inspires you."

Doo-wop music, which originated in the large urban centers of the United States, was also a part of Zappa's musical learning curve. Coming out of the poor, black neighborhoods of Chicago, Los Angeles, and New York, these groups usually sang a capella because they couldn't afford instruments, creating a need for deep voices as well as high. The music was simple and accessible, and held no barriers to age or gender. All you had to do was sing from your heart. Most of the songs written and recorded during the genre's best years, from 1940 to 1960, were about romantic love or heartache. The songs never touched on politics or anything overtly sexual. Zappa collected singles by the Penguins, the Spaniels, and the Cadillacs, among others.

In contrast to the sweet sounds of doo-wop, Frank Zappa was also attracted to blues music, particularly the artists who came out of the American South during the mid-fifties. Since Zappa was interested in playing guitar, it stood to reason that he would be attracted to blues musicians who were proficient on their instrument. The most influential among them were Guitar Slim (aka Eddie Jones) from Mississippi, Clarence "Gatemouth" Brown from Texas, and Johnny "Guitar" Watson, who was originally from Texas but grew up in Los Angeles.

Zappa loved the edgy, dirty sound of Guitar Slim, best heard on the hit single "The Things That I Used to Do," released on Specialty Records in 1953. He was always impressed by Brown's guitar playing as an extension of his own personality, which to Zappa was honest and direct. And when he heard Watson's classic instrumental "Space Guitar" (Federal, 1954), it proved such an epiphany that Zappa adjusted the tone of his guitar to match

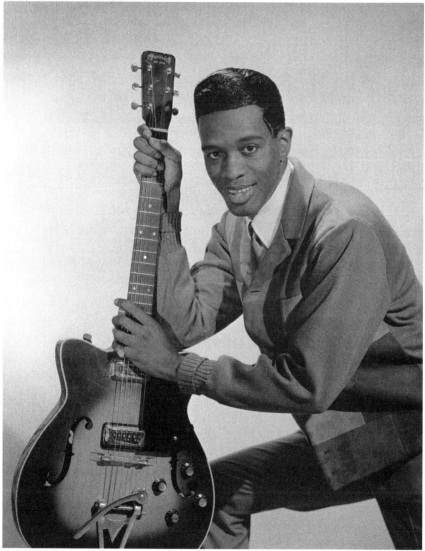

Publicity photo of Johnny Guitar Watson with his "Space Guitar."

CBS Photo Archive/Getty Images

Watson's when he started playing. Another big favorite was "Three Hours Past Midnight," released in 1956. Watson later participated in some of Zappa's own recordings, including providing the voice of "Brown Moses" on *Thing-Fish* and at a concert appearance in L.A., at the Palace Theater, in 1984.

On the inside cover of *Freak Out!*, the 1966 debut album by the Mothers of Invention, no fewer than thirteen blues musicians are named among the 179 "contributors," with Howlin' Wolf, Buddy Guy, and Slim Harpo included, as well as Guitar Slim, Brown, and Watson. (Arnold Schoenberg, Igor Stravinsky, Charles Ives, and Edgard Varèse are also on the list.)

Frank Zappa's Desert Island Picks

This still-popular party trick was played on Frank Zappa in 1989 on a weekly KCRW radio show hosted by John McNally called *Castaway's Choice*. McNally, a Brit who immigrated to the US to attend UCLA in 1977, was inspired by the long-running BBC radio show *Desert Island Discs*. He was impressed by what a person would reveal about themselves through their favorite music. In a story published in the February 25, 1987, issue of *Corsair*, the Santa Monica College newspaper established in 1929, writer Janet Newman asked McNally why his show was different from the British version. "Because American people are very giving when they talk about themselves," he replied, "they are much more open."

Unfortunately, the program itself is no longer available, but Zappa's list of picks was published in the Norwegian music magazine *Monster* in 2002.

1. Octandre (1923) by Edgard Varèse
2. The Royal March from *L'histoire du Soldat* (1918) by Igor Stravinsky
3. *The Rite of Spring* (1911) by Igor Stravinsky
4. Allegretto from Piano Concerto No. 3 in E-Major (1945) by Bela Bartok
5. "Stolen Moments" from *Blues and the Abstract Truth* (Impulse!, 1962) by Oliver Nelson
6. "Three Hours Past Midnight" (Federal, 1956) by Johnny "Guitar" Watson
7. "Can I Come Over Tonight" (Onyx 512, 1957) by the Velours
8. "Bagatelles" from String Quartet, Op. 9 (1913) by Anton Webern
9. Symphony, Op. 21 (1927) by Anton Webern
10. Piano Concerto No. 3 in G-Major (1931) by Maurice Ravel

Zappa didn't keep his love for this music a secret. He even included some of it in the set list of the 1988 tour. "Stolen Moments" is featured on *Broadway the Hard Way*, in a mash-up with Sting singing "Murder by Numbers." Portions of the Bartok piece and the Stravinsky "Royal March" are heard on *Make a Jazz Noise Here*, seguing into a Zappa instrumental called "Sinister Footwear." His tribute to Ravel is heard on the big band's version of "Bolero" from *The Best Band You Never Heard in Your Life*. And the Mothers of Invention occasionally performed "Octandre" on their 1968 tour.

One of the surprises on the list, though, is the single by the Velours. The Velours originated in the Bedford-Stuyvesant neighborhood in Brooklyn, New York. The single only went to #83 on *Billboard*'s Hot 100 chart when it was released in 1957. Four years later, the group disbanded after failing to make an impact on the music scene. But their recording did make an impact on Zappa. In the June 1975 issue of *Let It Rock*, a British music magazine, Zappa remarked, "Listen to the bass singer [Marvin Holland] . . . he's singing quintuplets and septuplets. And considering where it came from and when it was made, it was amazing."

3

A Day That Will Live in Infamy

Mother's Day 1965

In the first volume of Mark Lewisohn's superb biography of the Beatles, *Tune In*, he tells the story of how John Lennon and Stuart Sutcliffe came up with the band's name. To them, the importance of a name that stuck with fans—known in today's parlance as "branding"—also gave its members a focus for all of their hard work as a musical group. Associating yourself with a group, as any good anthropologist will tell you, gives you something you can get behind as a collective, especially when you're in your troubled teens and in need of a social connection. In other words, a clear and concise band name can make you feel a part of something bigger.

The Beatles' name was influenced by the Crickets, the small group led by Buddy Holly. Lennon wanted his band's name to have a double meaning, so he changed Beetles to Beatles, which satisfied both the Holly reference and, more importantly, the musical reference to "beat." If only it were that simple for Frank Zappa.

The family tree that sprouted the future Mothers of Invention had its roots in a group known as the Soul Giants, a Los Angeles–based R&B band formed by bass player Roy Estrada and drummer Jimmy Carl Black. Black and Estrada actually met in a pawnshop in L.A., where Black was selling his cymbals in order to buy food. Desperate for cash, Black had only been in southern California (by way of Wichita, Kansas) for two weeks. The Soul Giants were Black's saving grace because they were a working band playing local clubs on the L.A. and Orange County circuits.

Born in 1943 of Mexican-American heritage, Roy Estrada was a seasoned bass player on the L.A. music scene in 1964. He worked in cover bands, playing R&B hits of the era by such jukebox artists as Wilson Pickett. One of his most successful bands was the Viscounts, formed around 1962 with sax player Dave Coronado and guitarist Ray Hunt.

When the Viscounts lost their drummer, Jimmy Carl Black got the gig, and Estrada decided to change the name of the band to the Soul Giants. After a successful audition at a club called the Broadside in Pomona, California, Ray Collins joined the group as lead vocalist. Collins, who was a carpenter by day, had been singing professionally since 1957. He first met Frank Zappa in 1962, and the pair actually worked together as a duo for a short time. Ray Hunt, who was lead guitarist with the Surfmen, a surf-rock band modeled on the Ventures, joined the group in 1964.

The Soul Giants got steady work as a cohesive unit that year, doing what was expected of them by profit-hungry bar owners by playing Top 40 songs with an R&B bent suitable to Collins's range as a vocalist. Over time, however, internal rifts between Collins and guitarist Ray Hunt, who often argued about the band's musical direction, came to a head. The latter member left the group in the winter of 1965. Shortly after that, Collins called Zappa and asked him to play with the Soul Giants.

It's important to note that, by now, Zappa was already writing his own songs and film scores. He also ran Studio Z (formerly Pal), where you could record your band for $13.50 an hour, in Cucamonga, California, a suburban city in San Bernardino County, but he was struggling to keep the business going. The chance to pick up some extra money playing with the Soul Giants was an opportunity he quite literally couldn't afford to miss. So, when Ray Collins called to see if Zappa was interested in playing with his band, he jumped at the chance to join as lead guitarist.

Zappa was immediately impressed with his new band's drummer. As he recalls in *The Real Frank Zappa Book*, "The Soul Giants were a pretty decent bar band. I especially liked the drummer, Jimmy Carl Black, a Cherokee Indian from Texas with an almost unnatural interest in beer. His style reminded me of the guy with the great backbeat on the old Jimmy Reed records." (Black was actually of Cheyenne ancestry, and Reed, a blues musician from Mississippi, recorded some memorable tracks on Vee-Jay Records with drummer Earl Phillips.)

Three months into his tenure with the Soul Giants, Zappa pitched the band with a risky idea to start playing his original music in an effort to get a record contract and earn some "real" money. In Barry Miles's 2004 biography of Zappa, Frank is quoted as saying, "Initially it was a financial arrangement. When you're scuffling in bars for zero to seven dollars per man, you think about money first . . . and if you didn't sound like the Beatles or the Stones you didn't get hired."

Jimmy Carl Black remembered it a little differently. "Zappa said if you'll play my music, I will make you rich and famous," he told Miles. While the lack of a guarantee didn't faze all of the members of the Soul Giants, it did mark the end for Dave Coronado. He left the band because every time they played one of Frank's songs, people stopped dancing, which in turn made them drink less, thus annoying bar owners who only wanted to hear Top 40 cover songs. Consequently, the group—now a quartet of Ray Collins, Roy Estrada, Jimmy Carl Black, and Frank Zappa, the *de facto* leader—hardly worked for a while, especially during the period they were operating under the ridiculous name Captain Glasspack and His Magic Mufflers. A name change was definitely in order.

When Zappa offered up "the Mothers" to his fellow bandmates, it was an easy sell. A sly reference to the term "motherfucker," which was actually a phrase reserved for really good musicians, it was an edgy moniker. In an interview with *Zig Zag* magazine in 1968, Zappa claimed that the name and the plan to play only his own compositions was "eighteen months in the making." The fact that the Mothers were named on Mother's Day—May 9, 1965—is coincidental to the story, but as legend it remains a part of rock history. Once the name was agreed to, Zappa had business cards made up with his name, a phone number, and a simple "The Mothers" in type on the front. A short time afterward, Herb Cohen was hired to manage the band and book gigs. Prior to this, Zappa had asked Mark Cheka, a Greenwich Village pop artist, to manage the group and book their concerts. Cheka introduced Zappa to the freak movement that was growing in L.A. at the time. But by the end of 1965, Herb Cohen became full-time manager and Cheka was out.

First Recording Contract

In 1966, the Mothers finally secured their first record contract with the label MGM/Verve, which had once been billed as a home for "Music to suit every taste." Twenty years earlier, MGM (Metro-Goldwyn-Mayer) had started issuing soundtracks from its motion pictures. Now it wanted to branch out and secure a place in the new youth market. In May, before the release of their debut album, *Freak Out!*, the first instance of interference by a record executive in Zappa's career took place, with the band's name the central issue. As Zappa told BBC-TV reporter Nigel Leigh, "Some pinhead there decided that this [the Mothers] was a bad name for a group and that no radio stations would ever play our records because our name was too risqué." And so the Mothers were renamed the Mothers of Invention—not by the new leader of a former R&B band, but by a staffer at MGM records.

By the mid-sixties, record companies were well tuned to the value of marketing music with a carefully prepared image of its artists. Brian Epstein, for instance, knew the Beatles would be far more appealing to a wider audience in suits instead of the scruffy leather clothes they wore in Hamburg, Germany, so the astute manager made them dress in tailored clothes for every public appearance, photo session, and album cover. The only thing that was radical about their look was the length of their hair. Encouraged by the Beatles' dress and success, everybody from the Byrds to the Hollies to Paul Revere and the Raiders created a costumed look to go along with their music. It was a perfect combination of visual appeal and (in some cases) some pretty good songs. To Frank Zappa, they were known as "beautiful groups."

The Mothers of Invention never looked that beautiful. As Zappa remembers in his autobiography, "We were all ugly guys with weird clothes and long hair: just what the entertainment world needed." Sarcasm aside, Zappa understood the importance of marketing one's music. In his first *Rolling Stone* interview from 1968, he explained his plans to Jerry Hopkins. "The appearance of the group is linked to the music the same way an album cover is linked to the record. It gives a clue to what's inside. And the better the packaging, the more the person who picked up that package will enjoy it."

Zappa never formally told his bandmates what to wear onstage or on album covers. Likewise, the Mothers of Invention weren't going to be shaped by a trendy stylist or packaged by a hip designer, even though their leader took on a definitive look himself, with the iconic handlebar moustache and soul patch inspired by R&B legend Johnny Otis. The fact of the matter was that the band never had enough money to eat, let alone clothe itself properly. In an interview with a radio DJ in Dallas, Texas, Zappa recalled that on their first trip from the warm California sun to New York City in the winter of 1966, following the release of *Freak Out!*, "We were grubby and long-haired and stuff . . . and we had to go to a used clothes store in Los Angeles before we left Los Angeles to get some old overcoats to wear. We looked like a bunch of immigrants standing out there in the streets . . . and the cabs wouldn't pick us up to take us home. We had to walk home in the snow every night after the job." Nevertheless, the "immigrant" look helped to distinguish the band from all of the groomed and polished groups at the time. Ten years later, the stylized punk movement, with its piercings and torn clothing, would follow a similar path as a shot against the tailored look of disco.

An early print interview with the band appeared on December 8, 1965, in a music newspaper published by radio station KFWB in Los Angeles. On page two of the paper, Zappa offered up his new group's mission statement: "We, the Mothers, promise to assist whatever public we come in contact with, in a swift and orderly return to realistic values." The article—which reads more like a press release—offered commentary on Bob Dylan, Barry McGuire, and the importance of free speech in the band's music to "reach more people." It also offered up lyrics from a song called "Watts Riot," later retitled "Trouble Every Day," which would appear on *Freak Out!* As Zappa says in the same piece, "We consider ourselves therapeutic workers massaging the brains of people dancing to our music."

Zappa Finds an Audience

Zappa decided to market his band to a specific group of people in L.A. known as the "freaks." Freak culture opened the door to Zappa's need to attach his non-conformity in music to a younger, non-conformist social class. This notion worked for a lot of groups in San Francisco, such as the Grateful Dead. In his excellent book *The Dangerous Kitchen*, author Kevin Courrier puts the hippie vs. freak scene into its proper perspective. "In the mid-'60s, L.A. was in a state of transition. There was much racial and social unrest, and an emerging freak scene, which evolved as a reaction to the perceived corruption and evil perpetrated by the city's inequities. This attitude was different from the hippie scene growing in San Francisco."

In 1965–66, the "City by the Bay" was home to young people interested in peace, free love, smoking dope, and a mode of dress that matched American Indian motifs. L.A., to the north, was a little more "mercenary," according to Neil Slaven in *Electric Don Quixote*. "They emphasized the second word of 'show business,'" he writes. "Freaks were more individualistic and ego-driven, taking 'love' where they found it and equating 'tolerance' with 'every man for himself.'" They also cared about their appearance and that notion carried some weight in creating the image of the Mothers of Invention. The cover of *Freak Out!* bears this out.

In 1967, Zappa boasted to reporter Frank Kofsky about the nature of his audience: "Our initial appeal is to the outcasts, the weirdoes . . . the people that we hear about that like us—I could show you some of the fan letters. They're just unique, man. These are really the cream of the weirdoes of each town, and they're coming from all over. We're getting letters from very strange places." He respected the new fans but also exploited them for public gain, going on to explain his establishment of a fan club, known as United Mutations, which was open to all the young people interested in joining a community where they were recognized and appreciated for being "different."

According to Barry Miles, "the trajectory of the Byrds" was a business plan in the making. Following the success of the hit single "Mr. Tambourine Man" and the album of the same name in the summer of 1965, the group, led by Roger McGuinn, had a growing fan base on the popular club circuit known as the Strip in Los Angeles. As Miles writes, "The Byrds were closely associated with Vito [Paulekas] and the freaks and Karl Franzoni, the leaders of a group of about thirty-five dancers whose antics enlivened the Byrds early gigs." They had a look and attitude that appealed to Zappa and the Mothers because of the common ground they shared as non-conformists. Besides, as any record executive will tell you, to tap into *any* audience for your new music would have been considered a marketing coup. By associating with the freaks, the Mothers had regular gigs and a growing fan base. They even started to adapt a similar look: long, messy hair; colorful, mismatched clothing; and, as directed by Zappa, an improvised presentation onstage.

The name the Mothers of Invention (or the Mothers) appears on eighteen albums, not including archival releases. Concert posters, ads, and ticket stubs all continued to bear the name years after Zappa started recording as a solo artist, while even some of the publicity stills issued in the mid-seventies by Herb Cohen, Zappa's manager, were labeled "Frank Zappa and the Mothers." But by May 1976, after a tumultuous year of touring with a lineup that changed several times, the Mothers of Invention "brand" was dropped for good. Shortly thereafter, Zappa fired Herb Cohen and his brother Martin for stealing funds from DiscReet, the record label they had co-founded three years earlier. The year was capped off when Zappa filed a lawsuit against Warner Bros. and Herb Cohen and declared himself a "free agent." While the litigation proceedings continued, however, he wasn't allowed to use the name Mothers of Invention. His next album, *Zoot Allures*, was duly issued under his own name.

4

Unemployable

The Mothers of Invention

Group Hug

Many die-hard fans remember the Mothers of Invention as a *band*. This is a short history of the original group from 1965 to 1970.

The Mothers of Invention released seven albums *led* by Frank Zappa. His promise to make them all "rich and famous" with a recording contract reflected an era when record companies held the purse strings to any band's desire for success. Unlike today, in those days the notion of self-funding wasn't even a consideration. Record companies had the money, the distribution, and the marketing power most rock musicians sought. For Frank Zappa, playing bars and clubs in Hollywood wasn't enough because he wanted to reach a larger audience—and he needed to make a living at it. So, by 1965, the attraction of making a record was not only an artistic desire but a financial one as well. Nevertheless, it was a real challenge, playing original music unlike anything the people of California, let alone the world, had heard before. Consequently, the Mothers were basically "unemployable" at first.

When the Mothers made the commitment to play Zappa's compositions exclusively, there were only a few clubs in which to play that really mattered in the music business. In Los Angeles, A&R reps would check out bands on a regular basis, looking for the next big thing in rock 'n' roll. As Zappa writes in his autobiography, "One was called the Action, one was called the Trip, and the other Whisky a Go Go . . . there were a few other clubs in town, but they didn't have the same status as those places." The thinking was: if you play any one of these clubs at the right time, you were going to be "discovered." For the Mothers, that day arrived in late 1965, when the group's manager Herb Cohen brought producer Tom Wilson to hear the band, mid-set, at the Whisky.

The first lineup of the Mothers lasted for the better part of six months from Mother's Day 1965 and consisted of Frank Zappa (guitar), Roy Estrada (bass), Jimmy Carl Black (drums), and Ray Collins (vocals), with guest appearances by guitarist Alice Stuart, drummer Denny Bruce, and keyboard players Van Dyke Parks and Mac Rebennack, aka Dr. John. In November of

One of the earliest images of Zappa and the Mothers at a club in L.A. around 1966.

Michael Ochs Archives/Getty Images

that year, the band added Henry Vestine as a second guitar player. Vestine, a blues musician, was from Washington, D.C., and only stayed with the band until January 1966, leaving when Zappa's music became too difficult for him to play. In a British documentary by Prism Films produced in 2008, *Frank Zappa and the Mothers of Invention in the 1960s,* Jimmy Carl Black says that the deal-breaker was specifically the song "Who Are the Brain Police?" Vestine went on to form the blues-rock band Canned Heat with Bob Hite.

Following Vestine's departure, the Mothers picked up guitarist Elliot Ingber, who played with the band until November of 1966, when he was fired for smoking too much marijuana during performances. Ingber joined the L.A. group Factory, which soon morphed into Fraternity of Man, a blues-based, psychedelic rock band whose first self-titled album (Edsel, 1968) featured a recording of "Oh No! (I Don't Believe It)," penned by Frank Zappa.

In November 1966, the Mothers of Invention expanded to an eight-piece band with the inclusion of Billy Mundi (drums), Bunk Gardner (woodwinds), James "Motorhead" Sherwood (saxophone), and Jim Fielder (guitar). Fielder played on *Absolutely Free* (1967) but left the band to play bass for Buffalo Springfield and, later, Blood, Sweat and Tears. Billy Mundi was from San Francisco and only played with the band for a few years, but that period included the all-important *We're Only in It for the Money.*

The most talented addition to the band was keyboard player Don Preston, from Flint, Michigan. According to Barry Miles's biography of Zappa, Preston "had started his musical career in the military when he was stationed in Trieste, Italy, with Herbie Mann, and had years of experience with the likes of Elvin Jones, Carla Bley, and Charlie Haden." Preston was the first musician with a strong background in jazz and an enthusiastic interest in electronics and their use in synthesizers to join the band.

Bunk Gardner, whose real name was John Leon Guanerra, was from Cleveland, Ohio. He had proficiency in a number of woodwind instruments, including clarinet, tenor and soprano saxophone, and bassoon. James "Motorhead" Sherwood, who befriended Zappa in high school, was the band's roadie, lugging equipment for concerts and rehearsals. But he could also play tenor saxophone and dance on demand for the live shows.

In 1967, Ian Underwood joined the band simply by asking Zappa for an audition after seeing the Mothers of Invention in concert at the Garrick Theatre in New York. Underwood—a graduate of Yale (1961), with a BA in composition and a master's degree from Berkeley School of Music

(1966)—was a highly skilled musician who Zappa would utilize on many tours and recordings. He was proficient on piano and various wind instruments, including bass clarinet. In a bold attempt to fuse better relations within the group, Underwood suggested he take the job of music director for the band. Consequently, he played a key role in leading the rehearsals, giving Zappa more time to compose. (Years later, the person who held this risky position became known as the "clonemeister.")

At the end of 1967, the band's lineup changed again with the arrival of Arthur (Art) Tripp III from Athens, Ohio, to replace Billy Mundi. Tripp was an experienced percussionist who had earned a degree from the Cincinnati College Conservatory of Music in 1961. He served an apprenticeship with the Cincinnati Symphony Orchestra, with whom he performed works by John Cage and Karlheinz Stockhausen. Tripp hooked up with Zappa in November of '67, on the recommendation of Richard (Dick) Kunc, the recording engineer on *We're Only in It for the Money*. Tripp recorded six albums with the band before moving on to Captain Beefheart's Magic Band in 1970.

At this time, Zappa was the *de facto* leader of the group alongside manager Herb Cohen. The pair decided to pay the musicians $250 per week—whether or not they worked. It was a business decision that secured good players but brought a certain amount of economic grief if the band wasn't touring regularly and earning money.

Show Me the Money

At the beginning of 1968, after a steady series of tours of the US, Canada, and England, two albums, and a slew of publicity, fans from around the world began to take notice of the Mothers. Frank Zappa and his dedicated (and well paid) musicians may not have gotten rich, but they did get famous. Two years earlier, when they signed with MGM/Verve, the band received a $2,500 advance against royalties. The release of *Freak Out!*—only the second two-record set in rock music history, following Bob Dylan's *Blonde on Blonde*—was followed by the equally challenging *Absolutely Free* (recorded with a budget of $11,000) in June of 1967. That record was overshadowed by the release of *Sgt. Pepper's Lonely Hearts Club Band* by the Beatles. It was also the same year the Doors debuted, as well as David Bowie, although few people took notice of the latter's first record.

The MOI, from left to right, Ian Underwood, Bunk Gardner, Motorhead Sherwood, Roy Estrada, Frank Zappa, Jimmy Carl Black, Don Preston, Art Tripp.   *K&K Ulf Kruger OHG/Getty Images*

The real success—and presumably the money—came with Zappa's satiric shot at *Sgt. Pepper*. The Mothers of Invention went over the top with the cover for their September 1968 release *We're Only in It for the Money*. This is the album most fans refer to as the definitive Mothers of Invention lineup, both for its musical content and its gatefold cover art, with a picture of the band in drag on the outside and a mock *Sgt. Pepper* image on the inside.

The band continued to tour heavily throughout 1968 and well into 1969. The demanding schedule and Zappa's continuing growth as a composer brought two more players into the fold, namely Bunk Gardner's brother Buzz, born Charles Guanerra, on trumpet, and the one and only Lowell George, guitarist and vocalist extraordinaire. George was hired to replace Ray Collins, who left the band following a dispute with Zappa and went back to working as a carpenter. George was a good replacement for Collins, having gained experience with a group called the Standells, whose biggest hit, "Dirty Water," charted on *Billboard*, reaching #11 in 1966. George appeared on *Burnt Weeny Sandwich* and *Weasels Ripped My Flesh* but left the band in late May 1969. After that, the group hit the road again for what was to be their last tour, although they didn't know it at the time.

The end came in August 1969, two months before the release of Zappa's second solo record, *Hot Rats*, on the Bizarre/Warner label. Upon returning home to California after three concerts in Montreal, Quebec (which took place on the same weekend as the Woodstock Festival), Zappa and Herb Cohen called a meeting at Zappa's home in Laurel Canyon in southern California to explain that the group was "disbanding for financial reasons."

For Jimmy Carl Black, Don Preston, Art Tripp, Bunk Gardner, Buzz Gardner, Roy Estrada, Ian Underwood, and Motorhead Sherwood—the original Mothers of Invention—this marked the end of one of the most popular alternative bands of the sixties. According to Don Preston and Jimmy Carl Black, who were interviewed in 2008 for a series produced by Prism Films, they were shocked and hurt by the announcement. As Black stated, "It was pretty heavy; it was pretty cold, but he always said he was losing money." Preston agreed, adding, in a follow-up interview for the same documentary, "Everybody was in complete shock . . . all of us really had a really strong feeling of camaraderie . . . a group of people with special talents that was quite amazing."

The financial considerations weren't lost on Preston, who questioned whether the ten-member line up as too expensive a venture anyway. "It was wrong for many reasons . . . we didn't have to accept [the breakup] but we thought we had to and so we did." Bunk Gardner said he was disappointed and astonished that the band was losing money in spite of its success on the concert circuit, but nonetheless accepted that the band was going through an "evolution" and that their leader needed to grow musically and artistically.

To a certain extent, Zappa's financial reasons for breaking up the band were true, as confirmed by his secretary, Pauline Butcher. In her insightful memoir, *Freak Out: My Life with Frank Zappa*, Butcher writes about the organization as she saw it. "The Mothers of Invention were now a business as much as a band. Frank and Herbie [Cohen] owned both the management and record companies [Bizarre and Straight] and as such had complete power over the group. If any of the band failed to show up for rehearsal, they must present a doctor's letter or have wages docked. Yet, while Frank's lifestyle and expenditure soared, the Mothers still languished . . . despite their tours selling out everywhere." Butcher adds that Zappa had been beginning to tire of the band a year earlier as a result of their inability to play his music, which was becoming more complex. The public was unaware of the breakup until it was confirmed in an October 1969 press release. The last original Mothers of Invention album, *Weasels Ripped My Flesh*, was released in 1970. But Zappa still used the name on touring posters and publicity stills until 1976, including the variation "Frank Zappa and the Mothers."

Years later, Zappa told Neil Slaven that he felt very little nostalgia for the original band.

> I think that, in an ideal way, the nostalgia for the band is for the concept of the band and also for the fact that such a thing could exist as a touring musical entity in spite of everything that was going on. You really have to put your mind back to what else was on the road at that period of time. It's quite unbelievable that a band like that could get work anywhere for a period of years. I think that what it represented to a lot of people was the idea that there's a certain type of freedom that's involved in doing weird stuff just because you feel like it, and getting paid to do it.

On October 10, 1969, Zappa released *Hot Rats* on the Bizarre/Warner label. It was his second solo album, the first being 1967's *Lumpy Gravy*. It reached #173 on the *Billboard* charts in the United States but did better in Europe, especially in Holland, the following winter. Ian Underwood and Lowell George were the only members of the Mothers of Invention to appear on the record. George went on to form Little Feat, the eclectic rock band from Los Angeles, California, with Bill Payne, Roy Estrada, and Richie Hayward. Underwood continued to play with Zappa until the mid-seventies.

5

Noodling

Zappa and the Jazz Influence

I n the September 1994 issue of *Downbeat*, the magazine's critics elected Frank Zappa to the Hall of Fame. It was a timely choice, coming less than a year after Zappa died. Zappa is one of six guitarists on the current list. To some fans, his inclusion may have been construed as false praise, given that they paid little attention to his music when he was alive, but it did reflect the critics' acceptance of Zappa as a musician and composer. Zappa didn't think much of such tributes; hearing his music was a reward in itself most of the time.

Downbeat was established in 1934. Its slogan is "Jazz, Blues, and Beyond," which could also be a definition of Zappa's music. Every year, the magazine surveys its readers to find out what they're listening to; Zappa polled highest in the "Pop Musician of the Year" category in 1970, 1971, and 1972. In 1974, the readers voted Zappa and the Mothers of Invention best "Rock/Pop/Blues

Group." He never topped a poll again until he was entered into the Hall of Fame twenty years later. Nevertheless, as far as the critics were concerned, Zappa deserved to join the esteemed company of Miles Davis, Billie Holiday, Bill Evans, and Charles Mingus.

In an essay from the same issue of *Downbeat*, titled "Legacy of a Cultural Guerilla," John Corbett offers a cheeky yet earnest tribute to Zappa, whose "mind was full of ugly beauty." The writer goes on to conclude,

Zappa's favorite jazz record, produced by Tom Wilson.

"His influence on musics of all sorts—from political rock to electric jazz—is indelible." The idea of "music that lasts" certainly applies to jazz as much as it does to Zappa's work. He once remarked that "jazz isn't dead; it just smells funny." It was a prescient comment, because in 2015 sales of jazz recordings have considerably shrunk in a world more interested in disposable pop. But jazz isn't for everyone, and the critics and readers at *Downbeat* have always known its audience appeal was limited, if not "odor free."

Growing up in Lancaster, California, Frank Zappa first heard jazz in the same way he did other styles: by popping coins in a jukebox. He listened to recordings by blues greats such as Howlin' Wolf and Johnny "Guitar" Watson, as well as singles by bebop innovator Charlie Parker. When Zappa first heard Parker's remarkable style, he called it "noodling," and he didn't like it because he couldn't hear a "tune" in the music. But he did like composer/bassist Charles Mingus and Oscar Pettiford's band for their unusual sounds. It was interesting to the ear, he said, and it had some "balls to it."

Tom Wilson, who produced *Freak Out!* and *Absolutely Free* by the Mothers of Invention, also produced one of Zappa's favorite albums of new music, *Jazz in Transition* (TRLP 30). The record was a sampler featuring artists on the Transition label, as founded by Wilson in 1955. It includes tracks by pianist Cecil Taylor and bandleader Sun Ra, two of the leading composers working outside the conventions of jazz during the post-bop era after 1949. *Jazz in Transition* also features tenor sax great John Coltrane and the late Horace Silver, who formed one of the most important groups from that era, the Jazz Messengers.

Zappa never really used the word "jazz" as we know it today to identify his music—unless he was making fun of it. Zappa defined the Mothers of Invention as performers of "electric chamber music" that featured a lot of instrumentals often thought of as jazz, usually by narrow-minded or uninformed critics and journalists. Zappa's band offered listeners the most important element of jazz: improvisation. But in the late sixties, if you played loud electric music, you were automatically labeled "rock musician." Zappa believed in the creative freedom of improvisation in any music genre, not just the exclusive category known as jazz. You can hear an affinity for jazz in his work, especially in instrumentals such as "The Son of the Monster Magnet," "Peaches En Regalia," and "Black Napkins," as well as the one song most jazz musicians cite for its inspired modal changes, "King Kong."

Making a Jazz Noise

Jazz fans often point to a couple of Zappa albums as their favorites: *Waka/ Jawaka* and *The Grand Wazoo*. They came out in July and November of 1972, respectively, and they were the last releases on Zappa's Bizarre label. To consider them as a delayed two-record set would not be out of line because they were both recorded in Los Angeles, California, at Paramount Studios, in the spring of that year. The band featured some jazz musicians, including Sal Marquez (trumpet), Bill Byers (trombone), Ernie Watts (tenor saxophone), George Duke (keyboards), and Mike Altschul (flute and bass clarinet). The drummer was Aynsley Dunbar from England, and the bass player was Alex Dmochowski, aka Erroneous, who also played with Dunbar in the short-lived progressive rock band the Aynsley Dunbar Retaliation.

These two records came about after Zappa suffered a serious injury. On December 10, 1971, an angry audience member pushed Zappa off the stage at the end of a concert at London's Rainbow Theatre. Zappa fell hard, nearly fifteen feet, and suffered a broken ankle, a broken leg, and contusions to

Designer Cal Schenkel goes big.

the head. He was laid up in a London hospital for a month before he was able to return to the United States to recover. The cast on his leg prevented him from walking, so he used a wheelchair to move around. He canceled all remaining tour dates and settled in to write more music. What he came up with was completely removed from the work of the Mothers of Invention and the recent touring band featuring singers Flo and Eddie.

In April 1972, Zappa went into the studio with some finished charts arranged for a sixteen-piece band. It was probably the best band Zappa had led up to that point. Most of the musicians cut their teeth playing jazz, so they were all good improvisers, and they could quickly learn new music when it was placed in front of them. (The rehearsal sessions were subsequently issued in 2004, on *Joe's Domage*.) In a rare collaboration, Sal Marquez wrote and arranged all the horn parts with Zappa, who played guitar and conducted the band from his wheelchair. The results were extraordinary.

Waka/Jawaka

Waka/Jawaka, or *Hot Rats II*, as it was also known, opens large and wide with one of Zappa's longest compositions, "Big Swifty." The sound will immediately embrace anyone familiar with the music of Miles Davis from *In a Silent Way* (Columbia), the precursor to *Bitches Brew*. The texture of electric piano, muted trumpet, and a rhythm section laying down the beat makes for a powerfully funky sound. Zappa's guitar sound is much cleaner, and the improvisation among the players is bright and buoyant. It sounds like an impromptu jam session, but it's not. Like the overdub-laden songs Zappa recorded for *Hot Rats*, this track features only a sextet but sounds like a big band.

Just in case you thought Zappa was going jazz, he drops in two songs between the instrumentals: the blues-inspired "Your Mouth" and a satiric country song, "It Just Might Be a One-Shot Deal," sung by Janet Ferguson and Sal Marquez. Zappa liked variety on all of his records, and these two tracks are in keeping with what the fans expected, but what makes them unique is the fact that they only appear on this album. The record closes out with "Waka/Jawaka," featuring Don Preston, formally of the Mothers, playing the Minimoog synthesizer with its new frequency shifter. Preston's life-long interest in electronic music—and the instruments available to make it—adds a lot of color to the piece. This track highlights Zappa's insistence on being able to improvise without the restrictions imposed by jazz theory.

The Grand Wazoo

The Grand Wazoo features the larger ensemble without the overdubs of the previous album, and the band is solid on all five cuts. The title track jumps out of the speakers, as if we've entered the middle of the group's set unexpectedly. "The Grand Wazoo" is one of the catchiest riffs in the Zappa canon, and the band picks up the funky beat easily, until Zappa stops the action and moves into new musical territory. Unlike *Waka/Jawaka*, this album is busier in scope, with more complex arrangements and musical humor. Dashes of gospel, R&B, and hard rock adorn "Cletus Awreetus-Awrightus," which is closer to Spike Jones than it is to Charles Mingus, but if you listen carefully, you can hear both influences.

"Eat That Question" has a tougher edge to it, with Zappa's distorted guitar sound leading the way, but the song breaks free with a great electric piano solo by George Duke, whose musical chops enhanced Zappa's music for many years (see: *One Size Fits All*). As Zappa's solo winds out, the song enters a dynamic, slower passage, repeating the main musical line before entering a climactic finish with the entire ensemble. It's big and bold. The album closes with one of Frank Zappa's most beautiful compositions, "Blessed Relief."

Zappa's enthusiasm for the ensemble on these two records motivated him to put together a ten-piece touring band fondly known as the Petit Wazoo. The band only played twenty-one dates from late October to mid-December of 1972 in the United States and Canada. The recordings were finally released after Zappa archivist Joe Travers went looking for the tapes in Zappa's basement. The result was the album *Imaginary Diseases*, released in 2006. The live album isn't as interesting as the studio recordings, but it does capture the group's skills as improvisers, as well as the element of surprise, which is the way Zappa liked it. The sixteen-minute version of "Farther O'Blivion," for instance, features a tango in the middle of it. To show off the versatility of the Petit Wazoo, Zappa takes a poll of the audience to find out how they would like "D.C. Boogie" to finish: with a march, a polka, or a dog-food jingle. Zappa may have put forth a serious jazz concert, but he never left his facetious presentation far behind.

In the original liner notes to *Freak Out!*, Zappa lists Eric Dolphy, Roland Kirk, Cecil Taylor, Bill Evans, and Charles Mingus as "contributors." So, while he remained in the idiom of his own making, his appreciation and rapport for jazz was never very far away.

6

Beefheart vs. Zappa

A Clash of Icons

In July 2015, Captain Beefheart and Frank Zappa graced the cover of the British music magazine *Prog*. The article, entitled "Zappa's Bongo Fury," included a quotation from each man on either side of a picture of Zappa.

"He asked for a job," says Zappa. "He flunked the audition."

"Zappa?" says Beefheart. He's not even as hip as a fool!"

Why would a magazine seek out a new understanding of the relationship between two high-school buddies who bonded over their love of R&B? According to the magazine, "It was the definitive love/hate relationship. [They] shared a fierce rivalry, a twisted yet lifelong friendship and an unrivaled musical genius . . . those times never lasted long."

In any discussion of Frank Zappa, the name Captain Beefheart (or Don Van Vliet) almost always comes up. Therefore one could say that they are synonymous in the history of rock music. Their peculiar relationship has been written about in various biographies, but three events emerge as defining the complicated relationship between Beefheart and Zappa: the recording and release of *Trout Mask Replica* in 1969, the 1975 *Bongo Fury* tour, and the contractual hijinks surrounding Beefheart's 1976 album *Bat Chain Puller*, which wasn't formally released until after both men had died.

Frank Zappa had a lot of acquaintances and employees, and he had his immediate family around him, but he never really had many "friends." He admits this in his autobiography, and while he's flip about it, he does reveal an insecurity about himself that would make good fodder, as he suggests, for a PhD student in psychology. (Zappa actually calls for a "famous doctor" to study it.) Perhaps the pursuit of his art didn't allow for the building of friendships when he was putting so much time into running a band, composing music, and tending to the needs of his family, whom he describes as "totally unbelievable" and, in his mind, "way better."

This notion of a strong sense of individuality could go a long way to explaining Zappa's complex relationship with Don Van Vliet. So, while their relationship grew from their first meeting in 1958, over time it soured, before eventually recovering when Zappa was on his deathbed in 1993. But the creative highlights of that friendship have stood the test of time, beginning with the writing and recording of *Trout Mask Replica*.

In 1969, Captain Beefheart had two moderately successful albums under his creative belt with the Magic Band: *Safe as Milk* (Buddah) and *Strictly Personal* (Blue Thumb). Both albums had an original blues-rock sound that was rooted in Van Vliet's personal interest in mixing the two genres along the same lines as Al Kooper and Mike Bloomfield, who were also exploring the fusion of rock and blues on their album *The Live Adventures of Al Kooper and Mike Bloomfield* (Columbia). Van Vliet's take on the music was much more experimental, and he felt his record company was too heavy-handed in deciding how his music should sound. That, and quite possibly the fact that Van Vliet was taking LSD, stifled any progress the Magic Band was making at the time. By the end of 1968, Zappa decided to help Beefheart crawl out of his artistic funk by inviting him to work together on another album free of the corporate restrictions that both men found too imposing on their music.

In the winter of 1969, Zappa invited Beefheart to record for his recently formed label, Straight Records, which he had founded with his manager Herb Cohen. Zappa guaranteed Beefheart complete artistic control over the music, while Zappa acted as producer. But the ever-pragmatic Zappa wanted the band to rehearse as much as possible, to save precious studio time, even though he was flush with cash following his success with the Mothers of Invention, who by now had three albums on the market and were about to go out on tour. Beefheart took him at his word and hired new musicians for the Magic Band.

Collaboration?

The idea for Zappa and Beefheart to collaborate on an album together probably stemmed from their shared love for R&B, over which they had bonded some ten years earlier. In the interim, Zappa had even become Don's road manager for awhile, when Beefheart and the Magic Band were booked for a music festival in France. But to those who knew them both, the idea of them working together came as a surprise. As Don Preston recalls in Kevin Courrier's book *Trout Mask Replica*, "Both Frank and Don had two very extreme personalities, and how they ever did anything together is a mystery to me."

On one level, Preston was right, because Zappa had a formal knowledge of music while Beefheart's, according to Courrier, was much more instinctual. While pushing the limits of satire, Zappa was much more formal about his compositions. Beefheart was much more organic in his approach to songwriting. He couldn't read or write music, but he did convey what he wanted to the Magic Band—the group that gets the least recognition, according to some rock historians, in the story of Beefheart and Zappa. On paper, that creative mix could work—under the right circumstances, and perhaps with the right producer—but Zappa was the producer for this album, and a bit of a control freak, while Beefheart was steadfast in his artistic vision of mixing Delta blues with free jazz and absurdist poetry.

Beefheart's writing process and his infatuation with grinding out material for *Trout Mask Replica* is nicely rendered in Courrier's book, leading one to conclude that Beefheart was just as much of a control freak as Zappa. There was no formal structure to the rehearsals for the album; Beefheart simply worked the Magic Band to death, until he got what he wanted in the music. John French, the drummer in the band, helped focus the songs by recording everything Beefheart wrote or said on a cassette recorder and then formalizing Beefheart's ideas into musical terms the band could understand. French and guitarist Bill Harkleroad went a long way to arrange the tracks into something cohesive to record while maintaining Beefheart's vision.

When Zappa returned from his tour in late February 1969, he found that Beefheart had sequestered the group in his house until they had nearly two dozen songs in shape and ready to record. So, in March, the Magic Band, Beefheart, and Zappa went into the studio to begin recording *Trout Mask Replica*. The rigorous rehearsals paid off: they completed all the instrumental tracks in a single six-hour session at Whitney Studios in Glendale, California. Dick Kunc, who had also worked on the Mothers of Invention's *Freak Out!*, engineered the recording. Beefheart's vocals were added over the course of the next few days, after which Zappa took the tapes home to edit and mix the album—without Beefheart's input.

Beefheart had recorded the vocals without the use of headphones—which were a major technical obstruction, in his view—so many of the tracks had to be synchronized by Zappa. This technical glitch created one of the

Ice cream for crow? Zappa and Beefheart grace the cover of *Bongo Fury*.

most volatile moments between the two artists, but in retrospect it is one of the most appealing things about the album. When Zappa finished the album in April he invited the band to a playback session at his house, with the response to his mix overwhelmingly positive. On June 16, 1969, *Trout Mask Replica* was released as a two-record set on Zappa's Straight Records label.

The relationship between Zappa and Beefheart waned after the album came out, with Beefheart bitching about being marketed as a freak alongside labelmates Alice Cooper and Wild Man Fischer. He also claimed non-payment of royalties. In an interview with Nick Kent of *Freindz* magazine in 1972, he said, "Zappa is the most disgusting character I have ever encountered." Beefheart stopped talking to Zappa and decided to self-produce his next album, *Lick My Decals Off, Baby*. Another four records followed as Beefheart tried his best to find more commercial success. Unfortunately, these attempts alienated his existing fan base and failed to attract any new listeners, because the music simply wasn't up to the level of *Trout Mask Replica*.

The lineup of the Magic Band changed a number of times over the next few years as players dropped out of the group or Beefheart fired them. Art Tripp, who was hired by Van Vliet for the Magic Band after the Mothers disbanded, described him as "endowed with a magnetic personality, high intelligence, and a tremendous imagination." Tripp suggested that, as an only child, Van Vliet was doted on by his mother and knew how to get what he wanted. (Tripp spoke from experience because he, too, had no siblings.)

For Beefheart's 1974 release, *Bluejeans & Moonbeams* (Virgin), no personnel are listed in the liner notes. By the end of the year, it looked like he and the Magic Band were done. Van Vliet decided to take a break and pursue a career as a painter and illustrator. Zappa, meanwhile, was enjoying some of the most creative and critical successes of his career, with *Over-Nite Sensation*, *Apostrophe (')*, and *Roxy & Elsewhere* all released during 1973–74 to wide acclaim.

The Bongo Fury Tour

According to Beefheart biographer Mike Barnes, Van Vliet contacted Zappa and apologized for what he had said about him in the press in early 1975. Zappa was preparing for another short American tour, due to start in April of that year, and gave his crusty old friend a job in the band, despite his "flunking the audition." According to guitarist Denny Walley, who was interviewed for the same book, "The rehearsals with Don were not your average rehearsals. His attention span was about a second. You'd spend a good bit of time corralling him and getting him to focus. But most of the time he would just nail it."

Barnes reports that Beefheart didn't sing on every song during the tour and often sat in a chair onstage, drawing in a book, until it was his turn to perform. "He had a stack of sketch pads with a marker pen and while Zappa was playing a guitar solo, he would draw pictures of him as the devil and show them to the group and audience."

By the time the tour ended on May 23, 1975, Zappa was once again no longer speaking to Beefheart. When the album *Bongo Fury*—named after Beefheart's excellent spoken-word segment on "Sam with the Showing Scalp Flat Top"—came out the following year, one might have thought all was well between the two musicians . . . until Zappa credits Beefheart, on the closing bars of "Muffin Man," with "vocals and soprano sax and madness."

The body language on the cover photo also reflects the tension between them: Zappa sits with his legs crossed, his right hand in a fist and an ice-cream cone in his left, with a look of disdain in his eyes; Beefheart is to his left, wearing a large-brimmed black hat, looking down, with a soda in his right hand, indicating some discomfort about being in Zappa's company. In the liner notes, Beefheart is listed as playing "harp, vocals, and shopping bags"—the latter a reference to the bags he carried with him at all times during the tour. According to Mike Barnes, they contained sketchbooks, lyrics, and other "paraphernalia" that he "had a habit of mislaying and would then frantically try to relocate."

Bat Chain Puller

In 1976, a reinvigorated Beefheart went back into the studio to record *Bat Chain Puller*, which was scheduled for release by Zappa's new label, DiscReet Records, in October of that year. But then, in May, Zappa fired his longtime manager Herb Cohen and filed suit against him and his brother Martin, accusing them of stealing money from DiscReet. Cohen had financed the Beefheart project with his royalty checks, which annoyed Zappa so much that he filed suit to break with Cohen and the label they had co-founded. Cohen then signed Beefheart to Virgin Records for the release of *Bat Chain Puller* in the UK, but Zappa intervened before the release. Beefheart and Cohen thought that *they* should be paid an advance instead of Zappa, who, to them, had had little to do with the album in the first place. Zappa with-held the master tapes, insisting that his litigation against Cohen needed to be settled before Virgin could release the album. The legal hassle put the record in proverbial mothballs until 2012; at the time, it deeply wounded the already broken friendship between Zappa and Beefheart. When the suit between Cohen and Zappa was finally settled in 1982, Beefheart tried to get the master tapes back, so that he could add some of the tracks to what would be his last record, *Ice Cream for Crow* (Epic). But the animosity was too great, and Zappa refused to hand over the tapes because he thought the album would have been more successful if it was issued intact.

Beefheart quit the music business altogether as a result and settled in California with his wife to once again pursue his first love, painting, as Don Van Vliet. In the years that followed, his art was exhibited in Germany, New York, and Los Angeles.

Final Days

In 1993, Van Vliet was diagnosed with Multiple Sclerosis (MS), although this wasn't made public until after he died in 2010. According to biographer Mike Barnes, when Van Vliet learned that Zappa had prostate cancer, he called him up once a week and played some of the R&B records they had enjoyed in their youth down the line. It was his way of making peace.

After Zappa died, Van Vliet appeared in Anton Corbijn's short biopic, *Some YoYo Stuff*, in 1994. A frail Captain Beefheart appears onscreen with various images and phrases projected behind him, to which Corbijn has asked him to respond. When the word "Zappa" flashes up, Van Vliet says, "He's the only Frank Zappa I knew."

7

Mr. Dad, Frank Zappa

The Artist as Parent

Frank Zappa has gained considerable notoriety for his music, his look, his irreverent attitude, and his politics, but that's nothing compared to the publicity and commentary his immediate family has received. With four talented children with unusual names and a second marriage that lasted until his death in 1993, Zappa's personal life has been often described in the manner of a crowd looking at animals in a zoo. In the popular press, he was constantly asked to defend the names of his children. But the fact of the matter is that Zappa held his family close, even if he raised his kids in what some might feel was a slightly unusual way.

In her insightful memoir of her role as Zappa's secretary from 1967 to 1970, *Freak Out! My Life with Frank Zappa*, Pauline Butcher recalls asking Zappa about his relationship with his parents, whom she occasionally met, and how it influenced his behavior as an adult. "Basically you get to a point and you see that your parents are behaving in a way that is either illogical or irrelevant," he replied, "and you may not wish to argue with them."

Zappa went on to explain that he wouldn't have had a good time if he followed all of his parents' rules and restrictions, and while that may sound banal to today's youth, it influenced his role as a parent in later life. As he told Butcher, "In our house if I say 'no' and any one of the kids disagrees with it and they can logically prove that I'm wrong, they win." Zappa placed a lot of value on negotiation and logic. They were a strong part of his personality, and, for better or worse, shaped his style of parenting.

Frank, Meet Gail

In 1966, Frank Zappa met Gail Sloatman through a mutual friend, Pamela Zarubica (aka Pam Z.). Sloatman, born in 1945, was the daughter of a nuclear physicist who worked for the United States Navy, and, like Zappa, she had moved around a lot at an early age, winding up in London, England, as a teenager. While she was there she attended a Catholic girls school, eventually graduating, moving out, and working in the city as an American with a visa. Her first roommate was Anya Butler, who was very active in the growing British music scene of the sixties. Butler worked as a secretary for Chris Stamp and Kit Lambert, who managed the Who. Curious by nature, Sloatman got to know many of Britain's early hit-makers simply by being in the company of Butler.

When her work visa expired in 1965, Sloatman returned to the United States and settled in New York. Like most young people in the mid-sixties, she was a free spirit, keenly interested in music, musicians, and an alternative lifestyle, which prompted her to leave New York and head to California, with Butler by her side. She met Frank in Los Angeles after a promotional tour with the Mothers of Invention, and they immediately connected. By the fall of '66 she had moved in with Zappa and become his constant companion. In 1967, she became pregnant with their first child, Moon (or Moon Unit), who was born in September, while Zappa was on tour. By all accounts, it was a marriage made in heaven: he the hard working musician and she the attractive artist. She took a keen interest in fashion design, all while raising a child and managing her husband's schedule. By looks, the young couple had grown into a conventional family.

On October 7, 2015, Gail Zappa died, after a long illness, at the age of seventy at her home in Los Angeles, surrounded by her family. In an official statement released on Facebook, Gail was described as a matriarch who was "motivated by love in all aspects of her life, kept her authenticity intact, unbowed and, simply put, was one bad ass in the music business and political world."

The Children

Frank and Gail had three more children: sons Dweezil (aka Ian Donald Calvin Euclid), born in 1969, and Ahmet, born in 1974 and named after Ahmet Ertegun, the founder of Atlantic Records, and daughter Diva, born in 1979.

In his autobiography, Zappa devotes several humorous pages to his notion of fatherhood, in a section titled "Marriage (as a Dada concept)." While the chapter is short on detail, one gets the sense, by reading between the lines, that Zappa was a dedicated parent who cared about his kids.

And although they had unusual names, it was "their last name that would probably get them in trouble." One endearing passage in the book reveals some of Zappa's guarded affection for his kids. "I don't have any time for social activities," he writes. "I do, however, have a wonderful wife and four totally unbelievable children, and that, folks, is way better." He goes on to talk about his kids, his philosophy of dealing with "a person shorter than you," and his parenting style. He writes about his youngest daughter Diva, who at the age of nine wanted to go out and play in the rain. After getting permission to do so, she put on her raincoat and boots and spent an hour singing in the backyard, about which Zappa observed that kids "have a natural sense of mysticism, and a feeling of being connected to nature" because "it's all brand-new."

Moon Unit Zappa

The most revealing story came from Moon when she was thirteen years of age. Not wanting to disturb her father at work in his home office, she slipped a note under his door one day, indicating that she wanted to do her "Encino accent" on his next recording session. Frank took her up on the offer and used her voice on the song "Valley Girl," which became his biggest hit and the Zappa song most familiar to people who are not fans of his music. The record was a rare father/daughter collaboration and an early example of Moon's creativity. The song poked fun at the girls in the San Fernando Valley, of which Frank knew very little, but by the summer of 1982, "Valley Girls" would be the butt of jokes around the world. In recent years, Moon has pursued a career in writing, stand-up comedy, and acting. She even made a "disguised" appearance in Larry David's *Curb Your Enthusiasm*, dressed in a niqab, in the episode "The Blind Date."

Dweezil Zappa

Unlike his sister, Dweezil Zappa took to music at an early age, inspired by his father's creativity. He attended school and played baseball but was also encouraged to play guitar and try his hand at photography. A photograph he took from a hotel window appears on the cover of *Zappa in New York* (1977).

At twelve years of age, Dweezil jammed with a cover band of kids known as Fred Zeppelin. By the time he was thirteen, he had released his first single, December 1982's "My Mother Is a Space Cadet," a highly charged rock record featuring a solo inspired in shape and sound by Eddie Van Halen, who produced the song under the pseudonym "The Vards." Four years later, Dweezil issued a full-length album, *Havin' a Bad Day* (Barking Pumpkin), which was produced by Frank Zappa and engineered by Bob Stone. The record also features contributions by Zappa alumni Chad Wackerman (drums) and Scott Thunes (bass guitar) and several singers, including comedian Bobcat Goldthwait, sister Moon Zappa, and Bob Rice.

Dweezil first appeared onstage with his father in 1984, jamming on the song "Whipping Post," a recording of which appears on the album *Does Humor Belong in Music?* He has released several solo albums over the years, including two with his younger brother Ahmet under the group name Z, and has made several contributions as a guitarist on recordings by Ozzy Osbourne, Todd Rundgren, and, believe it or not, Pat Boone, who released an album in 1997 called *In a Metal Mood, No More Mr. Nice Guy* (Hip-O), which features Dweezil on a version of "Smoke on the Water."

In 2006, Dweezil released a solo album called *Go with What You Know* (Zappa Records), featuring a mash-up of "Peaches En Regalia," one of the most popular instrumentals in the Frank Zappa songbook. This first-rate version marked a turning point in Dweezil's musical career, acknowledging his father's composition while blending his own signature style with Frank's formidable original. Suddenly he was coming out from a shadow that had been both a blessing and a curse with a desire to play his father's difficult music.

That same year, Dweezil announced the formation of the consummate cover band Zappa Plays Zappa, with the aim to bring his father's music to a new audience of music lovers around the world. The band tours regularly to this day. The group's version of "Peaches" won a Grammy Award for "Best Rock Instrumental Performance" in 2008. In 2015, in association with the public funding website PledgeMusic, Dweezil released his first solo album in ten years, *Via Zammata*. He also continues to hold guitar workshops online and in person.

Ahmet Zappa

Ahmet Zappa (full name Ahmet Emuuka Rodan), named after Ahmet Ertegun, the founder and producer for Atlantic Records, was born prematurely in 1974 and spent the first few weeks of his life in intensive care. In his autobiography, Frank Zappa writes openly about his son's struggle to breathe properly at birth, which was later diagnosed as hyaline membrane disease. Ahmet survived and grew up with an interest in drawing and performing. He made his first appearance on one of his father's works as a guest vocalist on the 1981 album *You Are What You Is* and wrote the lyrics to "Frogs with Dirty Little Lips," which appears on Frank's album *Them or Us* (1984).

At the age of twelve, Ahmet started auditioning for roles on television sitcoms, later making appearances on *Rosanne* (ABC) and guest hosting a number of MTV programs. He's also taken up writing on a full-time basis. In 2006, he released a novel aimed at the youth market, *The Monstrous Memoirs of a Mighty McFearless*, published by Random House, which was also released as an audiobook. He also wrote the story that formed the basis of the 2012 Disney Studios film *The Odd Life of Timothy Green*, which stars Jennifer Garner. In July of 2015, he became head of the Zappa Family Trust, taking over from his mother, Gail.

Diva Zappa

Diva Zappa, whose full name is Diva Thin Muffin Pigeen, was born in 1979. She was named Diva because of her loud voice as a baby. At the age of five, in a father/daughter collaboration, she co-wrote "Chana in De Bushwop," which appears on the album *You Can't Do That on Stage Anymore, Vol. 3* (1989). By the time she was twelve, Diva won an award for her design of a poster to raise awareness of child abuse and neglect for the Los Angeles based group known as CARE. When she turned seventeen, she started an acting career that has led to a number of supporting roles and walk-ons, including one in the 2006 Paris Hilton film *Pledge This!*, in which she appears as the character Babs Cohen, whose best line in the movie is, "Nice legs. What time do they open?" She also appeared on the CBS television series *CSI: NY* and is currently a cast member on the comedy show *HOARS (Home Owners Association Regency Supreme)*. Most notably, she played the role of Janet the groupie in the live 2013 stage performance of her father's film *200 Motels*, featuring the Los Angeles Philharmonic conducted by Esa-Pekka Salonen, with former Zappa alumni Ian Underwood and Scott Thunes in the band. A thirteen-member ensemble cast recreated Zappa's score from the original movie, which he co-directed with Tony Palmer.

All of Frank and Gail Zappa's children were encouraged to seek out their creativity in the arts, and this was fostered to the point where each child was taken out of high school at the age of fifteen and given the California High School Proficiency Examination. Zappa completely mistrusted the education system, much as he mistrusted all government institutions, for creating a generation of "mediocre" people. At the time, his decision to order his kids to drop out of high school and take their chances without going on to college like most American youth was probably seen as either irresponsible or too imposing. Nevertheless, Zappa's children have forged their own artistic careers, in spite of the last name "that would get them in trouble."

8

No Dope-Heads

Zappa's Drug-Free Zone

When he first arrived on the music scene, everybody thought Frank Zappa was weird: his music, his cover art, his look, and the look of his bandmates all screamed it. For most listeners and critics, who didn't understand his music, especially his early recordings, the only conclusion to be reached was that he "must be on drugs" or that his personal behavior was deviant in some way.

Nothing could be further from the truth. As Zappa told *BAM* magazine in 1978, "I believe people use drugs as a license to act stupid; the same way other generations use alcohol." If a band member was using drugs and it affected the performance of his music, he fired them. He didn't care what they did in private, as he explained to writer Michael Snyder of *BAM Magazine* in January 1978. "What people do on their own time is their business. Once you start a tour, you're working in a professional situation from the time you leave the airport and your home base to the time you get back at the end of the last date. Everybody that's in that touring unit relies on everybody else, from the roadies right on through." Although he tried marijuana and enjoyed the occasional beer, Zappa's only vices were cigarettes and black coffee. (He often called them "food.")

In his autobiography, Zappa remembers soft drugs coming into his life as a musician. "Between 1962 and 1968, on maybe ten occasions, I experienced the 'joys' of socially circulated marijuana. It gave me a sore throat and made me sleepy. I couldn't understand why people liked it so much."

That's not quite what Howard Kaylan recalls in his memoir, *Shell Shocked: My Life with the Turtles, Flo & Eddie, and Frank Zappa, etc*, however. "I smoked pot with Frank Zappa," he writes. "Not once, not twice, but at least three times. It was a closely guarded secret." During their 1970–71 tour together, Kaylan says, Zappa occasionally came to his room looking for pot when "he was feeling particularly low or even fabulously good."

Nevertheless, Zappa's abhorrence for drugs was immovable, as was his attitude toward the people who used them. In a CBC television interview in 1971, when asked about an anti-drug stance that, according to the host of the public-affairs program *CBC Weekend*, was the antithesis of many rock musicians at the time, Zappa gave a succinct opinion on the effect of drugs on teenagers. "It's taken away a lot of their ambition. I think we have yet to reap the benefits of the so-called 'acid generation' as the burn-outs turn up more frequently." He also thought that rock musicians had a hand in supporting drug culture.

Zappa took his anti-drug stance to the airwaves in the sixties for the Do It Now Foundation, which still exists and aims to tackle important issues such as drugs and guns among youths. The public service announcements heard on radio were unscripted and effective, according to the foundation. Here was a guy who looked like a dealer, ostracizing drug users. (Years later, for those who got the inside joke, Zappa was cast as a drug dealer in a 1986 episode of the NBC television series *Miami Vice*.)

The myths surrounding Frank Zappa often brought more fans to his music than his actual recordings, particularly at the beginning of his career with the Mothers of Invention. Drugs and drug use were certainly a part of the counterculture of the San Francisco and L.A. music scenes in the sixties, and even though Zappa was the exception, the common belief that he used drugs to create his weird music was a myth that he never really shook off. To him, ignorance of his work and its roots was the reason so many people wrongly labeled him a drug user. Consequently, his strong disdain for the drug culture coincided with a larger disdain for American society and the use of drugs and alcohol. In his autobiography, he goes to great lengths to explain that, in his view, the chemical makeup of beer is far more harmful to men because it creates a "pseudo military behavior" that leads them to get drunk and turn violent.

For Ben Watson, author of *Frank Zappa: The Negative Dialectics of Poodle Play*, a deeper conclusion is that "people seem to need some biographical weirdness to explain why Zappa's music should be so strange." Watson's hefty tome is a serious attempt to bring context to Zappa the person and the irony of his songs, especially the ones he wrote about drugs. For Watson, Zappa's subversion is often the contradiction between the common knowledge about him and his relatively banal lifestyle. For Zappa, writing songs about America's relationship with drugs and alcohol from the comfort of his straight-up domestic home was subversive in itself.

Along with coffee, Frank considered cigarettes food.   *Paul Bergen/Getty Images*

Zappa's Songs About Drug Use

Zappa wrote several songs that were often misinterpreted as celebrating drug use but were actually critiques of the drug culture and its users. "Cocaine Decisions" and "Pygmy Twylyte" poke fun at the ritual of drug use and its effects, while the satirical lounge song "America Drinks and Goes Home" offers an inebriated critique of bar crowds, in front of which Zappa spent some of his "formative" years playing. "Cocaine Decisions," from *The Man from Utopia* (1983), takes shots at doctors, lawyers, accountants, movie producers, and politicians, all of whom, in Zappa's opinion, negatively affect society by using cocaine to develop what they think is a cool lifestyle. "Pygmy Twylyte," from *Roxy & Elsewhere* (1974), is a rhythmically complex musical trip into the world of Quaaludes and their limited effect on the drug user. Drugs were not a part of Zappa's lifestyle, in spite of the myths surrounding him and the fans who supposedly enjoy the use of drugs while playing his records at home. That lifestyle was a mystery to Zappa, but his sense of the drug culture went deeper.

In an extensive radio interview in 1977, transcribed in a discontinued magazine called *Nuggets*, Zappa went to considerable length to make the connection between the lost youth of the fifties who came to life in the sixties (Summer of Love, et cetera) and the CIA's attempt to control them by making LSD the drug of choice. Zappa believed that the government was afraid of this new generation because of its political power. To him, the government was fearful of a growing youth movement that had money and was politically astute. Drugs and other commercial products were a way of controlling that movement, and Zappa's reasoning, albeit reductive, has some merit. "All this stuff not only gives you a physical sensation, it gives you a social sensation; it gives you the impression that you have social worth in a certain circle of friends, because you have all the mannerisms of a certain lifestyle and because that is different from certain other lifestyles you must therefore be better. It just tends to reinforce feelings of self-worth in instances of people who might not have too much self-worth and need some."

Zappa went on to say that the Summer of Love was full of antidotes to the troubled teen, but always at a price, and he often blamed the federal government for tapping into the pained lives of youth and tampering with the medication, especially the CIA. "LSD was manufactured by the CIA. We already know that; they were using it on people in the Army to test it and the connection that was dealing with people in San Francisco in those days was probably working for the Government and he was using the whole teenage population in order to test that drug . . . I believe that part of that whole situation during the sixties was government manufactured. That stuff's been around for years—way before Haight-Ashbury. Haight-Ashbury was just the logical extension of their testing." It's a complicated theory but one that really drove Zappa's thinking against drug use and other aspects of government intervention. Zappa was a strong believer in the First Amendment of the US Constitution, but he felt that certain freedoms were illusory.

9

Welcome to the Machine

Zappa and the Record Business

To suggest that Frank Zappa hated the record business wouldn't be fair: he also mistrusted it. He understood how it worked but he struggled to keep his music available to his fans under somebody else's rules. When he promised to make the Mothers "rich and famous" in 1965, he knew record companies held all the financial, manufacturing, and marketing resources necessary to promote his music, but not necessarily *his* way.

Unlike a lot of musicians in the fifties and sixties who were either cheated of royalties (such as Little Richard), or naïve about who controlled their publishing rights, Zappa understood early on in his career that deferring the business side of his work to a corporate entity was the wrong choice. By learning about and getting involved in the management of his recordings, as well as his tours, he was in control. As a businessman, he often talked about his work and the financial struggles it entailed. One of his most poignant songs about it is "Outside Now," from the album *Joe's Garage*, released in 1979.

In *The Negative Dialectics of Poodle Play*, Ben Watson observes, "Zappa has always been explicit about the business side of his art, which is probably why he is often accused of being motivated by money." For Zappa, the connection between the two parties wasn't separate and distinct or hidden by the artists themselves, who, in the radical sixties, had to prove to their fans that they weren't part of the commercial establishment. As such, managers were rarely mentioned in liner notes or seen in group photographs. That was not the case for Zappa and the Mothers of Invention, whose manager was the former publicist and club owner Herb Cohen. He was not just some unidentified guy working in the wings. Cohen openly partnered with Zappa on all things related to the business by working with existing labels like MGM/Verve and creating the Bizarre and Straight labels in 1969. Zappa understood how important it was to tap into the resources of the corporate machine while maintaining some artistic independence. From a business point of view, the Zappa/Cohen partnership was aggressive in carving its own niche into a competitive marketplace.

Much of Zappa's business acumen was gained through his own experiences as a young entrepreneur in his early twenties. In her remarkable memoir, *Freak Out! My Life with Frank Zappa*, his former secretary, Pauline Butcher, recalls him telling her, "Don't be discouraged by failure. People who are afraid of failure are people who think themselves so great, they can't fail." During her short, intense tenure with Zappa, Butcher felt encouraged to let her creativity break out. "He not only believed his own horizons were infinite; he ascribed this attitude to those around him. Work hard, believe in yourself, use failure as a positive force, and you will succeed." In many ways, this was Frank Zappa's overarching philosophy about his career, and it easily translated into his method of running his own business.

The first manager of the Mothers, Mark Cheka, introduced Zappa to Herb Cohen in 1965, following a performance by the band at a party. Cheka didn't have the connections to take the band very far, but Cohen was a well-connected Los Angeles "businessman" who was already successful managing rock bands and folk musicians. He owned two clubs in the L.A. hub of new music known as the Sunset Strip—the Unicorn and Cosmo Alley—where the Mothers could play regularly between occasional performances at bigger and better-paying clubs such as the Whisky a Go Go. Cohen was never afraid of a challenge, including promoting a new band whose music wasn't like anything else at the time. Managing the Mothers was an opportunity he couldn't resist. By October of 1965, he made the band join the musicians' union, the AFM, which cost them money in dues but allowed Cohen to charge club owners scale for their gigs (and take 15 percent commission). Soon, the Mothers were making better money on the club circuit, gaining a fan base, and moving in the right direction, business-wise.

On March 1, 1966, the Mothers signed a two-year, five-album record deal with Verve records, a division of MGM, which purchased the famous jazz label from its founder, Norman Granz, in 1961, and is currently owned by Universal Music Group. The band received a $2,500 advance against royalties and a remarkable budget of $21,000 to record their first album.

The sizable budget surprised everybody, including Zappa, as he recalls in his autobiography. "The average budget for an LP in those days was six to eight thousand dollars . . . the other industrial norm was that most groups didn't really play their own instruments for the basic tracks on their albums. We played all of our own basic tracks on *Freak Out!*, with studio musicians added only for orchestrational color."

Under the terms of the contract, Zappa had control over the recording process with producer Tom Wilson, but the label still held control over the final package and the master tapes. A staffer at Verve/MGM, worried about the implications of the group's name, had them change it from the Mothers to the Mothers of Invention.

Zappa was able to release *Freak Out!* and the follow-up, *Absolutely Free*, as he intended; the real interference came when the record company decided to edit and remix *We're Only in It for the Money*, the band's third album, without Zappa's input. As a result of that, plus the controversy over the artwork, which parodied the cover of *Sgt Pepper* by the Beatles, Verve executives withheld its release until March 4, 1968.

Zappa was not amused, as reported by Barry Miles in his detailed biography, *Frank Zappa*. "The test pressing was censored [and] the equalization was changed removing the highs and boosting the bottom [frequencies] to obscure the words," said Zappa. "I called them up and said 'you can't put this record out.' And they'd already pressed 40,000 of them." The label also decided not to exercise its option to renew its contract with the band. So Zappa and Herb Cohen established their own label, Bizarre, which would offer the freedom Zappa needed to release his work, his way, and develop new artists as well. From 1968 to 1972, Zappa released eleven of his own albums on the Bizarre label, beginning with *Uncle Meat*, with distribution by Reprise Records, a division of Warner Bros.

Bizarre Records

The establishment of Bizarre Records was a serious business venture for Zappa and Cohen. The company had several divisions, including publicity, advertising, music publishing, and artist management. It had its own logo, designed by Cal Schenkel, featuring a surreal mix of cartoon and science-like graphics. The logo depicts a cylindrical bell jar on top of a wooden end table to which a vacuum pump is attached. Schenkel worked with Zappa on the cover designs for most of the records that were released by the label.

In a statement announcing the new label, Cohen and Zappa wrote, "We make records that are a little different. We present musical and sociological material which the important record companies would probably not allow you to hear. Just what the world needs, another record company." At the age of twenty-eight, Frank Zappa had full control of his music, publishing, album design, and packaging—a rarity in those days, except for the Beatles, who had established Apple records in the same year.

The contractual agreement with Warner Bros. was a good one, according to Zappa. As he told *Creem* magazine in January 1972, "We got a good deal all the way round from Warners. One of the most interesting aspects of our deal is that we own our masters. At the end of the contract with Warner Brothers we get our masters back and that's what I call a good deal. That's one of the most appealing things anybody could write into a contract."

The contract also included the delivery of a certain number of finished productions by the Mothers of Invention and any new acts Zappa and Cohen came up with to fulfill it. It meant that Zappa and Cohen had to seek out new artists worthy of Bizarre, meaning unusual and non-commercial music. Interestingly, the first of these releases was an album by the well-known comedian Lenny Bruce, *The Berkeley Concert* (with liner notes by Ralph J. Gleason). Also on Bizarre was *Permanent Damage* by the GTO's, an all-girl groupie band from Los Angeles (one of whom, Pamela Z., was Moon Zappa's babysitter) who were encouraged to perform and record even though they had little musical talent; *An Evening with Wild Man Fischer*; and the debut album by folk singer Sandy Hurvitz, *Sandy's Album Is Here at Last* (produced by Ian Underwood after an artistic dispute between Hurvitz and Zappa).

Straight Records

In late 1969, a sister label to Bizarre was established to release music by so-called "mainstream" artists mostly under Herb Cohen's management. Straight Records put out a total of sixteen albums, including the first two recordings by a new band from Phoenix, Arizona, called Alice Cooper. Zappa recalled his first meeting with the band on *The Mike Douglas Show* in 1976. The group auditioned for him at his house in Laurel Canyon, California; they impressed him, but the turning point came when they opened for the Mothers of Invention. "Invariably, when they would play,

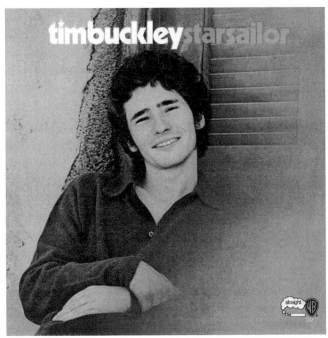

Tim Buckley's new sound released in 1970.

thousands of people would leave the room, and I knew they had something."
Alice Cooper's debut album, *Pretties for You*, was produced by Ian
Underwood and Herb Cohen and released in June 1969. It barely cracked
the *Billboard* 200, peaking at #193, but it still sold more copies than the follow-up, *Easy Action*, which was produced by David Briggs.

The two most important releases on the Straight label were *Trout Mask
Replica* by Captain Beefheart and *Starsailor* by Tim Buckley. The former is
still in print and made *Rolling Stone*'s list of the Top 100 Albums of All Time
in 1987, placing at #33. The release by Buckley is fondly remembered as
being his most experimental and creative because the commercial expectations of the label, and therefore Cohen and Zappa, were few. The backing
band included two former original members of the Mothers of Invention,
Bunk Gardner and Buzz Gardner. It features the tune "Song to the Siren,"
which offers free-form production colors not previously associated with
Buckley's earlier folk/roots recordings. *Trout Mask Replica* is now recognized
as one of the most visionary albums of all-time, a counterculture musical
feast that author Kevin Courrier describes as a record "that continues to

The most successful and famous release on Straight Records.

resonate because it forces us to hear things that can change our way of listening."

The last album on the Bizarre label was *The Grand Wazoo* by Frank Zappa, released on November 27, 1972.

DiscReet Records

In 1973, Zappa released *Over-Nite Sensation* on a new label called DiscReet. The red logo was a kind of throwback to the stylish designs of the early sixties. According to a newspaper story at the time, Zappa, Cohen, and a third partner at Bizarre, Zach Glickman, had "realigned" their custom label, with continuing distribution from Warner Bros. The story offered some cryptic reasoning behind the changes, which had evidently been made "because Zappa's former label titles do not lend themselves to commercial support of upcoming releases."

In his anthology on Zappa, *Cosmik Debris*, Greg Russo offers up a deeper explanation for the change. "Frank Zappa took a back seat in production and business arrangements, which were handled by manager and president Harold Berkman, and [because] many of the artists signed by Herb Cohen without Zappa's knowledge exhibited little or no talent on record." Creatively, DiscReet was far more adventurous about the music it wanted to release than Bizarre or Straight. In an interview for the Warners-owned promotional publication *Circular* in December 1973, Zappa called DiscReet "one label for all different kinds of product, an independent distribution deal on more favorable terms with WEA and for more dollars."

From 1973 to 1979, the DiscReet label released seventeen albums, including Zappa's most popular works. It also released the last two albums by Ted Nugent and the Amboy Dukes, *Call of the Wild* and *Tooth, Fang & Claw*, and the last two recordings by Tim Buckley, *Sefronia* and *Look at the Fool*. The label also released two albums by L.A. vocalist Kathy Dalton, *Amazing* and *Boogie Bands and One Night Stands* (featuring members of Little Feat), which had limited financial success, and the debut recording by Brenda Patterson, *Like Good Wine*, which fetches no more than $20 on eBay at the time of this writing.

Except for releasing eight important Zappa releases, DiscReet failed to succeed on many levels because Herb Cohen ran it without much input from his very busy partner, leading to a messy ending in 1976 when Zappa filed suit against Herb Cohen to dissolve the partnership. Zappa was able to cut a separate deal with Warner Bros. for the release of *Zoot Allures*, which was not part of the DiscReet obligations. In exchange for that record, however, Zappa handed over finished tapes for three albums, without notes and artwork, to fulfill the DiscReet/Warners contract, without the participation of Cohen.

DiscReet records shut down in 1979 as a result of a dispute between Zappa, Herb Cohen, and Herb's brother Martin. Zappa believed that Cohen was mishandling the label and taking profits for himself, even though they were legally equal partners. Once again, Zappa's relationship with the music business was in flux. To fulfill the terms of the contract with Warner Bros., Zappa submitted the tapes for a quadruple album known as *Läther*. But Herb Cohen intervened to block it because it was due out in Europe on Phonogram, aka Mercury Records, a division of Capitol/EMI. So, after the release of *Zappa in New York* (heavily edited and much delayed) in 1978,

Dweezil's Polaroid graces the cover of the album as issued by Warner Bros.

Warner Bros. told Zappa he had four more albums to submit, per his contract. The company rejected the four-record set that would become *Läther* and instead issued three albums—*Sleep Dirt*, *Studio Tan*, and *Orchestral Favorites*—with no liner notes and artwork by American illustrator Gary Panter that was not approved by Zappa in order to get a financial return on its contract with DiscReet. Zappa went on a short crusade, asking fans not to buy any of the albums, since to him they were unauthorized. To spite Warner Bros. (and, quite possibly, Capitol/EMI), he offered fans the chance to home-record *Läther* from KROQ radio in Pasadena, California, when he played test pressings of the album on air. The end result of all of this was the formation of a new independent label, simply called Zappa Records, distributed by Polygram.

Zappa Records

On March 3, 1979, the first album released on Zappa Records arrived in the form of the highly successful *Sheik Yerbouti* (first titled *Martian Love Secrets*), which peaked at #21 on the *Billboard* 200 that year. It was released between two Warners albums, *Sleep Dirt* (January) and *Orchestral Favorites* (May). Suddenly, Zappa was competing with himself for shelf space in record stores around the world. Undeterred, he released two more albums on the Zappa Records label that year, *Joe's Garage Act I* in September and *Joe's Garage Acts II & III* in November. He also produced and released the debut album by violinist and composer L. Shankar, *Touch Me There*, which features three songs co-written with Zappa, including the heavy, satirical track "Dead Girls of London."

Zappa had eventually regained control of his current projects and the financial means to move forward with tons of unreleased music. The contract with Polygram ended in 1980, sparked by the company's refusal to release a single by Zappa called "I Don't Wanna Get Drafted," which took aim at President Carter's urge to make young American men register for the draft. It was released on Zappa Records on April 28, 1980.

Barking Pumpkin Records

Zappa's next-to-last label was his most successful business venture. It was called Barking Pumpkin, and it put out twenty albums between 1980 and 1988, with another four issued between 1992 and 1994. The label was named for Frank's wife, Gail, whom he used to call "Pumpkin." When she quit smoking and developed a loud cough, "Barking Pumpkin" was born. The colorful logo features a Halloween pumpkin with its mouth open to say "arf" at a terrified black cat, which responds, in Chinese, "Holy Shit."

The label was fully independent, with Zappa signing distribution deals first with CBS and then Capitol, until the advent of CDs in 1984, at which point Rykodisc took over. Rykodisc was the first CD-only music label, and until 2002 it was home to the complete Zappa catalogue, often in different mixes and configurations not heard on the original vinyl. The label enjoyed timely releases of Zappa projects that were already "in the can," such as the six-volume series *You Can't Do That on Stage Anymore.*

In early 1993, when Zappa's health was in decline, he insisted that his wife Gail get out of the record business entirely. He didn't want her to inherit the burden of years and years of the kinds of financial headaches with record companies that he had experienced. At the time, Rhino Records was interested in the late composer's catalogue, but the undisclosed price tag was too high for the company. Rykodisc, having produced a successful run of CD releases while Zappa was alive, was in a position to make a deal for everything, and it completed that deal in October 1994, for a reported $20 million. The following year, the label began a major marketing and distribution campaign that brought all of Zappa's albums back in front of the buying public, including the release of a new compilation, *Strictly Commercial*. These fifty-three authorized releases were often remixes of the original vinyl plus new live recordings from Zappa's archives, which he called the Utility Muffin Research Kitchen (or UMRK).

Vaulternative Records

In 2002, Vaulternative Records was created to release Zappa's huge archive of live recordings under the new management of the Zappa Family Trust, led by Gail Zappa, her son Dweezil, and Joe Travers, head archivist (or "vaultmeister"). This corporate move effectively gave control of all of Zappa's works, image (including a trademark on his iconic moustache), and licensing to the family—a legacy that Gail Zappa oversaw until 2015, when she relinquished control to her son Ahmet, who now heads the Zappa Family Trust. To enhance the Zappa brand, the website www.zappa.com was launched in the same year, making his music available to the world without record company interference. But the digital revolution complicated matters, and in 2008 Gail Zappa filed suit against Rykodisc for copyright infringement, with the aim of stopping the company from releasing Zappa's music in any non-CD format. Once again, control of her husband's music was back in corporate hands, because the Warner Music Group had purchased Rykodisc two years earlier and now wanted to distribute Zappa's music on iTunes.

The dispute wasn't settled until 2011. A steady series of archival releases followed until a new deal was announced in 2012. Now, in a move that may not have impressed Zappa himself, the Zappa Family Trust signed an exclusive licensing deal with Universal Music Enterprises to reissue sixty albums in the catalogue, this time using the original analog masters. This numbered series taps into the vinyl mixes as they were originally intended, with reproductions of the original liner notes and sound quality considerably better than had been available on the Rykodisc releases from twenty years earlier. This was a musical feast to the purists, who preferred cleaned-up CDs to their old LPs. At the same time, Zappa's music was released on iTunes for a little more than a buck-a-song, ruining the album concept as the composer had originally intended it but offering up choice cuts to a new generation of listeners around the world.

Interestingly, in an interview with Mike King for the October 2010 issue of *Music Business Journal*, Gail Zappa had been dismissive of iTunes because of its compressed audio and parent company Apple's business practices. "I am not a fan of iTunes. I am not a fan of their growth through their overbearing means by which they have a reduced value of music. First, they [Apple] taught everyone how to steal it and then they said, 'Oops, sorry here's how you can pay for it really cheap!' So you know, I'm not a fan of that and I'm not a fan of price-fixing, which is something they do."

One year later, the Kobalt Music Group—"a leading independent music publisher and music services company"—made a deal with the ZFT to administer all of Zappa's songs, scores, and movies around the world. Asked about the agreement for a story in *Billboard* magazine dated August 1, 2013, Gail Zappa said, "We are forever laughing at the absurdity of this business and we are pleased to be doing it in the company of Kobalt." The company's New York offices are on Madison Ave.

Two years later, on July 29, 2015, the Zappa Family Trust made a major announcement regarding Frank's collection and future releases. Ahmet Zappa had taken over as the head of the ZFT, replacing Gail, and had signed a new deal with Universal Music (UMe) for "long-term licensing and global rights management." According to Gail, the new agreement meant a lot to her and the integrity of the music and the UMRK archives. "I am universally thrilled with this partnership because the fans will have unparalleled access to Frank Zappa's Works; the doors to the Vault are now officially WIDE open." In September, sixteen albums were made available exclusively as downloads through iTunes.

10

Liking the Sound of His Own Voice

Choice Quotations

Frank Zappa did hundreds of interviews during his lifetime. Even though he was busy composing or rehearsing his band or playing concerts, he always found the time to talk about his work or his guitar playing, often offering his political views in the same conversation. The following is a list of Zappa's finest commentary, with sources and context included.

The "all-American dissident curmudgeon."

On His Ability as a Guitar Player

"I think that I shouldn't be rated as a guitarist. That's a stupid hobby, rating guitar players. My technique as a guitar player is . . . fair. There are plenty of people that play faster than I do, never hit a wrong note, and have a lovely sound."

—*"The Lost Interview,"* Read Magazine, *1999 (originally conducted in 1984)*

"There's a lot of good guitar players out there. I'll guarantee you that I am the only person doing what I am doing, though. Because I don't approach it as a guitar star. I go out there to play compositions. I want to do compositions instantly on the guitar."

—*To John Swenson,* Guitar World, *March 1982*

"I'm not a virtuoso guitar player. A virtuoso can play anything and I can't. I can play only what I know, to the extent that I've developed enough manual dexterity to get the point across, but that has deteriorated over time"

—The Real Frank Zappa Book, *Chapter 8*

"Nothing is more blasphemous than a properly played distorted guitar. It is capable of making blasphemous noises, and that's what first attracted me."

—*To Bill Milkowski,* Downbeat, *February 1983, in response to a question about his fascination with the guitar in his youth*

On His Intentions as a Composer

"What I do isn't designed to reinforce your lifestyle. It's coming from a different place: it's not product. Ultimately everything that gets released by a record company turns into product, but the intent of what I do is not product oriented. I've got something to say. I've got certain ways that I want to say it and I take great care of the preparation of the material. I see it through all the way to the mastering process."

—*To John Stix,* Guitar World, *September 1980*

"The crux of the biscuit is: If it entertains you, fine. Enjoy it. If it doesn't, then blow it out your ass. I do it to amuse myself. If I like it, I release it. If somebody else likes it, that's a bonus."

—*To* Playboy, *May 3, 1993*

On the Subject of Drug Use

"Never having tried crystal methedrine . . . I will say that fucking is theoretically superior to anything chemical that you can stick in your body."

—*To* BAM, *January 1978*

"In Los Angeles, during the height of the drug frenzy, we had people who thought they could fly. People who thought they could walk through walls, and all the rest of the stuff. People who were in communication with the larger portions of the cosmos, because the LSD had convinced them of this."

—*To Headley Gritter,* RAM *(Rock Australia Magazine),
issue 131, April 1980*

On What Critics Say About Him

"I don't expect to have everybody like what I do. I don't expect them to understand it and I don't give a fuck. If I set a challenge for myself, the thing that matters is meeting that challenge by the time the event is completed. And I grade myself harder than anybody else is going to grade me. I know what I want to do when I start doing it. I know what I'm doing while I'm doing it. I know what it's supposed to be when it's done. I'm watching all the time."

—*To* BAM, *January 1978*

"Most rock journalism is people who can't write, interviewing people who can't talk, for people who can't read."

—*In conversation with Pierre Boulez at Schoenberg Hall,
UCLA, May 23, 1989*

On Himself

"I'm sure I'm quite eccentric by quite a lot of different types of standards. But by my own standards I'm normal. I think that's a prerequisite for being eccentric. In order to be a true eccentric you have to think that what you're doing is just perfectly normal and weird to somebody else, because if you think you're eccentric then you're manufacturing it."

—*To Karl Dallas,* Melody Maker, *January 28, 1978*

"I thought of myself as a creep because people always saw me as a creep. I don't think that many people would want me in their homes."

—To Eve Brandstein, Blast, *December 1976*

"I like carrying things to their most ridiculous extreme because out there on the fringe is where my type of entertainment lies."

—To Playbor, *May 2, 1993*

"I'm a cottage industry, and since I'm not funded by any foundation or government grant, and since I'm usually the one that is ultimately responsible for paying for these things, the projects are kind of at the mercy of what my income is like and what my overhead is doing to me at the time I undertake the project."

—To M.I., *November/December 1979*

On His Relationship with the Media

"Media is all a logical extension of government, as controlled by government. All you need to know is that's the way it is. If you believe and understand—what's to be afraid of? You know it's fucked. The media understands me fine. They understand me as well as I understand them. I'm just, a person living his life doing what he does and they do what they do, except— I'm a good guy and they're the bad guys."

—To Eve Brandstein, Blast, *December 1976*

On Education

"The ability of Madison Avenue to persuade people will rise proportionately as the educational system deteriorates."

—To Florindo Volpacchio, Telos, *May 16, 1991*

On the Purpose of the Mothers of Invention

"We're involved in a so-called war against apathy."

—From a 1968 BBC television program

On Other Music

"I've heard a lot of that kind of music and there are always things in it that crack me up. There are things in Schoenberg that are equally funny as the words to Wooly Bully, but don't tell him that."

—*To John Dalton,* Guitar, *1979, when asked if he found stupid things in the works of classical composers*

"Disco was a functional type of music. We may be using the term music loosely here. Disco was designed for a specific function. It was wallpaper to be used in the background of the lifestyle of the people who inhabited those disco places. And those places were basically meatracks. The function of this music was to provide this rhythmic dance texture while people went to the meatrack. If you are going to have a meatrack why would you have anything more intelligent than disco? It seems to me to be perfectly designed for its usage.

—*In conversation with Tom Graves,* Rock & Roll Disc *magazine, December 1987/January 1988*

"I think the music of the Fifties is really good. I suspect it's much better musically than much of what's available now. Not in terms of production, but in terms of content. One good believable song about some guy's girlfriend and how they broke up—a sincere one—is better than twenty albums of English rock that's ever been produced. Or better than one hundred albums of laid-back L.A. studio acoustic-guitar swill."

—*In conversation with Dave Rothman,* OUI *magazine, April 1979*

On the Punk Movement

"No musical trend has ever survived unless you can dress up to it."

—*From* The Dick Cavett Show, *June 14, 1980*

On Working with Eric Burden and the Animals (for whom Zappa arranged some songs)

"I found that not only were they not particularly original, but were hung up in that R&B bag, which is deadening when you get little white boys trying to be little black boys, screaming the blues and being funky and all—that's shitty."

—*To Frank Kofsky,* Jazz & Pop, *September 1967*

On Composing

"I earn a living by producing merchandisable manifestations of portions of my imagination."

—*From* Zappa!, *a special edition of* Guitar Player *1993*

On the Republican Party

"When God created Republicans, he gave up on everything else."

—*To Alan Thicke on* Thicke of the Night, *April 28, 1984*

"If they could get rid of that other fascist shit they've picked up over the years, I would register as a Republican. I'm talking about the evil influence the radical right has had on the Republican Party. If Abraham Lincoln came back today, he would not recognize the Republican Party as he knew it."

—*In conversation with Ron Chepesiuk,*
Gallery *magazine, June 1989*

Signing Off

"Goodnight Austin, Texas, wherever you are."

—*From* Bongo Fury, *1975*

Zappa and His Fans

A Cultivated Audience

In 1965, when Zappa and the Mothers of Invention (MOI) arrived on the music scene with their particular brand of music and look, they needed to find an audience to succeed. Zappa understood that his music wasn't for everyone, and that building a fan base for it required patience, luck, and marketing savvy. Young, middle-class fan clubs were pretty big business in the sixties for the Beatles, the Monkees, and the Rolling Stones, but those fans weren't necessarily the people Zappa wanted to reach. His music was different, his band was different, and he was different, so it stood to reason that his audience would be different, too. Even in the growing pop music industry of the sixties, the MOI's audience wasn't the so-called hippies, because they were from L.A., not San Francisco, where bands like the Grateful Dead had appeal with the editorial help of *Rolling Stone* magazine. So Zappa developed a relationship with the people of L.A.'s freak scene.

The freaks were the complete opposites of the hippies in dress and attitude. While the hippies valued tolerance and the notion of community, the freaks were much more self-centered, ego-driven, and non-conformist. They weren't as politically involved, either, choosing to leave that activity to university students instead. About the only thing they had in common was long hair. The freaks were free spirits who moved in many directions politically and socially—much like Zappa's music. They loved to dance and they didn't take drugs as a means of escapist behavior. They simply gave themselves permission to behave as freely as possible, without any ties to a code or culture beyond self-expression.

As Ben Watson concludes in *The Negative Dialectics of Poodle Play*, Zappa understood this audience as being a "transitional culture between the Beats and the Hippies." It was also an audience ready to accept everything that was handed to them, politically, culturally, and musically. This unfiltered reaction fueled Zappa and the MOI, so much so that the band became part of a movement. Consequently, this provided Zappa with an audience, and a focus, for his music. The MOI's first album, *Freak Out!* (1966), was as much a musical statement as it was political, but it was also part of Zappa's marketing plan. He considered freak culture, as outlandish as it was, as his target audience, and it worked.

United Mutations Fan Club

To Zappa and the Mothers of Invention, this was the start of a beautiful relationship—one that led to the creation of a fan club, United Mutations. Fan mail was always a part of Zappa's connection with his audience. He encouraged fans to write letters that were eventually answered with the help of his wife, Gail, and his secretary, Pauline Butcher. According to Butcher, the fan mail piled up over a year before she was hired, "waiting for the proper stationary" in order to reply to it all. But United Mutations took priority. Zappa actually took out magazine and comic-book ads to solicit membership, providing a sign-up form with a return address in Hollywood, California. Applicants had to answer a few questions about themselves, including name, age, sex, height, weight, address, state, zip, father's name and profession, and mother's name and profession. They also had to complete a short survey that included these questions:

- Who is God?
- ESP? (Extra Sensory Perception) Yes? No? Describe.
- Best way to describe my social environment is . . .
- If I had my way I would change it to . . .
- How will you change your social environment?
- When?
- What are you afraid of?
- What sort of help can the Mothers give you?

Quite the laundry list, but for three dollars you could join and get some photos, a signed membership card, and copies of the US Constitution and Bill of Rights. The club only lasted a few years but it established a means by which Zappa could at least identify his audience and sell his music.

Audience Relations

Zappa had a mix of contempt and respect for his audience. On some of the live recordings, for instance, you can hear him scolding them for not paying attention or praising them for bringing signs with slogans like "Fuck the draft," as one fan did at a show in Buffalo, New York, in 1980. Zappa didn't offend his audience so much as try to shake them out of complacency with insults. *Tinsel Town Rebellion* (1981), for example, features an extended audience-participation section in which Zappa asks for the women in the audience to throw their underwear onstage. He was actually collecting it for a quilt artist by the name of Emily James, but there is, understandably, some reluctance from the Buffalo audience, which causes Zappa to retort, "Perhaps you're a little bit too intellectual here." It's all in good fun, though, and perhaps the audience expected edgy patter from Zappa, much like an audience who finds a caustic and insulting comedian "good fun."

Zappa leads a dance contest on the same album, with equally mixed results. Stage antics of the sort that Spike Jones had in his shows often went from the sublime to the ridiculous. Audiences usually expected Zappa's concerts to be lively, and they expected to have a good time. But things sometimes turned unpredictable, as they did with the near hysteria at his often-boisterous New York Palladium shows on Halloween, where fans dressed up and tended to be in high spirits, or when a riot broke out at a concert in Palermo, Sicily, in 1982.

In the April 1989 issue of *Relix* magazine, Zappa talked about his audience compared to others', and the misconception that he only appealed to former fans of the Mothers of Invention. "Our audience has always been really mixed, in terms of age, in terms of geographical backgrounds, whatever. We have strange appeal, it's really hard to describe. For example, the age range at our concerts could be anywhere from fourteen to sixty, with a preponderance of the individuals in the concert right around eighteen to twenty-five. I don't think very many other groups have that kind of range. Most of the ones who come are new customers."

Zappa understood that his fans were, if nothing else, loyal. He was happy to release his music to as many people as possible but he also knew the value of being honest with them, too. Such was the case on October 31, 1977, when he went on Pasadena radio station KROQ-FM and invited listeners to tape their own copies of his latest record, *Läther*—which Warner Bros. wouldn't pay him for and had blocked EMI from releasing in Europe after Zappa cut a distribution deal with the label—from the radio.

When he released *London Symphony Orchestra Vol. 1* (1983), an album of his classical works conducted by Kent Nagano, Zappa offered fans a caveat in the liner notes: "With every performance of new music, errors will occur. Every effort has been to remove these, but without a much larger budget for rehearsal and recording time, the possibility of perfection . . . is somewhat remote."

Zappa had a limited budget to rehearse and record the LSO in London, and consequently this record and a second volume, released in 1987, were heavily edited. He wanted to be fair to his fans by letting them know that the recordings may not be up to their expectations. Rather than make excuses after the fact, his open relationship with his fans allowed him to be up front about it. He may not have offered a money-back guarantee, but at least he wasn't trying to hide behind what some might consider to be an inferior performance.

Money was so tight for the LSO project that only 6,000 LPs were pressed upon its initial release. But in 1995 the album was completely remixed and re-sequenced for issue on CD by Rykodisc, which said as much, in fine print, in the album's booklet. With its digital sheen removed, the very mistakes and errors Zappa had apologized for on the LP version were now fully exposed. To some fans that was a benefit, to others an anomaly, but Zappa's loyal audience never stopped buying his music. (It's not known if an apology was issued for making fans buy the same stuff twice.)

Mail Order, Zappa Style

When Zappa started Barking Pumpkin, it was more than just a label for his recordings. It was also a mail-order business, designed to meet customer demand for his music while giving him the freedom to issue his vast library of recordings on his own terms. When he released the double LP *Tinsel Town Rebellion* in May 1981 through regular corporate distribution, Zappa put an ad for the "hard core fan" on the inner sleeve for an exclusive three-volume set called *Shut Up 'n Play Yer Guitar.* Fans simply requested one or all three volumes, and in six weeks they had their product. According to an interview with Bill Milkowski in the December 1981 issue of *Good Times*, the campaign was a great success. "Within two weeks of the first orders coming in, the album had paid for itself," Zappa reported, "so I intend on putting out some more."

Although Zappa wasn't necessarily a pioneer of taking control of his own work and bypassing the corporate system, at the time it was considered a very bold move. By 1987, he had plans to release seventeen albums in the course of just six to eight months, which was unprecedented. Today, any musician can write, produce, raise money, and issue their music over the Internet via Bandcamp or iTunes for a fee, or on YouTube without charge. Zappa hated the corporate model and the way it decided when and how music was produced, marketed, and distributed. With the means available to any composer or musician today, can you imagine what he could be doing *now* to reach his audience?

12

Send-Ups

Zappa Lampoons the Beatles, Bob Dylan, and Michael Jackson

B y taking shots at politicians, hippies, groupies, record companies, and the religious right, Frank Zappa wasn't afraid to offend some people with his music. But he also took pleasure in mocking three of the biggest artists in pop: the Beatles, Bob Dylan, and Michael Jackson. Was this out of spite, or was he simply trying to poke holes in the balloons of star-crazed fans? Part of the answer lies in Zappa's desire to criticize American culture using the art of satire, an often-tricky device that relies on an audience being bright enough to get the references.

Zappa often felt that people didn't get the bigger joke lying behind a topical song directed at specific artists or a group of people, so he wrote both lowbrow and highbrow satiric music. The problem wasn't his alone: just ask Randy Newman, whose song about prejudice called "Short People," from the album *Little Criminals* (Warner 1977), was taken too literally by a misunderstanding American public, even though he was telling the story from a biased narrator's point of view. In fact, he *likes* short people— "They're just the same as you and I." (See chapter 13 for a more detailed look at Zappa's satire.)

The Beatles

On June 1, 1967, the Beatles released *Sgt. Pepper's Lonely Hearts Club Band*, an avant-garde collection of songs and soundscapes that, to some, was the new gold standard in rock music. At the time it was considered the first "concept album," opening the door to long-form compositions in a genre previously restricted to the three-minute, radio-friendly pop song, even though *Freak Out!*, which did the same, was released a year earlier.

Frank Zappa held an unusual position in his consideration of music as an art and as a business. He understood early on that record companies were only interested in making money and not in advancing a new art form. Consequently, even though he liked a couple of songs on *Sgt. Pepper*, he felt it was playing to the notion of universal brotherhood *for profit*.

In July 1969, the monthly British music magazine *Beat Instrumental* asked Zappa about the Beatles and their music. "He said he liked 'one or two songs' on the Beatles' *Sgt. Pepper* . . . but the best Beatles songs were 'Paperback Writer,' 'Strawberry Fields,' and 'I Am the Walrus.' 'I don't like the rest too much,' he said." Zappa went on to evaluate the notion of pop music's real appeal: "People require escapist entertainment, and the escapist potential of Hendrix and the Beatles is fantastic. The further away from nasty reality you get the better, the more it will sell. That is the attitude, but, worse still, it is called great art."

Zappa clearly wanted to demystify the music business by taking a satirical shot at the Beatles' best-selling album. The Mothers of Invention brought his point home with the release of *We're Only in It for the Money* on March 4, 1968, in an ambitious gatefold cover that imitated the famous album art created for the Beatles by Peter Blake and Jan Haworth. Instead of a flower garden, *Money* features a vegetable garden; in lieu of the Beatles' military-like silk costumes, the Mothers are wearing a mix of sloppy drag, large boots, and clumsy wigs. And while the Beatles stand in front of a uniform set of cutouts of famous people from politics, film, and music, the Mothers stand in front of some sixty-five images of such dubious characters as Lee Harvey Oswald, pictured as he was shot in Dallas; Lyndon Johnson, the unpopular US president; and a host of blacked-out faces barely familiar to anyone outside of designer Cal Schenkel's imagination. (A complete list can be found at http://wiki.killuglyradio.com.) As Zappa states in the album's liner notes, "This whole monstrosity was conceived and executed by Frank Zappa as a result of some unpleasant premonitions, August through October, 1967." For Zappa, it was time to take a shot at the commercial idealism of American culture as presented by the Beatles.

Zappa actually contacted Paul McCartney by phone to request permission to use the artwork. McCartney referred him to the band's label, Capitol/EMI. The company believed Zappa had infringed on the copyright image on *Sgt. Pepper*, so the Mothers' album was delayed while an alternative image was produced for the outside gatefold cover, which featured a large color image of the band in drag. The famous parody cover, which cost Zappa

The inner cover featuring Jimi Hendrix, Gail Zappa, and designer Cal Schenkel, bottom right, holding egg carton.

about $4,000 to create, was safely put inside. The album reached #30 on the *Billboard* 200 chart. But Zappa wasn't done yet.

After the Beatles released "All You Need Is Love" in 1967, Zappa wrote lyrics to an instrumental called, "Oh No," which eventually appeared on the album *Weasels Ripped My Flesh* in August of 1970. Having had the time to digest the success of the Beatles' hope to save the world through song, Zappa took issue with their dream: "You say love is all we need . . . I think you're probably out to lunch." It was a direct hit on an anthem for a generation. Nevertheless, Zappa understood the success of the Beatles from a cultural point of view, according to his secretary, Pauline Butcher. In her book *Freak*

Out! My Life with Frank Zappa, she writes about the hysteria the Beatles created in the sixties, and Zappa's reaction to it. "In London he had told me, 'The Beatles have shown other teenagers that anyone can achieve success regardless of their start in life.'" She mentions that he liked *Abbey Road* (Apple, 1969), but only for the engineering, not for the music. Ironically, Zappa later cast Ringo Starr as Larry the Dwarf in his film about life on the road, *200 Motels.* John Lennon, who played with Zappa in New York in 1971, was quite taken with him too, according to Butcher. "I may be popular," Lennon reportedly said, "but he is the real thing."

In spite of Lennon's praise, Zappa expressed a more pointed opinion of the Beatles in 1984, in an interview with *Capitol,* the weekly magazine of the *Columbus Dispatch.* In an extensive conversation with Barbara Zuck, he said of the Fab Four, "I didn't hate them. I actually like two or three of their songs. I just thought they were ridiculous. What was so disgusting was the way they were consumed and merchandised. No music has succeeded in America unless it was accompanied by something to wear, something to dance or a hairdo. A phenomenon is not going to occur unless you can dress up to it." Despite this poisonous commentary, Zappa actually performed a great version of "I Am the Walrus" with his 1988 big band, featuring Ike Willis singing the lead vocal. (It's available on *Beat the Boots III.*)

Zappa's best use of the Beatles' songs, for better or worse, was the 1988 band's performance of the "Texas Medley." In February of that year, he took three songs by Lennon and McCartney and rewrote the lyrics to take a satirical shot at Louisiana televangelist Jimmy Swaggart, evangelist Pat Robertson, and assorted members of President Reagan's cabinet. He changed "Norwegian Wood" to "Norwegian Jim," following it with "Louisiana Hooker with Herpes" (a new version of "Lucy in the Sky with Diamonds") and "Texas Motel" (which he based on "Strawberry Fields Forever"). Only bootlegs exist of this "suite," which was never released on any official Zappa recording—quite possibly for copyright reasons.

Zappa's final shot came with the posthumous release of *The Lost Episodes* in 1996. This album features a wide range of outtakes, early studio recordings, and a mix of previously unavailable songs, including a remarkable twelve-minute version of "Sharleena" featuring Sugar Cane Harris. Zappa worked part-time on the compilation for eighteen months, beginning in 1992. In the liner notes, Spencer Crislu, the engineer who put together the final version, writes, "Frank always understood his fan base . . . this is a sort of tribute to his fans, a sort of dropping of the veil." The release of the album, less than a year after the television debut of *The Beatles Anthology* in November 1995, was intended to poke fun at the Beatles' heavily publicized and profitable documentary series.

Bob Dylan

On a rainy night in southern California in December 1982, Frank Zappa met Bob Dylan. Zappa relates the circumstances in Neil Slaven's book *The Electric Don Quixote*. "I get a lot of weird calls [at the house] and someone suddenly called up saying, 'This is Bob Dylan, I want to play you my new songs.'" After confirming that this was indeed Dylan at the door, Zappa led him into the studio, where, as Slaven describes it, Dylan "sat at the piano and played eleven songs and then asked Frank to produce his next album."

Zappa was attracted by the possibilities of doing something outside of Dylan's scope. "I said he should do a complete synthesizer track and Dylan should play guitar and harmonica over the top." The project never materialized, and Dylan ended up cutting the songs for *Infidels* (Columbia) with co-producer Mark Knopfler.

This was the only time the two men met, but it wasn't the first time Zappa had heard Dylan's music. Zappa respected Dylan from the time he heard "Subterranean Homesick Blues" in 1965, and, more importantly, had Tom Wilson, the producer of Dylan's influential single, work on the Mothers' debut, *Freak Out!*, the same year. (Dylan also makes the famous "list" on the jacket liner notes.)

Zappa gave further praise to Dylan in an interview with *Hitline* magazine in 1965. "Bob Dylan is the only guy who really feels what he is saying, Barry McGuire is a phony," he said, McGuire having a hit single at the time called "Eve of Destruction." When Zappa heard "Like a Rolling Stone," he added, he was ready to quit the music business. Dylan, he said, "wrote songs that reflected the times in which he was living; he was a realist, if you will, whose glimmer and shock value, as suggested by his electric period, soon faded." In an interview with *Playboy* in April 1993, Zappa talked about the disappointment he felt after Dylan released *Blonde on Blonde* in 1966.

"It started to sound like cowboy music," Zappa said—as opposed to the hard-edged rock Dylan had been making previously. According to author Ben Watson, Zappa felt "betrayed" by the early promise of Dylan's success as a non-conformist, and as a consequence now had a reason to mock Dylan's music, which he did effectively on a song called "Flakes," from his 1979 album *Sheik Yerbouti*. The song features an interval by Adrian Belew, who, as "Bob Dylan," toots on his harmonica and spews the lines, "No matter what you do, they're gonna cheat and rob you . . . that'll get you so crazy till your head'll go through the ceilin'." It's an empty complaint about "the man" that targets Dylan personally. Percussionist Ed Mann can be seen singing the part on the 1981 concert DVD *The Torture Never Stops*.

Michael Jackson

Considering all of the peccadilloes and unusual behaviors that have sustained gossip newspapers and magazines over the years, it's a wonder Frank Zappa had anything more to say about Michael Jackson. But the fact of the matter was that Zappa felt that Jackson was a victim of his own corporate generated success. "Who wants to go through life with a tiny nose and one glove on?" he asked *Gallery*'s Ron Chepesiuk in June 1989, while offering his opinion of Jackson. "You could take the average kid next door and give him the marketing and packaging that Michael has gotten and turn him into another Jackson clone."

Jackson is further criticized in one of Zappa's most poisonous songs, "Why Don't You Like Me?" from *Broadway the Hard Way*, which he released that same year. Zappa takes everything we know about Jackson's eccentric behavior and blows it up by a thousand pixels. He even goes the extra step by incorporating Jackson's hit song "Billie Jean" into the music as a means of naming people in the audience who are not related to him, which was the point of Jackson's refrain, "The kid is not my son." The lyrics question everything from Jackson's confused identity (resulting from his many plastic surgeries) to the odd relationship he had with his pet monkey. Zappa also goes as far as to question the identity of Jackson's siblings, all while screaming for a Pepsi—the company that backed a tour by the Jackson 5 in 1984 following the success of the multi-million-selling *Thriller*. In one three-minute song, Zappa deconstructs Jackson's entire image, leaving nothing behind.

With his tongue planted firmly in his cheek, Zappa questioned his own success in relation to that of Michael Jackson in an interview with Gary Shay for the November 1984 issue of the short-lived music magazine *Songwriter Connection*. "The word genius is used as a value judgment by some people to describe the difference between what one guy does and another guy does, okay? To some people . . . what's the name of the guy with the glove? Oh yeah . . . Michael Jackson. Michael Jackson is a genius, okay? He's a genius because he sold thirty million albums. If you compare me to Michael Jackson, I'm a schmuck."

In many ways, Jackson was the poster boy for everything Zappa hated about the commercialization of the music industry and its infatuation with celebrity instead of the music itself. As he reveals in *The Real Frank Zappa Book*, "The manner in which Americans 'consume' music has a lot to do with leaving it on their coffee tables, or using it as wallpaper for their lifestyles, like the score of a movie. It's consumed that way without any regard for how or why it's made. Then, when it's merchandised, the emphasis shifts to the pseudo-personality of the artist; a magnification of the stage persona." He asks rhetorically, "Do we really want to know how Michael Jackson makes his music? No. We want to understand why he needs the bones of the Elephant Man and, until he tells us, it doesn't make too much difference whether or not he really is 'bad.'"

To Zappa, mocking Jackson reflected his disdain for the fans and media who were more interested in Jackson's personal foibles than his records, which he felt were simply there to be consumed for superficial pleasure and nothing more.

13

Today's Lesson

Does Humor Belong in Music?

When Frank Zappa was eight years old, he was given a most precious Christmas present: the new 78 single by Spike Jones and His City Slickers, "All I Want for Christmas Is My Two Front Teeth." Released on Victor-Bluebird, it was the big Christmas hit of 1948, selling over a million copies with the backing of various radio stations. It was written from a kid's point of view by Donald Gardner, a second-grade teacher from Smithtown, New York, who noticed that most of his young students had lost their baby teeth, which created a temporary lisp and interfered with their ability to whistle. Spike Jones got the song at the end of 1947, but it wasn't much of a composition, so his bandmates Eddie Brandt and Fred Morgan added a couple of verses, a bridge, and an ending to fill out the work.

The song's charming presentation, featuring George Rock's joyful vocals, appealed to a lot of kids. The eight-year-old Zappa liked it so much that he wrote a fan letter to the label, requesting an autographed photo of Jones. Instead he received a headshot of George Rock. Nevertheless, it was one of the most important records in Zappa's young life—one that opened a door to what was possible in music with a sense of humor.

Spike Jones

Born in Long Beach, California, in 1911, Lindley Armstrong "Spike" Jones grew up in a Methodist household near a noisy railway depot. His first instrument was the trombone, but the young boy, who suffered from asthma, eventually took to the drums instead. He absorbed the sounds of his environment and incorporated them into his music, much like the American composer Charles Ives. Jones's father worked for the Southern Pacific Railroad as an agent, so frequent trips to work in his company put

Jones the younger on trains, where he met the cooks and black stewards who worked on board and entertained him by hitting pots and pans with wooden spoons. This experience left a big impression on Jones, leading to his parents buying him his first set of drums when he turned eleven.

Jones loved to play and was forming his own groups by the time he reached high school. By twenty-five he was leading his own jazz bands, doing standards and pop songs of the day, which eventually landed him legit work as a percussionist with John Scott Trotter and His Orchestra, who backed Bing Crosby on the original recording of "White Christmas" (Decca) in 1942.

Jones formed the City Slickers as a large band of mostly jazz players who were not only good on their respective instruments but were also comics who weren't afraid to entertain an audience to the point of embarrassment. Their first hit was "Der Fuehrer's Face" (Victor-Bluebird), which took America by storm after it was released in September 1942. The United States had only recently entered World War II, and its citizens were ready to poke fun at the enemy. "Der Fuehrer's Face" was the perfect musical jab, expressing exactly how most people felt about Germany's chancellor at the time. The song was made a hit by one man: Martin Block at WNEW in New York. In an effort to sell war bonds to raise funds for the federal government's war chest, Block, a popular DJ at the time, played the song every time he hit a plateau in sales. Block also gave a copy away with the purchase of a $50 bond, which helped raise $60,000 in the first two weeks of the campaign.

The US government soon took notice, and before long Jones and his band made radio appearances and toured the States in support of the war effort. By the end of the decade, Jones's recordings could be found in the homes of most working-class people in Europe and North America. That popularity and label support gave Jones the creative freedom to parody familiar classical themes while developing his own brand of novelty songs. Like Frank Zappa, Jones wasn't for everyone, but his music sold very well, making him a radio star and a chart-topper for Bluebird records.

Jones's singular approach to "murdering the classics" made for an accessible, amusing, and remarkably clever brand of music. To some, the City Slickers were a talented band who defined the novelty song while breaking down the barriers of classical music, which was previously considered to be the preserve of serious audiences only. For those who loved the classics in their purest form, the City Slickers were the musical equivalent of the Three Stooges—face-slapping included. For Jones, music with humor was an

Spike's bright two-step hits the world.

intentional art form designed to insult the highbrow audience. With "Der Fuehrer's Face," Jones found an audience ready, willing, and able to laugh along with him while fully understanding the craft of his presentation. He enjoyed a long recording career with RCA-Victor, one of the leading classical-music record companies. He was signed to Victor's Bluebird imprint, which released jazz, specifically to distinguish his music from the label's classical output. (Unlike Jones, Victor wasn't interested in insulting the "high-brow" record buyer.)

Jones's commercial success eventually led him and his act to the new medium of television in the mid-fifties. Those TV shows, along with a great recording career, continued to inspire Zappa into his teens. For Zappa, the larger-than-life performances—featuring jugglers, dancers, and gymnasts, plus some of the best musicians in the business—made for a circus-like presentation that was funny and entertaining as Jones and the City Slickers satirized classical composers such as Rossini ("William Tell Overture") and Strauss ("The Blue Danube"). Jones also made fun of commercial pop songs like "Cocktails for Two," which featured gunshots and car horns.

What Zappa heard and saw in those TV shows was the perfect combination of performance art and comedy, which opened a door to express his own sense of humor in music. This contrasting mix of the bizarre with the serious would become an essential part of everything Zappa wrote and presented, particularly in his early shows with the Mothers of Invention. Upon closer scrutiny, almost every Zappa recording contains a nod to Spike Jones in some unexpected way, from *Freak Out!* (1966) to *Broadway the Hard Way* (1989). But perhaps the definitive tribute to Jones is on "The Adventures of Greggery Peccary," from the album *Studio Tan* (1978), which contains all of the elements most closely associated with Spike Jones and his grand presentation: a simple story linked by musical quotes from other works, including his own, with a cheeky narrator (Zappa) telling the story and illustrating it with sounds. A radio play, in other words. A close second would be "Billy the

Mountain," a longer, more theatrical piece with a satiric story linking the sophisticated musical elements together, from the album *Just Another Band from L.A.*, released in 1972. The big difference between them is that the former is a beautifully edited studio track, while the latter was performed live. The fact that Billy appears in character as Greggery Peccary on both ties the two works together as an example of Zappa's "conceptual continuity" (explored in more detail in chapter 26).

In 1956, Jones released his first stereo LP, *Dinner Music for People Who Aren't Very Hungry* (Verve). Taking advantage of new recording technology, Jones re-recorded a couple of his early hits, "Cocktails for Two" and "Chloe," in addition to another ten tracks with satirical titles. Featuring alongside the pair of familiar hits from the forties are "Duet for Violin and Garbage Disposal," "Black and Blue Danube Waltz," and "Wyatt Earp Makes Me Burp," with a vocal by Mousie Garner (as Sir Frederic Gas). Zappa's song titles alone owe something to Spike Jones—think of "Prelude to the Afternoon of a Sexually Aroused Gas Mask," "Bossa Nova Pervertamento," and "The Return of the Son of Monster Magnet," to name but three. To Zappa, this "low-rent Americana" would form an important part of his compositional style. It not only allowed for other band members to become involved in the material but was also part of his sophisticated formula for writing. Used effectively, humor can punctuate and distinguish a composer's music—a notion that wasn't lost on Zappa or his fans.

The Flo and Eddie Band (1970–71)

After Zappa broke up the Mothers of Invention in August 1969, he released three albums—*Hot Rats, Burnt Weeny Sandwich,* and *Weasels Ripped My Flesh*—featuring performance recordings from the archives. Moving forward, he recognized the importance of financing anything new by going out on tour. It was, in fact, part of his business plan. So, in the spring of 1970, he set up some dates in Europe, the United States, and Canada that would carry him through the year, with a few breaks in between bookings in which to record. He had George Duke (keyboards), Jeff Simmons (bass), Ian Underwood (woodwinds), and Aynsley Dunbar (drums) alongside him, but Zappa still wanted new musicians to augment the group and distance it from the original Mothers of Invention. As it turned out, humor would play a large role in the music and the presentation after he hired two members of the Turtles.

Howard Kaylan met Mark Volman at Westchester High School, Los Angeles, in 1963. They were in the same a capella choir class, but Kaylan also spent his time playing tenor saxophone with his instrumental pop band, the Nightriders, who played cover songs made famous by surf bands such as the Ventures. Mark Volman liked the band and wanted to join but he couldn't play an instrument; Kaylan convinced his fellow Nightriders to add Volman on the condition that he learn to play the alto sax. Volman jumped at the opportunity, later adding his voice to the proceedings once the Beatles landed in America in 1964. The subsequent popularity of the British Invasion such as the Dave Clark Five and Herman's Hermits, whose songs were becoming the mainstay of Top 40 radio, provided the impetus for many young people to start their own groups and make music. (And, as history would have it, the Turtles would appear as the opening act for Herman's Hermits at the Rose Bowl, Pasadena, in August 1965.)

Kaylan and Volman decided to change direction and add cover tunes to their set, including songs by Lennon and McCartney. The Nightriders changed their name to the Crossfires and, as Kaylan writes in his memoir, *Shell Shocked*, "learned the hits of the day and spewed them back at a waiting public with great accuracy and passion." Inspired by the popular folk group the Kingston Trio, Kaylan began looking for songs from the growing folk music scene, led by Bob Dylan. As their set list grew, so did their performances in Westchester and beyond, including house parties on the California coast and a steady gig at a club called the Revelaire. But they weren't making any money. As Kaylan tells it, "Two guys in suits had been watching us [at the Revelaire] approached me . . . they said they were starting up a new record label and that our new version of the Byrds hit 'Mr. Tambourine Man' had so impressed them that they wanted us to go into the studio and make a record."

Kaylan and the band took the two men up on the offer and chose "It Ain't Me Babe," written by Bob Dylan, as their first single, backed by a Kaylan original, "Almost There." The Crossfires wasn't going to cut it as the band's name, however, so the manager of the Revelaire, Reb Carter, rechristened them the Turtles. It was 1965; Kaylan and Volman were barely out of their teens when they signed with White Whale Records that year. Released in August, their debut single reached #8 on the *Billboard* Hot 100.

The Turtles

In October, the Turtles' debut album, *It Ain't Me Babe*, was released, featuring two more songs penned by Kaylan. It was produced by Bones Howe, who later worked with the West Coast session band known as the Wrecking Crew. The album sold well enough to reach the #98 position on the *Billboard* 200, but the songs weren't strong enough, as far as the band's label and management were concerned, to push the group forward. Nevertheless, the band's second album, *You Baby*, released in 1966, did much better, as the title track peaked at #20 on *Billboard*. The album featured more original material from the group, but they were still looking for that #1 record.

In the months that followed, the Turtles started getting songs from a variety of sources, including Brill Building writers like Carole King and the songwriting duo of Gary Bonner and Alan Gordon. They listened to hundreds of demos, one of which was "Happy Together," which had been turned down by the Grass Roots and the Vogues. The Turtles didn't record the song for several months, concentrating instead on perfecting their sound on the road. It was time well spent. When the Turtles released their recording of the song in February 1967, four months before Howard Kaylan's twentieth birthday, "Happy Together" became a mega-hit around the world, knocking "Penny Lane" by the Beatles off #1 on the *Billboard* Hot 100 and staying there for three weeks. It was immediately followed by "She'd Rather Be with Me," which reached #3. The band rode the wave of success from those songs for the better part of two years, releasing their original song "Elenore" in 1968, which carried them through to 1969. It all came to an end as quickly as it began, however. According to Kaylan, the band's label, which owned the publishing rights, took all the money, leaving the group with nothing. Court proceedings followed, with suits and countersuits preventing the Turtles from signing any new contracts that might grant them an income. As far as Kaylan was concerned, "The Turtles were done."

Flo and Eddie

The Turtles' brand of positive, good-time music had wide appeal in the late 60s, as Howard Kaylan recalls in his memoir. Both he and Mark Volman lived the lifestyle of sex, drugs, and rock 'n' roll that most people their age could only dream about. Kaylan's book is a chronicle that would make Keith Richards blush, considering all the alcohol, cocaine, and marijuana he used during his time with the Turtles. The book often reads like a continuous party, with the occasional concert and TV appearance in between. But it does give us insight into the outrageous times in which Kaylan lived, the many women he bedded, and how that lifestyle came to inform the music he and Mark Volman would make with Frank Zappa.

Kaylan, Volman, and Zappa knew each other because Zappa's manager Herb Cohen was Howard Kaylan's cousin. Zappa talked about the relationship to author Neil Slaven for his book *The Electric Don Quixote*. "We'd worked some gig with them when they'd been the opening act as the Turtles. We had a lot of laughs backstage, so it wasn't inconceivable that I could imagine going on the road with them . . . they had the 'road rat' mentality." Zappa was referring to their experience in the Turtles and the fact that they could handle the stress of the run of one-nighters, TV appearances, and festivals that were on Zappa's touring schedule. Kaylan and Volman could cope with irregular hours, groupies, and long flights and bus rides to get to the next city and the next concert. So, after Zappa played his *Contempo 70* concert at the Pauley Pavilion on the campus of UCLA on May 15, 1970, two weeks after the Turtles broke up, he asked Kaylan and Volman to join his new band. They first auditioned as saxophone players but failed to make a good impression on their instruments, so Zappa hired them as his new lead singers. As Kaylan recalls in his memoir, "He placed sheet music before us on stands and counted us off. We did what we could. Then he put on a tape of classic MOI songs for us to blorp along with. We did what we could. And then he turned off the machine and told us to put our instruments away . . . [he said] you won't be needing those."

In some ways, the end of the Turtles granted Zappa, who was in transition as a solo artist, the freedom to start something new with his music and his band. He was working with two vocalists with whom he was already familiar, so he wasn't exactly starting from scratch after the demise of the original Mothers of Invention. That said, it took a week of intense rehearsals to get the songs to performance level. But according to Neil Slaven, the band didn't really mesh until their Bath Music Festival gig on June 28, 1970. "This was a new Zappa," Slaven writes, "for whom most of us were unprepared . . . the air of vaudeville clung to many of the songs." Zappa was patient. "There's a group spirit that transcends just friendship among the members of the group," Slaven continues, "and there is now a certain devotion to some mythological cause and I think it comes across onstage."

Zappa's confidence in his new band led to them undertaking a recording session over two days in late August 1970. Flo and Eddie sang six new works that were released on *Chunga's Revenge* in October: "Road Ladies," "The Nancy & Mary Music," "Tell Me You Love Me," "Would You Go All the Way?," "Rudy Wants to Buy Yez a Drink," and a new version of "Sharleena," first recorded with Don "Sugar Cane" Harris in March 1970 but not released until 1996 on *The Lost Episodes*.

As Zappa states in the liner notes, "All the vocals in this album are a preview of the story from *200 Motels*. Coming soon." Kaylan and Volman's stories about their adventures on the road with the Turtles provided more material for Zappa's first major motion picture, which was, likewise, about a rock band's life on tour. With these new songs added to the set list, the band hit the road again in September for concerts in the United States and Europe that continued until mid-December. This leg of the tour helped polish the stage presentation. The "vaudeville" band, as some fans called it, offered concertgoers a mixture of jokes, one-liners, and audience participation, all directed by Frank Zappa.

Mark Volman described these performances to Dave Thompson in the November 2002 issue of *Goldmine* magazine. "With Howard and I up there, Frank had two Punch and Judy dolls who could personify all the ugliness that the Mothers was: the comedy, the satire, the vast pudgy rock stars, the drugs. And Frank could stand on stage and whip out his guitar solos; he could put his cigarettes on the end of the guitar, look disdainfully at the audience and play a seven-minute guitar solo that would make everyone cheer and then put his hand out to us, and say, 'Take it away, you fat, dopey clowns.'"

Billy the Mountain

In spite of the way Zappa directed the shows, Volman told Thompson that the whole presentation was part of a creative process. "From the early days, with pieces of the old Mothers . . . we kept moving until we eventually had the *Fillmore* album, aiming toward *200 Motels* and then 'Billy the Mountain,' until we had a whole new show, two-and-a-half hours of our own material. It took a while to get to, but we did it." This transition can be specifically heard on *Just Another Band from L.A.*, recorded in August 1971 at the Pauley Pavilion and released in March 1972, as well as on the archival releases

Playground Psychotics (1992), featuring John Lennon and Yoko Ono, as recorded at the Fillmore East on June 6, 1971, and *Carnegie Hall* (2011).

All three albums include a performance of "Billy the Mountain," a satirical work with music and storytelling about a mountain named Billy and his girlfriend Ethel, who is a tree. They reside in a place between Rosamund and Gorman, near Zappa's second home of Lancaster, California. The two make their living by posing for postcards. One day, they decide to cash in a royalty check and take a vacation to New York City (signified here by the theme from *The Tonight Show*, starring Johnny Carson). But since Billy is a mountain, his size pretty much lays ruin to the countryside, until he and Ethel get to Columbus, Ohio. There, he receives his draft notice, but Ethel doesn't want him to serve in the army. She is immediately labeled a communist by the government. Billy and Ethel, our heroes, take on the establishment, represented by Studebacher Hoch, who does everything in his power to stop Billy from burning his draft card and resisting the government. Billy gets his revenge by sending Hoch into the rubble at the foot of the mountain.

Zappa's extended work needed the input of Flo and Eddie to succeed as a satiric shot at the Nixon administration, popular culture, and the continuing war in Vietnam, because the work was constantly changing from city to city. On the version from *Just Another Band from L.A.*, the lyrics reference TV jingles, local fast-food restaurants in Los Angeles, and current events.

"Billy the Mountain" is a sizable work that shows off Zappa's use of humor in the best tradition of Spike Jones, but with far more contemporary references. As Volman recalled in his 2002 interview with *Goldmine* magazine, "Every time we played it, 'Billy' had little idiosyncrasies about the town [they were in at the time], all the psychedelic dungeons, the places you'd go to eat, the hip pseudo-intellectual spots where pot was smoked, the professors who were in trouble because they messed around with girls in class. It made the show very three-dimensional, because it wasn't just us performing . . . it brought [the audience] into the show."

The End of the Vaudeville Band

As the concert tour continued into the fall of 1971, the band, which included George Duke, Aynsley Dunbar, Ian Underwood, and Jeff Simmons, was now attracting new fans and pushing out the old ones. This is the featured group in Zappa's film *200 Motels*, which opened in October during the European leg of the tour. The movie went a long way toward casting Zappa's music in a purely satirical context, rather than the blend of satire and progressive rock and other theatrical elements that the older fans had enjoyed with the original Mothers of Invention.

By the time the Flo and Eddie band performed in the town of Montreux, Switzerland, on December 4, 1971, one fan could no longer hold back his enthusiasm. According to Howard Kaylan's memoir, "A joker in the back of the crowd wanted to show his appreciation for the show with a bang and sent a flare straight up and into the bamboo [rattan] ceiling, which ignited like tinder." Kaylan's book includes pictures of the fire from the safety of his hotel and the aftermath.

The band and audience escaped unharmed, but the group's equipment was completely lost, except for a cowbell that Volman salvaged from the fire. The whole event, including the music, was made available on a pair of bootlegs called *Swiss Cheese* and *Fire!*, which Zappa subsequently released on *Beat the Boots 2* in 1992. The British rock group Deep Purple, who at the time were making their album *Machine Head* in Montreux using the Rolling Stones' mobile studio, made these events famous in their classic song "Smoke on the Water."

After the fire in Montreux, Zappa wanted to quit and go home, even at the risk of canceling a sold-out two-week run in the UK. Kaylan and Volman, with the support of the other members in the group, convinced their bandleader to at least honor the dates in England. (It was, after all, the only way they could get paid.) Zappa relented, and the band borrowed equipment from the Who and Led Zeppelin to finish the tour. But on December 10, 1971, following the first of two shows at London's Rainbow Theatre, Zappa was attacked by a fan onstage and pushed into the orchestra pit some fifteen feet below. He was hurt badly and hospitalized for several months, resulting in him being confined to a wheelchair for most of 1972. And so, after eighteen months, the much-loved vaudeville band was finished.

It may have been the end of the band but it marked the beginning of the Flo and Eddie project, with the duo signing with Reprise records in the spring of 1972. In his book, Kaylan says he wanted to compose and perform straight-up acoustic rock songs in the vein of the Turtles, concluding that "the Zappa years had been but a momentary distraction." Mark Volman was a little more introspective. In the *Goldmine* magazine interview with Dave Thompson, he recalled, "Spiritually it was the lowest [Zappa had] ever sunk.

And I honestly think the effect of the fire and the incident at the Rainbow made him start to reevaluate spiritually what he was doing."

Zappa continued to compose music during his recovery, resulting in two instrumental albums, *Waka Jawaka* and *The Grand Wazoo*. The sarcastic and critical humor that defined the Flo and Eddie band was deferred for the better part of a year, until the release of *Over-Nite Sensation* in 1973, which features some of the funniest and most poignant songs in Zappa's catalogue, among them "Montana," "Zomby Woof," and "Dirty Love."

Ed Palermo

Ed Palermo, a New Yorker, is a bandleader and composer whose album *Oh No! Not Jazz* (Cuneiform) featured songs by Zappa arranged for big band. In an e-mail exchange with the author, he recognized the need for humor in music. "Humor, like music, is the best thing in life. We can't live without either of those two. Why not have them join forces? When someone comes to hear my band, they're going to have a good time whether they like Zappa's music or not. At the very least, they're going to have a good laugh."

Palermo's love for Zappa started when his older brother brought home a copy of *Absolutely Free* in 1967. He was "drawn in" by the song "Duke of Prunes," with its mix of beautiful harmonies and orchestration—the perfect combination for a future big-band leader. By 1969, Palermo had seen the Mothers of Invention in Philadelphia, and "it was love!"

For author Kelly Fisher Lowe, "Duke of Prunes" is "very serious music juxtaposed with completely nonsensical lyrics." In his excellent book *The Words and Music of Frank Zappa*, Fisher Lowe states that Zappa has three categories of lyrics: truly stupid, slightly less stupid, and sort-of funny. This, for Fisher Lowe, was the result of Zappa being "put out" by record companies demanding conventional pop songs that might get radio play. He was annoyed by these restrictions because he believed it was possible to write instrumental music that was funny and had audience appeal, much like the work of Spike Jones. In retrospect, he was right. While anyone's sense of humor is completely subjective, Zappa's music can still make people laugh even if you don't know his work. The best example of this came with the hit single "Valley Girl" in 1982. The razor-sharp wit of that satirical song still lingers in the zeitgeist today, in the form of lyrics written and delivered by Zappa's daughter, Moon.

Zappa understood from the get-go that the use of humor in a song or instrumental work went a long way to distinguish his music from the mainstream—which was exactly his point. In his autobiography, Zappa talks briefly about his approach to using sound effects or musical quotes in his own work. He called them "modules," or musical clichés, and they were designed to be familiar to anyone in tune with music history or current events. There are many examples, but some of the best can be heard on the album *Broadway the Hard Way* (1989), which features references to Elvis Presley, Michael Jackson, the Religious Right, Richard Nixon, and Madison Avenue careerists. One of Zappa's most sophisticated records, *Cruising with Ruben & the Jets* (1968), is considered a mock-up of fifties doo-wop sounds with appealing melodies and ridiculous lyrics that satirize love songs from an era of music that greatly influenced the harmonies Zappa wrote. In many ways, Zappa's rhetorical question about humor "belonging" in music offers fans the chance to answer it for themselves.

So why does humor belong in music? As one fan from the United States who goes by the name Debutante Daisy (from the song "Florentine Pogen") explained to the author in an e-mail, "Humor belongs in all aspects of life. Without humor, I'd probably need to be highly medicated and locked up in a rubber room somewhere. Humor belongs in music because some music (not all) is better with lyrics so why not have a laugh while you are enjoying beautifully composed music at the same time? For me it is a win-win when it is done right!" For Daisy, who first heard Zappa in concert at the age of fourteen, the fact that his music was funny offered a door into his work and life.

Another female fan I contacted, Ms. S. in Canada, offered the following explanation: "I was always drawn to his [Zappa] questioning . . . I believe strongly that it [humor] does [belong] . . . music is not created in a vacuum; it comes from our experience as humans. Our culture informs it. Humor is part of that. Why should music not include one of the great aspects of being human? Also, satire can be one of the most dangerous forms of comedy. It fits perfectly with music and its contribution to challenging norms." For this fan, who first saw Zappa on NBC's *Saturday Night Live*—one of the most important comedy shows in the history of television—the fact that he was funny made his music more appealing.

Zappa liked funny songs—that's why he wrote them—but there was always a bit of wit and social commentary attached. As with Spike Jones's use of sound effects, humor was one of the many tools Zappa used to make a point about human behavior or politics *and* entertain his audience. In the words of the great Billy Connolly, the purpose of poets and comedians (and presumably musicians) is "to make light of the darkness."

Zappa's Topical Songs

From the start of his career in music, Frank Zappa wasn't afraid to voice his opinions on the changing political face of the United States through song, just as he did in "Hungry Freaks, Daddy" from 1966. While he made fun of the strange behavior of men and women with songs about sex (See *You Can't Do That on Stage Anymore, Vol. 6* for edited performance of these songs), he also took a political position on a number of topics that offended his sense of "practical conservatism," as he calls it in his autobiography. Musician Nigey Lennon, author of *Being Frank: My Time with Frank Zappa*, said in an interview with broadcaster Bobby Marquis in 2013 that "a lot of people still remember his topical songs [because] he took people to task, a little like Mark Twain . . . he had a lot to say about the human condition and he could do it in a funny way."

Here's a sampling of Zappa's topical songs.

"Promiscuous"

On Zappa's most politically charged album, *Broadway the Hard Way*, recorded during the US election year of 1988, he takes hold of the growing fears he thought were being falsely created by the government about AIDS. In "Promiscuous," he takes a shot at the surgeon general of the time, Dr. C. Everett Koop. Koop was appointed by Ronald Reagan in 1982 and served in the role until 1989. (Taking the "general" part seriously, he often spoke to the media in a military uniform.)

Although the AIDS crisis was growing in the United States at the time of his appointment, President Reagan was sluggish in taking action. But rather than seek a better understanding of the disease—something that might lead to a cure or a vaccine—Koop issued a pamphlet called *Understanding AIDS*, which detailed the dangers of anal sex and the risks being taken by the gay community that could spread the disease. Koop's pamphlet gave Zappa the fodder with which to criticize the government for its lame response to the AIDS threat at the time and Koop's directive regarding sex education for kids, which he believed should start as early as the third grade. (As head of US public health initiatives, Koop did indeed launch such a program.)

Zappa's "Promiscuous," written as a rap song, questions the government's rationale while pointing the finger at Reagan, Koop, and the American Medical Association for misleading the public. When asked about it in a 1993 interview with *Playboy* magazine, Zappa criticized Koop's "science" regarding the origins of AIDS as being so "thin" that "it's up there with *Grimm's Fairy Tales*."

"I'm the Slime"

Zappa's most striking commentary about the medium of television appears on *Over-Nite Sensation*. It's a creepy tune featuring his closely miked vocal up front in the mix so that the listener can't avoid the narrative about what's "oozing out" of the television. Zappa watched news programs when he found the time in order to see which way the world was turning. Written in the first person, "I'm the Slime" portrays the TV set as a ghoulish enemy of the people ready to crawl along your living room floor and take over your mind. In his book *The Words and Music of Frank Zappa*, Kelly Fisher Lowe describes the song as expressing Zappa's concern about "the collusion of the government and the entertainment industry." That may be true, but musically the sting of the anger is tempered by the sound of "horn" bands popular at the time like Chicago. Recorded in 1973, "I'm the Slime" still holds up as a relevant commentary on the influential power of media. Imagine what Zappa would be saying today about the power of smart phones and Twitter.

"I Don't Wanna Get Drafted"

During a rehearsal session with Tommy Mars and Ike Willis back in 1979, Zappa learned that President Carter was thinking about reinstating the draft to force young men to register (as was officially proclaimed on July 2, 1980). As Tommy Mars recalls in the liner notes to *The Lost Episodes*, Zappa was so angered by the news that "he canceled rehearsal and the next day he comes in with this song."

As a single, the record made very little impact on the record-buying public, not making the *Billboard* charts, but it did reach #3 in Sweden, of all places. Nevertheless, Zappa's lyric, with the catchy refrain, is effective because it's told from the point of view of a potential draftee, who exclaims, "I'm too dumb and stupid to operate a gun." On the 1980 concert recording *Buffalo*, Zappa spots and reads out a sign in the audience that says

"Fuck the draft," so his message was reaching some fans. According to www.zappateers.com, which has a complete record of the Zappa shows, the song was regularly performed during most of the concerts on his 1980 tour.

"Heavenly Bank Account"

One of Zappa's favorite topics was the growing popularity and power of the religious right in the United States, as represented by an organization called the Moral Majority, led by its charismatic leader Jerry Falwell (1933–2007). Dedicated to aligning church and state, the organization folded about ten years after it formation in 1979, but not before infiltrating the Republican Party and helping Ronald Reagan win two presidential terms and his successor, George H. W. Bush, win one.

For Zappa, who spoke out against the organization, this song best reflects his outrage at how the fundamentalist Christian movement would take people's money and dictate the policies of the Republican Party. Arranged as classic gospel song, the lyrics reveal Zappa's disdain for televangelism, which he calls out as a scam. Zappa questioned the motives of Falwell and his cohort Pat Robertson, who lived in mansions and traveled in private planes while promising to help the poor. As he says while introducing the song on the live DVD *The Torture Never Stops*, "There's a difference [between] kneeling down and bending over." The song was never issued as a single, but a great B-side would have been "The Meek Shall Inherit Nothing," which talks about the pipe dream that some religions offer to the destitute.

"Poofter's Froth Wyoming Plans Ahead"

Here's an under-recognized song about the 1976 Bicentennial, heard only on *Bongo Fury* and sung by Captain Beefheart. Here, Zappa warns people not to buy the red, white, and blue banners, beer cans, and hats that were about to proliferate the marketplace to celebrate America's two-hundredth birthday. As he says on the album, the government had been "planning it for years." Zappa believed that jingoistic celebrations of this kind bring out the worst in Americans because they didn't know how to celebrate a political anniversary without getting drunk and buying everything in sight. The lyrics are a straight-up list of the cheesy souvenirs Americans were being encouraged to buy that would end up feeding "trash compactors" after the party ended. Written as an up-tempo country song, loosely based on a tune by Cindy Walker called "Set Up Two Glasses, Joe," "Poofter's Froth Wyoming Plans Ahead" is an irresistibly alliterative rhyme in spite of the fact that "poofter" is a derogatory term in Britain for a male homosexual.

Beefheart's performance here is excellent. When asked about writing songs for Beefheart in an interview with journalist Mick Farren at the *NME*, Zappa said, "The way he relates to language is unique, the way he brings my text to life."

Zappa's topical songs often expressed his immediate concerns for the changing world around him. It was his best method of expressing a dissenting point of view in an entertaining way.

14

The Recordings

A Curated Look at the Zappa Collection

Welcome to the Frank Zappa listening party. You're about to enter a world of laughter, absurdity, and a whole lot of serious music. As of 2015, one hundred official releases make up the Frank Zappa discography. For the first-time listener—to whom this chapter is directed—getting into the music may seem overwhelming, and to an extent it is. Although Zappa's music didn't evolve in the traditional artistic sense (trial and error, growth of the writer's skills, and so on), you could start with the first record, *Freak Out!* (#1), and move sequentially to the most recent, *Dance Me This* (#100). Or you could work your way backward, from the one-hundredth album to the first.

My approach is to group the albums into a series of levels, from primary to post-graduate, to make it easier to enter "the dangerous kitchen" and then let the music speak for itself. It's my way of breaking down selected albums of the Zappa collection into easily digestible vegetables or parts. Vocalist Bob Harris, who recorded with Zappa in 1980, said, "Anybody could grab the 'vibe' of Frank, even if you couldn't grasp the compositional stuff. It was all about the vibe. The vibe of freedom. That's what he shared with people."

Note: the Official Release (O.R.) numbers correspond to the 2012 reissues and the mail-order releases from www.zappa.com.

Primary Study

This first section establishes the building blocks of understanding and getting accustomed to Frank Zappa's music. To a certain extent, these "primary" recordings are the most accessible in his extensive output. They are also considered "must-haves" because they are universally appreciated by Zappa fans around the world.

Over-Nite Sensation (O.R. #17, DiscReet, 1973)

A wide cast of characters awaits you here, from the "Zomby Woof" to "Dinah-Moe Humm" and Frenchie the Poodle, by way of "Montana" and a new way of growing dental floss. One of the best starter records in the collection, *Over-Nite Sensation* is a must-have for any fan of Frank Zappa. It opens with the story of "Camarillo Brillo," a woman with a pseudo-hairstyle modeled after the black cultural icons of the early seventies. It's a really accessible song with a straight-ahead groove by one of Zappa's best ensembles. Zappa takes a shot at the fakeness of the counterculture movement, which he saw as a phony commercial enterprise disguised as cheap insight.

One might say that *Over-Nite Sensation* is a reaction to the hype and publicity surrounding cultural change in the United States at a time when women's rights, political activism, and a general distrust of authority had become an enterprise for American capitalists bent on making a profit out of anything that was "hip." Zappa certainly thought so, as the songs on this album reflect his general disdain for suspect fortunetellers; the "back to the land" movement, as depicted in "Montana"; and the growing openness of free love, as represented by "Dinah-Moe Humm." Zappa, of course, removes the idealism and fantasy of the commercial world and takes it to the extreme by debunking the romance or idealism of love and describing sex as a purely physical and pleasurable act. But he does it with a sense of humor, which is key to appreciating and enjoying the merits of this album.

One Size Fits All (O.R. #20, DiscReet, 1975)

Now celebrating its fortieth anniversary on the hit parade, this album is arguably one of Zappa's most intricate records. The classic opener "Inca Roads," about UFO sightings, is one of the best songs on the album, alongside the tale of a modified dog named "Evelyn." According to Zappa, the opening track started life as a complex instrumental, and it took him several years to add lyrics to it. The result is a song that pokes fun at UFO prognosticators and the notion that gods in chariots visited the earth—a popular concept in 1975. But this record succeeds because of the diversity of rhythm to be had on every track.

"Inca Roads" is probably among the most sophisticated and difficult songs in Zappa's songbook in terms of the stops and starts that create tension within the music, only to be released during the guitar solo, which was inserted from a recording made at a concert in Helsinki, Finland, months earlier. We then move on to a set of songs that are character studies of the southern California populace Zappa loved to make fun of, including "Florentine Pogen" and "Andy," with the latter offering a great example of the changes in tempo and blues changes that grace the whole record. *One Size Fits All* is a sonic delight to the ears and one of the best recordings in the Zappa catalogue. The cover art is reduced on the CD version, but if you can find a vinyl copy, be sure to visit http://members.shaw.ca/fz-pomd/ stars.html for a complete description of the star map that Cal Schenkel created for the back cover.

Freak Out! (O.R. #1, Verve, 1966)

This is where it all started, in June 1966, with the second ever double album in rock music. (The first one was Dylan's *Blonde on Blonde* (Columbia) released in May.) The record kicks off with the punk-like "Hungry Freaks, Daddy," an opening political statement that sets the tone for the whole album, or at least the first disc. Zappa's point of view is best seen as cynical and suspicious. On the one hand, he's cynical of the Johnson

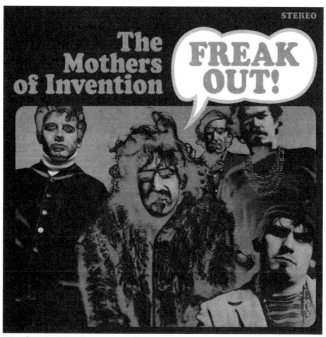

The $21,000 budget was well spent.

administration's "Great Society," which leaves young people out of the equation, while on the other hand he's suspicious of the idealism of pop culture. While these two ideas don't collide on Zappa's late works, they do link all of his music together in subtle ways. For instance, Zappa takes a different view of the idealism of love on "How Could I Be Such a Fool," one of the most revengeful songs on the album. Yet the record is balanced with some satirical pop, too, including the clever "Wowie Zowie" and "Any Way the Wind Blows," both of which showcase Zappa's strongest influence, doo-wop music. By the time we get to "The Return of the Son of Monster Magnet," we enter Zappa's world full on. It's a world built with electronic sounds, spoken word, and improvisation, with a mix of sci-fi sound effects thrown in.

In many ways, *Freak Out!* is the launching point in the art of Frank Zappa. Almost everything he did with the Mothers of Invention starts here, and it's all fully developed and well executed. Its mixture of the avant-garde with spoken word, R&B, and doo-wop, with a nod to the political climate of the day, makes for great repeated listening—especially the stereo version, where the sounds have more clarity. You'll never think of cream cheese again without thinking Zappa. Listen, too, for Zappa's use of tape-speed variation on a few cuts. "The Return of the Monster Magnet" is considered one of the most jazz-oriented compositions in Zappa's early catalogue, while "Trouble Every Day," about urban violence in America's cities, remains relevant fifty years later. It's hard to believe that Zappa was only twenty-five years old when it was released.

Hot Rats (O.R. #8, Bizarre, 1969)

This was Zappa's first "solo" album, following the demise of the original Mothers of Invention. His imaginative use of a new 16-track recorder on the classic instrumental "Peaches En Regalia" is a work of art. Captain Beefheart makes an appearance on "Willie the Pimp," and the instrumental "The Gumbo Variations" is a sonic delight. But what makes *Hot Rats* so successful is Zappa's sense of himself as a musician and composer. This record is full of self-confidence and certainty as Zappa shapes his blues-heavy guitar playing into new realms of rock music. He called it "a movie for your ears," but that could easily be said of his first solo venture, *Lumpy Gravy*, as it could for this album.

Hot Rats reached only #173 on the *Billboard* charts, but it soon hit #1 in the hearts and minds of Zappa fans around the world for its inventive and accessible music. Most of the album is instrumental, with some blistering solos from Zappa, especially on "Willie the Pimp." But the record also marks a new beginning for Zappa, who had split up the original Mothers of Invention six weeks earlier. *Hot Rats* is written in the first person. Here, Zappa brings all of his editing and technical skills to bear rather than pleasing the audience with the tried and true. Politically, Zappa wasn't going to lament the tumultuous decade with a nostalgic trip down memory lane. While the Doors, the Beatles, and many of the hit bands from the sixties were done, Zappa was just getting started.

Broadway the Hard Way (O.R. #53, Barking Pumpkin, 1988)

This album was released immediately after the 1988 big-band tour ended abruptly following a dispute within the band. Zappa had lost a lot of money and needed to recoup the costs. The result was an extraordinary album that offers something for every Zappa fan, including some new songs, such as "Planet of the Baritone Women" and "Rhymin' Man," about the Reverend Jesse Jackson. Zappa had intentionally toured during an election year because, in his view, the political face of America was changing for the worse. This album stands as a remarkable snapshot of the United States during that fateful year, but it also predicts the rise of the so-called religious right, whose TV evangelists filled the airwaves. Sting makes an appearance to sing "Murder by Numbers," as the band vamps to Oliver Nelson's "Stolen Moments." Priceless. Another highlight is Ike Willis's vocal on "Outside Now," originally heard on *Joe's Garage*. It's a poignant reminder that very little had changed in the recording business by 1988, and Zappa's extraordinary guitar solo enriches the dismay he was feeling for the American political process and the lack of involvement by its citizens. Try the follow-ups, *The Best Band You Never Heard in Your Life* (O.R. #55) and *Make a Jazz Noise Here* (O.R. #56), to get the full effect.

Joe's Garage (O.R. #28 and #29, Zappa, 1979)

Originally released in two stages across three LPs, these recordings were finally brought together as a single work with the two-CD edition from 2012. It's not one of my favorites, but it certainly reached a lot of fans for its honest assessment of the record business and the threat to creativity by the

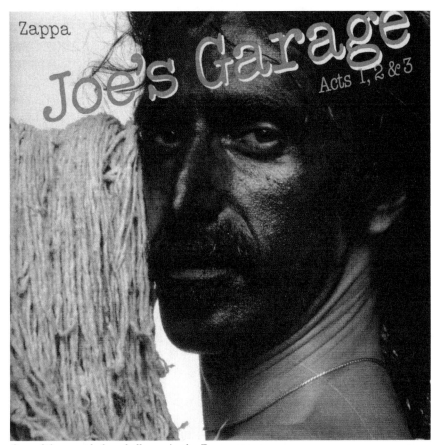

One of the most beloved albums in the Zappa canon.

powerful "machine"—the same one Pink Floyd referred to on 1975's "Welcome to the Machine."

Zappa considered *Joe's Garage* a "cheap kind of high school play" about a time when music has been outlawed. Its strongest asset is Ike Willis, who sings lead and whose heartfelt interpretation of "Outside Now" is considered the gold standard of Zappa's late-seventies output. The album also features the controversial song "Catholic Girls" and a visit to the "First Church of Appliantology," where vacuums dance with one another. It's a slightly absurd work, but with careful deconstruction the album is worthy of further study. In fact, Kelly Fisher Lowe does a fine job of sifting through the album in *The Words and Music of Frank Zappa*, calling it a "masterpiece" on the basis of it being musically strong, politically savvy, and full of Zappa's clever satire on American culture.

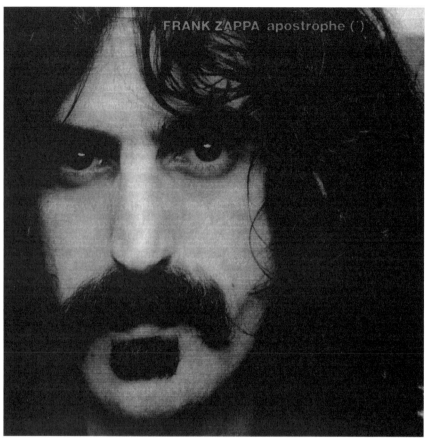

For your dining and dancing pleasure.

Apostrophe (') (O.R. #18, DiscReet, 1974)

A member of Zappa's Petit Wazoo band coined the phrase "don't eat yellow snow" in 1972 while on a bus to a gig. Who knew it would become one of the most famous quotations in Zappa lore? But it did, and you'll find it here on one of Zappa's most popular "concept" albums. To some fans, it's a dream realized; to others, it's a nod to *King Lear* by William Shakespeare. But the upshot of the fantasy is that it gave Zappa free range to express all manner of ideas. In spite of the short running time (just over thirty minutes), the album contains a wealth of interesting music. "Cosmik Debris" is one of Zappa's funniest songs about soothsayers, while also taking a stab at America's infatuation with the new age in popular culture. If you dig a little deeper, Zappa also comments on race in "Uncle Remus," which reflects his thoughts on the civil rights movement and whether it has made a difference in changing the lives of African Americans. He concludes that there still is a lot of work to do.

Sheik Yerbouti (O.R. #26, Zappa, 1979)

Upon its release in 1979, this album sparked the kind of publicity that a record executive could only dream of. The controversial nature of one song, "Jewish Princess," had Zappa defending his satiric tune from the Anti-Defamation League and women's groups who were upset by the lyrics and their characterization of women. But the record also takes a shot at Peter Frampton ("I Have Been in You"), gay A&R reps ("Bobby Brown"), and dancing fools like Zappa himself. Zappa was genuinely interested in

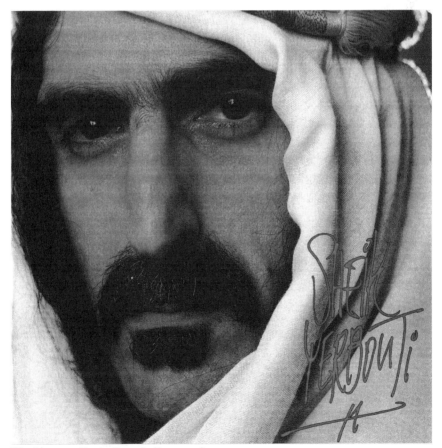

The biggest seller in Zappa's discography.

criticizing the myths around so-called rock stars. Among his targets was Frampton's follow-up to his platinum-selling *Frampton Comes Alive* (A&M, 1976), *I'm in You* (A&M 1977), which sold very well on the back of its hugely successful predecessor. Zappa felt that the idiotic lyrics to the title track of Frampton's album needed some comment, so he wrote "I Have Been in You," with equally nonsensical lyrics.

Much of *Sheik Yerbouti* is accessible to the newcomer, but this album stands out for its poisonous comments on everything that was trending in 1977, from feminism to gay rights. European audiences latched on to "Bobby Brown," especially in the dance clubs of Scandinavia. "Dancin' Fool" was also a big hit in Europe—so much so that CBS records issued an extended version as a 12-inch single in 1979. The song reached #45 on the *Billboard* 100, making it the second-highest-charting single in Zappa's career. But *Sheik Yerbouti* isn't just a couple of hit singles and controversial lyrics; it is Zappa's strongest test of the US Bill of Rights and the laws surrounding freedom of speech. The fans agreed, as the record peaked on the *Billboard* 200 at #21. It remains his biggest-selling album of all time.

Guitar (O.R. #50, Barking Pumpkin, 1988)

This highly edited instrumental album puts Zappa's guitar solos up front and personal. Even though the solos are lifted from complete songs recorded in performance, one gets the real essence of Zappa's sound and technique as he "sculpts the airwaves" onstage. You also get the chance to hear Zappa's growing interest in changing up the rhythms from straight 4/4 rock to the more subtle feel of reggae, so there's lots of variety on this two-disc set. One of the highlights is "It Ain't Necessarily the Saint James Infirmary," which merged two jazz standards to great effect, proving that Zappa could play something accessible and straight-ahead.

Cruising with Ruben & the Jets (O.R. #5, Bizarre, 1968)

This album is one of the best ways to get into Zappa's music. It's uncomplicated, straight-ahead doo-wop with a Zappa touch. The lyrics are subversive, though, in the sense that they don't celebrate romantic love as much as admonish it. Zappa loved the harmonies of groups like the Penguins and the Orioles, but he wasn't fond of the songs' idealism. He punched a hole in that era with the release of this album in 1968, but it wasn't well received at the time. Critics didn't understand the connection between Igor Stravinsky's exploration of neo-classical music and Zappa's neo-doo-wop, as it were. The album offers a key insight into the style of the Mothers of Invention, rooted as it was in R&B, but make sure you get the original LP or the 2012 reissue of the original mix. Alternately, check out *Greasy Love Songs* (O.R. #87) or *Joe's Corsage* (O.R. #74).

Secondary Study

Nearly half of Zappa's output is made up from performance recordings, including the multi-volume series *You Can't Do That on Stage Anymore.* Zappa placed a high premium on his band's ability to play his difficult music. This is a list of the most entertaining performances in the current catalogue. The good news is that there are more to come as archivist Joe Travers continues to sort through the hundreds of hours of tape in Zappa's vault. It's Travers's job to choose which tapes to issue next based on their content and their condition—a worthwhile (if time-consuming) process that yields some special music, especially from the original Mothers of Invention.

Road Tapes, Venue #1 (O.R. #93, Vaulternative Records, 2012)

This outstanding performance by the Mothers of Invention, recorded in Vancouver on August 25, 1968, and released as a two-disc set, features one of Zappa's favorite compositions by Edgard Varèse, "Octandre." It was often performed in concert but never made it to CD until 2012. What makes this recording special is the strength of the band and the musicians' ability to improvise at a moment's notice. Zappa was constantly challenging the Mothers to come up with as many musical ideas as possible without repeating themselves. By 1968, the Mothers were at the height of their powers and pushing the limits of what could be considered rock music versus performance art. This concert embraced both worlds effectively, and although it was recorded in mono on a rented reel-to-reel machine, the sound is excellent, thanks to a high-resolution digital transfer. Studio recordings of the Mothers are often much more forgiving than the live performances, but here the band excels as an ensemble. Zappa also has a decent rapport with the audience, which granted him more options regarding the set list. There's a good chance that attendees were expecting to hear

"Hungry Freaks, Daddy," not the Edgard Varèse composition so close to Zappa's heart.

The Best Band You Never Heard in Your Life (O.R. #55, Barking Pumpkin, 1991)

Arguably the best ensemble Zappa ever had, the 1988 big band was the last touring group of his career and also one of the most documented. This two-CD set will amaze, entertain, and keep you coming back for more.

The album is launched by a sparkling version of "Heavy Duty Judy," followed by Zappa's story about meeting Johnny Cash in the hope of securing a guest appearance by the country-music legend, but what makes this album great is the careful editing by Zappa of the individual tracks into one continuous concert experience. The seamless flow of the songs on the first disc is superb, while the second is equally satisfying to the ear.

The bonus track is the band's rendition of Led Zeppelin's "Stairway to Heaven." Part tribute and part satire, it has the Jimmy Page guitar solo transposed to the horn section, with masterful results. The song usually closed the show, and the version on this record is actually an edit of three different performances.

Add the companion album, *Make a Jazz Noise Here* (O.R. #56), as soon as possible.

You Can't Do That on Stage Anymore, Vol. 2 (O.R. #52, Rykodisc, 1988)

Also known as *The Helsinki Concert*, this two-CD album showcases the version of the touring group featuring George Duke, Napoleon Murphy Brock (who was ill at the time), Ruth Underwood, Tom Fowler, and Chester Thompson. The *One Size Fits All* band was the best five-piece ensemble ever led by Zappa, and this continuous performance proves it. All of the music was so well known by the players that Zappa thought "they could play it blindfolded," and he was right, considering some of the faster tempos and range of songs. The show was recorded during two nights in Finland in September 1974, with a set list including "Approximate"—one of the most difficult songs in the Zappa canon, and one he often chose to audition new musicians. In spite of poor sound equipment and faulty stage gear, the band played on with a highly skilled and enjoyable performance.

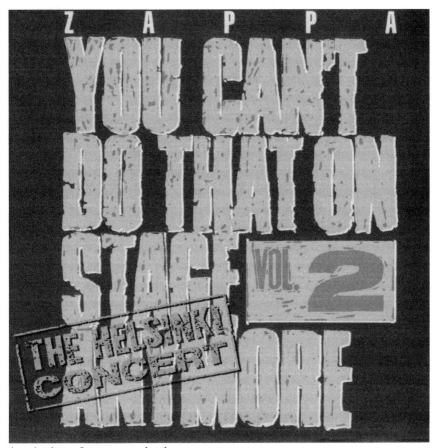

A majestic performance under duress.

Roxy & Elsewhere (O.R. #19, Discreet, 1974)

One of the most beloved albums in the Zappa collection, this one was recorded over three nights at the Roxy in Hollywood, supplemented by tracks from shows in Chicago and Edinboro, Pennsylvania. The eleven-piece group rises to the occasion as Zappa leads a show full of cheeky patter, including a reference to some gym socks donated to him by his brother Carl. Most of the songs on this album would become concert favorites on subsequent tours.

This two-record set is distinguished by the overall performance of the band and the freedom with which they could perform without necessarily taking direction from Zappa. In other words, the whole is bigger than the sum of the parts. Zappa is certainly the front man, but his extended monologues, which introduce most of the songs, have a lighter air about them. He's more interested in telling a tale than lecturing his audience, and consequently the album is less heavy-handed and more fun. The fans responded in kind, sending the album to #26 on the *Billboard* 200 after its release in 1974.

Additional songs from these shows can be heard on *Roxy by Proxy* (O.R. #99). In October 2015, a fully restored movie of the concert was issued on DVD for the first time as *Roxy: The Movie*.

Hammersmith Odeon (O.R. #89, Vaulternative, 2010)

Recorded over four nights at the famous London venue, this three-CD set features the 1977–78 touring band with Adrian Belew, Tommy Mars, Peter Wolf, Ed Mann, Patrick O'Hearn, and Terry Bozzio. Some of these tracks also appear on *Sheik Yerbouti*, but with significant overdubs. This set is an often-intense listening experience, mostly due to Terry Bozzio's inspired performance on the drums. It really kicks! Zappa challenges his band with an intense retrospective of his career, pulling out the best and most popular songs in his repertoire to date. The agility of the band is showcased on what was originally a live radio broadcast in the United States on January 27, 1978, although Zappa subsequently re-edited the album to include performances from another show on February 28. What we have here is the best continuous concert experience in the Zappa catalogue, presented in one sitting, with no overdubs.

Tinsel Town Rebellion (O.R. #30, Barking Pumpkin, 1981)

This set features a dance contest and a panty-throw presented by a most forthright bandleader. Zappa's sarcasm is palpable, and his irreverent cutups are razor sharp. The title track takes a creative—and, to some fans, accurate—shot at punk bands from Los Angeles at the time who had been seduced by the riches of the record business. A splendid time is guaranteed for a few.

Buffalo (O.R. #80, Vaulternative, 2007)

This first-rate concert recording showcases a band ready and willing to play to the best of their ability. Recorded at the Memorial Auditorium—aka the

More music for your dining and dancing pleasure.

Aud—in Buffalo, New York, the set opens with one of the primo versions of the instrumental "Chunga's Revenge." Bass player Arthur Barrow is especially good, driving the bus on the band's version of "You Are What You Is." The two-disc album also features Zappa's new stunt guitarist at the time, Steve Vai.

Ahead of Their Time (O.R. #61, Barking Pumpkin, 1993)

This is one of the most historically significant performances by the Mothers of Invention, as recorded at the Royal Albert Hall in London, England, on October 25, 1968. Less concert and more performance art, the band improvise short, nonsensical skits between songs. Fourteen members of the BBC Symphony Orchestra accompanied the Mothers for the festivities, which were also filmed for the movie *Uncle Meat*, as released on Honker Home Video.

Just Another Band from L.A. (O.R. #14, Bizarre/Reprise, 1972)

When Frank Zappa decided to hire Marc Volman and Howard Kaylan of the Turtles, they had to change their names for legal reasons. At the time, they were engaged in a lawsuit against their label, White Whale Records, over breach of trust. The label countersued for breach of contract, because "the Turtles and Howard Kaylan and Mark Volman" still owed it an album. As a result of the original deal they had signed individually, the singers couldn't use either the band name or their own names. Consequently, they took on the nicknames of two roadies and became Flo and Eddie (a contraction of "The Phlorescent Leech and Eddie").

This recording, from Pauley Pavilion at UCLA in 1971, features "Billy the Mountain," a radio play about a mountain named Billy (naturally) and his tree-girlfriend, Ethel, defying the corporate forces of a fictional company named Studebacher Hoch. The twenty-four-minute work is considered a nugget in the discography of Frank Zappa, mostly because of its self-indulgence, but the piece that originally filled an entire side did in fact make the repertoire of Zappa Plays Zappa in 2010 (as heard on the Razor & Tie release *Return of the Son of . . .*). In complete contrast, the album also features a song about sexual assault called "Magdalena," so proceed with caution.

Make a Jazz Noise Here (O.R. #56, Rykodisc, 1991)

This second volume from the 1988 big-band tour features a more eclectic set of tunes and instrumentals, with the band getting to wind out and improvise making "jazz noises" along the way. This two-disc album incorporates music by Igor Stravinsky and Bela Bartok, plus one of the best versions of "City of Tiny Lites," featuring Bobby Martin on lead vocals, and guarantees that it is "100 percent live with no overdubs." Zappa often said he preferred writing instrumental music over straight-ahead rock songs, and this album certainly makes his point, but he adds a couple of terrific performances of "Cruising for Burgers" and "Advance Romance," originally released on *Bongo Fury*, for good measure.

Graduate Study

Zappa's huge output wasn't limited to traditional rock music. He learned the rudiments of composition after high school, but he wasn't interested in "cookie-cutter" harmonies and structures, so he quit school and decided to teach himself formal composition. He also absorbed the modern sounds of Igor Stravinsky, Edgard Varèse, and Anton Webern from his personal collection as a teenager. The results are mixed, but these records still hold up under scrutiny.

Illustration by Larry Grossman.

Frank Zappa's 200 Motels (O.R. #13, Bizarre/United Artists, 1971)

The soundtrack to the infamous motion picture isn't too easy to find, but it is worth the effort and expense if you discover it at a flea market or vinyl convention. Zappa's first foray into symphonic accompaniment and rock band came with the help of the Royal Philharmonic Orchestra. It's as ambitious as it sounds, and portions of the recording are completely under-rehearsed, especially to contemporary ears spoiled by high-fidelity CDs. Nevertheless, Zappa's raw skills as a composer began in earnest with this work.

The Yellow Shark (O.R. #62, Barking Pumpkin)

Based in Frankfurt, Germany, the Ensemble Modern wanted to play the music of Frank Zappa during their 1992 season. It was a good fit; contemporary music was their specialty. They were interested in performing new

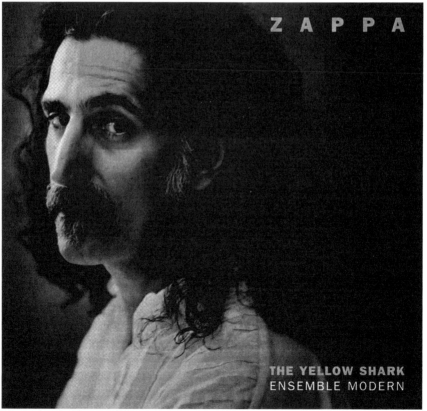

Music ahead of its time by an ensemble ready to play it.

music along with some old favorites in the Zappa catalogue, so, in the summer of 1991, Zappa was commissioned to write for them and invited to participate as rehearsal conductor and sound producer. The orchestra relocated to Los Angeles for several weeks as Zappa worked through his ideas. He also recorded the group and used their sounds to compose more music on the Synclavier.

By the time the concerts came along in 1992, Zappa and three sound engineers had designed an audio monitor system to ensure the "perfect" concert experience. The result is nothing short of brilliant on this engaging album. Listen for a quote from "Louie, Louie" by Richard Berry and a nod to the famous Varèse siren. Extensive liner notes are included with the 1993 CD version. The concert was made available on German pay-per-view television and videotaped from the Alte Oper in Frankfurt, which also featured Lalala Human Steps, the contemporary dance company from Montreal. As the show reveals, Zappa also conducted a couple of pieces, doing so with the mannerisms of a sculptor.

Orchestral Favorites (O.R. #27, DiscReet, 1979)

This album was recorded in Royce Hall, UCLA, over two days in September 1975. The Abnuceals Emuukha Electric Symphony Orchestra was, in spite of the unusual name, a legitimate ensemble based in Los Angeles, conducted by Michael Zearott. Zappa's limited budget only allowed for one concert followed by a recording session in Royce Hall. The rhythm section featured Zappa, Dave Parlato (bass), Terry Bozzio (drums), and Emil Richards (percussion). Highlights include "Duke of Prunes" and "Strictly Genteel." Two more tracks appear on the compilation *One Shot Deal* (OR #83): "Hermitage" and "Rollo." Warner Bros. first released this album without the approval of Zappa, along with *Sleep Dirt* and *Studio Tan*, but they are all now officially part of the Zappa discography.

The Perfect Stranger (O.R. #39, Angel, 1984)

One of Frank Zappa's favorite conductors and composers was Pierre Boulez, who's on the list of credits to the 1966 release, *Freak Out!*. In 1983, Boulez commissioned Zappa to write three works for his small orchestra, the Ensemble Intercontemporain. At the same time, Zappa was composing on the Synclavier, which gave him the chance to add his computer-generated tracks to the resulting album. Highlights include the thematic title track and "The Girl in the Magnesium Dress," which makes colorful use of a marimba part originally played by Ruth Underwood.

Dance Me This (O.R. #100, Vaulternative, 2015)

One of the benefits of listening to music in 2016 is context. The release of Zappa's last original album, twenty-two years after it was finished, may not have had the impact it has today had it not been for the explosive growth in "world music" since 1993. The wide variety of sounds now available to the informed listener has peppered the quality and quantity of music in broad strokes. To a certain extent, this is what Zappa's notion of composing music was all about.

In January of 1993, Zappa threw a house party with some very interesting guests, including Johnny "Guitar" Watson, the Irish group the Chieftains, and three singers known as Tuvans who hailed from the southern region

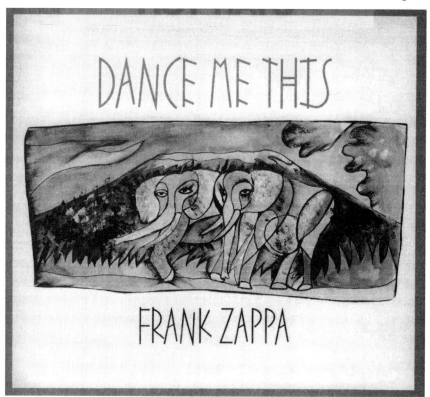

The last album released twenty-two years after it was finished.

of Siberia. The resulting jam session was one Zappa thoroughly enjoyed, as captured on a BBC TV documentary broadcast after his death. The chance to record the jam session was an opportunity he could not miss. Zappa was genuinely interested in music that had an ancient sound, and the results are remarkably bright, buoyant, and ethereal as he weaves the guttural voicing of Anatolii Kuular against that most Western of instruments, the piano (via his Synclavier, of course). The five-part soundscape called "Wolf Harbor" is the centerpiece of the album. This delicate suite of music is in sharp contrast to the harder edge of Zappa's earlier rock music. "Wolf Harbor" is a long way from "Montana," but the steady pulse of the bell in part one gives us a rhythmic pattern on which to hold as we move into something deeply emotional and old. It's a freeform work, suggesting choreography for a modern dance company in the manner of Stravinsky's collaborations with the *Ballets Russes* in 1913. In *Civilization Phaze III*, the character Spider talks about the universe as "one note" made up of "different octaves." *Dance Me This* is very much the musical explanation of that universe: connected and holistic.

On this, his final album, Zappa brings to life his notion of the "present day composer" refusing to die. *Dance Me This* is a subtle work, a quiet album of colors and textures closer to the villages of Mongolia than the streets of L.A. It's an album that reflects Zappa's relationship with sound in a most personal way: introspective, cosmic, dream-like. It's also mostly instrumental, with only three of its eleven tracks featuring vocals by Tuvan throat singers: the title track, "Goat Polo," and the closer, "Calculus." The latter was creating using algorithms, according to Zappa's engineer, Todd Yvega. The sound is excellent even by today's standards, Zappa having sculpted his music with great care and expression into a beautifully rendered masterwork.

London Symphony Orchestra, Volumes 1 & 2 (O.R. #38 and #48, Barking Pumpkin, 1983 and 1987)

These albums mark the debut of conductor Kent Nagano, who now leads the Montreal Symphony Orchestra. In an interview with the British fanzine *T'Mershi Duween* in 1990, Nagano said that the scores for this album had "extraordinary quality," adding that it was "very surprising that anybody could write something so original, much less someone who wasn't known in the classical music field."

In his autobiography, though, Zappa rants about the musicians on this recording, who he says failed to perform up to his expectations. Having hired the orchestra and Nagano and entered the studio to record these original works, he wasn't satisfied with the results, largely because of the limited rehearsal time available to them, and he offers an apology in the liner notes, admitting that the final version was heavily edited, especially "Strictly Genteel." To the experienced listener, this album may sound derivative, echoing as it does the music of Varèse and Webern, but to dismiss it for those reasons would be unfair. It's a challenging work for musician and listener alike.

Everything Is Healing Nicely (O.R. #69, Barking Pumpkin, 1999)

This album of rehearsal takes from Los Angeles, recorded in the lead-up to the *Yellow Shark* concert, requires a lot of patience on behalf of the listener. The music moves carefully, with a kind of hesitation that actually drags rather than enhances the experience. Consequently, it is much more contemplative—music for the mind, as it were. The highlight is "Roland's Big Event/Strat Vindaloo," which features Zappa playing electric guitar and L. Shankar on violin. The music takes on a mystical resonance that's very satisfying, offering fans a contrast to some of the edgier spoken-word pieces, in German, that also appear on the album.

Post Graduate Study

This level of Zappa's discography offers the connoisseur deep cuts into his music. These albums reward the listener because of their adventurous construction, musical sophistication, and humor.

We're Only in It for the Money (O.R. #3, Verve, 1968)

The first thing you notice about Zappa's third album is the cover art, with the Mothers of Invention in drag on the front and a parody of *Sgt. Pepper* in the gatefold. But there's much more to this record than a satiric arrow to the heart of the Beatles. This is an album to be "experienced" as a soundscape for America in 1968—one of the worst years in United States history. All of Zappa's pet peeves are on display and well presented. He holds nothing back when he cuts up hippie culture on "Who Needs the Peace Corps?" and

The "polite" cover graces the third album by The Mothers of Invention.

Nixonian oppression on "Concentration Moon." Listen for the psychedelia on "Flower Punk" and "Absolutely Free," which effectively mimic that now-dated sound. The album closes with a discordant piano and a few other unusual sound effects. Then, do not pass go and continue immediately to . . .

Lumpy Gravy (O.R. #4, Verve, 1968)

This record, which was Zappa's personal favorite, is the soundtrack to a movie of the mind. It's edited together to sound as though you're moving a dial on a radio, dropping in on conversations, monologues, jazz bands, and orchestras. The stereo ping-pong effect is often used to distinguish certain elements, but it's all tied together with a musical theme called "Oh No," which also turns up on *Weasels Ripped My Flesh* (O.R. #10), featuring a vocal by Ray Collins. Do not collect $200 and proceed to . . .

Civilization Phaze III (O.R. #63, Barking Pumpkin, 1994)

This is the consummate Frank Zappa album in so many ways, which makes it difficult to even attempt to describe it in words. The best thing to do is to give it your undivided attention; Zappa would have expected no less. If you have one of those fancy wireless hi-fi systems in your home, put it on every speaker and "let the colortinis fly through the air," as Tom Snyder used to say. Highlights include the earthy and ancient sound of Mongolian/Tuvan throat singer Kaigal-ool Khovalyq on the eight-minute masterpiece "Dio Fa," which, loosely translated, is Italian for "God is a liar."

Weasels Ripped My Flesh (O.R. #10, Bizarre, 1970)

The slightly nasty jacket art by Neon Park (aka Martin Muller) doesn't exactly encourage ownership of this album, but to judge this record by its cover would be completely unfair. *Weasels* is one of the most diverse albums in the Zappa discography. It was originally intended as a sampler for a twelve-record set called *The History and Collective Improvisations of the Mothers of Invention*. Had that anthology come out, it would have been the final word on the Mothers, because Zappa broke up the band a year before its release. But we'll never know. Highlights include Sugar Cane Harris's excellent performance on "Directly from My Heart to You," the vocal version of "Oh No" (featuring Ray Collins responding to the idealism of "All You Need Is Love" by the Beatles), and the adventurous "Prelude to the Afternoon of a Sexually Aroused Gas Mask." (Listen for Don Preston, on keyboards, playing a theme from Tchaikovsky's Symphony No. 6 behind pig-like grunts.) The album also features one of Zappa's greatest hits, "My Guitar Wants to Kill Your Mama."

Uncle Meat (O.R. #7, Bizarre, 1969)

Working with a Scully 12-track prototype recorder, here Zappa constructed an album of remarkable variety. All of his influences are present on this album, from doo-wop to the modern percussion sounds of Edgard Varèse, but this time it's all Zappa, all the time, because he takes full control of the

You know what they say, don't judge a Zappa album by its cover.

outcome. The album also marks the debut of Ruth Komanoff (who later married Ian Underwood) on marimba and vibraphone. Her performance, in partnership with fellow percussionist Art Tripp, brings a remarkable texture to the music that was previously absent. Subsequent releases by Zappa would all make significant use of the vibraphone or marimba. The tracks "Nine Types of Industrial Pollution," "The Uncle Meat Variations," and "We Can Shoot You" highlight Zappa's skills as an editor. The album is capped off with six variations of "King Kong," one of the most challenging and rewarding instrumentals in the Zappa songbook.

Läther (O.R. #65, Rykodisc, 1996)

Läther (pronounced "leather") is the album Zappa originally wanted to release as a four-LP set in 1977 on Mercury Records, but a contractual dispute between Warner Bros. and Mercury prevented its release in this form. Mercury, which had signed a separate deal with Zappa, actually made test pressings of this album, but Warners' impending litigation stopped it from going further with European distribution. Zappa was outraged by Warners' move and took his copy of the test pressing to KROQ radio in Pasadena, inviting listeners to tape it straight off the air. Meanwhile, Warner Bros. released most of the music from these sessions on three "unauthorized" (as far as Zappa was concerned) albums, *Sleep Dirt*, *Studio Tan*, and *Orchestral Favorites*. Fans were also treated to tracks from the album *Zappa in New York*.

By Dweezil Zappa—cover concept featuring Italy, Sicily, and Sardinia on the cow.

Twenty years later, in 1996, the original album was finally released as Zappa intended it. For the fans who had already heard the music on the previous releases, this remastered version offers up some of the same tracks in a completely different context. The music on this album could also be described as a recapitulation of Zappa's entire career in 1977. His touring bands are well represented right back to 1969, and the studio sessions from 1975 display the sharpness and wit of his composing style. Highlights include "The Illinois Enema Bandit," "Revised Music for Guitar & Low-Budget Orchestra," "The Adventures of Greggery Peccary," and "Duke of Orchestral Prunes." (Kevin Courrier provides some of the best scholarship on *Läther* in his book *Dangerous Kitchen: The Subversive World of Frank Zappa*.)

Jazz from Hell (O.R. #47, Barking Pumpkin, 1986)

This complex album echoes some of the sounds of Cecil Taylor and Eric Dolphy, whose pioneering free-style and borderless improvisations, heard in the late fifties, made some fans of jazz stand up and applaud while making others cringe. In a way, *Jazz from Hell*, composed and performed on Synclavier, pays tribute to Taylor and Dolphy by challenging our ears with music that is not only free of musicians (except for "St. Etienne") but also free of any melodic or harmonic restrictions whatsoever. Some of the musical intervals remind us of Eric Dolphy's work on his seminal Blue Note album from 1964, *Out to Lunch*. Considered in that context, this album is worthy of further consideration to any music student currently enrolled in a jazz program.

Thing-Fish (O.R. #41, Barking Pumpkin, 1984)

This is the Broadway musical to end all Broadway musicals. It takes everything Zappa hated—hypocrisy in politics, artistic conformity, and corporate imposition—and throws it back at the world without any heed to taste. *Thing-Fish* is a mix of stereotypes: Al Jolson, Amos and Andy, and the minstrel shows of the nineteenth century, which had white people dressed in blackface performing as black people. By today's standards, the minstrel show was racist and embarrassing behavior masked as entertainment. Here, Zappa takes minstrelsy and flips it upside down, while commenting along the way on American conformity in the arts, the growing AIDS crisis as a government plot, and infiltration of the religious right in US politics.

The presentation is a mix of the zany comedy of the Firesign Theatre and the edgy wit of Lenny Bruce, all controlled by the man behind the curtain, Frank Zappa.

That several songs from *You Are What You Is* are re-incorporated into *Thing-Fish* makes things more accessible, but it's still a challenging album. In Act One, one of the characters, Harry, asks facetiously, "What's the meaning of all this?" Good question.

15

Bootlegs

Zappa and the Power of Ownership

B ootleg recordings have been around since the advent of sound technology. Although he didn't know it at the time, Lionel Mapleson was the first ever bootlegger, having recorded performances by the New York Metropolitan Opera in 1901. Mapleson was the Met's librarian and had been given a Bettini micro-recorder and cylinder player. (Gianni Bettini, 1860–1938, was an Italian inventor.) He also owned an Edison Home Phonograph, used only for playback. According to archivist Dean Meader, Mapleson took to the fly loft above the stage and was able to record short pieces of performances. Cylinders in those days only held a few minutes of sound at a time, but despite this limitation, Mapleson recorded some passages one night and played them back to the members of the opera the next day. So, the very first bootleg was a recording of a concert. (Radio broadcasts and unissued studio performances are also a part of the bootleg genre. A "pirate" recording is released material in a different package, while a "counterfeit" recording is a copy of an official release with the same artwork.)

Mapleson's recordings set the technical standards for a bootleg—that is, poor or inconsistent sound quality and limited copies. After his death in 1937, it was revealed that he made over one hundred cylinder recordings at the Met between 1901 and 1904. They are now housed in the New York Public Library.

In rock music, bootlegs didn't appear until the end of the sixties, specifically with an album called *Great White Wonder* by Bob Dylan, which arrived in the form of two LPs wrapped in a plain white cover. The set of songs featured on it, which were recorded in 1967 by Garth Hudson of the Band during Dylan's hiatus in Woodstock, New York, later became known as *The Basement Tapes*. Following a motorcycle accident, Dylan and the Band had set up in a country house known as Big Pink and spent the summer writing

Zappa's 1977 radio broadcast illegally issued on LP.

and playing songs for their own amusement. Hudson ran a small reel-to-reel machine as a diary of their experience. The results were never meant for release to the public, but the bootleg recording of them became one of the most sought-after albums in music history.

Columbia released its own authorized version of the songs in 1975, but these recordings had been remixed, with overdubs by Dylan and Robbie Robertson, who also played on the tapes. Although the 1975 release sold well, Dylan fans yearned for the day they could get their copy of the original, unedited recordings. That day finally came on November 4, 2014, with the release of a boxed set containing all of the original "bootleg" recordings.

Zappa Fights Back

Frank Zappa never liked the bootleg "industry" very much, especially when it cut into his revenue stream, even though bootleg LPs usually had limited pressings of fewer than a thousand copies. One of the earliest Zappa bootlegs was a concert recording of *200 Motels* featuring Zappa, the Mothers of Invention, and the Los Angeles Philharmonic Orchestra conducted by Zubin Mehta.

The quality of the recording, from May 15, 1970, is good enough that it was probably a very popular bootleg at the time. (It can be heard today on YouTube.) The illegal recording was advertised for sale in the *Los Angeles Free Press*, with only a PO box number listed for interested parties to contact. Zappa tried to stop the sale and distribution of the album, attempting to discover the source by answering the ad and requesting his own copy, but the contents did not lead to the manufacturer.

Zappa generally thought that bootleggers were exploiting the name and music of the artist for their own financial gain, and he was right. But for fans, a bootleg is an historical artifact holding great value, and according to Greg Russo, author of the Zappa anthology *Cosmik Debris*, "The quantity of bootlegs available of Zappa material is staggering." A fan with some savvy could seek out and find Zappa concert bootlegs going back to 1968. Zappa blamed the ineffectual copyright laws of the United States for his lack of success in pursuing the bootleggers behind *200 Motels*, but he didn't give up. As far as Zappa was concerned, bootlegs interfered with his own release schedule, because they often contained versions of music he was plan-ning to release.

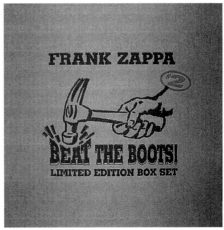

Cover designed by Geoff Gans.

In order to slow down the manufac-ture and distribution of bootlegs of his material, Zappa took action. First he hired T. B. Brown, a Zappa expert at Richard Foo's independent label Rhino Records, to sort and select some bootleg albums from the hundreds available from head shops and independent music stores. Brown shortlisted eight albums, including a pair of two-LP sets that were originally recorded between 1968 and 1981. Zappa didn't listen to any of them, but his sound engineers did some basic balancing and equalization treatments, which were necessary because much of the source material was several genera-tions removed from the original. Zappa then made a distribution deal with Rhino (which was later purchased by Warner Bros.), and in the summer of 1991, he released the ten-LP boxed set *Beat the Boots* on his own label, the appropriately named Foo-Eee.

The cover of *Beat the Boots* features an illustration of a hand with a hammer striking the word "beat" with a certain amount of force. The eight albums were all issued "as is," with printing errors on the jackets and spelling mistakes on the inner sleeves. In the spirit of bootlegging, the vinyl boxed set was limited to 600 copies. It also included a "Beat the Boots" T-shirt, as well as a pop-up display of Zappa and the Mothers. The collection was also issued as an eight-CD set, as eight individual CDs, and on cassette. Zappa also licensed the collection to distributors in the UK, Germany, France, and Japan. It may not have put a dent in the black market, but *Beat the Boots* sold over 20,000 units worldwide and became highly collectible among Zappa fans. Ironically, designer Geoff Gans was nominated for a Grammy Award for best recording package.

The success of *Beat the Boots* led to the release of a second volume of seven albums in June 1992, simply called *Beat the Boots 2*. This time, Rhino created a limited-edition eleven-LP boxed set, an eight-CD boxed set, and a seven-cassette set for the fans. Each came with a black beret with the Rhino logo, a pin, and a scrapbook designed by album-cover artist Cal Schenkel. This set contains concert recordings from 1968 to 1976, including the famous Montreux Festival "fire" concert immortalized in Deep Purple's song "Smoke on the Water."

In 2009, a digital download version of *Beat the Boots III* was made available by the Zappa Records label. It features six discs worth of concert recordings from various locations in the United States and Europe, including the last tour in 1988.

A complete list of Zappa bootlegs—and it's a long one—can be found at www.lukpac.org/~handmade/patio/bootlegs/.

16

The Gift That Keeps On Giving

Zappa's Archives and the UMRK

MRK stands for Utility Muffin Research Kitchen. The phrase comes from the song "The Muffin Man," as heard on the 1975 album *Bongo Fury*, and is the name of Zappa's home recording studio, which was completed in 1979. Zappa's first sound lab, however, was the PAL Studio, located in Cucamonga, California. It was owned and operated by an ex-marine by the name of Paul Buff. Zappa met Buff in 1960 with an interest in recording local pop and jazz bands, and Buff's experience as an electronics engineer made him the ideal tutor.

PAL Studio: The Early Years

From 1960 to 1965, Zappa was immersed in recording techniques, production, and arranging while recording singles for any group willing to pay the hourly fees. He learned as much as he could about microphones, amps, tape recorders, and mixing boards. Among the dozens of singles PAL Studio recorded and released, the most notable was by the instrumental surf-rock band known as the Tornadoes, who cut several singles and a couple of albums there.

In 1961, Zappa and Buff recorded and released their first single, "Sixteen Tons" b/w "Break Time" by the Masters (Buff, Zappa, and Ronnie Williams), which was released on the Emmy label. During off hours, Zappa took the opportunity to experiment with his own compositions and recordings that were a mix of music, sound effects, and improvised spoken word. He recorded and spliced together these recordings using magnetic tape as his audio canvas.

Zappa may not have known it at the time, but these early tapes laid the foundation of the archives housed in the UMRK. By the end of 1963, Zappa had moved into the PAL studio after Buff got a job as an engineer at a competing studio known as Original Sound. Zappa renamed it Studio Z and had the tools necessary to express his musical ideas. He devoted endless hours to trial and error in the recording studio, laying the foundation for his own artistic expression.

By 1966, when he and the Mothers of Invention went into the studio to record *Freak Out!*, Zappa was already well versed in recording technology. He understood multi-tracking, mixing, and editing. That first album set the template, with the credits stating, "Selections arranged, orchestrated, and conducted by Frank Zappa." He would later add "producer" to that list. Zappa would be considered a "control freak" in the modern parlance, but it was his name on the music, and he took immediate responsibility for his work and his archives.

The UMRK is as much a monument to Zappa's past as to his future, as he often dipped into the archives in order to create a new album for release. This was particularly evident in 1996, when he released *The Lost Episodes*, which features home recordings, PAL Studio recordings, and spoken-word elements dating back to 1958. (Engineer Spenser Chrislu was given the task of transferring and remixing the tapes for the project.)

The UMRK was built into the Zappa house where he and his family lived in Laurel Canyon near Los Angeles, California. When not on tour, Zappa usually worked sixteen hours a day, and he needed every recording, mixing, and editing device available to create the music he heard in his head. That meant a huge capital investment in a multi-channel mixing board, editing machines, computers, microphones, soundproofed studios, and instruments. This was Zappa's lab. He had to have it fully functional and available to him at all times, so in lieu of building it offsite, he had it built into the basement of his house. It's where he conducted business, held auditions, and wrote music. In another part of the basement, hundreds of reels of audiotape, videotape, and film were stacked floor-to-ceiling in a climate-controlled room. Zappa called it the Vault.

Zappa hired a staff of seven people to run the UMRK: technician Dave Dondorf, sound engineer Spencer Chrislu, music copyist Ali Askin, software and Synclavier engineer Todd Yvega, foreign language translator Simon Prentis, house mixer Harry Andronis, and videographer Van Carlson. They were responsible for keeping the equipment functioning, preparing sheet music, translating fan mail and cover art, and assisting in Zappa's use of digital technology. They worked for Zappa until his death in 1993.

The Vaultmeister

After Frank's death, Gail Zappa, his widow, hired Joe Travers to take over the UMRK archives as "vaultmeister." Travers was the drummer in Dweezil's band, Z, and had first met Frank after a concert in 1992. Zappa was impressed by his performance and his encyclopedic knowledge of his recordings. After Zappa died, Travers was given access to the archives and charged with cataloguing, restoring, and remastering the collection. He was humbled and honored to take the job, knowing that he would be responsible for some of the most important recordings in music history.

The vault contains performance recordings of the Zappa band since 1966. In an interview posted on YouTube and produced by Gail Zappa, Travers cites the early recordings, which date back to 1955, and the Studio Z sessions on 7-inch reels, as among his favorites. Those tapes represent a legacy of which he's now an important guardian.

Joe Travers, part-time drummer. Full-time Vaultmeister at the UMRK.   *Rex*

In 1995, archival albums started to trickle out under the strict supervision of Gail Zappa and Joe Travers. Travers was specifically interested in the '72 recordings of Zappa's instrumental ensemble known as the Grand Wazoo. These concerts were recorded and mixed by Zappa at the time but shelved for future release. Travers tracked down the original tapes and restored them for release as *Imaginary Diseases* and *Joe's Domage*. Most fans were only aware of two recordings from this period, *Waka/Jawaka* and *The Grand Wazoo*, released in 1972. These albums reflected Zappa's leaning toward more jazz-inspired compositions and arrangements, and in fact many of the musicians on them came from the jazz world, such as George Duke, Mike Altschul, and Sal Marquez. *Imaginary Diseases* captures the smaller, ten-piece touring group known as the Petit Wazoo, featuring Tom Malone, Dave Parlato, and Jim Gordon, with Zappa on guitar. We hear the band in six cities over the course of six weeks during the fall of 1972.

One of the advantages of the archives is that they make it possible to hear Zappa in action. For example, *Joe's Domage* is the perfect companion to *Imaginary Diseases* because it's a recording of the rehearsals for the tour, warts and all, as Zappa carefully works out the compositions with the band. *Joe's Xmasage* offers fans a compilation of recordings from 1962 to 1964 that provide the best examples of Zappa's personal learning curve at Studio Z. As Christopher Weingarten wrote in the April/May 2006 issue of *Relix* magazine, the album "contains fascinating insight into his earliest work-gothic R&B, go-go bar jams and some of his most visceral electroacoustic experiments ever." The album also contains "The Uncle Frankie Show," a satirical radio program voiced by Zappa from a recording made in 1964 about his upcoming rock 'n' roll opera, *I Was a Teen-Age Malt Shop*.

One of the biggest advantages of the vault releases is that they gave Zappa (and later his estate and archivists) creative control. For instance, the three-CD set known as *Läther* (pronounced leather), released in 1996, contains some of the most satiric and layered work in Zappa's history, but due to contractual obligations and record company ambivalence, it was never released as the four-LP set he intended. Some of the tracks did later show up on the albums *Zappa in New York*, *Sleep Dirt*, *Studio Tan*, and *Orchestral Favorites*, but not in the same context or format. To no surprise, the *Läther* material was also made available as a bootleg on Edison Records, but most fans kept their cassette tape versions until the official three-CD set appeared in 1996. Finally, they could hear the album as Zappa intended, with superior sound and annotated liner notes.

The Mothers of Invention Archives

The UMRK is also a goldmine for fans of the original Mothers of Invention, whose four-year career was, to some, way too short. To remedy the demand for the MOI, the famous concert at London's Royal Albert Hall from 1968 was released. *Ahead of Our Time* (1993) features members of the BBC Symphony Orchestra backing the MOI and some scripted material later used on *200 Motels* which he called the "Rock Versus Classical / Life Versus Art" confrontations. It's a high energy, kick-ass presentation with great sound that perfectly captures the Spike Jones influence in Zappa's work. This release is an excellent companion to Disc 1 of *You Can't Do That on Stage Anymore, Vol. 5*.

During his lifetime, Zappa officially released sixty-three albums. Since his death, another thirty-seven albums have been issued from the archives.

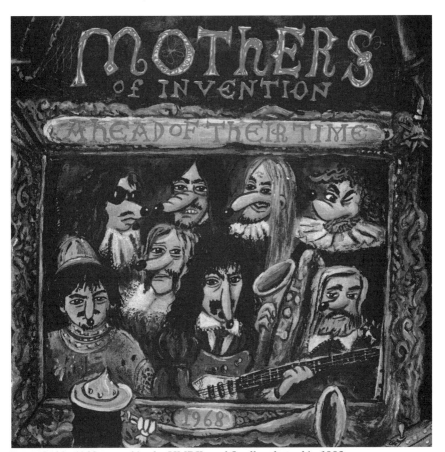

Recorded in 1968, stored in the UMRK, and finally released in 1993.

The daunting challenge for vaultmeister Joe Travers is to not favor one era over another or simply release the material in chronological order. He worked closely with Gail Zappa on sequencing and packaging. Liner notes are usually commissioned to trusted Zappa alumni, with Travers as annotator.

One of the sad things about dead composers such as Beethoven and Stravinsky is that everything they ever wrote has been heard; there's nothing left to discover. Thanks to digital technology and the storehouse known as the UMRK, though, we'll continue to hear the works of Frank Zappa for generations to come.

17

Modern Sounds

Zappa Goes Digital

I n 1982, Frank Zappa obtained a new toy: the Synclavier. It was invented in Vermont at the New England Digital Corporation, and it had a remarkable versatility: you could play it, compose on it, and record sample sounds of "real" instruments. The first prototype was made in 1973, with various components and features added between then and when the 8-track Synclavier II DMS was delivered to Zappa's house in Los Angeles. The system was built around twenty-four megabytes of memory; the price tag was $200,000.

In his autobiography, Zappa devotes a few pages about his use of the Synclavier as a composer's tool that "allows me to create and record a type of music that is impossible or too boring for human beings to play." As his music grew in complexity, the Synclavier became an important and invaluable tool, and it remained so for the rest of his life. Finally he could sample the sounds he wanted, add complicated rhythms, play them back, and, if he wanted to, have the music printed, because the system also included a software program known as SCRIPT. We now take this kind of thing for granted, since the advent of Apple's GarageBand and the dozens of other software applications that allow the user to record, mix, edit and compose music, but in 1982 it was adventurous technology for an equally adventurous composer.

The Synclavier was liberating for Zappa because he was willing to take the time to experiment with his new computer, just as he had with tape machines and other gadgets in Studio Z in the early sixties. With the help of a technician and a stack of floppy disks, Zappa could write pieces with difficult time signatures and create original sounds. He could write a drum track, for instance, that was so complicated that a human wouldn't be able to play it; the Synclavier could do so without ever getting tired. Similarly, he could write simple, repetitive woodwind music that would be too dull for a

The NED Synclavier VPK Velocity Pressure Keyboard.

Photo by Kevin Spencer, Creative Commons

human musician to play; the Synclavier would play those notes to infinity without taking a breath. Zappa generally preferred a human musician instead of a mechanical one, but the Synclavier offered him a swift, immediate, and efficient means of hearing his music without the trouble and expense of hiring an orchestra, which might not even get it right in the first place.

Perfectly Strange

In 1984, Zappa released a short seven-track album of chamber compositions called *Boulez Conducts Zappa: The Perfect Stranger.* The album featured the Ensemble Intercontemporain and a group called the Barking Pumpkin Digital Gratification Consort. The former was a twenty-nine-piece orchestra conducted by Pierre Boulez, one of Zappa's favorite music innovators. Boulez commissioned three of the seven pieces (specifically tracks one, two, and four on the album).

The "Consort" was in fact an alias for the Synclavier in Zappa's home studio, also known as the Utility Muffin Research Kitchen (UMRK). The casual listener probably wouldn't have known the difference between the "real" orchestra and the synthetic one, because the seven tracks on the album are similar in style and are seamlessly constructed. One reason for this, and why *The Perfect Stranger* is a good record, was Zappa's focus: the emotive sound of the composition. He doesn't let the Synclavier pull him into some electronic dead end where the music suffers and the listener is penalized for buying it. As Ben Watson surmises in his discussion of Zappa's use of the Synclavier in *The Negative Dialectics of Poodle Play*, "Composition is finally a matter of the listening ear. Thus Zappa bypasses one of the great conceptual cul-de-sacs of twentieth-century art music."

In an interview with John Diliberto published in the September 1986 issue of *Electronic Musician*, Zappa spoke extensively about the Synclavier, how he used it, and why it was, for him, the ultimate device for composing. "You don't sit down and write it out painstakingly over a period of years and have the part copied and hope that some orchestra will have enough time to devote to a rehearsal so they come within the vicinity of what your original idea is."

Three months after the release of *The Perfect Stranger* in August 1984, a slightly mysterious album called *Francesco Zappa* was released on the EMI Digital label. The cover features a painting of a dog in sunglasses by Donald Roller Wilson—the same dog that appears on the cover of *The Perfect Stranger*—while the back cover is a collage by Gabrielle Raumberger, with Frank Zappa credited as producer and orchestrator. This was a full-length album created entirely on the Synclavier. The music was by an obscure Italian composer, Francesco Zappa, who lived from 1717 to 1803. He was a cellist and conductor who worked mostly in The Hague, in the Netherlands, and whose musical career supplemented his income as a teacher. Gail Zappa, Frank's wife, discovered a listing for the composer in Grove's *Dictionary of Music* and learned that his compositions were available at the Bancroft Library at UC Berkeley and at the Library of Congress. Although they weren't related, Zappa was very interested and borrowed the Op. 1 Trios and the Op. 4 Sonatas by his namesake from the library.

Next, Zappa put his Synclavier to work. With the help of technician David Ocker, he entered each composition into the digital music system. Zappa did not use sampled instruments to recreate the music, so he had to experiment with certain synthesized sounds to get a result. It took months of work to finish it, but the harmonic choices were limited, and the music isn't sophisticated enough to engage the listener. As a technical achievement, though, the album reinforced Zappa's confidence in "La Machine," as he called it, as a means to an end.

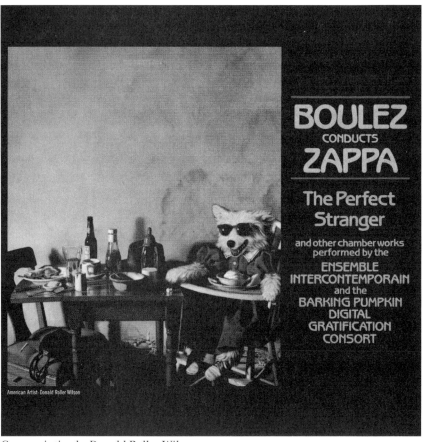

Cover painting by Donald Roller Wilson.

Jazz from Hell

In 1986, Zappa released the album *Jazz from Hell*, featuring instrumental compositions created using the Synclavier. By this time, the hardware and software had been updated to include more options for the composer. The result was an album that put electronic music on its head. The record opens with a heavy drum-synth tune called "Night School," featuring what sounds like a piano weaving its way on a musical journey up and down any scale or key signature it chooses. We then segue into a variation of those themes with "The Beltway Bandits," where the melody becomes more abstract.

By the time we reach "While You Were Art II," the sounds have become much more eclectic, with bits of violin, guitar, marimba, percussion, and harpsichord samples all vying for our attention like a bunch of school kids at recess. There's continuity, but it all seems scattered and unpredictable—which was probably Zappa's intention. The three-minute title track features samples of tenor saxophone, percussion, and electric bass that sound like they're competing with one another, as if jazz has been condemned to a life of constant improvisation. "G-Spot Tornado" is rightly named for its rapid beat and bustling energy, but relief comes when it ends cold and we segue into "Damp Ankles," a slower, stranger, and more mechanical-sounding journey of gongs, trombones, percussion, and clavinets.

The album closes much as it began, with a complicated drum track, but this time Zappa uses samples of human voices as instruments, with the slow, familiar synth sound underneath providing some momentum to the piece. Thirty-five minutes later, it's over. The ballad "St. Etienne" is a live recording from the Palais des Sports in St. Etienne, France, in 1982. The album won a Grammy Award in 1988 for "Best Rock Instrumental Performance," which seems ironic, assuming the judges actually sat down and listened to it.

Why so serious? Cover photo by Greg Gorman.

Zappa Tweaks His Own Recordings

The advent of the compact disc in the mid-eighties was a technological boon to the music industry because these 4.75-inch aluminum and plastic discs could hold up to seventy-four minutes of music. When it first arrived, digital audio technology held the potential to enhance a listener's experience with new tools for remastering old analog tapes and remixing master recordings, often to the delight of the creator.

For Frank Zappa, who was as much an audiophile as he was a musician and composer, the new technology allowed him to go back into his large catalogue to remix, re-edit, and even reconstruct or reinvent his works. According to Scott Parker, in *ZaFTIG: The Zappa Family Trust (Compact Disc) Issues Guide*, "It is not overstating the point to suggest that his life revolved around achieving the ultimate in sound quality for his vast album catalogue . . . when the opportunity to issue his albums in the new CD format came along, Frank jumped on it."

In 1985, Zappa released his first CD on EMI, the aforementioned *Boulez Conducts Zappa: The Perfect Stranger*, originally released on vinyl a year earlier. It was a good choice because the master was recorded digitally, and half the music had been created digitally on the Synclavier. Vinyl was still the format of choice for music in 1984 because record manufacturers weren't technically ready to adopt the compact disc, while record companies had doubts about the financial viability of the format at first. But when the bigger record companies saw how lucrative it would be to reissue their archives—without paying the artists—they decided to go ahead. Although new CDs were more expensive than LPs in 1985, the technology and supply of compact disc materials eventually caught up to consumer demand. (For example, my first CD player, made by Philips, was $500 in 1988. A new CD had a retail price range of between $15 and $30. Second hand CDs were usually $10 each.)

By 1992, the flood of new and back-catalogue albums on CD made it the standard format in which to buy music. The price-points changed, too, when the cost of manufacturing a back-catalogue CD shrank to about $4. Cassettes were pushed out of the marketplace once CD players became more affordable, and LPs became more plentiful in used record stores than in new ones, having generally been supplied by music lovers who had replaced their vinyl with new, smaller, and better-sounding format. (I worked in a music store in Toronto called HMV during the transition. Some customers often felt that they *had* to replace their collection. Often, at the risk of losing a sale, I advised them against it, because the technology had yet to prove itself.)

Zappa understood the transition to digital early on when he signed an extensive distribution and manufacturing deal with Rykodisc, the first CD-only label, founded in Salem, Massachusetts, in 1983. At the time, the label was fully independent—a factor not lost on the independent-minded Zappa. He signed a long-term contract with the label in February 1986 that saw the release of twenty-four titles from his discography over four years. In the May 1990 issue of *Billboard* magazine, Rykodisc founder Don Rose spoke highly of the importance of having Zappa participate in the new label. "We knew he had regained the rights to his entire body of recorded work, and therefore controlled his catalogue personally, which is rare. So it made perfect sense for us to go after such a forward-thinking artist who controlled his own material and was already digital-friendly."

Rose was correct, as Zappa confirmed in the same article: "This was all done in real time, by me in a chair operating the equipment. All the assembling and editing I did myself." Zappa used a either a Sony PCM 1630 or PCM 1610 processor that converted his analog tapes to three-quarter-inch digital video tapes able to hold more audio information and from which a CD could be mastered. Zappa also took the time to rerelease his back catalogue in an entirely new way, rather than simply reissuing the original LPs on CD as is. Just as he enjoyed the reworking of his songs onstage, Zappa could now tweak his original masters by replacing tracks on the existing mixes, such as the bass and drums he added to the 1984 edition of *Cruising with Ruben & the Jets*. Zappa looped Arthur Barrow's bass and Chad Wackerman's drums onto the CD version, replacing the original tracks by Roy Estrada and Jimmy Carl Black. According to author Scott Parker, it was Zappa's intention "to create CD masters that were different enough from the original vinyl albums to give fans who already owned the albums a reason to buy them again on CD." Much like the finicky artist whose painting is never really finished, Zappa constantly thought of his work as something that could be improved and enhanced.

Rykodisc issued the twenty-four titles in bundles, beginning in August 1986 and continuing until May 1990, when the last set was issued. These releases did not arrive in chronological order, however, because Zappa worked first with the tapes that were in the best condition to remaster.

While Zappa made tweaks to some of the recordings, he didn't change the original track sequencing. The changes were much more subtle—often to the detriment of the recording. For example, he often added too much digital reverb to some of the flawed master tapes, as he did on the Rykodisc version of *The Grand Wazoo*. When it came to the mastering and rerelease of *You Are What You Is*, he cut his guitar solo from the song "Dumb All Over," allegedly because he didn't like it. (He could, of course, have spliced another solo from another concert in its place.)

It's important to keep in mind that digital technology in the eighties really wasn't up to the standards we enjoy today. Record companies were happy to make money by pressing whatever masters they had, adding compression to the digital copy to cover audio flaws or putting the warnings on the covers of CDs, like this one from MCA, "May contain some tape hiss and anomalies that exist with analog recordings," or EMI's "Because of its high resolution, the compact disc can reveal limitations of the source tape." Zappa's first CD releases never had such qualifiers. (You can read a comprehensive assessment of his compact-disc releases in the book *ZaFTIG* by Edward Komara and Scott Parker.)

Zappa continued to release new recordings on CD through 1987, including the aforementioned *Jazz from Hell*, a remixed version of *Freak Out!*, and *Uncle Meat*, which was originally a two-LP set when it came out in 1969. The CD version included over forty minutes worth of new material from the archives. But the real prize of 1987 was the issue of *Hot Rats*, Zappa's second solo album, and one of the most beloved by fans. Originally released in 1969, the mostly instrumental album was thoroughly remixed by Zappa from the original master tapes. He revamped "Peaches En Regalia" with much better-sounding drums, although it's a little shorter than the original version. By contrast, he extended the version of "The Gumbo Variations" by some four minutes. "Son of Mr. Green Genes" puts Zappa's guitar solo a little lower in the mix, but in the beautiful instrumental "Little Umbrellas" we hear a short recorder solo in the bridge. All of this to say that, unlike the other 1987 CD rereleases, which many audiophiles, including Scott Parker, thought had inferior sound quality, *Hot Rats* is outstanding for its sound and remixing. As Kevin Courrier points out in *Dangerous Kitchen: The Subversive World of Frank Zappa*, "The CD has a sonic brightness that the [original] album lacked."

The Touring Bands Come Alive

As a long-time editor, right back to his days in Studio Z in the late fifties, Zappa found in the new CD format and digital editing technology the freedom to pull together concert material from his archives and to restructure it to create the audio illusion of one complete performance. The results of his and his technician's efforts are best experienced on the prodigious six-volume series titled *You Can't Do That on Stage Anymore*. This series of live recordings, issued in two-CD sets, allowed Zappa the chance to mash up versions of the same song, such as the two performances of "Montana" on *Vol. 4*, which has a 1973 version edited together with one performed in 1984. Similarly, Zappa could juxtapose a performance by the Mothers of Invention from 1969 against his 1982 ensemble with Steve Vai, as he did on *Vol. 5*, creating a kind of "battle of the bands." On *Vol. 4*, he surprised his fans with the blues-based "original version" of the song "The Torture Never Stops," recorded on May 21, 1975, in Austin, Texas, with a great vocal by Captain Beefheart that did not appear on the *Bongo Fury* album. Or he could issue a full-length show without overdubs or fancy editing, as he did on *Vol. 2* (aka *The Helsinki Concert*), which features a complete performance by Zappa and the Mothers from 1974. As Zappa told writer Jim Bessman for *Billboard* in 1990, "This is what I've been waiting for since the day I got into the record business: the chance to present whatever quality of material I do to the consumer in its most listenable format."

After Zappa died in 1993, Rykodisc began releasing his entire catalogue in chronological order. The label even hired a "catalogue development manager" by the name of Jill Christiansen to oversee the process. The 1995 CDs offered fans the "FZ approved masters," which, except for improved artwork and booklets, remained essentially unchanged from the earlier pressings of the mid-eighties. The equalization had been adjusted on some of the titles, such as *Over-Nite Sensation* and *Apostrophe (')*, and a newly configured version of *Läther* came out in 1996, but the real gem was the issue of *The Lost Episodes*, featuring previously unreleased tracks from the archives. Suddenly the UMRK was being tapped for rich audio artifacts dating all the way back to Zappa's days in Studio Z in 1959. Rykodisc also issued the superb compilation *Strictly Commercial*, featuring single versions of "Don't Eat Yellow Snow," "Montana," and the title track from *Joe's Garage*. The last Zappa rereleases appeared in 1997: *Have I Offended Someone?*, with excellent liner notes by Edward (Ed) Sanders of the New York rock band the Fugs;

and *Mystery Disc*, another collection of archival material, originally released in 1998.

Warner Bros. Buys Rykodisc

In 2006, Warner Music Group purchased Rykodisc for the princely sum of $67.5 million. That deal not only secured the current Zappa catalogue but also the prized master tapes Frank had worked on. Gail Zappa then acquired ownership of the masters following the creation of a new entity called the Zappa Family Trust (ZFT). The deal, which took a few years to finalize, returned the master tapes to their rightful owner and deferred liability to the ZFT instead of the immediate family. Consequently, the ZFT under Gail's supervision could reissue the entire Zappa catalogue and take advantage of the latest digital technology to improve the Rykodisc issues for the new century.

In 2011, the Zappa Family Trust signed a distribution deal with Universal Music Group (aka UMe), which included the restoration of the official Zappa albums to their pre-digital form (excluding those albums that were originally recorded digitally, such as *The Perfect Stranger*). In 2012, Zappa archivist Joe Travers was put in charge of the massive task of restoring and digitally remastering some fifty albums using the Direct Stream Digital technology often used in the production of Super Audio CDs or SACDs. In short, Travers had to go into the UMRK vault, pull out the original tapes, repair and restore the damaged ones, and then transfer them to a digital format.

On July 31, 2012, Universal started its rolling program of reissuing the entire Zappa catalogue, in batches, on a monthly basis, beginning with *Freak Out!* and ending with the release of *The Lost Episodes* on December 18. Forty-seven of the sixty-eight albums released by Universal are considered definitive by author Edward Komara, because they represent Zappa's "original intention for a given title."

18

A Man's Man

What Women Think About Zappa's Music

Dinah-Moe Humm," "Harry You're a Beast," "Crew Slut," "Catholic Girls," "Valley Girl," and "Jewish Princess" are just some of the many songs that have gotten Frank Zappa into trouble for their negative depictions of women. During his lifetime, it was often pointed out to him in interviews that songs like those mentioned above were "sexist." Zappa answered his critics in his autobiography, in which he writes, "If you were to take all the lyrics I've ever written and analyze how many songs are about 'women in demeaning positions,' as opposed to 'men in demeaning positions,' you would find that most of the songs are about stupid men. The songs I write about women are not gratuitous attacks on them, but statements of fact . . . such creatures do exist and deserve to be 'commemorated' with their own special opus."

One woman who challenged Zappa on this notion was his former secretary, Pauline Butcher. In her terrific memoir, *Freak Out! My Life with Frank Zappa*, she tells the story of the time she asked him about the subjects of his "acidic tongue." For the most part, Zappa defended his songs and their content by saying, "I'm the reporter. The messenger." To some people that may be a cop out, to others a legitimate position, considering the endless number of topics on which someone could write a song.

In an interview with Canadian broadcaster Bobby Marquis, Butcher recalled the first time she challenged Zappa over his song "Brown Shoes Don't Make It," from the album *Absolutely Free*, released in 1967. Hired by Zappa to type out the lyrics for the forthcoming album, Butcher took offence to the lines about a thirteen-year-old girl being covered in chocolate syrup. "I thought that that was immoral," she said, "and I told him so . . . he didn't take umbrage; he didn't take sides and actually debated with me. This was amazing, because in 1967 men did not listen to what women had to say,

Frank & Moon Zappa
Valley Girl

FOR PROMOTION ONLY. SALE IS UNLAWFUL

Zappa peaks the Billboard 100 at number 32.

in those days . . . so for Frank to give me the time of day and consider my words was quite riveting to me."

Zappa preferred to write songs about the unusual habits of people in general, not just women. "Crew Slut," a song Butcher thought offensive, was for Zappa one that actually "praised" girls who "live for the privilege of doing the laundry and performing other services for men who put up the PA system and focus the lights on stage." He wrote songs from his experience as a touring musician playing clubs, concert halls, and arenas around the world. Rather than write a song about some imaginary person, he chose a subject near and dear to his heart—or, at least in this case, the hearts of his road crew. Butcher goes on to say that Zappa "would chose subjects no one else would touch." As Ben Watson observes in *The Negative Dialectics of Poodle Play*, "If the lifestyle of rock stars is not conducive to respect for women, Zappa is not going to present us with something cleaned-up and ideal."

A similar conclusion comes to Ed Sanders, in his liner notes to a compilation of so-called racy Zappa songs, *Have I Offended Someone?* Sanders considers the larger view by suggesting that Zappa challenged censorship by citing the US Bill of Rights, specifically Article I, regarding freedom of speech. "Frank Zappa started using that guaranteed freedom in ways no American recording artist and performer had ever done." Sanders suggests that there would be little objection in the current media climate of "compulsive confession and erotic ink" if Zappa simply wrote a book. But "something happens [however] when satiric or erotic texts are sung to powerful music which raises their ability both to thrill and excite as well as to prick censorious ears." Five out of the fifteen tracks on that CD are about women or girls, including the *Billboard* #32 hit "Valley Girl," which spawned a merchandising opportunity with Bloomingdale's, an unauthorized movie, and a coloring book. Clearly this was a satirical song, mostly written by Zappa's daughter Moon, who was fourteen years of age at the time; it might have been considered offensive to women, but most people got the joke. It became one of Zappa's biggest hits and is still fondly remembered by many first-time fans.

Sticks and Stones

One of the songs that got him into the most trouble was "Jewish Princess," from *Sheik Yerbouti* (1979). The Anti-Defamation League of B'nai B'rith actually filed a protest with the Federal Communications Commission (FCC) to ban radio play of the song. (Little did they know that Zappa barely got radio play in the first place.) Nevertheless, the complaints drew attention to the song and the album in ways even the best publicity machine couldn't muster.

Zappa explains the unwanted acclaim in his autobiography, in a chapter titled "Sticks & Stones." He defends his so-called "offensive" songs, including "Jewish Princess," in no uncertain terms. He wasn't afraid to write about certain types of women from his own point of view. In response to the complaint from the B'nai B'rith, Zappa offered this taut remark to Dan Forte in the August 1979 issue of *Musician*: "Would they like the song better if I converted to Judaism?"

In *The Words and Music of Frank Zappa*, author Kelly Fisher Lowe takes issue with Zappa's defense against accusations of anti-Semitism in "Jewish Princess." He writes, "Zappa's music has always been about forcing people to realize the relationship between freedom and responsibility and the relationship between systems and the individual." Zappa's satiric songs about women are often best understood as microcosms of his larger view of society. Zappa is all about freedom of speech, and if he expresses a view that might be misconstrued, it's not his concern. As author Kevin Courrier points out in *Dangerous Kitchen*, "Zappa's satire is often bitingly direct. But is ["Jewish Princess"] anti-Semitic? Not at all. Besides being an equal opportunity offender, Zappa tries to get at certain basic themes in his satire . . . if a culture needs to censor its critics, then how can it lay claim to the most cherished of democratic principles?"

The Women Respond

For most critics, Zappa's provocative songs offer up a cultural, political, and satirical context that some people might not fully appreciate without further study. One female fan from Germany, Bärbel Hoppe, told me in an e-mail that when she had the lyrics to *Joe's Garage*, her first Zappa album, translated into her native tongue, she was "shocked" by "Catholic Girls," considering it sexist. Years later, having learned more about Zappa's work, she came to the conclusion that "Zappa sings about what people are only thinking about. The words in his songs was not his opinion, it was the public opinion [and Zappa] was making jokes." She went on to conclude that he brought forward topics and character studies that other artists only "whispered about."

An American fan who goes by the name of Debutante Daisy (from the song "Florentine Pogen") explained that she believed Zappa was particularly good at observing human behavior, male and female, and that "women who take offense [to] Frank's lyrics either don't get it or have low self-esteem. I've never been easily offended and have a strong sense of self and confidence of who I am as a person . . . if anything, I am amused by those songs," she adds, citing "Dinah Moe-Humm" and "Crew Slut." Daisy got into Zappa at the age of fourteen when her older brother offered to take her to her first rock concert. She had a choice between AC/DC or Frank Zappa, choosing the latter without hesitation. It was her older siblings who first brought Zappa's music to her attention.

In an e-mail exchange, Daisy describes her favorite album, *One Size Fits All* (1974):

> I love the album cover art—the sofa, the constellations, every-thing about it. As for the music, I love the mix of hard rock, Ruth [Underwood's] amazing vibes, percussion, Napi [Napoleon Murphy Brock's] vocals/sax and flute, George [Duke's] vocals and keys, Tom [Fowler's] bass lines. "Andy," "Florentine Pogen," "Po-Jama People," the beauty of "Sofa"—I mean, what's not to love about this album? I chose Debutante Daisy as my avatar on the Zappa Forum back in 2004 and I've been know as that nickname ever since. It suits me. I also own the first reproduction of OSFA painted by Cal Schenkel himself. I received it as a gift from fifteen of my closest friends for my thirtieth birthday back in 1997.

Frank Zappa, Misogynist?

Two Canadian women I contacted went deeper into the mystique and controversy of Zappa's songs about women. In e-mails, they both reported that his music went beyond its satiric intentions when it came to women. One fan, Ms. R., had been introduced to Zappa's music by her father, who used to quote his lyrics around the house. Her first album was *Apostrophe (')*.

"The majority of Zappa's music was satirical," she writes, "and no doubt he wrote 'Dinah Moe Humm' with the same satirical edge. The problem is that I don't think he's making fun of patriarchy; I'm pretty sure he's making fun of women, which isn't cool with me." She went on to add that "fantasies and practices like those described in 'Dinah Moe Humm' are consensual and non-consensual realities for many. Violently misogynistic products of the porn industry shape our sex lives, and yet these products are invisible in day-to-day life. Music that documents reality provides opportunities for dialogue." Ms. R. concludes that she respects Zappa's honesty in his songs about women: "I'd rather Zappa write brutally about his sex life than pretend being a rock star [that] isn't actually about sex and power. Likewise,

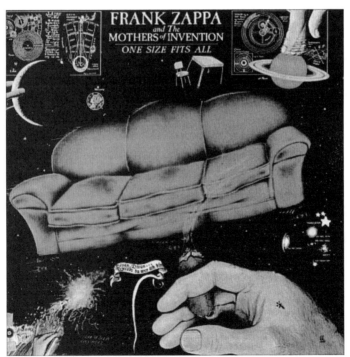

One of Zappa's most loved albums for men and women alike.

I'd prefer that people of all genders experience pornographic material out in the open, and engage in meaningful conversation around it."

Ms. R.'s friend L. answered the same question using the song "Crew Slut" as her point of reference. "[That song] might actually sound like a hot scenario if you're into that kind of fantasy! I'm not offended, *per se*, although I do tend to think badly of Zappa . . . his was a convenient (not malicious) misogyny." She concludes that he was as much a misanthrope as a misogynist, adding, "I am able to bear some of the worst Zappa lyrics when I choose to see him as someone who would want all humans to be allowed to do whatever the fuck they wanted, regardless of gender or sex."

In a sense, then, Zappa could be considered a liberator of sexist ideas by bringing them out into the mainstream, but he's not being left off the hook either. Like Ms. R., Ms. L. was introduced to Zappa's music by her father, around the time Steve Vai was in the band. One of her favorite albums is *Sheik Yerbouti*, featuring the song "Jewish Princess."

Another fan, Ms. S. from Toronto, who first saw Zappa on NBC's *Saturday Night Live* in 1978, puts her spin on the subject of women in his music:

> I am one of those who agree he was capable of misogyny. It was extremely disappointing to discover . . . with age, I have a deeper understanding. He grew up in fifties America. How could he escape the traditional views on gender? His anti-feminist stance was the norm. He and his music [were] not created in a vacuum. Also, as women, it is almost impossible to find music that does not include misogyny. From rap, opera, blues, classic rock, pop, it is everywhere. Is it fair to expect more from Zappa? I also felt he had an almost pathological need to offend/shock. He needed to oppose, regardless of the subject matter. I am sure living within the realm of the music business did nothing to encourage emotional growth or maturity.

Women, it seems, are not drawn to Zappa's music in the same way as men. A survey of these same female fans for this book offers a glimpse into the answer to the question: why doesn't Zappa's music have wider appeal to women? For Debutante Daisy:

> That is something I am still trying to figure out myself. I have spent my entire life listening to FZ and trying to turn friends onto his music. It is very complex and quite frankly (no pun intended) lots of men don't like his music either. I don't want to say women aren't smart enough to get it but if you look at audiences of most progressive rock artists, most of them are men (not sure why that is)? I get it, love it, live for it, why not other women? It is a mystery! Since FZ's music was

never that commercially popular, it just stands to reason that many women were never exposed to it. I have plenty of Zappasisters who are just as fanatic about the music as the male fans are. Once you get it, you get it, regardless of gender.

For Ms. S. from Toronto, the lack of appeal to women goes deeper. "He was always cerebral. He seemed to deride emotion, love, etc. I appreciate his need to move away from traditional music subjects, but he lacked vulnerability. There was a cynicism. I am sure idealism was underneath, but his smugness and contempt at times created a distance. I don't like to relegate women to the realm of emotion, but perhaps our intelligence in this area is different, and therefore makes it harder to connect to Zappa."

For Ms. L, it's also a question of musical taste.

> I refuse to rehash some dull story about the differences in "male" and "female" musical tastes, although it must be observed that the sociocultural atmosphere in Zappa's early seventies heyday certainly did not provide much space for sonically experimental and accomplished female artists (they were there anyway—Barbara Thompson [British sax player and composer] springs to mind) let alone welcoming environments for all but the toughest-skinned female audiences. A lot of women probably felt more comfortable in other scenes. But, come on. How many fans, male or otherwise, of Zappa's ambitious, self-congratulatory, genre spanning, audiophiliac music could there really be in the first place? When it comes down to it, I don't think he is that popular generally, sex or gender notwithstanding. Sure, he's a wizard king genius cult leader for a certain strain of rock fan, but for the rest of us . . . ?

Ms. L. cites the notion of a "man's world" in considering Zappa's lack of appeal to women:

> Zappa played rock 'n' roll, but his creative lineage is closely aligned with the Western art-music tradition. His rock music was tightly composed, directed, and produced, even when it involved collective improvisation. The art-music tradition is deeply patriarchal and hierarchical—there are few women composers pre-1950, and men still outweigh women in this area. Radical as he was, Zappa affirmed the existing social order by being a male composer in the primary control position of his ensembles. He fought for freedom in some places, but he didn't do very much to agitate the Old Boys' Club. Women can choose to fight their way into that club, but our efforts may be better spent tearing it down.

Zappa's songs have always been controversial, and his songs about women uncover a number of different opinions about the man and his work. As with all music, the listener brings his—*or her*—experience to the art form, which is the one thing Zappa understood about his audience. Zappa was an "equal opportunity offender," and while that doesn't excuse his offensive material, it does aid and abet a better understanding of the composer and the political and social context of his work.

19

A Guitarist's Guitar Player

Zappa as Instrumentalist

One of the best descriptions of Frank Zappa's technique as a guitarist came from his son Dweezil, who in a 2006 interview with Richard Gehr of *Relix* magazine likened it to "the battle between the chicken and the spider." That's quite the metaphor, but it remains the best way to understand the physical dynamics of Frank Zappa's hands on the guitar and his completely original style of playing.

Guitars have been around for a long time—for centuries, in fact. Originating in Spain in the eleventh century, they fall into two wide-ranging categories: acoustic and electric, although electric guitars only came on the scene in the thirties. Zappa got his first electric guitar, a Fender Jazzmaster, in 1958, and since he didn't take lessons he taught himself how to play it and developed a personal style that some enthusiasts consider to be revolutionary. In 2011, *Rolling Stone* magazine placed Zappa at #22 in its list of the 100 greatest guitarists. (Jimi Hendrix came first, so perhaps he was more revolutionary!)

Style and sound are two of the most difficult challenges for any guitarist—or for any musician, for that matter. It all depends on the sound equipment you have, the instrument you have in your hands, and your personality. Zappa never had a "signature" style, like Wes Montgomery or Chuck Berry, because he didn't hear music as narrow, linear sound. What he heard was a kaleidoscope of sounds, rhythms, textures, and timbres in context with one another. His foundation was the blues, but he never restricted himself to familiar blues licks such as bending the notes as a means of expression or standard chord changes. (The closest he comes is on the song "It Ain't Necessarily the Saint James Infirmary," from *Guitar*.) An educated ear can certainly hear blues scales in his playing, but Zappa also added a percussive component to his style that was unique to him. He was more interested in creating something new and spontaneous than showing off, especially in concert. But those rapid-fire solos could truly dazzle an audience.

As far as his sound was concerned, Zappa was one of the first guitarists to invest his money in the best equipment available to him. In the mid-seventies, he spent over $30,000 to build a guitar "rig" using studio-quality equipment. He also invested in portable electronic sound devices, also known as pedals, which he could activate with his feet. One of the devices he bought was a parametric equalizer (rather than a graphic equalizer), which he used to shape the tone of his guitar. A typical five-band graphic equalizer would consist of vertical sliders designed to add or subtract a fixed frequency of the sound, such as 10khz or the upper mid-range. (Boom boxes from the eighties had them, too.) A ten-band graphic equalizer would have five more vertical sliders, offering access to more frequencies and granting more tone control than a five-band. A parametric equalizer offered even more versatility in refining the parameters of the sound coming out of a speaker. Zappa was always interested in the science of his guitar's sound, and the parametric equalizer provided him with limitless choices depending on the composition and the size of the auditorium. On tour in 1988, Zappa used two customized Fender Strats with adjustable EQs built into them to aid him in controlling any feedback, pushing it right to the limit as if he was standing on the edge of a cliff.

To many fans, Zappa was a guitarist first and foremost. To appease the (mostly male) fans who didn't care to hear him sing and to spite the critics who thought guitar solos were completely self-indulgent in the age of punk, he released several albums of just his instrumental passages—a kind of songs-without-words set of recordings taken from different concerts. He called the albums *Shut Up 'n Play Yer Guitar, Shut Up 'n Play Yer Guitar Some More, Return of the Son of Shut Up 'n Play Yer Guitar* (all 1981), and *Guitar* (1988), the latter of which he said was not recommended "for children or Republicans." Fully annotated with notes listing the specific instrument he plays, these albums are compilations of his "solos" from 1977 to 1984. Then, during the last year of his life, Zappa put together the album *Trance-Fusion* (2006), featuring solos from his last tour in 1988.

Playing these albums back-to-back gives us a really good sense of Zappa's skill as a guitarist. He rarely plays the same lick twice, and he has a tendency to adjust his musical choices based on the rhythm of the piece or the chord changes or some sonic happening that he picks up on. His drummers

Zappa gets down to business with his Gibson Les Paul with DiMarzio pickups.

often suggested ideas. On the song "Republicans," from *Guitar*, recorded in 1984, the band vamps on a series of key changes as Zappa literally shapes his sound against a steady groove. It's a remarkable example of Zappa's sculpture of sound—a type of geometric representation, if you like, with multi-sided, three-dimensional objects floating in the air and inside your head. He does this by slurring rather than picking most of the notes that could be defined as his "style," but by the very next song he'll be playing something completely different.

YouTube provides a ton of performance videos from the Zappa catalogue, but one of the best can be found on the official DVD *Does Humor Belong in Music?*, which features footage from an outdoor concert recorded at the Pier in 1984. The New York show opens with "Zoot Allures," one of the most-played instrumentals in the Zappa songbook. As the camera zooms in, the first thing you notice is the way Zappa holds his pick between the thumb and two fingers of his right hand. By holding the pick in this position, Zappa literally "plucks" the strings, and therefore the notes, out of the instrument. This action gives the notes equal weight, allowing his solo to stand out from the rest of the band. Zappa's technique evolved over his career, and the video evidence, from among the thousands of clips on YouTube, gives us an important glimpse into his style and technique.

Zappa's Signature Instrumentals

Even though Zappa did not have a signature sound, he did have three instrumental works that, according to his son Dweezil, were "signature" pieces, namely "Black Napkins," "Zoot Allures," and "Watermelon in Easter Hay." Each one of these is a careful, uncomplicated ballad in different time signatures. While Zappa often wrote as many notes on the page as possible, these songs stand out for their simplicity and natural beauty. Interestingly, "Black Napkins" and "Zoot Allures" both appeared on the same album (1976's *Zoot Allures*), but almost every version of the latter is a good one because it showcases Zappa's use of controlled feedback. The version of "Zoot Allures" on *The Best Band You've Never Heard in Your Life* is particularly strong, with Zappa soloing against a reggae beat laid down by the rhythm section.

"Black Napkins" was named after a particularly bad Thanksgiving dinner the band experienced in Milwaukee, Wisconsin, which said more about the quality of the dinner than the food itself. The gentle 3/4 time signature makes it one of the more accessible Zappa numbers and grants him a lot of room to improvise, which is a key element in most of his compositions. It's not in the jazz idiom *per se*, but it is free of musical restrictions. One of the best versions is the original live recording from Osaka, Japan, heard on *Zoot Allures*, but the version by the '88 big band on *Make a Jazz Noise Here* is highlighted by the solos of Paul Carman (alto sax) followed by Walt Fowler (trumpet), Albert Wing (tenor sax), and then Zappa's own short recapitulation. Zappa actually reduced his solo on this version by editing it out, a decision that speaks either to his lack of ego or the excellence of his musicians. (Not every solo Zappa took during a performance was a masterpiece, despite what some experts would lead you to believe.)

"Watermelon in Easter Hay" seems to connect with the fans to the point of tears. As Neil Slaven writes in the introduction of his book *Electric Don*

Quixote, the song "says more about Frank Zappa than these words can." He's referring to the original version on *Joe's Garage*, which even Zappa admitted was the best song on the album. Dweezil Zappa resisted adding it to the set list of his ultimate tribute band, Zappa Plays Zappa, until he was emotionally prepared to play it. That day came in 2013, when Dweezil posted his first performance of the song on his YouTube channel. It's an excellent version.

Zappa's Gear

Considering his accomplishments as a guitarist, it's interesting to learn that Frank Zappa actually started as a percussionist in high school, around the age of twelve. He learned the rudiments of time and meter, eventually getting a snare drum on which to practice at home. His first set of drums was a second-hand set that he first played in 1956 with an R&B group called the Ramblers. In those days, rhythm 'n' blues was the "new" music for postwar kids in southern California. As Zappa, who loved R&B and bought 78 and 45 singles, explained to *Guitar Player* in January 1977, "The saxophone was the instrument that was happening on record. When you heard a guitar player it was always a treat [but] they only gave them one chorus, and I figured the only way I was going to get to hear enough of what I wanted to hear was to get an instrument and play it myself."

First Guitars

Zappa got his first guitar in an auction when he was eighteen. It was an archtop acoustic guitar of an unknown brand with a very high action. His first electric guitar was a Fender Jazzmaster, which he played for several years in the lounge act Joe Perrino and the Mellow Tones during the late fifties. In spite of the dullness of the music, Zappa learned how to play guitar in ensembles at an early age, while earning money along the way. The time he had invested in playing finally paid off with the acquisition of a Gibson ES-5 Switchmaster in 1962.

Gibson modeled the ES-5 after its own L-5 Jazz guitar, and it didn't skimp on power. The guitar offered three PAF "humbucker" pickups, with separate volume and tone controls. It was a bit of a monster in size and weight, but Zappa recorded his first three albums with that instrument, with a sound greatly influenced by Johnny "Guitar" Watson.

Gibson and D'Mini

By the seventies, Zappa's primary instrument was a Gibson SG with a cherry-red body and a mahogany neck. It was a modified guitar with P-90 pickups and extra tone controls. He played it on *Roxy & Elsewhere* in spite of the fact that it had a cracked neck and was difficult to keep in tune. In 2013, Gibson issued a signature model, simply called the Frank Zappa Roxy SG. It has all the bells and whistles of Zappa's original but without the cracked neck, including a Lyre tailpiece at the bridge and a switch that throws the pickups "out of phase" with one another.

By the early eighties, Zappa was using what he called "mini" guitars—instruments that were lighter in weight without sacrificing action and sound control. The models he used were the Les Paule and the Strate

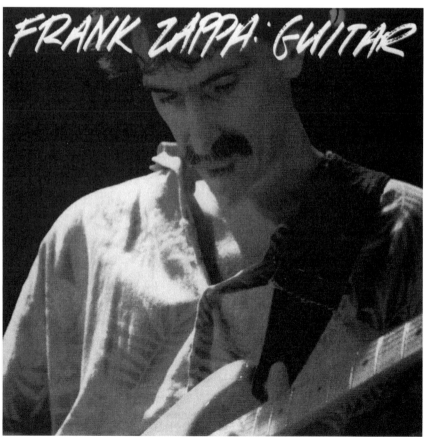

Zappa with his custom Strat.

(Stratocaster), both made by a company called Phased Systems. These guitars were modified as per Frank's specifications for pickups, tone arms, and volume controls. As he observed in an interview with *Guitar Player* magazine in 1983, "The D'Mini Strat that I have is unbelievable; you can't believe the noises that come out of that thing." He had it tuned up to F-Sharp, while his Les Pauls were tuned up to A. As any guitarist will tell you, tuning away from a standard E-tuning offers musical challenges, not only for the player but also for the music, which was Zappa's first order of the day. As he told *Guitar Player*, "I don't wear them; I play them."

The Hendrix Strat

Zappa was also the proud owner of the "Hendrix Strat." This was the sunburst Fender Stratocaster that Jimi Hendrix played, left-handed, and burned, according to www.groundguitar.com, either at a gig at the Astoria in London in 1967, or at the Miami Pop Festival the following year. There seems to be some doubt as to its origins. According to Zappa, who also played in Miami with the Mothers of Invention, Hendrix's roadie, Howard Parker, gave it to him. The guitar was beaten up and unplayable until Zappa took it off the wall of his basement studio and had it restored to working order. It can be heard on several tracks from Zappa's instrumental album of 1988, *Guitar*, on which he provides the name of every axe he uses on each track. His son Dweezil inherited the famous instrument and had it refurbished to its modified state. Zappa can also be seen posing with it on the cover of the January 1977 issue of *Guitar Player* magazine.

The Guitar Gallery

Zappa had about twenty-five working guitars in his collection, including a 1953 Gibson Les Paul Goldtop and a blonde Fender Stratocaster, the latter of which he played on his 1988 world tour. It was a heavier-than-usual Strat body with a custom neck and a Floyd Rose tailpiece, featuring Seymour Duncan pickups. As Zappa reported to *Musician* magazine in August 1988, "It's got a gain stage and two parametric EQ circuits built into it . . . that allows you to tune right into the feedback point of any room so you can really control what you're doing with feedback." One of the key features of Zappa's technique, best heard on the albums *Guitar* and *The Best Band You've Never Heard in Your Life*, is the way he controls feedback or recoil from his guitar. Have a listen to the instrumental version of "Duke of Prunes," from *Orchestral Favorites*, and you'll hear a sound he always favored for its musical effect in the context of the "environment" he was experiencing onstage. "Duke of Prunes" was recorded in 1976 at Royce Hall in Los Angeles, with Zappa backed by the Abnuceals Emuukha Electric Symphony Orchestra.

Zappa loved live performance for its spontaneity and the element of surprise, especially when it came to his solos. As he told Steve Rosen in *Guitar Player* in January 1977, "I usually play my best stuff on the road." Thankfully, most of the guitar solos on Zappa's albums are from live recordings that have then been spliced into a studio mix or another live performance far removed from its original context. Regardless of the source, the results are indicative of Zappa's talent as a guitarist and his effective use of technology to achieve it.

20

We'll Fix It in Post

Overdubs Galore

In the April/May 2006 issue of *Relix* magazine, Frank Zappa's former guitarist Steve Vai offered this memory: "In his studio, Frank was the most elite of audio gourmet chefs . . . his methodology included merging tracks recorded by separate bands with tracks borrowed from previous records, reassembling tracks from various live recordings, layering massive vocal overdubs, and processing sounds to an unrecognizable . . . sonic tapestry." It's quite the description, but it gives us insight into the size of Zappa's toolbox and his ability to create linear songs in a non-linear fashion.

One of the best parts of the old, non-digital technology was the tactile engagement between human and machine, tape, grease pencil, and a sharp razorblade. Since the advent of digital technology, including sophisticated software like Pro Tools, today's editors may have it easier, but they don't enjoy holding the sound information in their hands. Zappa made use of digital technology later in his career (notably the Synclavier), but the bulk of his music was recorded on analog equipment that made overdubbing and editing an art in itself. Sound editing today is done by one hand operating a mouse while watching a computer screen. Sound editing in Zappa's day was in front of a giant reel-to-reel tape machine with an edit block on top of the recording heads and a set of speakers. It was solitary work that took a lot of time, patience, and accuracy. The trick was knowing how the equipment worked and how to master it to create the results you wanted. So, when he wasn't touring, Zappa spent much of his time editing and creating music.

Burnt Weeny Sandwich

One of the best examples of Zappa's technique can be heard on the album *Burnt Weeny Sandwich*, released in 1970 (and not to be confused with the eighteen-minute fantasy film of the same name). It's a remarkable feat of

A triumph of Zappa's skill as an editor.

sound editing, matched by the cover art, created by Cal Schenkel and John Williams, which shows a photograph of a sculpture titled "Crucified on Technology," originally made for an Eric Dolphy album. The record features live and studio performances by the Mothers of Invention cut with instrumental pieces featuring Ian Underwood on harpsichord or piano.

Zappa's original music is "sandwiched" between two R&B cover songs: "WPLJ," originally recorded by the Four Deuces in 1956, and "Valarie," first recorded by Jackie and the Starlites in 1960. These versions feature Lowell George on guitar and vocals, as taken from studio recordings made in 1969. We then make our way through the album by way of the instrumentals "Igor's Boogie, Phase One" and "Overture to a Holiday in Berlin" to "Theme from Burnt Weeny Sandwich," recorded in 1967 in New York. We then hear phase two of "Igor's Boogie" (named for Stravinsky) before launching into

"Holiday in Berlin," a full-blown recording of the MOI, but it's not a linear, single performance because Zappa adds a guitar solo from a live performance in Boston in 1969. That's followed by a short interlude featuring Zappa playing acoustic guitar and Ian Underwood playing harpsichord.

The eighteen-minute "The Little House I Used to Live In" is actually a constructed piece that shows off Zappa's editing talent. The bulk of the song was recorded at London's Royal Albert Hall in 1969, but it's spliced together with a recording of Ian Underwood playing a solo piano piece at the beginning. At the 5:15 mark, the music slows to accommodate a killer violin solo from Sugar Cane Harris. As his solo comes to a natural end, we're suddenly launched into a slower, multi-tracked woodwind/harpsichord section that then gives way to a vari-speed organ solo by Zappa during the last four minutes of the song before it closes, amusingly, with some added-in applause. The album is rounded out with a nice MOI version of "Valarie." While this record doesn't sound as seamless as Zappa's later work, it all makes sense within the context of the "sandwich" and its layers. If you have the right tools, it seems, anything is possible.

Multi-Tracking *Hot Rats*

When Les Paul and Mary Ford released "How High the Moon" on Capitol in 1951, few people realized that it was the first hit single to use multi-tracking or overdubs. Paul, a jazz guitarist, wasn't happy with the sound of his recordings so he built his own studio and acquired an Ampex Model 200 reel-to-reel tape machine with which to record. This machine allowed him to play all of the guitar parts on "How high the Moon" and double-track Mary Ford's closely miked vocal as she sings harmony with herself. The result was a #1 hit single and a remarkable achievement in sound that still resonates with listeners today. It's not certain if Zappa was familiar with the technical wizardry behind "How High the Moon," but he must have been impressed. Records were no longer complete "captured performances." They could be layered compositions in their own right.

In 1969, Zappa produced *Hot Rats*, which he described as "an album more about overdubbing than anything else." It was recorded on a new 16-track tape machine, with different rhythm sections on each track, but the core musicians were Zappa and the talented multi-instrumentalist Ian Underwood. It was the first time Zappa had hired skilled jazz musicians over members of the MOI to lay down the bass and drum tracks first, which

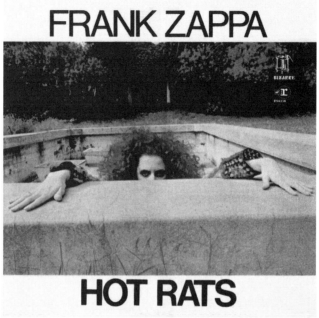

Zappa's second solo album.   *Photo by Andee Nathanson*

required only about ten hours of studio time. Zappa and Underwood then set about finishing the album by overdubbing their parts on the remaining tracks. Guest musicians such as Jean-Luc Ponty (violin on "It Must Be a Camel") and Captain Beefheart (vocals on "Willie the Pimp") recorded their parts separately on top of the existing rhythm tracks. The album's signature song, the technical *tour de force* "Peaches En Regalia," took one hundred hours to complete.

When Zappa reissued his back catalogue on CD in 1987, he remixed the whole record, except for "It Must Be a Camel." Some tracks are shorter in length than they were on the 1970 vinyl release. Fortunately, with the help of vaultmeister Joe Travers, the original analog mix was issued on CD in 2012. (Most collectors have both versions.)

Zappa and the Art of the Overdub

Overdubbing was a useful tool for Zappa throughout his recording career. He liked to mess with his music and dicker with his recorded sounds so much that by 1979, in the liner notes to *Sheik Yerbouti*, he specifically indicates what overdubs were made on each cut. His detailed explanation of

"Rubber Shirt" makes for some interesting reading. After a short description of how the song was put together, he states that "all of the sensitive, interesting interplay between the bass and drums never actually happened." That's quite a big reveal, considering all of the auto-tuning that's rampant in some pop music today (that not everyone admits to using). Zappa goes on to quantify the amount of overdubs for the eighteen tracks, which begs the question, "Does honesty belong in music?"

Creating the Perfect Concert Experience

With the release of the six-volume series known as *You Can't Do That on Stage Anymore* and the three albums featuring the 1988 big band, Zappa went to great lengths to assure the listener that there were "ABSOLUTELY NO OVER-DUBS" (his emphasis), as stated in the liner notes. Zappa began to celebrate and take pride in the hundreds of musicians that made music the old fashioned way, with no opportunity to correct mistakes or sweeten vocals, including his own.

In the notes to *The Best Band You Never Heard in Your Life* (1991), Zappa reiterates that the material is "100 percent" live, with no overdubs, before going on to comment more generally on the music scene of the day. "In a world where most of the 'big groups' go on stage and pretend to sing and play, we proudly present this quaint little audio artifact." Zappa does admit that the sequence of the music is culled from different performances during the 1988 tour, although he adds the city each time just to let us know. His steadfast editing on the series, and on the 1988 big band albums, is pure magic, as Zappa creates momentum with each segued track. Listen to the seamless music on Disc 2 of *The Best Band You Never Heard in Your Life* for a remarkable example of an "edited" performance.

21

On the Road

Opening Acts Get a Shot

From 1965 to 1988, Frank Zappa toured extensively around the world. It was an important part of his career as a businessman, musician, and entertainer. Along the way, a number of acts had the pleasure (or horror) of opening shows for him from time to time. This chapter covers a few of those performers and what they were up against when they had to play in front of Frank's fans.

The Sixties

A wide variety of bands opened for the Mothers of Invention. Some of them made musical sense while others made for some unusual shows and presumably irritated audiences keen to see their music heroes exclusively. Between 1966 and 1969, for instance, the following artists opened for the MOI: Tim Buckley, Canned Heat, the Blues Project, Otis Rush, Richie Havens, the Fugs, the Youngbloods, the Electric Flag, Brian Auger and Julie Driscoll with the Trinity, plus jazz musicians Don Cherry and Charles Lloyd. Alice Cooper, who was discovered by Zappa, opened some concerts, as did the Chicago Transit Authority, the Guess Who, the Buddy Miles Express, and, believe it or not, Simon and Garfunkel.

The latter pairing came about after Paul Simon and Art Garfunkel were having dinner with Zappa in New York and expressed interest in playing before a large audience because they missed being on the road. Zappa agreed to have them open an MOI show but pulled a fast one on his audience by asking Simon and Garfunkel not to play hits like "Homeward Bound" but instead play songs from their first incarnation as Tom and Jerry. The only show they did together was in Buffalo, New York. Joseph Fernbacher, who reviewed the concert for a local newspaper, the *Spectrum*, said that "one's mind stammered" at the sight of the duo playing sloppy versions of songs by the Everly Brothers, which came in sharp contrast to the Mothers of Invention, whose music "fell between the John Cage and Bill Haley and the Comets idiom." Zappa later reintroduced the duo as Simon and Garfunkel, and they sang "The Sound of Silence."

The Seventies

After disbanding the Mothers of Invention in 1969, Zappa went on the road every couple of months, putting together different ensembles each time. He toured Europe and North America throughout the seventies and even made it to Japan and Australia for a series of shows. During this busy decade there were fewer opening acts, granting Zappa the chance to extend his performances. But notable acts did open the odd show, including the J. Geils Band, Humble Pie, Livingston Taylor (brother of James), Chuck Berry, the Persuasions, Rory Gallagher, Fleetwood Mac (1971 edition), the Doors (in 1972, without Jim Morrison), Dr. Hook, Foghat, Steely Dan (on the 1972 *Petit Wazoo* tour), Jesse Colin Young, Taj Mahal, and Leo Kottke. Jimmy Buffett opened one concert in Houston, Texas, in 1974, while Dion opened a show in Washington, D.C., the same year. Comedian Martin Mull opened a few shows in 1973.

The acts were quite varied, and they were generally familiar to Zappa's audience. According to some fans, one of the best concert experiences they had was when the Mahavishnu Orchestra, led by John McLaughlin, opened eight shows for Zappa in the spring of 1973. Fans that I spoke to have never forgotten the impact that musical combination had on them. Attendees of the Toronto concert on May 4 of that year remember a remarkable opening performance by Mahavishnu that was as powerful as their album *Birds of Fire*, released on Columbia in March of that year. Zappa did not want to be outdone, so he changed his set to include more long-form pieces, with lots of room for him to improvise. Years later, in issue #64 of the fanzine *T'Mershi Duween*, bass player Tom Fowler reported that Zappa often wrote tunes on the spot, inspired by Mahavishnu's challenging time signatures. "I remember we were playing at the Spectrum in Philadelphia which is a basketball arena with the dressing rooms upstairs. I was down there listening to the Mahavishnu and I go upstairs and there's Frank writing odd-metered tunes on the spot that were heavily influenced by McLaughlin's stuff."

Perhaps the least familiar artist to open for Zappa in the seventies was Tom Waits. His manager at the time was Herb Cohen, who also handled the

Tom Waits in the early seventies.   *Gems/Getty Images*

affairs of Frank Zappa. Waits was new on the scene in 1973, having only released one album, *Closing Time*, featuring the song "Ol' 55." At the time, Waits's act was simply he and an upright piano. He'd tell stories and generally present himself as a strange lounge-singer you'd find at a smoky bar on skid row. Cohen and Zappa probably thought the audience would get Waits's brand of performance art, but it wasn't always the case. He would be booed and yelled at by the crowd, who didn't have the patience to sit through his set.

Waits recalled the nasty reception to writer Michael Barclay, in the April/May 1999 issue of *Exclaim!*

> It was a complete mismatch. We had the same manager and he said, "Aaaargh! Go to Canada with Frank! Frank will treat you right! In fact, go meet Frank in Canada! At a hockey arena!" After my cruel set, after the bleeding had stopped, I came back in the middle of his show and he would play "Ol' 55" and I'd tell a story. I had fun, some nights. But I had to have Frank on stage to keep them from hurting

me. They were Frank's people, you know? They didn't want to hear anybody. And they thought that whoever was coming out before Frank, Frank had designed it that way and wanted them to hurt me: pelt me, throw things at me and abuse me. And the chant: "We! Want! Frank!" or "You suck!" was also a big favorite."

Waits felt he was being used as a "rectal thermometer for the audience."

The Eighties

Zappa only went on five distinct tours during the eighties, and in fact, after a particularly grueling tour in 1984, he actually retired from the road for a four-year period. Then, when he started up again in 1988, it was without any opening acts. Instead he invited the occasional guest performer, such as his son Dweezil, or Sting, whose performance in Chicago of "Murder by Numbers," would become a surprise addition to the album *Broadway the Hard Way*.

22

The Woodstock Festival Without Zappa

The Mothers Make Other Plans

To many music lovers, Woodstock was the seminal musical event of 1969. It took place in Upstate New York on Max Yasgur's farm near the town of Bethel. With a growing and active youth movement protesting against the Vietnam War and adopting rock 'n' roll as its personal and political soundtrack, Woodstock became the highlight of the era for many young people of the so-called flower-power generation (an era that came to a crashing end in December at the Altamont Festival, headlined by the Rolling Stones).

According to its producers, Woodstock attracted around 400,000 people to its three days of "peace and music," but it wasn't the first rock-music festival—it was simply the most commercial and newsworthy. Musically, it helped launch Crosby, Stills and Nash; solidified the Who as a legitimate rock act; and confirmed Jimi Hendrix in the musical zeitgeist. Its eclectic mix of folk, R&B, and Indian classical music played by Ravi Shankar offered its young audience a chance to discover new music while enjoying the familiar bands of their generation. Missing from the bill, however, were Frank Zappa and the Mothers of Invention.

During their touring years in the late sixties, the Mothers of Invention played at a lot of festivals. They were often hired to headline a festival or participate in larger musical concerts. One of their first was in 1967, when they played the Bread for Heads festival at the Village Theater in New York City. That same year, they played the Fantasy Faire and Music Festival, held in Devonshire Meadows in Northridge, California. (Keep in mind that there were very few producers around with the financial and artistic know-how necessary to put on a big show. At the time, Bill Graham was the leading expert and rock music entrepreneur who ran the Fillmore West in San Francisco and the Fillmore East in New York City to great acclaim.)

By 1968, the Mothers were booked in a variety of music festivals in the United States, and Europe. They played the Miami Pop Festival with Jimi Hendrix in May, and they played a German festival called the Internationale Essener Songtage in September.

By the spring of 1969, the Mothers of Invention had been touring regularly for about eighteen months, appearing all over the United States, Canada, and the UK. In spite of the constant touring, Zappa believed his music wasn't reaching the right audience. "The kids are going to be confused by what we are moving on to," he told *Beat Instrumental*, "because people don't know how to listen to music." It was also becoming an expensive operation. Nevertheless, the band forged ahead, hoping to find a new audience more open to their free-form presentation. In April, they played the Boston Globe Jazz Festival, taking to the stage between sets by the Newport All-Stars and the Dave Brubeck Quartet. According to newspaper reports, Roland Kirk, the extraordinary reed player, jammed with the Mothers of Invention to great success.

At the invitation of George Wein, the Mothers were invited to play a series of Jazz Festivals in Charlotte, Miami, and the prestigious Newport Jazz Festival on July 5 in Rhode Island. At this point, the Mothers of Invention were playing only a few songs and then breaking out in a mix of improvisation that blended a lot of different genres, often at the same time. As Don Preston remembered to Barry Miles, "We sometimes during a concert only played three or four songs. The rest would all be improvisation. That's the way the band was working. And working real well that way."

Clearly the band and their music were changing. Zappa kept writing, and the Mothers kept on performing, despite enduring a series of poor venues, lousy PAs, and the threat of rain at virtually every outdoor gig. Around this time, an offer to play the Woodstock Festival was made to the Mothers of Invention, but Zappa wasn't interested. They were booked to play three concerts in Montreal, Quebec, on the very same weekend as Woodstock, including an appearance on CJOH TV in Ottawa on August 19 to close out their summer tour. A couple of weeks later, Zappa disbanded the group.

Woodstock was an invitation Zappa turned down quite possibly because he no longer had any respect for the audience to which the festival was

The Mothers of Invention, Montreal, 1969.
Photograph by Gordon Beck, VM94-TH9-282-002. Archives de la Ville de Montréal.

directed. In an interview with Scott Cohen in the December 1975 issue of
Circus Raves, Zappa talked about his disdain for the Woodstock generation.
"By that point [1969] all the hippies were so impressed with themselves that
they didn't know which end was up. They got to the point where they were
taking themselves so seriously that they thought they were going to rule the
world . . . and if you didn't have two fingers up in the air, some beads around
your neck, a scarf tied on your head and a couple of flowers in your pocket,
then you didn't have any peer group status."

By 1990, Zappa's cynicism was even more biting. In an interview with
RockHEAD, a European rock-music journal, Zappa remarked, "If you look
at pictures from the Woodstock movie and see these people squatting in
the mud, you'd say, 'What are they going to grow up to be?' . . . they turned
out to be Wall Street."

23

Best to Prepare

Auditioning for Frank Zappa

After Frank Zappa broke up the Mothers of Invention in 1969, he had to find new musicians to play his music, one by one. Sometimes he would discover them at a club, as he did when he found vocalist Ray White in Hawaii and guitarist Adrian Belew in Nashville. But for the most part he would audition players at his house in Los Angeles, California, or a nearby rehearsal studio.

Auditioning was usually a competitive process. Zappa was formal about it, preparing lyrics for a vocalist or charts for a drummer, keyboard player, or bass player, depending on what he needed at the time. Zappa preferred musicians who could read music and play different styles, but he also looked for something special in the person. When Ian Underwood auditioned for Zappa and the MOI, he was asked a question that would become standard practice: "What can you do that's fantastic?" Here are some of their stories.

Ike Willis

Ike Willis, the consummate Zappa vocalist and guitarist, met the bandleader before a concert at his college in St. Louis, Missouri, having been introduced to Zappa's music years earlier by his friend Jeff Hollie. When Zappa finished his sound check for the concert that evening, Willis, who was part of the house crew, simply walked up and started talking to him. The conversation lasted several hours; Willis talked about his interest in music, especially R&B and classical, which appealed to Zappa. Willis played Zappa a song at his request, and eight months later, Zappa invited him to audition in Los Angeles. Willis arrived on a Tuesday to a packed room full of players eager to get into Zappa's upcoming band. Zappa asked him to help audition the musicians by doing the vocal parts. Two days later, Willis was asked to join the band. It was something of a formality, because he'd already been working with Zappa during the other auditions. According to Willis, the audition lasted less than a minute.

Tommy Mars

Zappa often took recommendations from existing band members when a position came up. One time, in 1977, percussionist Ed Mann put in a word for his friend Tommy Mars, an experienced keyboard player and vocalist. Mars and Mann had been members of a jazz-rock fusion group called World Consort in 1973. By 1977, Mars was doing the lounge circuit, crooning for people who usually had too many cocktails during his set. Mars resented the fact and used to make up songs with vulgar lyrics, all directed at patrons who weren't necessarily paying attention.

That skill came in handy when he finally auditioned for Frank Zappa, because the audition didn't start very well. Mars didn't know much about Zappa's music except for the instrumental "King Kong," so when he was handed pieces of incomplete sheet music and asked to play it, he screwed up. (Zappa later finished these pieces into a composition titled "Sinister Footwear.") After sweating out the challenge of playing the written music correctly, Mars was asked to sing a song. Fatigued by the whole experience, he improvised a song as if he were back at the lounge. Zappa was immediately impressed, and Mars passed the audition.

For Mars, who went on to play with Zappa from 1977 to 1982, it was a momentous start. Bobby Martin, his bandmate in the 1981 touring group, said Mars completely understood Zappa's music. His ability to quickly grasp the technical and conceptual parts of the songs made him a valuable part of the band.

Arthur Barrow

For bass player and music-degree holder Arthur Barrow, the audition process was different, because it required homework. Barrow was working in California, at Disneyland, doing Top 40 songs for scale. He met ex-Mother Don Preston through a mutual friend, which led to them playing in a short-lived band called Loose Connection. Preston also gave Barrow Frank Zappa's phone number, and when he heard about auditions he called Zappa to introduce himself.

Zappa gave Barrow the assignment of learning the part to "St. Alphonso's Pancake Breakfast" from *Apostrophe (')*. Barrow learned the bass line by recording the track to a reel-to-reel tape machine and slowing it down to half speed. Two days later, he played it for Zappa, who was impressed but non-committal. Barrow knew some other Zappa songs, though, and became part of the rhythm section as auditions continued. Zappa hired him for a week instead, but after two days he told Barrow he could stay on. He was paid $500 a week, plus a *per diem* when the group toured.

Warren Cuccurullo

When Brooklyn native Warren Cuccurullo auditioned for Zappa, it was a dream come true—literally. In an interview with Phil Coulter for CBC Radio in 2009, the guitarist described their first meeting. "I get up to the house and it looked just like a dream I had once, that I was there. There was a room that went down to the basement, the stairway that was in my dream; I was connected to the house somehow . . . anyway, we sat in the living room with our guitars. He would play something, just a riff, and see if I could play it back . . . and I think that I was the first kid who could spit stuff out, like him."

For Cuccurullo, all of those years playing guitar in the solitude of his bedroom, learning Zappa's solos from *Over-Nite Sensation*, had finally paid off. As he told Coulter, "My lifetime achievement was getting hired in Frank's band." Cuccurullo worked for Zappa from 1978 to 1980.

Terry Bozzio

Drummer Terry Bozzio was twenty-five years of age when he auditioned for Zappa during a "cattle call" in Los Angeles. He was going for a job in one of the most difficult chairs in Zappa's band, one that required a highly developed skillset. Zappa was very demanding of all musicians but held particularly high expectations for drummers because most of his music was composed with the drummer in mind. When the call went out in 1975, Terry Bozzio wasn't working at anything, let alone music, but he nonetheless decided to try for Zappa's band.

Bozzio didn't know much about Zappa's music, so he purchased two albums, *Roxy & Elsewhere* and *Apostrophe (')*, three days before the audition. The sheer complexity of the music and the level of the players and what he

Zappa wrote "The Black Page," a fan favorite, specifically for
Bozzio.   *Rex*

was up against overwhelmed him. When he arrived in L.A. and made his
way to the rehearsal studio in Hollywood, his stress levels were very high. To
add to the tension, he then entered a room with dozens of other drummers
waiting to take their turn. He had to read the difficult music to
"Approximate," with its odd time signatures. Zappa threw as many different
patterns as he could at the young drummer to see how he might respond.

Bozzio closed out his audition with a simple blues shuffle to demonstrate
his feel on the drums. Zappa liked what he heard. After he finished, Zappa
asked if anyone else was interested in playing. The story goes that the other
drummers in the waiting room all took a pass after hearing what Bozzio
could do. So, to his surprise, Terry Bozzio was hired. He played with Zappa
for nine years.

Robert "Bobby" Martin

The multi-instrumentalist Robert Martin met Zappa in 1981 after a stint playing in Etta James's band. He received a telephone call from Zappa's soundman, David Robb, who knew Martin from his work as a session player. Zappa was looking for one more musician to fill out his touring group that year. Martin knew the audition for Zappa was going to be a challenge, but he didn't prepare anything, choosing instead to "wing it." He was, after all, a classically trained musician whose parents were opera singers. He also had a degree from the Curtis Institute of Music in Philadelphia.

For the audition, Martin started on keyboards, and was given some sheet music titled "Envelopes," which he was able to read and play. His ability to play the French horn was also challenged when Zappa asked him to transpose and play some new music that was equally difficult. He then played alto sax on a short piece that led to his vocal audition: "Auld Lang Syne" in the key of A. Zappa was so impressed he hired Martin on the spot.

In an interview with *Downbeat* magazine in May 1978, Zappa was asked about musicians and what he expected of them. "The kind of musicians I need for the bands that I have doesn't exist. I need somebody who understands polyrhythms, has good enough execution on the instrument to play all kinds of styles, understands staging, understands rhythm and blues . . . when I give him a part, he should know how it works in the mix with all the other parts." His expectations may have been high, but Zappa always managed to find the right players in spite of it.

24

Playing Zappa's Music

Insights from His Musicians

In the June 1968 issue of the now defunct *Hit Parader* magazine, Frank Zappa was asked to list the best instrumentation of his ideal band:

The instrumentation of the ideal Mothers rock and roll band is two piccolos, two flutes, two bass flutes, two oboes, English horn, three bassoons, a contrabassoon, four clarinets (with the fourth player doubling on alto clarinet), bass clarinet, contrabass clarinet, soprano, alto, tenor, baritone and bass saxophones, four trumpets, four French horns, three trombones, one bass trombone, one tuba, one contrabass tuba, two harps, two keyboard men playing piano, electric piano, electric harpsichord, electric clavichord, Hammond organ, celeste, and piano bass, ten first violins, ten second violins, eight violas, six cellos, four string bass, four percussionists playing twelve timpani, chimes, gongs, field drums, bass drums, snare drums, woodblocks lion's roar, vibes, xylophone, and marimba three electric guitars, one electric twelve-string guitar, electric bass and electric bass guitar and two drummers at sets, plus vocalists who play tambourines. And I won't be happy until I have it.

For a musician, to make the Zappa band was a triumph. But the grueling audition process, which stressed out even the most skilled players on the planet, was only the first step. Playing Zappa's music required humility during the rehearsal process, which usually lasted five days a week for several months at a time. New band members had to relocate to Los Angeles, usually for three or four months of rehearsals, to learn up to one hundred songs. Zappa expected his band to play his songs correctly every time, which meant constant repetition until everything was ready. In an interview with broadcaster Jason Wilber in 2012, guitarist and singer Adrian Belew described his rehearsal time with Zappa as "immersed in his music," adding that once he went on tour, it was "like going from the black-and-white version of *The Wizard of Oz* into the color version of *The Wizard of Oz*."

Ruth Underwood was Zappa's percussionist from 1970 to 1977. She loved to play Zappa's music because it was always a little off center. In an interview with Phil Coulter of CBC Radio in 2008, she talked about her "most memorable" piece of Zappa's music, a song called "Oh No," which had an "unsettling meter . . . that just cut through my heart and soul, when I heard that." For Underwood, the mix of dramatic contrasts in Zappa's music had great appeal as a musician, which was a big draw for a lot of players in Zappa's bands.

Arthur Barrow, bassist and vocalist with the Zappa band in 1979, held one of the most important positions in the group. He was the "clonemeister," or concertmaster, responsible for leading the rehearsals and teaching the band Zappa's new music, which was always in a state of flux. Rehearsals usually continued for eight hours a day. Zappa would show up for the second half of the rehearsal to find out what the band knew and to introduce new music or changes to the existing song list.

Barrow's job was to take notes, prepare the changes for the next day, and walk the band through everything. He used a cassette recorder for playback and to keep track of the process; the musicians had to learn the songs as written, knowing they could be changed on a moment's notice. At first glance, Barrow's job seemed tedious, but he found it fun, because nobody knew what to expect from Zappa. The band was Zappa's tool for creating new music as much as playing the catalogue. In 2008, Barrow told CBC journalist Phil Coulter that Zappa "would push you and push

Ship arriving too late to save a drowning witch

1982 EUROPEAN TOUR

Forty-five cities from Aarhus, Denmark, to Palermo, Sicily.

you to see what your limits were . . . because he made use of the musicians he had and their particular talents."

For guitarist Warren Cuccurullo, the impact of playing Zappa's music only dawned on him years afterward. "Notes and pictures . . . every note had a picture and he was always thinking stories, pictures, always." Cuccurullo told Phil Coulter that, in spite of the fact that he only played with Zappa for a couple of years, he understood Zappa's "language" and how he took all of the best parts of jazz, classical, and rock music and put them all into "his new thing." In 1995, Cuccurullo released his first solo album, *Thanks to Frank*, which features a mix of styles he employed while playing with Zappa. It's full of weird sounds and some pretty versatile music, all played with no overdubs. Zappa's work ethic also inspired Cuccurullo to write and record as many ideas as came to him. Cuccurullo was twenty-two when he started playing for Frank Zappa, so it was more than just a job: it launched his career and helped him mature as an artist.

Playing Zappa's music was always a rewarding struggle for some musicians, including drummer Chad Wackerman. Wackerman first played with Zappa at age twenty-one, from 1981 until the final touring band of 1988. Wackerman tells his story on his website, where he says that it was his "feel" on the drums that Zappa really liked. Recalling his audition, he writes, "Frank [then] had me play in just about every style imaginable; heavy metal, swing, funk, New Orleans style rock (he called it a Delta groove), a Weather Report type feel, Latin styles, swing reggae, straight reggae, ska, punk . . . then it was combining an odd time and a ska feel or a reggae feel."

Tom Fowler played bass for Zappa from 1973 to 1975. In a radio interview with Bobby Marquis on CKCU-FM, first broadcast in June 2014, Fowler talked about Zappa's openness to his ideas. "He basically couldn't do all the instruments all of the time so we had to invent ways to play it together . . . and he [Zappa] would write it out so that we could play with each other as perfectly as we could." Fowler also said that Zappa had "no barriers to what he wanted to do," because he was always thinking about music and he was always writing it down. "I saw him sit down on a plane one time and write out a whole chart [score] and copy and when we got to New York, we play it. . . . he was really prolific."

When Zappa was working on the song "Fine Girl" in August 1980, he hired Iowa native Bob Harris to do a vocal. Harris was a friend of Zappa's engineer at the time, Mark Pinske, whom he had worked with in Florida the year before with another band. Zappa needed someone to sing the falsetto vocal parts on the song. Zappa played Harris the basic tracks and Harris took direction from him regarding the doo-wop-style vocals that he wanted. The experience later got Harris a job with the 1980 touring band, but what most impressed him about Zappa, as he later told Bobby Marquis, was that "he would bring out the best in people, usually. People would either flourish or fold in front of Frank. I was lucky enough to flourish. When we did 'Fine Girl' . . . I realized Frank was a total balance of genius and common sense."

Harris's experiences working in the studio with Zappa left a huge impression on him, and in his conversation with Marquis, he recalled how much he, Ike Willis, and Ray White laughed during their downtime, often while Zappa was "losing it." As Harris observed, "He could access his 'inner-child' at a moment's notice."

25

Annus Horribillis

1988

I n late 1987, Frank Zappa decided to hit the road for one last tour. He was motivated in part by politics: the United States was entering an important presidential election, drawing to a close the Ronald Reagan era, which Zappa detested. In an effort to encourage his audience to participate, Zappa started a voter-registration campaign in all the American cities he played. The League of Women's Voters set up tables in the lobbies of concert halls, and according to Zappa, up to 20 percent of the audience registered to vote in the 1988 election.

Politics was always a part of Zappa's life, and this tour was going to be his "campaign," along with a chance to show off a new group and a slew of new songs critical of the current political system. But the big-budget tour ended ten weeks early and would prove to be Zappa's last.

Zappa Chooses Musicians

Frank Zappa always put a new band together when he went out on the road, and the 1988 tour was no different. But this time he was interested in mixing up the sound and arrangements of his old hits, so he augmented his regular band with a five-piece horn section. The tour was named Broadway the Hard Way, with concerts lined up in the United States for most of the winter and fall and European dates in the middle, during the spring. Zappa called in a few alumni of bands past: Ike Willis (vocals/guitar), Chad Wackerman (drums), Scott Thunes (bass), and Bobby Martin (vocals/keyboards/alto sax) from the 1984 touring group. He also added Ed Mann (percussion), who had played with him in the late seventies, Bruce Fowler (trombone) and his brother Walt (trumpet), Albert Wing (tenor saxophone), Paul Carman (alto, soprano, and baritone saxes), and Kurt McGettrick (baritone sax and

Zappa leads the '88 Big Band with Scott Thunes, left, on bass.   *ulstein bild/Getty Images*

contrabass clarinet). The newest member was Mike Keneally, a twenty-five-year-old New York–born guitarist and vocalist. Keneally's role was that of "stunt" guitarist, there to play some of the more intricate music written by Zappa. (The incomparable Steve Vai held the same job on the 1980 tour.)

Rehearsals began in a Los Angeles studio in the fall of 1987 with an ambitious 120-song repertoire. Consequently, the band kept a grueling schedule from October through January 1988, rehearsing five days a week, eight hours per day. The most important job in Zappa's band was that of "clonemeister," whose role it was to lead the rehearsals and teach the musicians how to play their parts correctly. (Ian Underwood was the first clonemeister of the original Mothers of Invention in 1967.) Scott Thunes was first given the assignment in 1984, succeeding fellow bass player Arthur Barrow, and in the interest of continuity, he was given the job again for the 1988 big-band rehearsals.

Ed Mann, who had been hired back to play for this group, held the position in 1978. In an interview with the May 1991 issue of the British fanzine *T'Mershi Duween*, he described the challenges he faced. "It's like this: there is the band and there is the guy who runs the band, and then Frank. And the guy who runs the band teaches the rehearsals and all that stuff, and if it's not the right energy, it doesn't come across, it doesn't work somehow . . . but it makes a difficult position for the guy who has to run the band."

Having held the job before, Thunes knew what was expected of him. Zappa was a hard taskmaster, and Thunes had the tough job of running the first half of every rehearsal, since Zappa only appeared in the afternoons.

Scott Thunes, Bass Player

Thunes was born in 1960 and grew up in San Anselmo, California, northwest of San Francisco. He started playing electric bass at the age of ten, when his brother and mother needed a new band member for their family folk group. He had such a talent for it that, by the age of fifteen, he was accepted into Marin County College to study music. While at school he learned the rudiments of music, composition, and jazz fundamentals. He was also exposed to contemporary classical music, including the works of Bela Bartok, which greatly inspired him. Unfortunately, he was turned down by the San Francisco Conservatory of Music, and instead ended up playing in new-wave groups in the region, while supplementing his income as a car-jockey.

In 1981, Scott's brother Derek heard that Frank Zappa was holding auditions for his upcoming touring band. Thunes had started listening to Zappa as a child and went to his first concert in 1975, so he considered himself a huge fan. After some apprehension, Thunes rang Zappa and asked for an audition. When he arrived at Zappa's house, keyboard player Tommy Mars was already there to help with the session; Thunes did so well that Zappa recorded part of the session for the song "Cocaine Decisions," which he released on *The Man from Utopia* in 1983. Thunes was paid for his efforts and then assigned "homework" by Zappa: he was to learn the bass part to "Mo 'n Herb's Vacation" from a transcription of the piece's clarinet music. Thunes auditioned with two other bass players but did not get an answer from Zappa for another week. Steve Vai put in a good word for him, though, and eventually Thunes was hired. He remained as Zappa's bass player until 1988.

Group Dynamics

If you've ever played in a band or some musical ensemble, you'll know that personalities often clash, which can create tension within the group. That tension can be useful, leading to better art, or destructive, if somebody says the wrong thing. The history of music is filled with break-up incidents and stories, and you don't have to look very far to find examples of personality conflicts (aka "creative differences") putting an end to successful groups in music. The Beatles ended when Paul McCartney went to court to dissolve the band after the argumentative mood of its members started to erode the whole group. The members of Cream detested one another by the time Eric Clapton, Ginger Baker, and the late Jack Bruce called it a day in 1968, and the infighting of Fleetwood Mac is legendary, the band's members breaking up and reuniting like the change of seasons.

Frank Zappa's bands were different, in the sense that he was the boss and everybody knew it. When you joined his touring band, you weren't a member: you were an employee, getting paid to play his music. That relationship may seem cold to some people, but Zappa was never sentimental about his musicians. He enjoyed their company onstage and he appreciated their talent and effort, but he was also a pragmatic bandleader.

When Zappa reported that the 1988 band "self-destructed" in his liner notes to *The Best Band You've Never Heard in Your Life* (1991), fans were curious to know what he meant. In interviews that followed, Zappa was vague about what had caused the issue but angry about his losses, which added up to $400,000. In *Zappa the Hard Way*, British author Andrew Greenaway explains why the 1988 big band prematurely stopped touring after finishing the European dates, offering details regarding the volatile band members, some of whom blamed Scott Thunes for the break-up. Thunes was known to have a rather caustic personality that rubbed some of the musicians the wrong way. Mike Keneally recalls the first time he saw Thunes, describing him as "a tall, head-shaven, impolite force of nature skateboarding into and all around the enormous facility" and a "combination punk-rocker / marine drill sergeant on wheels."

When the rehearsals started, Thunes's weak conducting skills began to irritate the horn section, especially when they came to some of the more difficult arrangements he had written for them (with Zappa's approval). Instead of taking a break or pausing to let the musicians learn their parts, Thunes would lose his temper, which created animosity, especially with the Fowler brothers and Albert Wing. According to Ike Willis, Zappa was aware of the personality clashes, and for the last month of the rehearsals asked Willis to lead them instead of Thunes. The breaking point came when drummer Chad Wackerman became annoyed with Thunes over the music. By the time the tour was due to commence, the tension between Thunes and most of the rest of the band had eased, but it never fully went away.

Tour Begins in the United States

Two full-size buses carried the band members from city to city, in a manner typical of most groups working the continental United States. In the case of this tour, the buses were divided into "smoking" and "non-smoking." Zappa, Thunes, McGettrick, the Fowler brothers, Mike Keneally, and Zappa's bodyguard and road manager were on the smoking vehicle. Everybody else was on the non-smoking bus. This separation helped improve the band's mood for the first month of the tour. Most of the concerts were sellouts, with enthusiastic audiences present at every show. Zappa even brought in new arrangements or changes in lyrics to reflect the day's news. But when the group arrived to play in Springfield, Massachusetts, a meeting was held to air complaints. Thunes was caught by surprise when Chad Wackerman complained that the rhythm section wasn't supporting the horn section during their solos.

Ironically, since it was the drummer who made the observation, it meant Thunes was the rhythm player not holding up his end of the music. Thunes took this personally; Zappa tried to appease him by asking him to mellow out and enjoy himself, but Thunes took the comments as an affront against his commitment to the tour, and he wouldn't let it go. Consequently, Thunes began to resent some of the other musicians, especially Ed Mann and Wackerman.

Things came to a head in the middle of a concert in Allentown, Ohio, in March, during a performance of "King Kong." Percussionist Ed Mann told writer Andrew Greenaway that, during the improvised part of the song, "I blew my lid on mic at Thunes . . . for those of you who might not know the whole is the sum of its parts . . . no single part can be a whole all by itself unless it's a fucking black hole." Mann went on to make references to Nazis that Thunes thought were directed at him. Thunes was angry, flipping the bird at Mann, while Zappa just laughed.

Bound for Europe

The American leg of the tour finished up on March 25, 1988, at the Nassau Coliseum in Uniondale, New York. Two weeks later, the tour resumed in France. Sometimes a change is as good as a rest, but not this time. By now, Scott Thunes had only one friend left in the band—Mike Keneally. Everybody else hated him, and for good reason. Thunes had a habit of running around onstage, sticking the end of his bass guitar in the butts of the horn players while they were playing. This childish behavior continued with sarcastic comments during the pre-show huddles or at the sound check. One time, Zappa took Thunes aside and asked him to "cool it," reminding him of the great expense of the tour and how he didn't need dissenting personnel. But it was too late.

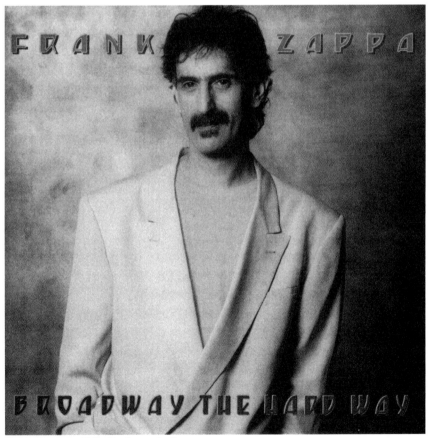

Zappa's most politically charged album.

The feuding was beginning to affect the performances, which is ironic because to the fans, everything was fine, as evidenced on the subsequent CD releases from the tour. Zappa's well-rehearsed band started having troubles in Rotterdam, in the Netherlands, during the first of two shows at the Ahoy on May 5, 1988. Zappa's music is prone to mistakes from time to time, with a missed lyric here or some messed up passages there. It comes with the territory. But with the growing acid feelings within the band, they became magnified, and the bandleader wasn't impressed.

One night, Zappa called out Ed Mann for a major mistake he made during "Dickie's Such an Asshole," which an astute fan had noticed and brought to his attention. Mann was asked to play the really quick phrase on marimba, as written, and then reproduce the mistake. Ike Willis forgot some of the lyrics to the same song, causing Zappa to comment during the second half of the show that the band needed more rehearsal. Apparently four months wasn't enough. Things were beginning to sour, onstage and off.

The Beginning of the End

Scott Thunes was now pissing off the crew, too, resulting in him being the victim of one or two incidents. Every band member wears a laminated ID card around their necks so that the local security can identify the musicians from the fans. Thunes usually freed himself of the pass during the show, leaving it on the tech stand offstage and then picking it up afterward. One night he found the laminate had holes where his picture used to be. Another time his face had been cut out altogether, most likely by a crewmember.

The tour rolled on in spite of the bad behavior and juvenile antics. And then they reached Austria, which was where it really got personal. On May 27, 1988, the Broadway the Hard Way Tour arrived in Linz, ahead of a show at the Sporthalle the next night. In an expression of gratitude, the locals baked a cake and put the names of every band member on it. Scott Thunes arrived a little late and found that his name had been scratched off the cake. Rather than let this pass, the bass player and bane of everyone's existence on the tour took a wooden spoon and lifted the names "Ed Mann" and "Chad Wackerman" off the cake, too. Zappa reprimanded him again, but it didn't stick. Thunes's anger got the better of him on the bus after the show. Bruce Fowler was giving him grief over the incident and Thunes responded by dropping his pants and exposing himself.

By the time the band reached Genoa, Italy, on June 9, the performances were beginning to suffer. Zappa had previously tried to make light of this by dropping in lyrics that made fun of the "drama," as he did in Barcelona, Spain, the previous month. But now it was affecting his all-important solos. In his book *Zappa the Hard Way*, Greenaway reports Zappa saying, "On a good night, the ideas for guitar solos came out. On a bad night it was me versus the band." Zappa decided to poll the band informally about the dysfunction and what to do about it. To an extent, everybody was to blame for the breakdown, and Zappa was trying to gauge the prospects for moving on. What he learned was that the band didn't want to complete the upcoming US leg of the tour with Scott Thunes.

When he heard this, Thunes offered to quit, largely out of respect for Zappa, but the bandleader didn't see him as the problem. In fact, he wanted to keep Thunes. He liked him, and he liked the way he played bass. To the pragmatic bandleader, the real problem would be finding a replacement for Thunes and then going into rehearsals again so that the new bass player could get up to speed on the repertoire. The complexity of the show, as far as Zappa was concerned, was too much for someone to be able to learn it in a short period of time. So, rather than continue with Thunes and a band that was beginning to deteriorate onstage as well as off, Zappa canceled the remaining concerts, at a loss of $400,000. Zappa exercised his right as the boss to make the final decision and not acquiesce to the whims of the band.

Epilogue

After the tour ended, Zappa went into the studio and assembled the best performances from the tour for the *Broadway the Hard Way* LP, which he put out in October. It was released on CD the following May. In April 1991, Zappa released a double-CD set featuring more songs from the tour, *The Best Band You Never Heard in Your Life*, quickly followed by *Make a Jazz Noise Here*, another double CD featuring more instrumental tracks. In all, over five and a half hours worth of music from the 1988 big-band tour was released by June 1991.

Meanwhile, on November 8, 1988, Republican candidate George H. W. Bush defeated the Democrat Michael Dukakis in the US presidential election. Bush earned 53 percent of the popular vote and carried forty states, including Zappa's home state of California.

26

Music Theories

Zappa's "Conceptual Continuity"

n the liner notes to *You Can't Do That on Stage Anymore*, Frank Zappa offers a checklist of the eight criteria that determined the release of the archival performances in the six-volume series. The first five criteria relate to the chosen track, influenced by the quality of the band, Zappa's guitar solo, or some "folkloric significance" to the performance. Item number six reads, "Will it give 'Conceptual Continuity Clues' to the hard-core maniacs with a complete record collection?"

"Conceptual continuity" and its companion term, "Project/object," help us understand the way Zappa thought about his own endeavors.

Project/Object

Project/object is Zappa's big-picture phrase to describe his work in different mediums, be it radio, film, video, albums, songs, or concerts. Conceptual continuity is the thread linking all of the projects in the object. For example, one object might be a new album; the songs (projects) make up the album (object). If Zappa does a radio interview about the same album, it too is a project that forms part of the object, because it's related to the original project.

Project/object is not confined to any one medium. Zappa compared his theory to a writer who makes up a really interesting character so good that he needn't be limited to one book, so he shows up in a future novel. For example, the great Canadian author Mordecai Richler wrote a hilarious novel called *The Apprenticeship of Duddy Kravitz* in 1959 to wide acclaim. Duddy Kravitz became a much-loved character, mostly for his tenacious search for money in order to buy land. Throughout the book, Duddy works the system, as only he can, to fulfill his grandfather's wish to obtain land

and become a "somebody" and enter a higher social class. Kravitz shows up again in Richler's later novels *St. Urbain's Horseman* (1971) and *Barney's Version* (1997), demonstrating the same spirited qualities he showed on his debut. To Richler, these characters were like his repertory company, and since they all lived in the same neighborhood or district in Montreal, where the books were based, it was likely they would see each other from time to time.

Zappa takes that notion a littler further by referencing a lyric, subject, or character from one song in another to bring together his whole output. Zappa compared it to Rembrandt's use of the color brown in his art. The Dutch painter used layers of brown at the sketch level and built his portraits using light and shading techniques, thereby creating an image that looked like it was emerging from dark to light on the canvas. In order to do this effectively, Rembrandt put a touch of brown in every color of his palette.

Conceptual Continuity

In a profile of Zappa in the April 29, 1974, issue of *Circular* magazine, writer Barry Hansen defines conceptual continuity as "Zappa's belief that everything he creates and performs in any medium is part of a single continuous artistic and communicative experience." At first glance, that "singleness" of design is most obvious when you listen to his albums, as one element segues directly into the next without a break. This was certainly a new way of listening to recorded music for most people when *Freak Out!* arrived in 1966. (The Beatles did it a year later on *Sgt. Pepper*). As a musical technique, though, it wasn't new. For instance, Beethoven's String Quartet No. 14, Op. 131, finished in 1826, is a seven-movement work that's played without a break. Tempo changes shift from one movement to the next, making the work one of the most difficult compositions to perform. Opus 131 actually starts in one key, C-sharp minor, and ends in another, C-sharp major. The last movement quotes some phrases of the opening movement, which was unusual to audiences at the time. Beethoven was clearly changing the way music should be heard by bending the rules.

Zappa probably wasn't thinking of Beethoven when he decided to join together all of the songs on an album, but the listening experience is similar in scope. By the time one idea is expressed and developed, we're on to the next, and so on. It's like watching waves of water approach a beach: they vary in size and weights yet continually flow at the will of the wind, or, in the case of LPs, a turntable locked in at the right speed. We hear the whole work while enjoying its component parts as we go.

Zappa didn't limit himself to simple technical devices to get his theory across. He used a ton of references and clues to feed the "maniacs," as he called them, who loved to seek out instances of his conceptual continuity. A kind of *Where's Waldo?* for the fans. On the Zappa website Zappa Wiki Jawaka, you can find a subject index of 105 of them. (Users of this site have to open an account and sign in to add information, just like Wikipedia.) The index includes phrases, song titles, animals, body parts, body functions, and things like "Elvis Presley," all annotated for your conceptual continuity entertainment. Like Stephen Hawking's unified theory of the universe, conceptual continuity ties together everything in Zappa's oeuvre.

The Canine Connection

One of the best clues to Zappa's theory is his reference to dogs. The canine list includes names like "Fido" and "Evelyn," breeds like "poodles" and "huskies," and the leashes and collars on the jacket of *Absolutely Free.* The album jackets for *Francesco Zappa, Them or Us,* and *The Perfect Stranger* feature a painting by Donald Roller Wilson of a dog, named "Patricia," wearing sunglasses. Cal Schenkel designed three Zappa albums with the band members depicted as dogs: *Cruising with Ruben & the Jets, Just Another Band from L.A.,* and the posthumous release *Ahead of Their Time.* Two of Zappa's strongest works are "Dog Breath, in the Year of the Plague" and its instrumental component, "Dog Breath Variations," and they come up repeatedly in different performances in Zappa's discography. The list goes on.

Further explanation of conceptual continuity surfaced in 1984, when Zappa released a limited-edition book named after his album release of the same year, *Them or Us.* London publisher Pinter & Martin reprinted the book in 2010. It's a facsimile edition of Zappa's original work, which he produced on a dot-matrix printer at his house. It was only available by mail order in 1984, although Zappa's fans soon scooped up all 5,000 copies. As he writes in the dedication to the 350-page tome, "This cheesy little homemade book was prepared for the amusement of people who already enjoy Zappa music. It is not for intellectuals or other dead people."

Zappa goes on to express appreciation for the fans interested in conceptual continuity and also those who understood the sense of "absurdity" in his work. Written as a screenplay, *Them or Us: The Book* is Zappa's elucidation

Cal Schenkel's dogs.

based on his interest in the "unified field theory" or UFT. That theory is best suited to experts in physics, but it suggests that the world of particles and fields of energy could be related, rather than being individual parts of the universe acting independently of one another. Albert Einstein coined the phrase when he was thinking about his general theory of relativity, published in 1915, and electromagnetism.

Zappa's book *Them or Us* is his story of conceptual continuity, so familiarity with his music is essential in appreciating its "absurdity." Real and imagined characters show up, and Zappa's cast includes Billy the Mountain, Thing-Fish, and Francesco Zappa, all living in the same universe and colliding with one another.

Xenochrony

When Zappa was in the editing suite, he had an archive full of recordings including music and spoken-word pieces to use. It wasn't uncommon for him to edit a spoken-word segment and match it up with another recorded in a completely different year. His album *Civilization Phaze III*, for example, uses dialogue recorded in 1967 and 1991, edited together to sound like a single conversation. He called the method "xenochrony": the synthesis of recorded events from different times and places. To form the word, Zappa took the Greek *xeno*, which means alien, and linked it with the Greek word for time, *chrono*. He also used xenochrony when he spliced a guitar solo from a past era into the middle of a new recording.

The criterion for such a bold creation was based around the rhythmic fit of the piece. For instance, on the song "Yo Mama," from the album *Sheik Yerbouti*, Zappa took a 4-track recording of his guitar solo from a completely different concert performance and placed it in the middle of the basic track, which was recorded in the Hammersmith Odeon, London, in 1978. On the same album, Zappa overdubbed a bass part by Patrick O'Hearn from a 1974 live show onto a new recording of "Rubber Shirt." He also took another version of the solo from a later recording, slowing it down to create a track that sounds like two bass players and a drummer sharing the stage. The result is a "xenochroneous" creation that's no less beautiful than if it had been a single complete session.

27

Not a Place to Stay

200 Motels

On October 29, 1971, Frank Zappa's first major motion picture was released in select theaters. *200 Motels* was a personal story about life on the road and how it can drive you crazy. The title relates to the touring schedule of the Mothers of Invention, who played for five years and did about forty shows per year that required a stay in a motel.

When *200 Motels* came out, young audiences were already accustomed to seeing their favorite bands on the big screen. Richard Lester's Beatles film *A Hard Day's Night* (1964) was a huge box office success that inspired a slew of movies about rock bands, including *Head* (1968), starring the Monkees, and *Gimme Shelter* (1970), featuring the Rolling Stones. But Zappa wasn't interested in perpetuating the myths of music stardom. He defined his film, instead, as a "surrealistic documentary." It offers a very different treatment of the rock 'n' roll lifestyle, depicting the feel and atmosphere of life for a touring rock band.

Zappa the Filmmaker

Frank Zappa started making films during his high-school days in Lancaster, California. He loved the editing process and often mixed music and time-lapse images in a collage of colors and shapes to produce short artistic films. On April 30, 1969, he introduced his eighteen-minute film *Burnt Weeny Sandwich* on KQED-TV in San Francisco. He was also working concurrently on the *Uncle Meat* project, which was released as an album in 1969 but, due to poor funding, wasn't finished as a film until 1987, when it was made available on Honker Home Video.

Zappa started working on *200 Motels* years before shooting commenced. He even took piles of blank sheet music on the road so that he could work on the score. In fact, he wrote the script and the score in the very motels in which the band stayed.

It took Zappa three years to put the music down on paper. He finished a first draft of the score shortly after he broke up the original Mothers of Invention in August 1969, but he needed an orchestra in order to hear it. Following a chance encounter at radio station KPFA-FM, Zappa met Zubin Mehta, the new conductor of the L.A. Philharmonic. Mehta was always interested in new music for the orchestra but turned down Zappa's offer to take a look at his score because he was too busy at the time. The orchestra's manager, however, was not, and he liked the score so much he convinced Mehta to give it a try. According to Pauline Butcher, Zappa's secretary, $7,000 was spent to hire a team of copyists to write out the individual parts for the orchestra.

Three months later, a concert was set for May 15, 1970, at the acoustically challenged Pauley Pavilion on the campus of UCLA. Zappa hired some of his former bandmates for the performance: Ian Underwood, Don Preston, Jim "Motorhead" Sherwood, Ray Collins, and Billy Mundi. Jeff Simmons and Aynsley Dunbar played bass and drums, respectively. The concert was billed as the *Contempo 70 Festival*. Since the score called for rock band *and* orchestra, several days' rehearsal was required, but the sound was still a problem right up until the performance. Regrettably, due to union rules, Zappa could not record the concert for his own use, but a bootleg version of decent quality was released illegally (and can be heard on YouTube).

Although the concert received mixed reviews, Zappa was generally pleased with the results. The show also impressed two members of the Turtles, Mark Volman and Howard Kaylan, who were among the audience of over ten thousand people. Two weeks later, they joined Zappa's band as Flo and Eddie.

The Pitch

In November 1970, Zappa approached David Picker, the head of United Artists, in search of funding for his film. All he had was a ten-page treatment, a tape with about thirty minutes of music, and some photographs prepared by Cal Schenkel, the film's art director. Five days after the meeting, United Artists agreed to finance the picture when Zappa gave the studio the rights to the soundtrack album. Pinewood Studio was booked for ten days in late January 1971, so Zappa had only a short time to pull a cast together and book the Royal Philharmonic Orchestra to record the score and appear in the movie.

The Cast

200 Motels features the 1971 lineup of the Mothers, playing themselves, complaining about money and their boss while enjoying the company of groupies in between picking fights with customers in bars. Ringo Starr—disguised as Frank Zappa in a wig and moustache—plays the part of Larry the Dwarf. He also narrates the story. Keith Moon of the Who appears dressed as a nun by the name of Pamela, a groupie in training, while ex-Mother Jimmy Carl Black plays Lonesome Cowboy Burt. Don Preston, who appeared as the mad scientist in *Uncle Meat*, reprises his role for *200 Motels*. The only true actor was Theodore Bikel, who in addition to being a well-established folk singer was often seen on American television programs playing villains or doctors.

Elgar Howarth conducted the Royal Philharmonic Orchestra, with the movie also featuring members of the Monteverdi Choir under the pseudonym the Top Score Singers. Dancers, mimes, and Zappa family babysitters Janet Neville Ferguson and Lucy Offerall play groupies.

The film was one of Zappa's biggest projects. United Artists was probably impressed with the casting of Ringo Starr and Keith Moon, two of the biggest names in pop at the time. According to director Tony Palmer, they thought the Beatles were going to be in the film, too—an honest mistake, perhaps, considering UA had produced *A Hard Day's Night* in 1964. But when Starr was cast in the movie, the Beatles had only recently broken up. (Coincidentally, Aynsley Dunbar of the Mothers and Starr's chauffeur, Martin Lickert, were also natives of Liverpool.)

The Movie Is Made

The film was given a budget of $630,000 and was the first movie to be shot on two-inch videotape before being transferred to 35mm film stock. Zappa had just enough money to book ten days at Pinewood Studio in London, which had the dimensions and crew necessary to make the picture. British filmmaker Tony Palmer took on the bulk of the work. His claim to fame at the time was *Cream: Farewell Concert*, a stylized film of the British band at their final show in 1968. He was also responsible for bringing in Ringo Starr and the Royal Philharmonic Orchestra, under conductor Elgar (Gary)

Zappa looms large in his first major motion picture.

Howarth, and the TV crew. Palmer oversaw proceedings from the television remote truck while Zappa directed the action in the sound studio.

When *200 Motels* opened, audiences were treated to a mix of concert performances of Zappa's band featuring Flo and Eddie, a cartoon, and imaginative dance sequences. In the commentary to the 2009 DVD release, Tony Palmer said he had a book of images by the Spanish surrealist Salvador Dali with him during the shoot. He wanted to create "a visceral experience as if the viewer was at a concert," so he used the four video cameras and accompanying switcher board to create the effect of a Dali painting. The performance footage of the Mothers features extreme close-ups, distorted colors, and fast cuts between cameras, resulting in a music video–like effect.

The film's narrative suffers because the band members look too self-conscious about what they are doing in every scene. Nevertheless, the highlights include an animation sequence by Cal Schenkel called "Dental Hygiene Dilemma," featuring a mystic in a wig on television. The wide range of music showcases Zappa's newfound orchestral scoring techniques and some well-rehearsed performances by the Mothers.

Not available on iTunes.

In the liner notes to his 1970 release *Chunga's Revenge*, Zappa notes that some of the songs are a preview of the story, but none were used in the finished movie. The songs that were introduced in concerts leading up to the filming of *200 Motels* were "Bwana Dik," "Penis Dimension," and "Magic Fingers." Zappa's orchestral score, however, was much more akin to Arnold Schoenberg's *Pierrot Lunaire* (1912), a short melodrama of twenty-one poems set to music. The simultaneous release of the soundtrack on United Artists featured the new songs, the original orchestra and choir, and dialogue from the film. It peaked on the *Billboard* album chart at #59.

The Critics Weigh In

The response to *200 Motels* was decidedly mixed. In his review for the *New York Times*, dated November 12, 1971, film critic Vincent Canby called it "an anthology of poor jokes and spectacular audio-visual effects, a few of which might expand the mind, but all of which, taken together, are like an overdose of Novocain." Canby did enjoy the score by Zappa, who he called "the Orson Welles of the rock music world," but the bustling presentation and inconsistent performances left him exhausted. Roger Ebert was even less forgiving in his review for the *Chicago Sun Times*, now archived on the late critic's web site. "In a way, maybe, overbearing is the word for this movie. It assaults the mind with everything on hand."

The strongest reaction came from the director himself. In a scathing commentary for the *Guardian*, published November 7, 1971, he practically disowned the movie as "one of the worst films in the entire history of the cinema." Perhaps the movie aged well for him, though, as he would later embrace the picture when it was released on DVD in 2009. On the commentary track, Palmer dispels the myths surrounding his participation, such as that he supposedly walked out in anger during the shoot and destroyed some of the videotapes. He had high praise for Theodore Bikel, whom he says was "calm, professional, and supportive" during the shoot. He went on to conclude that he felt "privileged to be a part of it."

After the Credits Rolled

Some of the musicians and production team went on to big things after *200 Motels*, including conductor Elgar Howarth. Howarth, a noted instrumentalist, was part of the brass section that played on "Magical Mystery Tour" by the Beatles in 1967. He played trumpet in the Royal Opera House's house orchestra and composed music for bands including the Philip Jones Brass Ensemble. Today, he is semi-retired and living in England.

Another contributor to *200 Motels* was choreographer Gillian Lynne, who was responsible for the musical staging in the film. Dame Lynne went on to work as associate director on the acclaimed musical *Cats*, winning awards for choreography and direction. She was also hired to direct the musical staging and choreography of *Phantom of the Opera* in 1986 and *The Secret Garden* in 2000. Her 2011 autobiography, *A Dancer in Wartime*, was well received by critics.

Tony Palmer is still an active member of the music and movie scene. After *200 Motels* he produced and directed one of the most important television series on the history of American popular music, *All You Need Is Love* (1975). He also made documentaries about Maria Callas (*Tony Palmer's Film About Callas*, 1987) and Yehudi Menuhin (*Menuhin, a Family Portrait*, 1990). In 2010, his film about Leonard Cohen, *Bird on a Wire*, was rediscovered and released on DVD in its original form. In 2015, Palmer reissued a compilation of three short documentaries from 1972 as *The Pursuit of Happiness*, featuring archival interviews with John Lennon and Shirley MacLaine, among others. Originally broadcast on London Weekend Television in Britain, the collection offers insight into the attitudes of post-hippie culture.

Film as History

Zappa's *200 Motels* serves as a benchmark of his creative output and a step toward his video productions in the eighties. In his book *The Negative Dialectics of Poodle Play*, Ben Watson describes *200 Motels* as being about "the chaos and competition of life on the road becomes a metaphor for capitalism: people reduced to puppets within a schema [framework] they can't understand."

On October 23, 2013, forty-two years after the movie debuted, the Los Angeles Philharmonic conducted by Esa-Pekka Salonen brought the music of Frank Zappa to the stage of the Walt Disney Concert Hall in a rare concert performance called *200 Motels: The Suites*. A thirteen-member cast presented the story, in character, while the orchestra and band performed Zappa's complete score. Diva Zappa, Frank's youngest daughter, played the role of "Janet the Groupie" in a show that included former Zappa alumni Ian Underwood and Scott Thunes in the band. Six days later, the BBC Concert

Orchestra performed *200 Motels* at London's Royal Festival Hall, site of many concerts by the Mothers of Invention. Members of the Zappa family were in attendance, but this time Diva read the role of Lucy.

On April 18, 2015, as part of the annual Record Store Day celebrations, a limited-edition 7-inch single was released, on purple vinyl, featuring the Overture to *200 Motels* performed by the L.A. Philharmonic under Salonen. The B-side featured "What's the Name of Your Group?," as performed by the Royal Philharmonic Orchestra and conducted by Frank Zappa and recorded in 1971. In late July, the Zappa Family Trust issued a press release regarding their new distribution deal with Universal, which included a promise to issue the 2013 Salonen concert in the near future.

28

Steal This Video

Frank Zappa's Visual Productions

When Frank Zappa released his illustrious movie *200 Motels* in 1971, he went on the American game show *What's My Line?* to promote it. The host, Wally Bruner, quizzed him about the process of shooting a movie on videotape and transferring it to film, as it was the first time this process had been used.

The conversation revealed how well the thirty-one-year-old artist, better known for his music, understood the flexibility and creativity of working with videotape versus film. Zappa could easily have pursued an artistic career making movies exclusively but for the cost of doing so. Nevertheless, he produced and directed a number of interesting videos featuring performance footage and satiric commentary on pop culture. These are the official releases in the Zappa video catalogue.

A Token of His Extreme

On August 6, 1974, Zappa and the Mothers entered the sound stage of KCET-TV in Culver City, California, to perform two shows in front of a studio audience. The taping was produced and arranged by Frank Zappa with his own money. He wanted to capture the 1974 *Over-Nite Sensation* band with Napoleon Murphy Brock, George Duke, Tom Fowler, Ruth Underwood, and Chester Thompson. This band had already been on the road since the fall 1973 tour, and this stop was scheduled into a tour that continued until the end of the calendar year. The video, directed by Dick Darley, was Zappa's attempt to promote his band, his music, and the clay animation of one Bruce Bickford, whose creative pieces were spliced into the final video.

Bruce Bickford came from Seattle and moved to Laurel Canyon, not far from Zappa's house, in 1966. He had been enthralled by the clay he was

Zappa's television special.

given to play with as a child, and, in a radio interview with Bobby Marquis, first broadcast in December 2014 on CKCU-FM, he said he was also greatly influenced by the Disney animated film *Peter Pan*, which he first saw in 1953. "I'd never had an experience like that in my life. The colors and everything was so vivid . . . The characters like Captain Hook even had a diamond ring on his hook . . . I'd go to bed at night and think about it [hoping] to dream about it."

Bickford started making short films of his clay animation, and one day he dropped in on Zappa to introduce himself and show him his latest project. Zappa was so impressed by Bickford's Claymation that he actually put him on the payroll, granting Bickford a steady income and the chance to produce more animated films. Bickford worked by himself, molding clay figures and shaping stories in his tiny studio. Claymation in those days was a very slow, tedious process, often taking days to shoot a minute's worth of footage. Zappa admired Bickford's dedication to his craft and chose to add his short films to *A Token of His Extreme*. Bickford's work is showcased on "Inca Roads" and "Dog Breath Variations / Uncle Meat."

For several years after the initial broadcast on KCET, Zappa made the tape available as a syndicated special. French and Swiss television stations broadcast the program, but no other American stations were interested. In 2013, Eagle Rock Productions released a remastered version on DVD that also includes Zappa's 1976 appearance on *The Mike Douglas Show*. Douglas had aired a two-minute segment featuring Bickford's treatment of "Inca Roads" on his nationally syndicated talk show, which was probably the first time North American audiences had seen Bickford's work. As a film, *A Token of His Extreme* works hard at presenting one of Zappa's best bands in full force, and it generally succeeds.

Baby Snakes

In 1979, Zappa released a more ambitious video called *Baby Snakes*, "A movie about people who do stuff that is not normal," which he wrote, produced, and directed. The video mixes performance footage with backstage patter, soundtrack recordings, and rehearsals, and runs nearly three hours from start to finish. Animator Bruce Bickford is seen at work in his studio, where he is prompted by Zappa to talk about his ideas. The concert footage is taken from a run of shows at the Palladium in New York, October 28–31, 1977. This band features Tommy Mars, Terry Bozzio, Adrian Belew, Patrick O'Hearn, Ed Mann, and Peter Wolf.

The performance footage alone is spectacular, with Zappa and the band in great form. *Baby Snakes* gives us insight into Zappa's conducting techniques and his spontaneous creation of sound. The band members are fully attentive during "Managua," as Zappa shapes the length and breadth of each instrument. The audience participation segment offers us the "reenactment of the sum total of modern civilization," as directed by Zappa, who takes a shot a Warner Bros. in a spoken-word segment, followed by a rather sublime segment known as the "dance contest," a regular feature at Zappa's shows in the seventies. This film-within-a-film features a soundtrack of "The Black Page No. 2."

Just what the world needs, another movie by Frank Zappa.

The Torture Never Stops

When Zappa released this performance video of the 1981 touring band, everything changed in the presentation of his music. There were no more dance contests, and the Spike Jones circus atmosphere is nowhere in sight. Produced in cooperation with the fledging MTV, *The Torture Never Stops* is Zappa's most intricate and sophisticated presentation. It was broadcast on *MTV Live* with host Nina Blackwood, who called it a "nightmare" because Zappa didn't treat her respectfully. (None of this is on the DVD.) The band features Steve Vai, Ray White, Ed Mann, Scott Thunes, Chad Wackerman, Bobby Martin, and Tommy Mars.

The *Torture* set was recorded four years after the *Baby Snakes* shows of 1977, but the sound and complexity of Zappa's music is light years away from that picture. Zappa's performance is much more serious, and he's less physically congenial with the audience than before. This is Zappa in stark contrast to the nostalgic era of Ronald Reagan: edgy, assertive, and unrepentant. His performance on "Dumb All Over" is delivered with just enough cayenne pepper to make his point about televangelists effective, as he warns his audience, "Don't let them get ya." The playing is remarkably tight, the band having come to this concert with over two dozens shows under their belt, and the result is a visual testament to the exceptional talent Zappa was able to assemble under one roof.

Dub Room Special!

Released in 1982, this compilation video reaches back to performances from 1974, featuring some animation by Bruce Bickford and a segment in the dub room of a company called Compact Video, home to two-inch, one-inch, and three-quarter-inch tape machines. Zappa dons a special hat with a PZM microphone attached to it to introduce the various technicians who work at the company. *Dub Room Special!* was intended as a self-contained television show directed by Zappa and is more for the fans than for new audiences.

Does Humor Belong in Music?

This performance video from 1984 is much more buoyant and genuinely funnier than *The Torture Never Stops*. The addition of Ike Willis to the band adds levity to the show, which was taped in front a packed house at the Pier in New York. Interview footage is spliced into the presentation, too, as Zappa comments on the Republican Party and his two favorite foods, coffee and cigarettes. The video closes with a killer version of the Allman Brothers hit "Whippin' Post." It's not a slick production, but it is entertaining.

Video from Hell

This "concept video" from 1987 shows Zappa in full control of the medium from start to finish. It's a focused presentation that features a new piece written and performed on the Synclavier, "G-Spot Tornado," and a full-length video of "You Are What You Is" featuring an actor playing Ronald Reagan, who gets electrocuted. The video is essentially about Zappa's growing use of the Synclavier, and we get to see the computer device in action in his home studio. The video also features clips from *200 Motels*, some home movies taken by Zappa, and some rare footage of the Mothers of Invention rehearsing songs for *We're Only in It for the Money*. One of the highlights is a clip from Zappa's 1973 appearance on the Australian talk show *Adelaide Tonight*. The way he conducts the audience and the band gives us a better understanding of Zappa's process of composition. The video concludes with Zappa's testimony at the Maryland State Legislature in February 1986, during a debate over censorship laws (covered in more detail in chapter 30).

Uncle Meat

Work on this film first started in 1968, when Zappa decided he wanted to make a film of the original Mothers of Invention. The cinematographer was Haskell Wexler, who offered five days of his services for free. Wexler, an Academy Award winner, had used two of Zappa's songs in the documentary *Medium Cool*, released the same year.

Uncle Meat movie features concert footage from the Festival Hall in London, attached to a bizarre love story with Don Preston as a mad scientist and Phyllis Altenhaus (who worked at MGM Records as a secretary) as his love interest. Financial issues halted production, leading Zappa to turn to other projects, but it was finally finished and released in 1988. The film is characteristically bizarre, but the performance footage still holds up, even by contemporary standards.

The True Story of Frank Zappa's 200 Motels

In an effort to demystify and correct the public record about his first major motion picture, Zappa released this one-hour documentary in 1989. As of this writing, it is only available on VHS. The video reveals some of the confusion around shooting a movie with little rehearsal and only about a week of filming. Zappa shares some previously unseen footage, including a short conversation with Tony Palmer, the British director who helped Zappa realize the picture. Overall, it's a pretty good addition to the finished movie.

The Amazing Mr. Bickford

In an effort to celebrate the works of animator Bruce Bickford, Zappa released this compilation video. It features Bickford's Claymation films as well as some previously released material from *Baby Snakes* and *A Token of His Extreme*. The movie is soundtracked by music from Zappa's classical album *The Perfect Stranger*, conducted by Pierre Boulez. The result is a sound/picture study of Bickford's creations that often works well, although the incongruity of the music, which was written and recorded under a completely different circumstance, doesn't always supplement the moving images. Nevertheless, the world would not have heard of Bickford at all had it not been for Frank Zappa. Bickford continues to make animated films using a 35mm camera in his garage, in between creating graphic novels. He currently lives and works in the small town of SeaTac, Washington, a suburb of Seattle.

Classic Albums: *Apostrophe (') and Over-Nite Sensation*

Released after Zappa's death, this short video from 2007 gives us an inside look into how these albums were made and features interviews with Dweezil, Moon, and Gail Zappa, who enhance the story and Zappa's process. The DVD has a very good segment on the Vault featuring curator Joe Travers. Featured interviews with Alice Cooper, Steve Vai, and Warren Cuccurullo give a better sense of Zappa the man and how he worked with people. One of the many highlights is Zappa's performance of "I'm the Slime" from *Saturday Night Live* in 1976—the best three-minute version you'll ever see.

29

A Medium with His Message

Selected TV Appearances

F rank Zappa rarely turned down a TV appearance. He understood the reach of television and its power as a promotional medium, especially for his music. He was also a pretty good talker who wasn't afraid to express his ideas and political opinions, or anything else a host would care to talk about. A plethora of video clips are available online, but these selected TV appearances show off Zappa's candor and talent as an artist, and how he used other people's shows as his platform. As of this writing, all of these appearances can be seen on YouTube.

The Steve Allen Show

It all started on *The Steve Allen Show* on March 4, 1963. Allen was a successful comedian, musician, composer, and writer. He was the first host of NBC's *Tonight Show* from 1954 to 1957 (when it was based in New York). By 1963 he was in Hollywood, hosting a syndicated variety show with announcer Johnny Jacobs and bandleader Donn Trenner. Allen was famous for his quick wit, intelligence, and vast knowledge of music and dance.

Frank Zappa was twenty-two years of age when he appeared on the program as a novelty act of the kind audiences expected to see and hear on Allen's show. Zappa simply came and told the audience he could play a bicycle. But his appearance was significantly different because it engaged the band, the host, and two bicycles in a rich display of sounds and spoken word that was perfect for television.

Zappa came with a prepared tape from Studio Z featuring the sounds of his first wife Kay Sherman trying to play clarinet. His sixteen-minute appearance tells us a lot about Zappa and what he's up to. In the Q&A with

A young Frank Zappa with Steve Allen.   *Photofest*

Allen, he calls himself a "composer" and reveals that he's just finished scoring a movie called *The World's Greatest Sinner*, produced and directed by Tim
Carey and featuring a fifty-five-piece orchestra. He then demonstrates the
sounds he can get out of a bicycle, which is followed by a performance with
Allen playing one bike with a bow, Zappa on the other with drum sticks,
and the band making unusual, non-musical noises with their instruments.
Heard underneath is Zappa's audio recording, as produced in Studio Z. It's

a wonderful scene that actually succeeds on many levels, but most importantly it reveals Zappa's interest in experimenting with unusual sounds to make music. He made a follow-up appearance in 1968 with the Mothers of Invention.

The Mike Douglas Show

On November 11, 1976, Zappa was a guest on *The Mike Douglas Show*, a syndicated talk show produced in Philadelphia. The show was broadcast in the late afternoon on the East Coast and was probably seen by teenagers after school. Like Steve Allen, Mike Douglas came from the world of music, having been the singer in Kay Kyser's big band. He was a good listener, and his interviews were very conversational. He never used cue cards, and he dropped the use of a desk, as was common among other talk-show hosts, such as Johnny Carson. Removing this barrier likely allowed guests to feel more relaxed on Douglas's show. This is particularly true with Zappa's appearance, as Douglas is prepared to talk about his guest's musical origins, what he looks for in a musician, and what he listens to when he wants to "really relax." The two-segment appearance is highlighted by a performance of "Black Napkins" with the house band and a clip from Zappa's own television special, *A Token of His Extreme*. Zappa introduces the segment by animator Bruce Bickford for a portion of "Inca Roads." The segment was later included on the DVD release of the film as a bonus chapter.

Monday Conference

One of Zappa's most interesting appearances was on the ABC network in Sydney, Australia, on July 2, 1973, on *Monday Conference*, a weekly current-affairs program. The host was Robert Moore, who led a discussion with a panel of young men and women quizzing Zappa about the cultural implications of rock music from a social and political perspective. The questions are challenging, contemporary, and often funny. Zappa loved these open forums, especially if the audience was looking to have an adult conversation.

CNN Crossfire

Ted Turner's Cable News Network (CNN) was one of Frank Zappa's favorite channels to watch—and occasionally mock. *Crossfire*, which ran on the

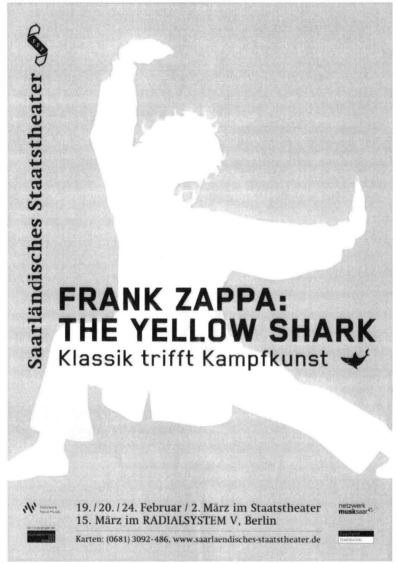

Advertisement for a performance of *The Yellow Shark*.

network for over twenty years, was a nightly thirty-minute debate program. In 1986, it was co-hosted "on the left" by Tom Braden and "on the right" by Robert Novak. The debate wasn't necessarily always balanced, but they did at least try. On the night Frank Zappa appeared he was put up against *Washington Times* columnist John Lofton on the subject of objectionable lyrics in pop songs. The program was caustic at times, but Zappa seems to prevail on the subject of censorship and the right to free speech, among other topics, in between interruptions from Lofton or Novak. It's one of the most popular Zappa segments on YouTube.

The Today Show

Frank Zappa's last television interview was broadcast on NBC on May 14, 1993. Katie Couric was the host and Jamie Gangel conducted the interview. This time, Zappa's health was the subject of the conversation, but Gangel does ask him about his use of the Synclavier and a recent performance of *The Yellow Shark* in Germany. Zappa's answers are short but candid.

30

User Discretion Advised

Zappa and the Politics of Censorship

F rank Zappa wasn't afraid to wear his political heart on his sleeve. The 1966 debut double album by the Mothers of Invention, *Freak Out!*, is laden with songs about freak culture but it also includes "Trouble Every Day," Zappa's comment on the infamous Watts riots, which had taken place in Los Angeles the year before.

The Watts riots were front-page news and made national TV broadcasts. Zappa's song reflected his feelings on the inequalities felt by many Americans and the sometimes-dangerous enforcement of the law. He had reason to be upset: thirty-four people died, more than 1,000 were injured, and some 3,438 were arrested. An investigation later revealed that there was serious unemployment in the community in the lead-up to the riots, which were triggered by social unrest and allegations of police discrimination, especially against the black residents. (The recent upheavals in Ferguson, Missouri, in 2014, and Baltimore, Maryland, in 2015, have a lot in common with the Watts riots.)

Politics

Frank Zappa had an engaging if sometimes contradictory take on politics. On the one hand, he was a firm believer in Article I of the US Bill of Rights, and he abhorred government interference in people's lives. On the other hand, he hated street demonstrations as a means of protest, peaceful or otherwise, believing that citizens should try to "change the system from within" by participating in democracy, either by voting or running for office. That did not necessarily tally, though, with the radical look of his band and the razor-sharp cutups of government officials and religious leaders in his songs. In other words, Zappa appeared to be *against* more things than he was *for*. To add to the confusion, he even admitted that he was a conservative during his appearance on CNN's *Crossfire* in 1986.

What do we make of all this? An answer can be found in Zappa's views on censorship.

Zappa and the Constitution

For Frank Zappa, Article I of the US Bill of Rights offered words to live by. Just before his testimony at the 1985 Senate hearing on regulation of lyrical content, he pulled out the exact text on a small piece of paper and read it into the record. These words were important to Zappa because everything he did in film, music, videos, concerts, and books challenged the very notion of freedom of speech. In his excellent liner notes to Zappa's handpicked compilation album *Have I Offended Someone?*, Ed Sanders of the Fugs states that Zappa was using his "guaranteed freedom in ways no other American . . . had ever done." For Zappa, any kind of censorship violated the Bill of Rights, and he spoke out against such violations in the United States and other countries.

One of the biggest tests of that defense came in 1985.

Tipper Gore and the PMRC Crusade

Tipper Gore was the wife of Al Gore, at the time, a state senator for Tennessee. One day, she walked into a record store to buy the album *Purple Rain* by Prince for her eight-year-old daughter and was later shocked and appalled when her daughter pointed out the song "Darling Nikki" and its overt lyrics about sex and masturbation. Gore reacted so strongly that she called a few of her D.C.–based friends and formed the Parents Music Resource Center (PMRC). Her co-founders were Susan Baker, Pam Hower, and Sally Nevius. The purpose of the organization was to draw awareness to what Gore and the others considered explicit content in rock songs. In a nutshell, they wanted some rules to govern the sale of music to children. The PMRC had no formal membership, but they did take donations. The group came up with a list of fifteen songs it considered offensive and dangerous to kids and used this list to promote its agenda. (None of Zappa's songs were on the list.)

Zappa's response to censorship, fully guaranteed.

In May 1985, the PMRC sent a letter outlining its concerns to the president of the Recording Industry Association of America (RIAA), whose name was Stanley Gortikov. Gortikov refused to participate in any action. The group then approached the president of the National Association of Broadcasters (NAB), Edward Fritts, who sympathized with their cause. Fritts unilaterally contacted record companies and asked them to send complete lyric sheets to radio station program directors, who could then judge for themselves which songs were suitable for broadcast.

It's important to note that the PMRC did not want to censor music, only to provide parents with the "tools" necessary for them to make the right purchases for their kids. All of this activity would have blown over but for a tiny piece of legislation being considered at the same time regarding a tax on the sale of blank cassette tapes, House Resolution 2911 (H.R. 2911). This bill was being considered in the House of Representatives at the same time the PMRC was making noise. One of the sponsors of the bill, which was set to add millions of dollars in revenue to record companies, was Al Gore.

This apparent conflict of interest seemed to go unnoticed by everyone except Frank Zappa. His fear was that the recording industry would overlook the implications of the PMRC to make sure H.R. 2911 was passed. Zappa was so incensed by what he viewed as the "extortion" taking place that he wrote a two-page letter to President Ronald Reagan, appealing to his steadfast position on constitutional affairs. The letter wasn't answered.

During the summer of 1985, Zappa took to the media. He appeared on talk shows such as *Larry King Live* on CNN, *Nightwatch* with Charlie Rose on CBS, and *Nightline* with Ted Koppel on ABC. Zappa was now speaking to middle-class households, standing up for freedom of speech, and he wasn't afraid to debate the issue. What he struggled with was the fact that Tipper Gore's campaign had nothing to do with Article I of the Bill of Rights. For Zappa, her campaign, and that of the PMRC, was a disguised moral crusade. However, President Reagan fully backed the organization's cause when he said in a speech that people in rock music were "pornographers." To some observers, Reagan commandeered the moral agenda for political gain when he ran for office. In the fall, when the publicity and national conversation increased, the Senate Committee on Commerce, Science, and Transportation decided to have a hearing on the matter.

Frank Zappa at the Senate Committee Hearings

On September 19, 1985, Zappa decided to put his money where his mouth was and testify before a Senate committee on special labeling for the lyrical content of records in a packed room in Washington, D.C. Senator John Danforth chaired the committee, which heard from Zappa, John Denver, Dee Snider of Twisted Sister, and the founders of the Parents Music Resource Center, PMRC, led by Tipper Gore, wife of then-senator Al Gore, who also sat on the committee.

As a strong believer in freedom of speech, Frank Zappa was disgusted by the idea of a movie-style ratings system for music, and he appeared before the committee to tell them so. He decided to take the high ground by appearing with short hair in a dark suit with a red tie. His five-page testimony offers some important insights into Zappa's skeptical political beliefs and his principles regarding the first amendment of the US Bill of Rights. The half-hour presentation, which included a short Q&A session with members of the committee, is full of the kind of sarcastic humor typical of a Zappa speech. He criticized the PMRC for its extreme measures regarding song lyrics, calling its plan an attack on free speech and the rights of artists to express themselves. Looking at the big picture—about which Zappa was fairly astute—he also stated that the PMRC was a diversionary tactic set up to see the passage of H. R. 2911, adding that record companies wanted that bill to go through because all they could see was dollar signs. It was also a bit of television theater, since the room was packed with photographers, reporters, and citizens, all curious to know what Mr. Zappa had to say. (The C-SPAN website's archives offer the four-hour session in its entirety, giving viewers the opportunity to get both sides of the story.)

Frank Zappa Meets the Mothers of Prevention

For the rest of the year and well into 1986, Zappa continued to be invited to discuss censorship on radio and TV talk shows and news programs in the United States, Germany, and Austria. He appeared on some local cable programs in L.A. and even on the new Joan Rivers show on FOX. To top it off, he released the album *Frank Zappa Meets the Mothers of Prevention* on November 21, 1985. The album was put together quickly, but it was Zappa's firm statement on the PMRC, the Senate Committee hearings of which he was a part, and the record industry, which had conceded to put stickers on its product to indicate whether "explicit" material was enclosed. (Apple's iTunes music service uses similar labels today, with some records, especially by hip-hop artists, offering clean or explicit versions for your entertainment dollar, and, presumably, the safety of your children.)

The highlight of *Frank Zappa Meets the Mothers of Prevention* is the twelve-minute "Porn Wars." Zappa obtained the complete audio transcript of the Senate hearings and spliced together a mash-up of the verbal exchanges and speeches made during his appearance. Underneath it all is an original soundtrack he created on the Synclavier, as well as excerpts from his album *Thing-Fish*. Zappa goes on to explain why he values freedom of speech and why his album won't hurt the customer. He then closes the guarantee with a shot at the PMRC and the "video fundamentalists" who he felt were only interested in taking people's money.

Frank Zappa Meets the Mothers of Prevention isn't the strongest album in his discography, but it does reveal his position on censorship loud and clear. And, in the spirit of full disclosure, he even added his own "Warning Guarantee" sticker to the jacket: "This album contains material which a truly free society would neither fear nor suppress."

The Religious Right

Talk of censorship soon moved to include another topic close to Zappa's heart: the rise of the Moral Majority on the religious right and its growing influence in shaping government legislation. It was a subject he hinted at years earlier when speaking to Wayne Manor of the *New Music Express* in an interview published on July 22, 1978. Zappa was beginning to connect the political dots, as it were. "I see that people are drifting toward the right today, in a very hypocritical way . . . the whole right-wing trend is people who want to look upstanding while they go home and do as much weird stuff as they can get away with." Presumably this included politicians.

Zappa wasn't necessarily a prophet but it's interesting to look at the politics of America today in the context of his comments. Space limits this author from going down that rabbit hole, except to cite one song that best describes Zappa's position: "Jesus Thinks You're a Jerk" from *Broadway the Hard Way*. It's a stinging indictment of the American system being hijacked by the lunatic fringe of the religious right. It's so funny it's frightening.

Frank Zappa wasn't afraid to engage in politics or hide behind the veil of artistic expression in lieu of real participation. He was an astute follower of American politics, and he always questioned the motives of politicians, especially when they threatened freedom of speech. He even considered running for office in 1992, but his failing health didn't allow it.

31

Yearbook Signing

Zappa Alumni

Frank Zappa liked musicians if they were on time, learned his compositions, and stayed away from drugs during tours and recording sessions. The latter rule was strictly enforced.

When Howard Kaylan joined the band in 1970, he got a stern warning from Zappa just before rehearsals were to start for an upcoming tour. Kaylan, one half of the Flo and Eddie duo with Mark Volman, talks about his first encounter with Zappa in his memoir, *Shell Shocked*. He and Volman were so excited about playing with Zappa that they arrived early to the first rehearsal. They were heavy pot smokers, however, so to cool their anxiety they smoked several joints beforehand. When Zappa arrived, he immediately took notice of the aroma in the studio and gave them a stern warning: "Around here we have rules . . . there is to be no marijuana smoking in this studio."

Kaylan understood this to mean that he and Volman could smoke "outside" the studio instead. But Zappa was unrelenting. "My music is serious," Kaylan recalls him saying. "This tour is serious . . . if I catch you guys smoking dope, I'll test you right then and there. And I'll never bail you out. You get caught at some border crossing, you're on your own; I don't know you. Get it?"

Kaylan and Volman certainly "got it." Some other musicians didn't, however, and continued to mess with the performance expectations Zappa required in order to play his music correctly. In 1966, Zappa actually fired guitarist Elliot Ingber just before a concert. The story, according to Don Preston, was that Ingber was so high that he was attempting to tune his electric guitar without turning on his amplifier. A watching Zappa quickly put the absurdity to rest and dismissed Ingber.

Zappa usually hired players who knew how to read music and were highly skilled on their instruments. The prolific composer demanded nothing less. One of the finest of these was Robert (or Bobby) Martin. Schooled at the prestigious Curtis Institute of Music in Philadelphia, Martin could read music for piano, French horn, and alto saxophone. He was able to quickly transpose Zappa's music into the right key in order to play it. In fact, at his audition in 1981, Martin was required to sight read, cold, music for all three instruments, as well as sing.

On top of this, Zappa required his musicians to memorize everything before going on tour. It was a gig that required a lot of discipline. In 1976, for instance, Zappa auditioned fifty people before he selected the final players. One of these was a female vocalist by the name of Bianca Thornton, who, as Zappa recalled in a March 1977 interview with the *International Times*, eventually had to leave the band because the work was so demanding. "She was a great singer, great through rehearsals, but just couldn't handle it."

In spite of all this, this selective list shows the depth and range of Zappa's band members. Their roles involved not only proficiency on a particular instrument but something unique about each player, such as an ability to juggle or make unusual sounds. Zappa's music was about breaking conventions and expectations, and he often looked for musicians ready to take risks to get his musical ideas across to an unsuspecting public.

Mike Altschul (b. 1945), piccolo, flute, clarinet, saxophone, and trumpet

Altschul was a session player who participated in Zappa's larger, jazz-oriented recordings from 1972 to 1981. Before he joined Zappa's Grand Wazoo band, he gained considerable experience playing for Don Ellis and Stan Kenton on a steady basis. Altschul plays on *The Grand Wazoo*, *Studio Tan*, and *Orchestral Favorites*. His most significant contribution is as multi-instrumentalist on "Waka/Jawaka." As an arranger, he was also a valuable member of the L.A.-based ensemble Abnuceals Emuukha Electric Symphony Orchestra, which played on *Orchestral Favorites* and *Lumpy Gravy*.

Arthur Barrow (b. 1952), bass

Barrow played bass in Zappa's touring band and made significant contributions to his recordings between 1978 and 1985. His most outstanding performance can be heard on the live album *Buffalo*, especially on "You Are What You Is." Barrow held the title of rehearsal director (or "clonemeister") in preparation for tours. In Zappa's bands, the clonemeister is the equivalent to the concertmaster of an orchestra. While it is a prestigious position in a symphony orchestra, it really wasn't in Zappa's band, because the job was primarily to act as the foreman of the group, pointing out musical mistakes and making sure the songs were played correctly from the original recordings, every time. Barrow often recorded the shows on a cassette recorder for playback to hear how the group sounded on certain songs. If a song sounded "shit," Zappa would take it out of the set, which gave Barrow a clue as to how to do the job.

In a 1992 interview with the Zappa fanzine *T'Mershi Duween*, Barrow revealed that Zappa insisted on having the band learn nearly 200 songs, from which a concert set would then be chosen. During the rehearsal stage, Zappa would indicate which songs were the strongest based on the amount of time invested in their rehearsal.

Barrow didn't like some of the songs Zappa wrote, so he pushed the band to practice only the songs that he liked to hear, such as "You Are What You Is." Says Barrow, "The songs that I didn't like, the songs that I thought were dumb, like 'The Torture [Never Stops],' my least favourite Frank Zappa song ever . . . I never rehearsed the band at all. And the ones I did like, such as 'Florentine Pogen' and 'Inca Roads,' we rehearsed the shit out of every day. Made them sound really good. So when Frank would call out 'Ms. Pinky,' he'd say, 'It sounds horrible; you can take that off the list,' and I would just chuckle to myself. So that meant the tour was comprised of all my favourite songs." Barrow continues to lead Zappa cover bands today, presumably playing his favorite songs.

Website: http://home.netcom.com/~bigear/

Adrian Belew (b. 1949), guitar, vocals

Belew's tenure with Zappa was short but significant. Zappa discovered him at a club in Nashville, Tennessee, and immediately him invited to audition. Belew had only one week to prepare but impressed Zappa with both his guitar wizardry and his Roy Orbison impression. His combination of unique guitar sound and strong tenor vocals are best heard on "City of Tiny Lites" from *Sheik Yerbouti*, released in 1979. Another fine example of his complementary guitar playing can be heard in full force on the three-CD set *Hammersmith Odeon*, recorded in 1978 but not released until 2010.

Adrian Belew.   *Photofest*

Belew went on to play with David Bowie, King Crimson, and the Bears. He continues to play in Europe and the United States with his own trio.

Website: www.adrianbelew.net

Max Bennett (b. 1928), bass

Bennett played for Zappa just after the breakup of the Mothers of Invention in 1969, appearing on *Hot Rats*, *Chunga's Revenge*, and *Studio Tan*. His claim to fame came when he got the chance to play with jazz legend Charlie Parker in 1950 after Parker's regular bass player, Tommy Potter, failed to show up for a gig. That unexpected career change launched Bennett into the jazz genre, which was America's music before the advent of rock 'n' roll. Bennett later played and recorded with Stan Kenton, Quincy Jones, and Peggy Lee.

While with Lee, Bennett took up the electric bass, which would get him more work during the sixties. He was working exclusively in Los Angeles by the time he got a call from his friend John Guerin, asking him to play on Zappa's *Hot Rats*. Guerin and Bennett are the rhythm section on "Willie the Pimp" and "Little Umbrellas," while Bennett also plays bass on "Son of Mr. Green Genes" and "The Gumbo Variations."

In a *Los Angeles Times* interview published in 1991, Bennett spoke highly of his time with Zappa, stating, "I was impressed with it; it was the forerunner of what the L.A. Express was going to be, in that contemporary vein of stretching out in a jazz-rock concept."

Bennett never worked for Zappa again, but in 1972 he joined the L.A. Express under leader Tom Scott. His versatility also got him work for a wide variety of singers and bandleaders in pop, R&B, jazz, and country. He's now retired from the music business. Guerin, meanwhile, later hooked up with Joni Mitchell and played with her touring band in the mid-seventies. He died in 2004 of a heart attack.

John Bergamo (1940–2013), percussion

Bergamo can be heard on *Zappa in New York*, *Studio Tan*, and *Orchestral Favorites*. His most important contribution to music may very well be the formation of a band called the Repercussion Unit in 1976. That group also included Ed Mann, who played for Zappa from 1977 to 1988. Bergamo knew Zappa and was inspired by his percussion-focused compositions, like "The Black Page." He introduced Mann to Zappa in 1974. In 1980, Bergamo founded the California Institute of Arts (CalArts) percussion program, which he led for the next thirty-three years, until his death in 2013.

Jimmy Carl Black (1938–2008), drums, vocals

"The Indian of the group," as he introduces himself on *We're Only in It for the Money*, Black was of Cheyenne ancestry and played with the original Mothers of Invention from 1965 to 1969. Originally from El Paso, Texas, Black had a background in R&B, which lent a particular style to Zappa's early music in the Soul Giants, but it was his entertaining personality that added value to the live performances of the MOI and the first few albums, especially *We're Only in It for the Money*.

After leaving the Mothers, Black continued to play Zappa's music in cover bands like the Grandmothers with great success in Europe, where he remained a fan favorite right up until his death from cancer in 2008. He is best remembered for his endearing, no-nonsense point-of-view and his light demeanor. In response to Zappa's promise to make the Soul Giants "rich and famous," Black famously retorted, "He took care of half that promise. He made me famous but he damn sure didn't make me rich." Stefan Hörterer, a fan based in Germany, maintains a website in Black's name at www.jimmy-carlblack.com. His memoir, *For Mother's Sake*, was published in 2013.

Terry Bozzio (b. 1950), drums, percussion, vocals

Terry Bozzio played with Zappa from 1975 to 1984 and could be considered the hardest working man in Zappa history. Zappa composed "The Black Page"—a sophisticated piece, first heard on *Zappa in New York*, for which every drum roll and tom and cymbal crash was written into the scores—specifically for him. In a 2010 video interview, Bozzio said, "I chipped away at it for about fifteen minutes a day for about a week before I could play it for him." It was to become his signature piece, not only with the Zappa touring bands of the late seventies but also with his own solo drum performances.

As well as appearing on *Zappa in New York*, Bozzio can also be heard on *Bongo Fury*, *Zoot Allures*, *Studio Tan*, *Sleep Dirt*, *Sheik Yerbouti*, *Joe's Garage*, *Orchestral Favorites*, *Baby Snakes*, and *Thing-Fish*, and on five of the six releases that make up the *You Can't Do That on Stage Anymore* series. Bozzio was a favorite of fans around the world for his unique rendering of "Punky's Whips," as seen in *Baby Snakes*. After his tenure with Zappa, Bozzio and

Jimmy Carl Black, the Indian of the group. *Rex*

his wife Dale formed the group Missing Persons, who were just as popular for appearance as their music. He currently tours solo with an enormous drum set.

Website: www.terrybozzio.com

Michael Brecker (1949–2007), saxophone
Randy Brecker (b. 1945), trumpet

The Grammy-winning Brecker Brothers, as they were known, appear on *Zappa in New York* (1976) and *Läther* (released in 1996). While their contribution to these albums was small, Michael and Randy made significant contributions to jazz as composers and performers and were among the most sought-after session players well into the nineties. They also followed separate solo careers as leaders and sidemen.

Website: www.randybrecker.com

Napoleon Murphy Brock (b. 1945), saxophone, flute, vocals

Zappa discovered Brock in 1973, at a gig in Waikiki, Hawaii. He was impressed by the range of Brock's voice and his showmanship, which would prove important for the band's stage presentations. As a lead singer, Brock became the *de facto* front man for Zappa's band, with his stage presence best seen and heard on the DVD *A Token of His Extreme*, recorded in 1974. Brock used everything he learned as a vocalist on Zappa's music, namely, gospel, R&B, and blues. He played and recorded with Zappa from 1974 to 1984, and can be heard on *Apostrophe (')*, *Bongo Fury*, *Roxy & Elsewhere*, *One Size Fits All*, *Zoot Allures*, *Sleep Dirt*, *Sheik Yerbouti*, *Them or Us*, *Thing-Fish*, and five volumes of the six-part series *You Can't Do That on Stage Anymore*.

Popular with the fans, Brock was invited to perform with the Zappa Plays Zappa band led by Dweezil Zappa in 2006. In an interview posted on www.gratefulweb.com in 2012, he revealed that he agreed to appear as a tribute to Frank to show gratitude for what he had done for him, but he had some harsh words about Dweezil. "He's okay, he's got the name, he's got Frank Zappa's name, but he really doesn't know the music, he really doesn't know it. He doesn't know the concept, that's the sad part."

Website: www.napoleonmbrock.com

Paul Carman (b. 1945), saxophone

Carman played soprano, alto, and baritone sax in Zappa's big band in 1988. Carman's claim to fame was his ability to play the famous Jimmy Page guitar solo to "Stairway to Heaven" by Led Zeppelin on his sax. Zappa liked it and asked him to arrange it for the horn section. A reggae version of the piece closes the album *The Best Band You've Never Heard in Your Life*. He currently leads the Paul Carman Quarket+1 and is a teacher at the Idyllwild Arts Academy in Idyllwild, California.

Vinnie Colaiuta (b. 1956), drums

Colaiuta auditioned for Zappa when he was twenty-two years of age and passed with flying colors, according to Steve Vai, who said the drummer was one of the best sight-readers "who ever existed on the instrument." This is Vai's eyewitness account of a rehearsal with Zappa of the complex song "Mo' and Herb's Vacation" from 1981, as recalled to *Drum!* magazine in 2013:

> It's unbelievably complex. All the drums were written out, just like "The Black Page," except even more complex. There were these runs of like 17/3 and every drumhead is notated differently . . . Vinnie had this piece of music on the stand to his right. To his left he had another music stand with a plate of sushi on it, okay? Now the tempo of the piece was very slow, like "The Black Page." And then the first riff came in . . . with all these choking of cymbals, and hi-hat, ruffs, spinning of rototoms and all this crazy stuff . . . Well I saw him look at this one bar of music, it was the last bar of music on the page. He started to play it as he was turning the page with one hand, and then once the page was turned he continued playing the riff with his right hand, as he reached over with his left hand, grabbed a piece of sushi and put it in his mouth, continued the riff with his left hand and feet, pushed his glasses up, and then played the remaining part of the bar.

Vai summed up the performance as "the sickest thing I have ever seen."

Colaiuta toured and recorded with Zappa from 1979 to 1983. He can be heard on *Joe's Garage, Tinsel Town Rebellion, Shut up 'n Play Yer Guitar, The Man from Utopia, Guitar, Buffalo,* and *Any Way the Wind Blows*, as well as Vol. 1, 4, and 6 of *You Can't Do That on Stage Anymore*. Schooled at Berklee College of Music in Boston, Massachusetts, Colaiuta has recorded with Joni Mitchell and Sting, and continues to work as a session musician to this day.

Website: www.vinniecolaiuta.com

Ray Collins (1936–2012), vocals, harmonica

Ray Collins first met Frank Zappa in 1962, when he was the lead vocalist with the Soul Giants, an R&B band that became the Mothers of Invention after Zappa joined. Collins was a versatile singer whose agile range and sweet falsetto graced the early MOI recordings. He is heard on *Freak Out!*, *Absolutely Free*, *Cruising with Ruben & the Jets*, *Uncle Meat*, *Burnt Weeny Sandwich*, *Weasels Ripped My Flesh*, and *Apostrophe (')*, and on selected tracks from *You Can't Do That on Stage: Vol. 5*. He can also be heard on some pre-Mothers recordings, including the first-rate *Joe's Corsage* (released in 2004). He died of a heart attack on December 24, 2012.

Warren Cuccurullo (b. 1956), guitar, vocals

Cuccurullo was a huge fan of Zappa's music in his teens and often travelled to concerts within a day's journey of his Brooklyn home. Following an introduction by Terry Bozzio, Cuccurullo was invited to audition for Zappa's 1978 touring band. He played with Zappa until 1980, when he left to form Missing Persons with Bozzio. He is seen on the video *Baby Snakes* and heard as second guitarist on *Joe's Garage*, *Shut Up 'n Play Yer Guitar*, *Tinsel Town Rebellion*, *Guitar*, *Any Way the Wind Blows*, and Vol. 1, 4, and 6 of *You Can't Do That on Stage Anymore*.

Website: www.cuccurullo.tv

George Duke (1946–2013), keyboards, vocals

George Duke was already a seasoned jazz musician when he met and auditioned for Frank Zappa in 1970. A graduate of the San Francisco Conservatory of Music, Duke apprenticed with the Don Ellis Orchestra and Julian "Cannonball" Adderley and knew Zappa's music well when he was asked to join the band with Flo and Eddie. He recorded and toured with Zappa until 1979, when he decided to pursue a solo career as a composer and sideman.

Duke appears as principal keyboardist and vocalist on *Chunga's Revenge*, *200 Motels*, *Waka/Jawaka*, *The Grand Wazoo*, *Over-Nite Sensation*, *Apostrophe (')*, *Roxy & Elsewhere*, *One Size Fits All*, *Bongo Fury*, *Studio Tan*, *Sleep Dirt*, and *Them or Us*. His remarkable lead vocal on "Inca Roads" is considered one of his finest performances in the Zappa canon. He also appears on *You Can't*

Do That on Stage Anymore, Vol. 2 (aka *The Stockholm Concert*) and the archival releases *Läther, Road Tapes, Venue #2*, and *Roxy by Proxy*, and in the videos *The Dub Room Special* and *A Token of His Extreme*. He died of leukemia in 2013.

Aynsley Dunbar (b. 1946), drums

Dunbar started his professional career at age seventeen, making a name for himself in pop and blues circles following a stint with John Mayall in 1967. He also led his own prog-rock band, Blue Whale, and hooked up with Zappa in 1970 after a jam session at a music festival in Belgium. Dunbar was a key member Zappa's band with Flo and Eddie, which toured extensively in the early seventies. He lived in the Zappa home for his first nine months in the United States. When Zappa introduced him to people, he always remarked that Dunbar sounded like "two drummers."

Dunbar is heard on *Chunga's Revenge, Fillmore East, June 1971, 200 Motels, Just Another Band from L.A., Waka/Jawaka, The Grand Wazoo, Apostrophe ('),* and Vol. 1, 3, and 6 of *You Can't Do That on Stage Anymore*. He's also heard on the archival releases *Playground Psychotics, The Lost Episodes, Joe's Domage,* and *Quaudiophiliac.*

Website: www.aynsleydunbar.com

Roy Estrada (b. 1943), bass, vocals

Roy Estrada was a member of the Soul Giants when guitarist Frank Zappa joined the band in 1965. He continued to play bass in the renamed Mothers/ Mothers of Invention until 1969, when Zappa dissolved the group. He went on to form Little Feat with Lowell George, and in 2002, he formed the Grandmothers with Don Preston to play the music of Frank Zappa. After two felony convictions for sexual assault, he took a plea bargain for child abuse in 2012 and is currently serving a twenty-five-year sentence without parole in Texas.

Estrada can be heard on *Freak Out!, Absolutely Free, We're Only in It for the Money, Lumpy Gravy, Cruising with Ruben & the Jets, Uncle Meat, Burnt Weeny Sandwich, Weasels Ripped My Flesh, Zoot Allures, Shut Up 'n Play Yer Guitar, Ship Arriving Too Late to Save a Drowning Witch, The Man from Utopia, Baby Snakes, Them or Us, Thing-Fish,* and Vol. 1, 3, 5, and 6 of *You Can't Do That on Stage Anymore*. He also appears as a character on *Civilization Phaze III* and on the archival releases *The Lost Episodes*, *Mystery Disc*, *FZ:OZ*, *Joe's Corsage*, and *Quaudiophiliac*.

Bruce Fowler (b. 1947), trombone

Fowler is one of three siblings who played with Frank Zappa; the others are Tom and Walt. Their father was jazz educator and musician William Fowler (1917–2009). Bruce first joined Zappa's instrumental group known as the Petit Wazoo and stayed with Zappa until 1979 before returning to play in the '88 big band. He can be heard on *Over-Nite Sensation*, *Apostrophe (')*, *Roxy & Elsewhere*, *Bongo Fury*, *Zoot Allures*, *Studio Tan*, *Sleep Dirt*, *Broadway the Hard Way*, *The Best Band You Never Heard in Your Life*, and *Make a Jazz Noise Here*. He's also in the horn section for the archival releases *Imaginary Diseases*, *Trance-Fusion*, and *Wazoo*. Like his brothers, Bruce remains an active recording musician on the L.A. studio scene, while occasionally adding his talent to the Zappa cover group Banned from Utopia, which also features Ike Willis and Arthur Barrow.

Tom Fowler (b. 1951), bass

The younger brother of Bruce and Walt joined Zappa's band in 1973, appearing extensively until 1975. He's on *Over-Nite Sensation*, *Apostrophe (')*, *Roxy & Elsewhere*, *One Size fits All*, *Bongo Fury*, *Studio Tan*, and every release except *Vol. 5* of *You Can't Do That on stage Anymore*. Fowler also appears on the archival releases *Roxy by Proxy*, *The Lost Episodes*, *Läther*, and *Quaudiophiliac*, and can be seen in the videos *The Dub Room Special* and *A Token of His Extreme*. Today, Fowler plays with Banned from Utopia.

Walt Fowler (b. 1949), trumpet, flugelhorn

Walt Fowler played with Zappa on live albums only between 1973 and 1988. He made his debut with the band on *Roxy & Elsewhere* and is also heard on *Broadway the Hard Way*, *The Best Band You Never Heard in Your Life*, *Make a Jazz Noise Here*, and Vol. 4 and 6 of *You Can't Do That on Stage Anymore*. He's also on *Civilization Phaze III* and *Trance-Fusion*. Fowler continues to work as an orchestrator on movie soundtracks and occasionally plays with the James Taylor band.

Website: www.waltfowler.com

Bunk Gardner (b. 1933), clarinet, saxophone, flute, piccolo, bass clarinet

Gardner's real name is John Leon Guarnera, and he was added to the Mothers of Invention when Zappa's compositions grew in complexity, requiring different and more diverse musical instruments than an ordinary popular-music band. Gardner recorded and toured with the MOI from 1967 until 1969. After that, he immediately hooked up with drummer Jimmy Carl Black to form Geronimo Black, who recorded one self-titled album in 1972.

Gardner appears on *Absolutely Free, We're Only in It for the Money, Lumpy Gravy, Cruising with Ruben & The Jets, Uncle Meat, Burnt Weeny Sandwich*, and *Weasels Ripped My Flesh*. He's also heard on the archival releases *Ahead of their Time, Mystery Disc, Finer Moments, Road Tapes, Venue #1*, and Vol. 1, 4, and 5 of *You Can't Do That on Stage Anymore*. In 1981, Gardner, along with vocalist/keyboardist Don Preston, formed the Grandmothers to perform music by Frank Zappa. In 2011, Gardner released a two-part audio memoir, *The Bunk Gardner Story*, also featuring musical contributions by Don Preston. It's available on iTunes.

Website: www.grandmothersofinvention.com

Buzz Gardner (1931–2004), trumpet, flugelhorn

Gardner's real name was Charles, and he was the older brother of Bunk (John), who joined the original Mothers of Invention in 1968. His army buddy Don Preston introduced him to Zappa. Gardner contributed to *Burnt Weeny Sandwich* and *Weasels Ripped My Flesh* and is heard on Vol. 1, 4, and 5 of *You Can't Do That on Stage Anymore*. He also appears on Captain Beefheart's *Trout Mask Replica* (1969). In 1981, he joined the Grandmothers with Don Preston and his brother Bunk.

Lowell George (1945–1979), guitar, vocals

George is best known as the co-founder of Little Feat, the preeminent rock band of the seventies. In 1968, Zappa needed a replacement for lead singer Ray Collins, who had quit the MOI over creative differences, for an upcoming tour, and George, who possessed a remarkable voice and captured the wide-ranging emotional textures of R&B, got the job. Zappa was particularly impressed with George's version of "Here Lies Love," originally recorded in

1955 by the Four Deuces. You can hear the MOI version featuring George on *You Can't Do That on Stage Anymore, Vol. 5*. George also appears on *Hot Rats*, *Burnt Weeny Sandwich*, and *Weasels Ripped My Flesh*, and can be seen in the movie *Uncle Meat*.

Website: www.littlefeat.net

Jim Gordon (b. 1945), drums

Gordon was one of the best-known session drummers of the sixties and seventies. He played for Delaney and Bonnie, George Harrison (*All Things Must Pass*), John Lennon (*Imagine*), Derek and the Dominoes (*Layla*), and Steely Dan (*Pretzel Logic*). Frank Zappa hired him to tour with the twenty-piece Grand Wazoo band in 1972. He appears on *Apostrophe (')*, *Läther*, and the archival releases *Imaginary Diseases* and *Wazoo*.

Gordon was a drug addict who developed undiagnosed schizophrenia. In 1983, during a serious bout of mental health, he murdered his mother, believing she was some kind of demon trying to kill him. Regrettably, California state laws at the time did not allow for an insanity defense, so he was sentenced to sixteen years in prison and was last known to be in a medical corrections facility in Vacaville, California.

Bob Harris (b. 1952), keyboards, vocals

Zappa hired two musicians named Bob Harris during his career. Harris I played with Zappa in 1971; Harris II, who was born in Iowa, joined the touring band in July 1980 and was nicknamed the "boy soprano" for the high range of his voice. Check out "Teenage Wind" and "Fine Girl." Harris can be heard on *Tinsel Town Rebellion*, *Shut Up 'n Play Yer Guitar*, *You Are What You Is*, *Ship Arriving Too Late to Save a Drowning Witch*, *The Man from Utopia*, *Them or Us*, *Thing-Fish* (as Harry), and Vol. 6 of *You Can't Do That on Stage*. He also appears on the archival release *Buffalo*.

Harris's wife Thana was invited to sing on a remix of *Sleep Dirt*. She wrote a memoir of her experience of working with Steve Vai and Frank Zappa called *Under the Same Moon*, in which she tells the story of a young artist coming into her own as a woman and as a singer. She also talks about Vai's daily marathon practice sessions and her working relationship with Zappa.

Don "Sugarcane" Harris (1938–1999), violin, organ, vocals

Harris got his nickname from Johnny Otis, whose look inspired the iconic image of Zappa with moustache and soul patch we know today. Harris's most important contribution to the Zappa catalogue is his remarkable vocal rendition of "Directly from My Heart to You," written by Little Richard, on *Weasels Ripped My Flesh* (1970). Harris can also be heard on *Hot Rats, Burnt Weeny Sandwich, Chunga's Revenge, Apostrophe ('),* and the archival release *The Lost Episodes.*

Ralph Humphrey (b. 1944), drums

Humphrey joined Zappa's band in 1973 following a gig with the Don Ellis Big Band. He appears on *Over-Nite Sensation, Apostrophe ('), Roxy & Elsewhere,* and Vol. 1, 3, 4, and 6 of *You Can't Do That on Stage Anymore.* He's also heard on the archival releases *The Lost Episodes, Läther, One Shot Deal, Understanding America, Road Tapes, Venue #2,* and *Roxy by Proxy.* He's currently the co-director of the drum department at the Los Angeles College of Music (www.lacm.edu).

Elliot Ingber (b. 1941), guitar

Ingber joined the Mothers of Invention in 1966 as second guitarist on *Freak Out!,* but his real claim to fame has to be his participation on an MGM single by Burt Ward, who played Robin on the ABC television series *Batman.* The single, "Boy Wonder I Love You" b/w "Orange Colored Sky," was written and arranged by Frank Zappa. Ingber was fired after he tripped out on LSD before taking the stage with the MOI. He later played with Captain Beefheart and the Magic Band as "Winged Eel Fingerling." He is also heard on *Lumpy Gravy* and the archival releases *The Lost Episodes, Mystery Disc, The MOFO Project,* and *Understanding America.* In 2001, Ingber released an album of his own works called *The 4,* which he made available on CD Baby (www.cdbaby.com).

Eddie Jobson (b. 1955), violin, keyboards

Jobson started playing piano at age seven and violin at the age of eight. By the time he met Frank Zappa in 1976, he was already a working musician, having done time with Curved Air and Roxy Music. In fact, it was during a tour with Roxy Music that Zappa gave him an audition, onstage, in Milwaukee.

Jobson's image graces the cover of *Zoot Allures*, but he's not on the album; he was simply in the band at the time the photo was taken. He can be heard on *Zappa in New York*, *Studio Tan*, *Shut Up 'n Play Yer Guitar*, and the archival releases *Läther*, *Have I Offended Someone?*, and *Philly '76*. He continues to compose and perform, most recently for the thirtieth anniversary of UK, the prog-rock band he formed with drummer and percussionist Bill Bruford (the original drummer in Yes).

Website: www.eddiejobson.com

Howard Kaylan (b. 1947), vocals

Kaylan was one of the founding members of the Turtles, one of the most successful Top 40 bands of the sixties. The group's claim to musical fame is the song "Happy Together," now a part of sixties radio stations and Internet streams around the world. Kaylan and fellow Turtle Mark Volman became known as Flo and Eddie when they joined Zappa's first band after the dissolution of the original Mothers of Invention in 1969. Zappa was reinventing the Mothers of Invention as a vaudeville act aimed at satirizing the entire pop music industry, which he felt was beginning to take itself too seriously in the new decade.

Flo and Eddie toured extensively with the Zappa band for about eighteen months, from 1970 to 1972. They also appear in Zappa's film *200 Motels* and can be heard on *Chunga's Revenge*, *Fillmore East—June 1971*, *Just Another Band from L.A.*, and Vol. 1, 3, and 6 of *You Can't Do That on Stage Anymore*. They also appear on the archival releases *Playground Psychotics*, *Carnegie Hall*, *Understanding America*, and *Finer Moments*.

In 2013, Kaylan released a memoir, *Shell Shocked*, in which he claims that Zappa smoked pot on more than one occasion, and reveals that he almost died in the infamous fire at the Montreux Jazz Festival in 1971, when the band lost everything, except for a cowbell. In the summer of 2015, Kaylan and Volman went on a short American tour to mark their fiftieth year in the music business.

Website: www.howardkaylan.com

Mike Keneally (b. 1961), guitar, keyboards, vocals

At twenty-five years of age, Keneally joined Zappa's last touring group, the 1988 big band. He filled the all-important role of "stunt" guitarist, a chair once held by Steve Vai. In the September 1988 issue of *Musician*, Zappa described the job to Alan di Pena as having two aspects: "to enable me to write guitar parts that I could never play myself" and "to reproduce guitar parts I've done on old records, because I can't sing and play lead guitar at the same time onstage."

Keneally is heard on *Broadway the Hard Way*, *The Best Band You Never Heard in Your Life*, *Make a Jazz Noise Here*, and Vol. 4 and 6 of *You Can't Do That on Stage Anymore*. He's also on the archival releases *Trance-Fusion* and *Understanding America*. Keneally was one of the guitar players to appear on *Zappa's Universe*, a Verve recording of a tribute concert held at the Ritz in New York City in 1991. (Joel Thome conducted the show in collaboration with Zappa, who was too ill to attend.) In 1996, he formed a prog-rock band called Mike Keneally and Beer for Dolphins.

Website: www.keneally.com

Ed Mann (b. 1954), percussion

Mann enjoyed one of the longest tenures in Zappa's band, from 1977 to 1988. He's heard on every album Zappa released during that time, from *Zappa in New York* to *Make a Jazz Noise Here*. He can also be heard on the archival releases *Halloween*, *Quaudiophiliac*, *Trance-Fusion*, *The Dub Room Special*, *One Shot Deal*, *Hammersmith Odeon*, and *Understanding America*, and on the soundtrack to *Baby Snakes*.

Mann succeeded Ruth Underwood—thanks to her personal endorsement—in the all-important role of percussionist, which shaped the sound of Zappa's music on record and in performance. Two great examples come to mind: Mann's complicated marimba run on "Dickie's Such an Asshole" (from *Broadway the Hard Way*) and Underwood's playing on "Inca Roads" (originally on *One Size Fits All* but also heard in a live version on *The Helsinki Concert*).

After Zappa's death in 1993, Mann joined Robert Martin to form the tribute group Banned from Utopia. He's currently in a group called the Z3, with whom he takes Zappa's music and turns it into funk. In a June 2015 story in the *Hartford Courant*, Mann put his band into perspective and explained why Zappa's music continues to engage him. "I like the power of it. I like how loud it is. It's the loudest band in the world. But the energy is really positive, and it's not introspective. They take the music seriously, but they don't take themselves seriously. The compositions are great, and they're a lot of fun to play, we get to do that. But it's really about the jam and the groove, which really hits both ends of it for me."

Website: www.thez3.com

Tommy Mars (b. 1951), keyboards, vocals

Mars, whose real name is Tommy Mariano, took up piano as a child and studied music formally at the Hart College of Music in Hartford, Connecticut. Both he and Ed Mann played in the jazz-rock fusion band World Consort in 1973. He didn't know much about Zappa's music when he was recommended by Mann to audition for Zappa in 1977, yet he was to tour and record with Zappa until 1982, starting with *Sheik Yerbouti*. He also appears on every part of the *You Can't Do That on Stage Anymore* series except Vol. 2, and was in the band that was captured in the video *The Torture Never Stops*, filmed at the Palladium in New York on October 31, 1981.

Mars co-led Banned from Utopia with Robert Martin in 1995, and in 2007 he recorded an album of new music inspired by Zappa called *Strange News from Mars* with guitarist Jon Larsen, featuring Bruce Fowler, and Jimmy Carl Black. In 2015, Mars joined former Doors guitarist Robbie Krieger's band to record a new album scheduled for release in 2016. Krieger's CD also features former Zappa alumni Arthur Barrow and Chad Wackerman.

Robert Martin (b. 1948), keyboards, alto saxophone, French horn, vocals

Bobby Martin's versatility as a musician and singer made him one of the most talented performers to play Zappa's music. He's a graduate of the Curtis Institute of Music in Philadelphia, alongside esteemed fellow alumni conductor Leonard Bernstein, composer Samuel Barber, and virtuoso pianist Lang Lang. Martin joined Zappa's 1981 touring group and participated in recordings from 1982 to 1988, from *Ship Arriving Too Late to Save a Drowning Witch* to *Make a Jazz Noise Here*. He also appears on five of the six volumes of *You Can't Do That on Stage Anymore*, and he's in the performance video *Does Humor Belong in Music?* Today, Martin leads one of the most popular Zappa cover bands, Banned from Utopia, featuring Ray White, Tom Fowler, and Albert Wing, who all played with Zappa during his lifetime.

Website: www.multimartinmusic.com

Billy Mundi (1942–2014), drums, percussion, vocals

Billy Mundi, aka Tony Schnasse, whose real name was Antonio Salas, was the second drummer of the original Mothers of Invention. He joined the band in 1966 during the recording sessions for *Freak Out!* but didn't appear on record until the second release, *Absolutely Free.* He's also on *We're Only in It for the Money, Uncle Meat, Burnt Weeny Sandwich, Weasels Ripped My Flesh,* and the archival releases *You Can't Do That on Stage Anymore, Vol. 5, Lumpy Money, Greasy Love Songs,* and *Understanding America.*

Mundi left the group when a better offer of money and a steady diet of work came from Jac Holzman at Elektra Records, who asked him to play in the band Rhinoceros. He later worked as a session musician, with credits including an appearance on Bob Dylan's 1970 release *New Morning* (Columbia) and Todd Rundgren's 1972 album *Something/Anything?* (Bearsville).

Patrick O'Hearn (b. 1954), bass, vocals

O'Hearn grew up in a musical house in Portland, Oregon. His parents had their own lounge act dedicated to jazz standards that greatly influenced O'Hearn's choice of first instrument: the double bass. After studying with Gary Peacock of the Keith Jarrett Trio, he began to play on the West Coast jazz scene in the early seventies.

O'Hearn met Frank Zappa in 1976 and was interested in learning more about electronics and the sounds one could create with a fretless electric bass. The musical freedom of that instrument created some interesting results on the Zappa recordings he participated in from 1978 to 1984. Most of these were live recordings, beginning with *Zappa in New York,* but he's also on *Joe's Garage, Sleep Dirt, Them or Us,* and *Ship Arriving Too Late to Save a Drowning Witch.* O'Hearn is still active as a composer and musician.

Website: www.patrickohearn.com

Dave Parlato (b. 1945), bass

Parlato cut his jazz chops with Don Ellis in the mid-sixties before eventually landing a job with Zappa's Grand Wazoo and Petit Wazoo instrumental ensembles. During the Petit Wazoo band's winter 1972 tour, Parlato spotted a dog urinating in the snow. His response? "Don't eat yellow snow." The rest is history.

Parlato can be heard on *Zoot Allures, Studio Tan, Sleep Dirt, Orchestral Favorites*, and *Tinsel Town Rebellion*. He's also on the archival releases *Läther, Quaudiophiliac, Imaginary Diseases, Wazoo*, and *One Shot Deal*. He is still active on the jazz scene today, and his daughter is the acclaimed jazz vocalist Gretchen Parlato.

Jim Pons (b. 1943), bass

Pons played with the Flo and Eddie band in 1971, by way of the Turtles. He's heard on *Fillmore East—June 1971, Just Another Band from L.A.*, and Vol. 1, 3, and 6 of *You Can't Do That on Stage Anymore*. He's also on the archival releases *Playground Psychotics, Carnegie Hall, Understanding America*, and *Finer Moments*. Pons left the music business in 1973 to work for the New York Jets football team as video director. He currently plays upright bass in the bluegrass group Deep Creek.

Jean-Luc Ponty (b. 1942), violin

Virtuoso violinist Ponty was one of the first world-renowned jazz musicians to record Zappa's music outside of his involvement with the Mothers. *King Kong: Jean-Luc Ponty Plays the Music of Frank Zappa* was released by Liberty Records in 1970 to great acclaim. Richard Bock produced it, with a sixteen-piece band featuring George Duke (piano), Ernie Watts (saxophone), and Art Tripp (drums). Zappa was the arranger.

Ponty joined the touring Mothers in 1973 following the release of *Over-Nite Sensation*. He also appears on *Apostrophe ('), Return of the Son of Shut Up 'n Play Yer Guitar*, and *You Can't Do That on Stage Anymore, Vol. 6*. He is also on the archival releases *The Lost Episodes, One Shot Deal, Understanding America*, and *Road Tapes, Venue #2*. Ponty made his mark in the fusion scene of the mid-seventies while working with the Mahavishnu Orchestra and as the leader of his own band. In 2011, Warner Bros. released *Electric Fusion—The Atlantic Years*, a four-CD set of his recordings from 1975 to 1996. He continues to write, record, and perform.

Website: www.ponty.com

Don Preston (b. 1932), keyboards, electronic devices, vocals

Don Preston was one of the most colorful members of the original Mothers of Invention when he joined the band in 1966 after the release of their first album. Zappa hired Preston after he learned the song "Louie, Louie"—his stock audition song at the time—which Preston played on the massive organ in London's Albert Hall during a concert in 1967. Preston was interested in electronics, and he often built his own keyboard devices specifically for use with the Mothers.

Preston is heard on all of the original Mothers of Invention records from 1967 to 1969 and was also invited by Zappa to play on *Waka/Jawaka*, *The Grand Wazoo*, and *Roxy & Elsewhere*. He can also be heard on all but the second volume of *You Can't Do That on Stage Anymore* and the archival releases *Playground Psychotics*, *Ahead of Their Time*, *Mystery Disc*, and five of the *Beat the Boots* albums. He also performs in the movies *200 Motels* and *Uncle Meat*. He co-founded, with Bunk Gardner, the Grandmothers, who continue to perform the music of Zappa today. In 2010, he wrote and performed incidental music for the audio book *The Don Preston Story*.

Website: www.grandmothersofinvention.com

Calvin Schenkel (b. 1947), illustrations, artwork

As album-cover designer, Cal Schenkel made one of the most important non-musical contributions to the works of Frank Zappa. In 1967, Schenkel was introduced to Zappa at his studio in New York. Zappa recognized the importance of a good album cover, especially with his adventurous and unorthodox style of music. Zappa encouraged Schenkel to work with him, even setting up a studio for him in the Laurel Canyon log cabin that Zappa and his young family lived in.

Schenkel made graphic contributions to just about every Zappa/Mothers release, from the infamous cover of *We're Only in It for the Money* (1968) to *Greasy Love Songs* (2010). He also acted as production designer on the movie *200 Motels* and was hired to design some of the covers for the Straight Label, co-founded by Zappa and Herb Cohen in 1969. These include the famous *Trout Mask Replica* cover, featuring Captain Beefheart.

Schenkel is still creating unique illustrations and graphics today.

Website: www.ralf.com

James "Motorhead" Sherwood (1942–2011), baritone saxophone, vocals

Sherwood met Frank Zappa in high school in Lancaster, California, in 1956. The two shared an interest in R&B and blues recordings, which inspired them to form the Omens with Don Van Vliet, and, later, the Blackouts, featuring Zappa on drums. Sherwood was given the nickname "Motorhead" for his proficiency with auto mechanics and the fact that he was the Mothers of Invention's roadie extraordinaire. He was a full-time band member from 1967 until 1969. Sherwood appears in the movie *200 Motels* as Larry Fanoga, on Vol. 1, 4, and 5 of *You Can't Do That on Stage Anymore*, on *Civilization Phaze III*, and on the archival releases *Ahead of Their Time*, *Läther*, *The MOFO Project/Object*, *Greasy Love Songs*, *Road Tapes*, *Venue #1*, and *Finer Moments*. In 1980, Sherwood joined Don Preston and Bunk Gardner in the tribute band the Grandmothers (of Invention). He died on Christmas Day, 2011.

Jeff Simmons (b. 1949), bass, vocals

Simmons, who was equally astute as a guitarist, was the bass player in Zappa's band featuring Flo and Eddie. When his band Easy Chair opened for the Mothers of Invention in 1968, Zappa was impressed and signed them to his first label, Bizarre Records. Simmons was then signed as a solo artist to Zappa's more adventurous label, Straight, to write and produce a soundtrack to the biker B-movie *Naked Angels*. Simmons was second guitarist during the 1974 world tour, which is captured on six different recordings from the *Beat the Boots* series. He's also on *Roxy & Elsewhere*.

Website: www.bluefoxrecords.com/portnoy.html

Bob Stone (1943–2005), sound engineer

Bob Stone was responsible for engineering and remixing Zappa's albums from 1981 to 1993. He's credited for remixing, for better or worse, some of the first digital reissues of the Zappa catalogue on Rykodisc at a time when digital sound technology was still in its infancy. Nevertheless, Stone helped Zappa break into the new compact disc format in the late eighties. Stone also had access to the massive Zappa vault at the Utility Muffin Research Kitchen. He also ran his own mastering and recording studios in Van Nuys, California, until his death from cancer in 2005.

Chester Thompson (b. 1948), drums

Born in the same city as Zappa, Thompson took up the drums at age eleven and was playing in bands two years later. His natural gifts as a drummer made him one of the most in-demand players in rock and jazz circles. He joined Zappa in 1973 and toured extensively with the Mothers for over a year. His most significant contribution as a drummer is on *One Size Fits All*, but he also appears on *Roxy & Elsewhere*, *Studio Tan*, *Sleep Dirt*, and the first four volumes of *You Can't Do That on Stage Anymore*. He's in the 1974 television special *A Token of His Extreme*, released on DVD in 2013.

Thompson joined Genesis in 1977 after Phil Collins took up lead vocals for the touring edition of the group. He continues to play, record, and teach as an adjunct professor at Belmont University in Nashville, Tennessee.

Website: www.chesterthompson.com

Scott Thunes (b. 1960), bass

Thunes started playing bass guitar at the age of ten. When he turned twenty-one, he auditioned for Frank Zappa, and he got the job. Thunes is on Zappa's studio recordings from 1982 to 1988. He can be seen on the DVD *The Torture Never Stops*, which captures the 1981 Halloween show in New York, and *Does Humor Belong in Music?*, from the 1984 show at the Pier. Thunes quit the music business when Zappa died in 1993 and went to work for a software developer. He occasionally attends the Zappanale Festival, which is held in Germany every year, and currently plays with the Mother Hips, a group based in San Francisco.

Website: www.motherhips.com

Arthur Tripp III (b. 1944), drums, percussion

Art Tripp met Zappa in 1968 by way of Richard Kunc, who was Zappa's first recording engineer. He recorded seven albums with Zappa, including *Cruising with Ruben & the Jets*, *Uncle Meat*, *Burnt Weeny Sandwich*, and *Weasels Ripped My Flesh*. He's also on the archival releases *Ahead of Their Time*, *The Lost Episodes*, *Road Tapes, Venue #1*, and *Finer Moments*.

Tripp was particularly good at improvisation, with his skills greatly enhancing the MOI's concert performances. The best example is the film *Uncle Meat*. According to Zappa, Tripp was the most skilled musician in the band at the time because he could read music, write parts for percussion, and attune himself to Zappa's intentions as a composer by adding a classical element to the band's R&B- and blues-based music.

Tripp also played with Captain Beefheart and His Magic Band for a few years, but had retired from the music business altogether by 1980. Three years later, he became a chiropractor and opened his own practice in Gulfport, Mississippi.

Ian Underwood (b. 1939), multi-instrumentalist

Underwood was one of the most versatile musicians in Zappa's band. He joined the Mothers of Invention in 1968 and helped Zappa develop his compositions for many years. Underwood was a multi-instrumentalist whose proficiency on woodwinds, piano, synthesizer, and guitar provided an important part of the Zappa sound. One of the best examples is the album *Hot Rats*, released in 1969, on which Underwood is multi-tracked playing piano, organ, flute, and all the saxophone parts, producing a sound not unlike a big band. Underwood was the only musician Zappa kept on after the dissolution of the MOI in 1969. He's heard on every Zappa release from 1968 to 1974, including five of the six volumes in the concert series *You Can't Do That on Stage Anymore*.

In May 1969, Underwood married Ruth Komanoff, who played as a percussionist with Zappa from 1970. They divorced in 1986. Today, he continues to compose music for films and work as a session musician.

Ruth Underwood (b. 1946), percussion, vibraphone, marimba

Ruth Underwood was the first woman to grace the Zappa band when she joined in 1970. Her excellent sound and technique on marimba and vibes alone added considerable depth and breadth to Zappa's music. Zappa wrote specifically with her in mind until she left the band in 1977. One of those works was "RDNZL," beautifully rendered on *You Can't Do That on Stage, Vol. 2* (aka *The Helsinki Concert*). The same album also features her remarkable playing on "Don't You Ever Wash That Thing?," during which Zappa remarks, "It sure is slippery in the percussion section today, [and Ruth is thinking], 'I hope I don't hurt myself.'"

Underwood plays on *Over-Nite Sensation, Apostrophe ('), Roxy & Elsewhere; One Size Fits All, Zoot Allures, Zappa in New York, Studio Tan,* and *Sleep Dirt.* She's also on Vol. 1, 2, 3, 4, and 6 of *You Can't Do That on Stage Anymore.* By 1980, she had basically retired from music to raise her two children. Just before he died in 1993, Zappa met with Underwood and recorded her playing vibraphone and marimba for future use. Her marimba sound (or sample) is a musical highlight of Zappa's last album for Synclavier, *Dance Me This,* released posthumously in 2015.

Steve Vai (b. 1960), guitar, vocals

In 1979, Steve Vai sent Zappa a cassette tape of his own music, along with a transcription of "The Black Page" that really impressed the bandleader. Zappa hired Vai to transcribe twenty-two compositions for *The Frank Zappa Guitar Book*, a tutorial for guitar players. He also asked him to join the band as "stunt" guitarist in 1980, employing Vai to play the guitar parts from the recordings as well as new parts not played by Zappa in concert.

Vai is considered Zappa's equal in dexterity and speed when it comes to playing the guitar, and he quickly became a feature of the live performances in the early eighties. The song "Stevie's Spanking," with its extended dueling guitar solos, was written by Zappa to showcase Vai's ability. You can hear Vai on every recording from *Tinsel Town Rebellion* (1981) to *Guitar* (1988). He's also featured on all but Vol. 2 of the *You Can't Do That on Stage Anymore* series.

As a guitarist, Vai held a unique view of Zappa's compositions and how they worked musically and rhythmically. His personal liner notes for

Steve Vai, "stunt guitarist."

the archival release *Imaginary Diseases* are particularly insightful. Vai participated in the 2006 tour by Zappa Plays Zappa and he continues to write, record, and teach his master class, Alien Guitar Secrets.

Website: www.vai.com

Don Van Vliet, aka Captain Beefheart (1941–2010), harmonica, vocals

A lot has been written about Van Vliet, aka Captain Beefheart, so there's nothing to new to add to the story of the man. Here, though, are three books to get you started: *Trout Mask Replica* by Kevin Courrier; *Captain Beefheart: The Biography* by Mike Barnes; and *Beefheart: Through the Eyes of Magic* by John French, who played drums for the Magic Band. It was Zappa who gave Vliet his nickname and released *Trout Mask Replica* on his Straight Label in 1969. Vliet also participated on *Hot Rats* ("Willie the Pimp") and the 1975 show in Austin, Texas, that was released as *Bongo Fury*. Like Zappa, Beefheart was a unique and unorthodox musician who challenged audiences as much as he annoyed them.

Mark Volman (b. 1947), vocals

One of the founding members of the Turtles, Volman was the other half of the duo Flo and Eddie, who joined Zappa in June 1970, touring extensively in a show that was as much a mockery of the Turtles as it was a celebration. Flo and Eddie put the vaudeville back into Zappa's presentations, adding just the right amount of humor and general onstage silliness. Volman often took to playing the horny female groupie to Kaylan's rock-star character, based on their experiences on the road with the Turtles. Their satiric act is in evidence on a sketch called "Do You Like My New Car?" from the *Fillmore East* album, released in 1971, which was also to be used in the film *200 Motels*. Volman appears as himself in the movie, as well as providing "special material" for the story.

Flo and Eddie can be heard on *Chunga's Revenge, Fillmore East-June 1971, Just Another Band from L.A.*, and Vol. 1, 3, and 6 of *You Can't Do That on Stage Anymore*. They also appear on the archival releases *Playground Psychotics, Carnegie Hall, Understanding America*, and *Finer Moments*. He continues to perform with Howard Kaylan at summer festivals in the United States and has made himself available online for questions about pursuing a career in music.

Website: www.professorflo.com

Chad Wackerman (b. 1960), drums

Chad Wackerman was the last person to sit in the prestigious drummer's chair in Frank Zappa's band. His father was a drummer and music teacher, so growing up and learning one of the louder musical instruments wasn't a problem. In 1978 he joined Bill Watrous's band, playing jazz and learning the rudiments of timekeeping and changes in meter. He auditioned for Zappa in 1981, passed, and stayed with him until the 1988 big band tour.

Wackerman played drums or supplied tracks to every Zappa release from *Ship Arriving Too Late to Save a Drowning Witch* (1982) to *Make a Jazz Noise Here* (1991). One of his best performances was captured on the DVD recorded at the Pier in New York in 1984, *Does Humor Belong in Music?*

Wackerman described his experience with Zappa in an interview with Dom Romeo for the music blog at http://standanddeliver.blogspot.com from May 9, 2004. "It encompassed so many different styles. It was like being in a rock 'n' roll band, it was like being in a great jazz ensemble, it was like being in a chamber orchestra as well." Wackerman was only twenty-one years of age when he joined Zappa's band in 1981. Years later, he went on to form his own jazz/fusion trio with Doug Lunn and Mike Miller. He continues to record, compose, and offer master classes in percussion.

Website: www.chadwackerman.com

Denny Walley (b. 1944), guitar, vocals

Walley was born in Pennsylvania but soon moved with his family to Lancaster, California, into the very same neighborhood as the Zappa family. He eventually met Frank in 1955. Walley took up guitar with a focus on learning blues licks and developing his "slide" technique. Twenty years later, he hooked up with Zappa, who was looking for a session guitarist. Walley filled the role from 1975 to 1979. He's heard on *Bongo Fury, Joe's Garage, Tinsel Town Rebellion, You Are What You Is, Thing-Fish*, and the compilation album *Guitar*. He's also on Vol. 1, 4, and 6 of *You Can't Do That on Stage*

Anymore and the archival releases *Halloween, Trance-Fusion, One Shot Deal, Understanding America*, and *Joe's Camouflage*.

Ray White (b. 1939), guitar, vocals

White's background as a gospel singer served him well when met Zappa in 1976. He knew nothing about the man and his music, save for the song "Montana," about which he said, "The guy who wrote this has to be the craziest white boy on the face of the planet." It was a fortuitous comment, because a short time later White auditioned for Zappa and was hired as a vocalist to complement Ike Willis, who was the band's lead singer at the time.

White joined the Zappa touring band in 1976 and stayed on until 1984. He can be heard on every release from *Zappa in New York* (1978) to *Guitar* (1988). He's also on the archival releases *The Lost Episodes, Läther, Trance-Fusion, Buffalo, One Shot Deal, Lumpy Money, Philly '76*, and *Understanding America* plus five of the six volumes of *You Can't Do That on Stage Anymore*.

White was a devout Christian but had no issues regarding the material he sang, only some of the bad habits of band members. In 2007, he was invited by Dweezil to play some selected concerts with Zappa Plays Zappa, but he left in 2009 to join Ike Willis in the Project/Object band.

Website: www.projectobject.com

Ike Willis (b. 1955), guitar, vocals

Ike Willis started playing guitar at the age of eight. His mother was a jazz singer, so he was encouraged to pursue music at an early age. Years later, Willis met Zappa after a concert at Washington University in St. Louis, and they immediately connected. Willis successfully auditioned and joined the Zappa touring band in 1978 and stayed on for the next ten years. He became known as "The Voice" for his portrayal of Joe in *Joe's Garage* and the character of Thing-Fish in Zappa's "opera" of the same name.

Willis's sound became synonymous with Zappa's music in the second half of his career. Just before Zappa died, Willis made a promise to keep his music alive as long as he could. As a result, he's currently associated with at least nine different Zappa cover bands, including Project/Object, and, for 2015, a group called Ugly Radio Rebellion. His memoir was published in 2016.

Website: www.ikewillis.com

Peter Wolf (b. 1952), keyboards, vocals

Wolf started playing piano at the age of four and aimed at a life-long career in classical music. But he was also interested in jazz and rock music, especially Frank Zappa. He immigrated to the United States in 1975, and, a year later, he auditioned for Zappa's band. He passed the test and was added as an additional keyboard player for the 1977 tour with Adrian Belew.

Wolf can be heard on *Sheik Yerbouti, Joe's Garage, Tinsel Town Rebellion, Shut Up 'N Play Yer Guitar, Baby Snakes, Guitar*, and Vol. 1, 4, and 6 of *You Can't Do That on Stage Anymore*. He's also on *Halloween, Quaudiophiliac, Trance-Fusion, One Shot Deal, Hammersmith Odeon*, and *Understanding America*. After his stint with Zappa he worked as a producer and arranger for a few years, only to return to Austria in 1994 to establish a solo career as a composer.

Allan Zavod (b. 1945), keyboards

Zavod is a classically trained pianist whose interest in jazz granted him a chance to meet and play for Duke Ellington in 1969. Ellington was so impressed that he arranged to have Zavod attend the Berklee School of Music in Boston. He stayed in the United States for the next twenty years. Zavod met Zappa in 1984 and joined the touring band. One of his best piano solos can be heard on "Let's Move to Cleveland" from *You Can't Do That on Stage Anymore, Vol. 4*. Here, Zavod gets to jam with Archie Shepp, one of the great improvisers from the progressive jazz world, and he really winds out at the end of the song.

During the 1984 tour on which Zavod participated, Zappa usually included "Let's Move to Cleveland" in the set list in order to show off the Aussie's skills as a musician. As Zavod recalled in an interview from 2003 with Avo Raup, "Once I'd played with Frank Zappa, I could do anything. He gave us confidence." He can be seen on the concert DVD *Does Humor Belong in Music?* and heard on Vol. 1, 3, 4, and 6 of *You Can't Do That on Stage Anymore*.

In his book, Zappa talks about Zavod's big finish after a keyboard solo that he named "the volcano," which made use of the sustain pedal. After his stint with Zappa ended, Zavod returned to Australia to play and compose. In 2009, he was made a doctor of music by the University of Melbourne.

Website: www.allanzavod.com

For a complete list of the people who played with Zappa, go here: http://globalia.net/donlope/fz/musicians/index.html

32

Father and Son

Zappa's Legacy, Part I

In 2006, Frank Zappa's eldest son, Dweezil, put together the best musicians he could find and went on tour to play his father's complex and sophisticated music. He called the group Zappa Plays Zappa, or ZPZ. It was a long time coming. Dweezil's father died of cancer on December 4, 1993, a few days shy of his fifty-third birthday, and suddenly the eldest son—an accomplished musician in his own right—had heavy shoes to fill.

Dweezil wasn't alone. His mother Gail, sisters Moon and Diva, and younger brother Ahmet shared the grief of their loss and moved forward. The creation of the Zappa Family Trust deferred certain legal and financial responsibilities to non-family members. But the musical legacy of Frank Zappa was an entirely different matter, and in 2006, thirteen years after the patriarch died, Dweezil and ZPZ decided it was time to go out on the road.

Dweezil Zappa

Dweezil was born on September 5, 1969, the second child of Gail and Frank Zappa. Growing up, he liked photography, baseball, and music. One might think that his father tutored him on guitar, but Dweezil was first attracted to the sound of guitarist Eddie Van Halen, whose remarkable technique and lightning-fast hands were a major influence. Dweezil found Van Halen's music significantly more accessible than his father's. His relationship with his dad was inspiring, nurturing, and engaging, in spite of the long absences when Frank was on tour, but Dweezil still had to find his own way in music and learning guitar. The Zappa album that first caught his ear was *Bongo Fury*, featuring Captain Beefheart. Growing up and discovering his father's recordings was as exciting to Dweezil as it was to the rest of the world. For Dweezil and his younger brother, Ahmet, it was like opening a treasure chest.

The house of Zappa must have been an active place for Dweezil to grow up in, especially with a 24-track recording studio in the basement. The flow of creative people visiting on a regular basis to work with Frank was probably dynamic and fun most of the time. In fact, both parents were working from home: Gail handled the business and Frank handled the music. It was certainly not a circus, but Dweezil's wasn't a home life based on a set routine. As Frank writes in *The Real Frank Zappa Book*, his son had his own room with a separate entrance that gave him the freedom to come and go as he pleased—"a unique little place in the house with a stairway going up the outside." The room was fully equipped with a computer, sound system, television, and guitar amp, providing Dweezil the tools necessary to develop his own life in music, distinct from that of his father. At twelve, he played with a garage band called Fred Zeppelin; at thirteen, he cut his first single (with the help of his father and a few of his bandmates), "My Mother Is a Space Cadet."

By the age of seventeen, Dweezil was more dedicated to learning and growing as a musician. He even started to attend his father's band rehearsals, where he experienced Frank's creative process, which was a combination of preparedness and spontaneity. Frank Zappa took rehearsals seriously; he often had new compositions for the band, but he wasn't afraid to add a spontaneous musical moment or funny situation into the day's work. Picking up on his father's process, Dweezil's released his first album, *Havin' a Bad Day* (Barking Pumpkin), in 1984. It was the same year he played on Frank's album *Them or Us*, specifically on the track "Sharleena," taking the guitar solo usually reserved for his father. It was an auspicious debut, proving his merit as a real player with his own style and sound.

ZPZ

Dweezil now leads the ultimate tribute band, Zappa Plays Zappa. On their first "Tour de Frank," the band featured three alumni of Frank's bands—Steve Vai, Terry Bozzio, and Napoleon Murphy Brock, who were added to the highly skilled band of young musicians personally selected by Dweezil. The first tour was documented on the two-DVD set *Zappa Plays Zappa* (Strobosonic), directed by Pierre and Francois Lamoureux under the supervision of Dweezil, who participated in the final editing and sound mixing. Since then, members of Frank Zappa's past groups have made guest appearances at selected shows, with mixed results.

In an extensive interview with John Collinge in the spring 2010 issue of *Progression* magazine, Dweezil outlined the obstacles he faced. "When I started this whole thing I really had no intention of having alumni in the band. But the first year out, promoters were of the opinion that nobody would come to see us if we didn't have alumni. I disagreed, but they didn't

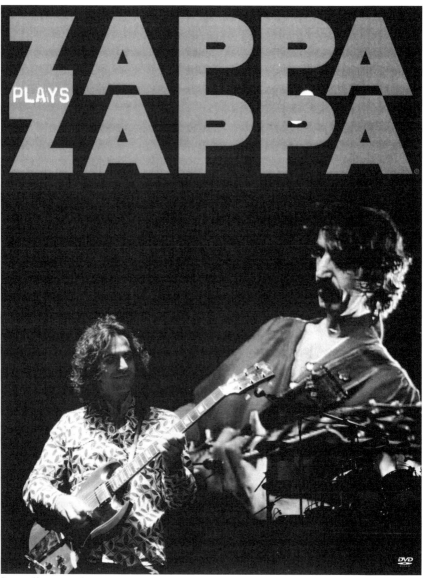

Dweezil carries the musical torch.

want to take that risk . . . but the core band was the real engine behind the whole thing."

Asked in the same interview for his view on the other Zappa tribute bands on the circuit, Dweezil refused to hold back. "I don't have anything good to say about them . . . those guys not only disrespected Frank while Frank was alive, they continue to do it in various ways after the fact. I'm really not interested in what they have to offer." Many fans would probably disagree, but that hasn't been a deterrent to the steady touring of Zappa Plays Zappa. As Dweezil has said over the years, his goal is to reach new audiences with his father's music. "If young kids appreciate Frank's music on the level of what is possible musically, that's what we hope for."

Dweezil and his band have released several CDs since their debut. In 2009, the group won a Grammy award for Best Rock Instrumental Performance for their version of "Peaches En Regalia," written by Frank Zappa, which appears on their self-titled record. Dweezil's goal to get his father's music back into the mainstream paid off, and he continues to lead a six-piece version of the band—now without alumni—on a steady international touring schedule. In November 2015, he released his first solo album in ten years, *Via Zamatta*.

2010 ZPZ Tour

In 2010, Zappa Plays Zappa refocused their set list and decided to take advantage of the "complete album" performance strategy that had worked so well for Steely Dan, among others, in recent years. To celebrate what would have been Frank's seventieth birthday, Dweezil and ZPZ chose to perform *Apostrophe (')* in sequence. The Toronto concert I attended really drew out the eclecticism of the record. This album is full of Zappa's mix of the sublime with the ridiculous, with sophisticated passages of music that require the listener to lean in and pay attention. (Author Ben Watson calls the record "Zappa's *King Lear*" and devotes considerable analysis to it in his book *The Negative Dialectics of Poodle Play*.)

2014 Tour

In 2014, Dweezil chose to celebrate the fortieth anniversary of the album *Roxy & Elsewhere*, another fan favorite, by playing the whole thing onstage. It was an interesting choice because the original album is actually a concert recording, taped at the Roxy Theater in Los Angeles. Dweezil opted to forego the cabaret-like atmosphere of the album by concentrating on the music. As a creative choice, it was the right one, because the songs on this record are some of the most complex arrangements in Zappa's catalogue. Zappa's 1974 audience expected to be insulted and embarrassed as part of the show; in 2014 it was less about recreating the past and more about celebrating the music. At the Toronto performance in October 2013, the show was quite strong without the frills and distractions of the original album. ZPZ were really comfortable with the material, and the crowd was totally supportive, resulting in a successful show, even if the hard edges of the original were measurably softened.

2015 Tour

In 2015, a six-piece version of Zappa Plays Zappa launched a world tour based around another of Frank's best recordings, *One Size Fits All*, to mark the fortieth anniversary of the album's release. In an interview with Courtney Devores of the *Charlotte Observer*, Dweezil talked about making fundamental shifts in his guitar playing in order to play Frank's songs. "I had to completely change my playing style, not only physically, but the mental approach." One of the hurdles he faced was the fact that he didn't read music, which presented a steep learning curve. "I learn everything by ear. I have to rewind and memorize stuff . . . I have to look at everything in small chunks and memorize them in smaller phrases." Considering all of the music Frank Zappa wrote, this probably meant learning about a hundred tunes.

The Legacy

When ZPZ went on the road in 2006, it was a nostalgia show that allowed older, mostly male fans eager to relive their youth and their connection with Frank Zappa. On that first tour, audiences bought T-shirts and CDs and consumed alcohol and other substances to get into the mood. The three hour and forty-five minute concert featured twenty-nine songs penned by Frank Zappa. It was definitely a love-in, as I experienced in Toronto on June 16, 2006, at the Hummingbird Centre. The audience was energized, attentive, and extremely enthusiastic about the band and the music. The concert wasn't just a walk down memory lane: it was a celebration.

Fast-forward to 2015 and the audience profile for the ZPZ shows has changed. In an interview with Jon Solomon for www.westword.com, published on April 23, 2015, Dweezil reported, "We've seen it shift to where you have college-aged kids and younger, and we have a lot more women at the shows than when we first started." It was his intention to introduce his father's music to a new generation of listeners and to do so in an open and benevolent way. Unlike Frank, Dweezil holds no contempt for his audience, and he never insults them. His presentation is much more relaxed, and he is much nicer to any kids in the audience. Zappa the younger is more interested in generating a fan base than losing one, and so far his tours have been a public-relations success. Dweezil gives master classes when he tours, attracting players of all levels to learn more about his technique and that of his illustrious father. After each concert, the whole band comes out to sign autographs and graciously meet the new and old fans. Audience goodwill is particularly important to Dweezil as he performs music he still considers to be ahead of its time.

33

Cover Bands

Zappa's Legacy, Part 2

In the December 2014 issue of the prestigious American music magazine *Downbeat*, readers voted to place Ed Palermo's Big Band tenth on a list of the best albums of the year with *Oh No! Not Jazz!!* (Cuneiform). One disc of the two-CD set features music written by Frank Zappa and arranged by Palermo for the sixteen musicians in the group. It was the bandleader's third album to feature the music of Zappa, but the first time *Downbeat* readers had pushed a Zappa record of any kind into the Top 10.

Oh No! Not Jazz!! is an album that captures Zappa's humor and, to an extent, the jazz sensibility prevalent in most of his music. In an e-mail exchange with the author, Palermo talked about the ease of arranging the music for a big band. "It all fits like a glove. Arranging his music is true joy for me. For one, I get the nostalgic high from hearing songs that I grew up listening to. On top of that, I get to arrange it in ways that tickle me *now*."

During his lifetime, Zappa always treasured good musicians who had the musical "chops" to play his difficult compositions. Getting the right people to play what he heard in his head challenged him because of the long and expensive rehearsal time his musicians needed to get it right. For Ed Palermo, who also looks for good players, Zappa's music continues to inspire him. Some of these ideas are best heard in Palermo's tune "Why Is the Doctor Barking?," a remarkable piece of music that pays tribute to his favorite composer with its witty hooks and complex time signature. In one full swoop, Palermo respects and advances ideas that Zappa included in some of his early works, such as "Peaches En Regalia."

The art of the cover or tribute band is to take on someone else's songs and either reproduce them note for note or go beyond that and reinvent them. Zappa's music is so versatile that rock bands, jazz bands, and classical ensembles can cover it with equal verve and, if inspired, write and arrange their own compositions with Zappa-like motifs. It's out of this organic mix

The Ed Palermo Big Band puts the swing in Zappa's music.

of appreciation and love for Zappa's works that musicians around the world continue to play his music. This chapter is a survey of some of those bands.

The Grandmothers

One of the first Zappa cover bands was the Grandmothers, led by drummer Jimmy Carl Black from the original Mothers of Invention. The band started in 1980, when Black teamed up with Don Preston, Bunk Gardner, Tom and Walt Fowler, and Tony Duran for Rhino Records. The band cut one unreleased album but broke up two years later. The project failed, according to Black, because of Tom Fowler's behavior toward Tony Duran.

Black and the Grandmothers reconvened in 1987 simply to rehearse Zappa's music, which eventually became a prominent part of the group's set list as well as their original compositions. "We're a family," Black told the fanzine *T'mershi Duween* in the spring of 1992. "Everyone appreciates everyone else. I've had this band for four years, rehearsing, not playing. We've had over three thousand hours of rehearsals. That's how tight the band is. They're so tight it's unbelievable. We can use telepathy. We know what's going to happen before it does happen." The band recorded seven studio albums during its existence, along with a steady diet of live performances that came to a formal end in 2000. (Black died in 2008.)

The Muffin Men

In 1990, the Muffin Men, named after a song by Zappa, debuted in Liverpool, England, led by Roddie Gillard and Mike Kidson. The band released their version of "Let's Move to Cleveland" as a single in 1992, with a debut album appearing the following year that featured Jimmy Carl Black on two tracks. The band still plays festivals and shows around the UK and Europe, often inviting Zappa alumni such as Ike Willis to play with them. As they proudly state on their Facebook page, they have enjoyed "more than twenty years of purveying fine interpretations of Frank Zappa's music to the most discerning of listeners."

Bogus Pomp

In 1994, guitarist Jerry Outlaw formed Bogus Pomp, named for a song on Zappa's *Orchestral Favorites*. Based in Tampa Bay, Florida, the group started as a jam session with Rick Olsun (keyboards), Alex Pasut (bass), and Tom McCowan (drums). With a fondness for Zappa's music, the band started to learn and rehearse on a steady basis, dedicated to the notion that to play Zappa's music well a musician had to put in the time to become proficient in its execution. Zappa fans would accept no less. Five years later, in a bold move, the group expanded from a quartet to a ten-piece, adding "Orchestra" to their name, and approached the Florida Symphony Orchestra, then conducted by Thomas Wilkins, to put on a program of Zappa's music featuring their band. The orchestra agreed.

It took nine months to prepare the program, beginning with securing authorization from the Zappa Family Trust along with corporate financing.

The concert was a critical and financial success. The band repeated the program a year later, and they were invited to play with the Buffalo Philharmonic Orchestra in May 2000, along with former Zappa vocalist Napoleon Murphy Brock. In 2002, the group released their versions of Zappa's best-known instrumentals on their own label on an album called *A Pungent Steaming Affair.*

In a March 2000 cover story about the band in the now-defunct *Buffalo Beat*, Outlaw talked about the importance of playing Frank's music. "There is absolutely no doubt that Zappa will eventually be placed alongside his classical music contemporaries, where he deserves to be. I truly feel that he was the greatest composer since electricity changed music." Today, Bogus Pomp still hosts an annual concert event called Zappaween, which marked its twentieth anniversary in 2015.

Project/Object and Banned from Utopia

While the number of dedicated musicians starting and maintaining tribute acts in the world of Zappa continues to grow, two groups stand out for their lineups of musicians who played with the bandleader, namely Project/Object and Banned from Utopia. The former was started in New York in 1996 by Andre Cholmondeley along with Zappa's longtime lead vocalist Ike Willis and original Mother Don Preston. Some fans consider them the preeminent Zappa tribute band, and they enjoy a steady touring schedule in the United States to this day. Since the group's formation, many former musicians who played and recorded for Frank Zappa have taken part in Project/Object. The 2013 lineup, for instance, featured Denny Walley, Ray White, Ed Mann, and Tom Fowler. (Willis also occasionally joins Pojama People, an Oregon-based tribute band.)

Banned from Utopia, who debuted in 1994 at the Jazz Open Festival in Stuttgart, Germany, feature most of the members of Zappa's last organized group from his '88 big band. Led by keyboard player Tommy Mars, the group has recorded three CDs and one DVD that capture Zappa's music in an upbeat way. As Bradley Torreano of the *All Music Guide* puts it, "Banned from Utopia is an extension of Zappa's emphasis on spontaneous music. Covering Zappa songs with a loose vibe and exploratory approach while also writing their own material, BFU (as they refer to themselves) lovingly recreate the wacky virtuoso approach of their former bandleader."

Ensemble Modern

Zappa tribute or cover bands extend beyond the traditional rock or jazz genre into more sophisticated musical collectives. One of the very best is Germany's Ensemble Modern, founded in 1980. This classical orchestra played an important role during Zappa's later years by recording an album of his works for orchestra called *The Yellow Shark*, released by the Barking Pumpkin label in November 1993. Today, the EM performs over one hundred concerts a year, with a program that not only includes the works of Frank Zappa but also those of his strongest classical influences, such as John Cage and Edgard Varese.

Ensemble Ambrosius

Another chamber group known as Ensemble Ambrosius from Helsinki, Finland, debuted in 1995 and plays the music of Zappa in a baroque style. It was a musical joke that paid off for the seven-piece band, and one that led to a well-received recording in 2000 simply called *The Zappa Album* (BIS/Northern Lights), which is still in print. The cover features a profile of a brown rabbit's head with a bubble thought stating "Arf," illustrated in tribute to the composer's notion of conceptual continuity.

Inventionis Mater

This two-member ensemble from Italy features Andrea Pennati (guitar) and Pierpaolo Romani (clarinet and bass clarinet). The classically trained duo has transcribed many works by Zappa including "King Kong," "Brown Shoes Don't Make It," and "Zomby Woof," and released two remarkable albums of Zappa compositions, *Does Humor Belong in Classical Music?* and *Kong's Revenge*. The effort required to break down Zappa's sophisticated music for two instruments is an inspiration for any musician.

Fattore Zeta

Another cover band from Italy is the six-piece ensemble Fattore Zeta, or Factor Z. They formed in 2005 and have released over a dozen recordings since their debut. Rooted in jazz, they play mostly Zappa instrumentals such as "Green Umbrellas" and "Blessed Relief," but they don't settle for

We can do Zappa with just two instruments!

note-for-note versions of Zappa's songs. They often break out in extended solos in a nod to Zappa's love for improvisation. Some of their performances are on YouTube, including a mash-up of "America Drinks and Goes Home" and "Theme from *Shaft*" by Isaac Hayes.

Zappanale Festival

Many fans of Zappa's music have taken the notion of celebrating the composer to a grander, more festive level. In 1990, in the spirit of the famed Venice Biennale for contemporary art, the first Zappanale was held in the town of Bad Doberan, Germany. Wolfhard Kutz, its founder, was actually spied on by the East German secret police (the Stasi) for influencing the German youth with Zappa's music. The Zappanale was a bold move to openly celebrate so-called subversive rock music to fight an oppressive state. To an extent, this political move by a life-long fan was in keeping with Zappa's support for freedom of speech and freedom of expression. For Kutz, who still oversees the festival every summer, listening to Zappa's records gave him the strength to fight the system, because he recognized in the songs the opportunity to express his own dissenting point of view.

In 1989, after the fall of the Berlin Wall, Kutz formed the Arf Society, a Frank Zappa fan club. (The fee to join is currently 50 euros.) In 2014, the Zappanale celebrated its twenty-fifth anniversary with a varied bill featuring not only bands that play Zappa's music, like the Muffin Men and the Grandmothers of Invention, but new experimental groups such as the Spanner Jazz Punks from England, who describe themselves as "the troublesome offspring of a frenetic marriage between sleazy punk jazz and psychedelic performance art." The twenty-sixth edition of the festival featured Napoleon Murphy Brock.

Zappa Down Under

One of the larger ensembles coming out of Sydney, Australia is Petulant Frenzy, a group specifically assembled to play Zappa's more complicated music like "Brown Shoes Don't Make It," originally heard on *Absolutely Free* in 1967. The band is tight and funny and has just enough irreverence to pull off Zappa's edgy early material. As their website proclaims, "We play Zappa and we mean it." The ten-piece band often struggle to find all of their musicians available to perform for demanding audiences—an experience that would probably not be lost on Zappa the bandleader, whose ensembles had a well organized and demanding rehearsal and touring schedule.

Recommended Reading The Real Frank Zappa Books

Pauline Butcher, *Freak Out! My Life with Frank Zappa* (London: Plexus Publishing Ltd., 2011)

Frank Zappa had a secretary! Who knew? This wonderful memoir is full of anecdotes by Pauline Butcher, who worked for Zappa from 1967 to 1973. She shares her personal experiences with the Mothers of Invention, Gail Zappa, and members of all-girl groupie band the GTO's. As a Brit working for a very popular American musician, Butcher's relationship with Zappa was not just about the work but also about a clash of manners. Butcher wasn't awe-struck by his fame and his fortune, so she was able to challenge his ideas, opinions, and lifestyle without being dismissed. Zappa respected Butcher, and her book reveals their unique relationship. Recommended.

Kevin Courrier, *Dangerous Kitchen: The Subversive World of Zappa* (Toronto: ECW Press, 2002)

Courrier's book is a must-read for any lover of music. The reason is because he loves music, too—especially the music of Frank Zappa. The book is thoroughly interesting and full of historical context, which is really important in understanding Zappa's life and work. Moving chronologically through every song of every album, Courrier writes critical assessments so well that you have to pull out the album and listen to it as you read. It's a fun exercise, and I've done it myself on several occasions. Regrettably, the book is now out of print, so visit your public library and borrow a copy. (In the interests of full disclosure, I've worked with Kevin on radio documentaries for the Canadian Broadcasting Corporation, among other projects. We've been "Zappa Brothers" since 1986.)

Andrew Greenaway, *Zappa the Hard Way* (Bedford, UK: Wymer Publishing, 2010)

The saga of Zappa's last touring band of 1988 is nicely chronicled in this short but interesting tome, featuring interviews with most of the musicians who played with Zappa. There's always been turmoil in musical groups, especially when personalities clash, regardless of genre. What makes this story ironic is the fact that some of the very best music to come out a Zappa tour came from the '88 band. I only wish the text presentation distinguished Greenaway's narrative from the comments of musicians. I felt like I was reading an uncorrected proof. One of the book's strengths is that it includes an appendix featuring every set list, including rehearsal songs, from every performance, as well the "secret words" Zappa introduced each night. (These secret words were little intervals or gimmicks used by Zappa during the tour. The fans caught on and started asking for them at every concert.) The last song the band played, by the way, was "The Illinois Enema Bandit."

Edward Komara with Scott Parker, *ZaFTIG: The Zappa Family Trust (Compact Disc) Issues Guide* (Waterbury, Connecticut: SPB Publishing, 2015)

Edward Komara is a librarian with the State University of New York at Potsdam. Scott Parker is a musician and author who has written extensively about Frank Zappa's recordings, specifically from a technical perspective. This highly readable book gives fans an overview of the one hundred albums in Zappa's catalogue, with annotated notes regarding every album in chronological order. As a reference book, it's first-rate, but what makes the book essential to your collection is the critical assessment of the CD reissues from 1987 and 1995 on Rykodisc in comparison with the 2012 reissue series by Universal. Komara and Parker assess the sound quality and track differences for each CD against the original vinyl releases. Parker also tells us the story behind Zappa's rationale for the changes he made to the recordings when they first came out in 1987 and the technical obstacles he had to overcome to issue his music on CD. These guys have done their homework, and by enlisting the help of Zappa archivist and vaultmeister Joe Travers, they've published a hefty book with information you can trust. This book is invaluable to the long-time fan and helps sort out Zappa's collection into easily digestible parts for the newcomer.

Kelly Fisher Lowe, *The Words and Music of Frank Zappa* (Westport, Connecticut: Bison Books, 2007)

This is a fine academic study of Zappa's satire and how he used words to effectively criticize everything about culture, men, women, groupies, politics, TV evangelists, sex, religion, and more. But the best part about the Bison Books edition is Fisher Lowe's introduction about his efforts to secure approval for the re-publication of Zappa's lyrics. In spite of the obstacles he faced, Fisher Lowe persevered with his commitment to bringing new fans to Zappa's songs. Sadly, he died in 2007, at the age of forty-one, just before this version of the book was published.

Barry Miles, *Frank Zappa* (London: Atlantic Books edition, 2004)

Barry Miles is one of the most prolific writers on musicians and poets from the sixties. He's written biographies of Allen Ginsberg, Paul McCartney, Bob Dylan, and Frank Zappa. In his Zappa bio, the attention to detail is extraordinary, but he makes too many judgments about Zappa's behavior, particularly in terms of his own family. Miles is totally involved with his subject and his work, yet what he gives with one hand, he takes away with the other.

Greg Russo, *Cosmik Debris: The Collected History and Improvisations of Frank Zappa (Son of Revised)* (Floral Park, New York: Crossfire Publications, 2006)

Russo's book is an indispensible guide to all things Zappa, from rare images to complete touring schedules and TV appearances. The layout and typesetting is horrible, but Russo's determination to get the facts right makes up for its rough look. You'll never find a better Zappa database in book form.

Neil Slaven, *Electric Don Quixote: The Story of Frank Zappa* (London: Omnibus Press, 1997)

Neil Slaven's well-written biography balances his personal love for the man while maintaining a safe, critical distance from his subject. The whole notion of the Don Quixote story perfectly describes Zappa's persona and his narrow-minded, obsessive focus. Slaven makes some interesting observations about Zappa's humor and how it changed over the years through his songs. Highly recommended.

Ben Watson, *Frank Zappa: The Negative Dialectics of Poodle Play* (New York: St. Martin's Griffin, 1996)

The Professor is in! Ben Watson's book is a mind-bending experience. It was written just after Zappa died and remains the gold standard of Zappa scholarship. His understanding and explanation of conceptual continuity is exquisite. But the book is not suited to a first year Zappa student, in my opinion. This hefty tome is what you graduate to after becoming familiar with the music; otherwise, your brain may start to hurt.

Frank Zappa with Peter Occhiogrosso, *The Real Frank Zappa Book* (New York: Poseidon Press, 1989)

No true fan of Zappa should be without this book. It's a great read, but not perfect. You would think that the man himself would write the last word on Frank Zappa. Not so. Zappa probably wasn't at his best when he finally decided to write a book and deliver it kicking and screaming to the publisher shortly after the failed 1988 tour. That said, his anecdotes, opinions, and ideas are on full display here, whether you like them or not, so get the Russo book as well so that you can cross-reference Mr. Zappa's facts, just in case. The illustrations in the book suggest a graphic novel would have been a great way to tell his story, too. Any takers?

Complete Discography

This is the official, complete list of Frank Zappa's recorded output as authorized by the Zappa Family Trust, with label plus original release date included for each record.

Freak Out! (O.R. #1, Verve, June 27, 1966)

Absolutely Free (O.R. #2, Verve, June 26, 1967)

We're Only in It for the Money (O.R. #3, Verve, March 4, 1968)

Lumpy Gravy (O.R. #4, Verve, May 13, 1968)

Cruising with Ruben & the Jets (O.R. #5, Bizarre/Verve, December 2, 1968)

Mothermania (O.R. #6, Bizarre/Verve, March 24, 1969)

Uncle Meat (O.R. #7, Bizarre/Reprise, April 21, 1969)

Hot Rats (O.R. #8, Bizarre/Reprise, October 15, 1969)

Burnt Weeny Sandwich (O.R. #9, Bizarre/Reprise, February 9, 1970)

Weasels Ripped My Flesh (O.R. #10, Bizarre/Reprise, August 10, 1970)

Chunga's Revenge (O.R. #11, Bizarre/Reprise, October 23, 1970)

Fillmore East—June 1971 (O.R. #12, Bizarre/Reprise, August 2, 1971)

Frank Zappa's 200 Motels (O.R. #13, Bizarre/United Artists, October 4, 1971)

Just Another Band from L.A. (O.R. #14, Bizarre/Reprise, March 26, 1972)

Waka/Jawaka (O.R. #15, Bizarre/Reprise, July 5, 1972)

The Grand Wazoo (O.R. #16, Bizarre/Reprise, November 27, 1972)

Over-Nite Sensation (O.R. #17, DiscReet, September 7, 1973)

Apostrophe (') (O.R. #18, DiscReet, March 22, 1974)

Roxy & Elsewhere (O.R. #19, DiscReet, September 10, 1974)

One Size Fits All (O.R. #20, DiscReet, June 25, 1975)

Bongo Fury (O.R. #21, DiscReet, October 2, 1975)

Zoot Allures (O.R. #22, Warner Bros., October 29, 1976)

Zappa in New York (O.R. #23, DiscReet, March 13, 1978)

Studio Tan (O.R. #24, DiscReet, September 15, 1978)

Sleep Dirt (O.R. #25, DiscReet, January 12, 1979)

Sheik Yerbouti (O.R. #26, Zappa, March 3, 1979)

Orchestral Favorites (O.R. #27, DiscReet, May 4, 1979)

Joe's Garage, Act I (O.R. #28, Zappa, September 3, 1979)

Joe's Garage, Acts II & III (O.R. #29, Zappa, November 19, 1979)

Tinsel Town Rebellion (O.R. #30, Barking Pumpkin, May 11, 1981)

Shut Up 'n Play Yer Guitar (O.R. #31, Barking Pumpkin, May 11, 1981)

Shut Up 'n Play Yer Guitar Some More (O.R. #32, Barking Pumpkin, May 11, 1981)

Return of the Son of Shut Up 'n Play Yer Guitar (O.R. #33, Barking Pumpkin, May 11, 1981)

You Are What You Is (O.R. #34, Barking Pumpkin, September 23, 1981)

Ship Arriving Too Late to Save a Drowning Witch (O.R. #35, Barking Pumpkin, May 3, 1982)

The Man from Utopia (O.R. #36, Barking Pumpkin, March 28, 1983)

Baby Snakes (O.R. #37, Barking Pumpkin, March 28, 1983)

London Symphony Orchestra, Vol. 1 (O.R. #38, Barking Pumpkin, June 9, 1983)

Boulez Conducts Zappa: The Perfect Stranger (O.R. #39, Angel, August 23, 1984)

Them or Us (O.R. #40, Barking Pumpkin, October 18, 1984)

Thing-Fish (O.R. #41, Barking Pumpkin, November 21, 1984)

Francesco Zappa (O.R. #42, Barking Pumpkin, November 21, 1984)

The Old Masters, Box One (O.R. #43, Barking Pumpkin, April 19, 1985)

Frank Zappa Meets the Mothers of Prevention (O.R. #44, Barking Pumpkin, November 21, 1985)

Does Humor Belong in Music? (O.R. #45, EMI UK, January 27, 1986)

The Old Masters, Box Two (O.R. #46, Barking Pumpkin, November 25, 1986)

Jazz from Hell (O.R. #47, Barking Pumpkin, November 25, 1986)

London Symphony Orchestra, Vol. 2 (O.R. #48, Barking Pumpkin, September 17, 1987)

The Old Masters, Box Three (O.R. #49, Barking Pumpkin, December 30, 1987)

Guitar (O.R. #50, Barking Pumpkin, April 26, 1988)

You Can't Do That on Stage Anymore, Vol. 1 (O.R. #51, Rykodisc May 9, 1988)

You Can't Do That on Stage Anymore, Vol. 2 (O.R. #52, Rykodisc, October 25, 1988)

Broadway the Hard Way (O.R. #53, Barking Pumpkin, October 25, 1988)

You Can't Do That on Stage Anymore, Vol. 3 (O.R. #54, Rykodisc, November 13, 1989)

The Best Band You Never Heard in Your Life (O.R. #55, Barking Pumpkin, April 16, 1991)

Make a Jazz Noise Here (O.R. #56, Barking Pumpkin, June 4, 1991)

You Can't Do That on Stage Anymore, Vol. 4 (O.R. #57, Rykodisc, June 14, 1991)

You Can't Do That on Stage Anymore, Vol. 5 (O.R. #58, Rykodisc, July 10, 1992)

You Can't Do That on Stage Anymore, Vol. 6 (O.R. #59, Rykodisc, July 10, 1992)

Playground Psychotics (O.R. #60, Barking Pumpkin, October 27, 1992)

Ahead of Their Time (O.R. #61, Barking Pumpkin, April 20, 1993)

The Yellow Shark (O.R. #62, Barking Pumpkin, November 2, 1993)

Civilization Phaze III (O.R. #63, Barking Pumpkin, December 2, 1994)

The Lost Episodes (O.R. #64, Rykodisc, February 27, 1996)

Läther (O.R. #65, Rykodisc, September 24, 1996)

Frank Zappa Plays the Music of Frank Zappa: A Memorial Tribute (O.R. #66, Barking Pumpkin, October 31, 1996)

Have I Offended Someone? (O.R. #67, Rykodisc, April 8, 1997)

Mystery Disc (O.R. #68, Rykodisc, September 15, 1998)

Everything Is Healing Nicely (O.R. #69, Barking Pumpkin, December 21, 1999)

FZ:OZ (O.R. #70, Vaulternative, August 16, 2002)

Halloween (O.R. #71, Vaulternative, February 4, 2003)

Joe's Corsage (O.R. #72, Vaulternative, May 30, 2004)

QuAUDIOPHILIAc (O.R. #73, Barking Pumpkin, September 14, 2004)

Joe's Domage (O.R. #74, Vaulternative, October 1, 2004)

Joe's XMASage (O.R. #75, Vaulternative, December 21, 2005)

Imaginary Diseases (O.R. #76, Zappa Records, January 13, 2006)

Trance-Fusion (O.R. #77, Zappa Records, November 7, 2006)

The MOFO Project/Object (Fazedooh) (O.R. #78, Zappa Records, December 5, 2006)

The MOFO Project/Object (O.R. #79, Zappa Records, December 12, 2006)

Buffalo (O.R. #80, Vaulternative, April 1, 2007)

The Dub Room Special! (O.R. #81, Zappa Records, August 24, 2007)

Wazoo (O.R. #82, Vaulternative, October 31, 2007)

One Shot Deal (O.R. #83, Zappa Records, June 13, 2008)

Joe's Ménage (O.R. #84, Vaulternative Records, September 26, 2008)

The Lumpy Money Project/Object (O.R. #85, Zappa Records, January 21, 2009)

Philly '76 (O.R. #86, Vaulternative Records, December 15, 2009)

Greasy Love Songs (O.R. #87, Zappa Records, April 19, 2010)

"Congress Shall Make No Law . . ." (O.R. #88, Zappa Records, September 19, 2010)

Hammersmith Odeon (O.R. #89, Vaulternative Records, November 6, 2010)

Feeding the Monkees at Ma Maison (O.R. #90, Zappa Records, September 22, 2011)

Carnegie Hall (O.R. #91, Vaulternative Records, November 17, 2011)

Understanding America (O.R. #92, Zappa Records/UMe, October 30, 2012)

Road Tapes, Venue #1 (O.R. #93, Vaulternative Records, November 7, 2012)

Finer Moments (O.R. #94, Zappa Records/Ume, December 12, 2012)

AAAFNRAA—Baby Snakes—The Complete Soundtrack (O.R. #95, Zappa Records digital download, December 21, 2012)

Road Tapes, Venue #2 (O.R. #96, Vaulternative Records, October 31, 2013)

A Token of His Extreme Soundtrack (O.R. #97, Zappa Records, November 25, 2013)

Joe's Camouflage (O.R. #98, Vaulternative Records, January 30, 2014)

Roxy by Proxy (O.R. #99, Zappa Records, March 13, 2014)

Dance Me This (O.R. #100, Zappa Records, June 19, 2015)

Compilations and Collectable Samplers (various formats)

*The **** of the Mothers* (Verve, October 13, 1969)

The Mothers of Invention (MGM, July 20, 1970)

The Worst of the Mothers (MGM, March 15, 1971)

Rare Meat (Rhino, February 7, 1983)

The Guitar World According to Frank Zappa (Barking Pumpkin cassette, June 1987)

You Can't Do That on Stage Anymore Sampler (Barking Pumpkin, April 1988)

Cucamonga Years (Japan, December 10, 1991)

Strictly Commercial: The Best of Frank Zappa (Rykodisc, August 21, 1995)

Strictly Genteel: A "Classical" Introduction to Frank Zappa (Rykodisc, May 20, 1997)

Cucamonga (Del-Fi, February 24, 1998)

Cheap Thrills (Rykodisc, April 28, 1998)

Son of Cheep Thrills (Rykodisc, April 27, 1999)

The Secret Jewel Box: Archives Vol. 2—Original Recordings of Frank Zappa (Light Without Heat Corp., December 11, 2001)

Threesome No. 1 (Rykodisc, April 23, 2002)

Threesome No. 2 (Rykodisc, April 23, 2002)

Zappa Picks by Jon Fishman of Phish (Rykodisc, October 15, 2002)

Zappa Picks by Larry LaLonde of Primus (Rykodisc, October 15, 2002)

The Best of Frank Zappa (Rykodisc UK, November 1, 2004)

The Frank Zappa AAAFNRAA Birthday Bundle (Zappa Records digital download, December 15, 2006)

The Frank Zappa AAA·FNR·AAA Birthday Bundle 21.Dec.2008 (Zappa Records digital download, December 21, 2008)

The Frank Zappa AAA·FNRAA·AA Birthday Bundle 21.Dec.2010 (Zappa Records digital download, December 21, 2010)

Paul Buff Presents the PAL and Original Sound Studio Archives: The Collection (Crossfire Publications, January 24, 2011)

Penguin in Bondage/The Little Known History of the Mothers of Invention (Zappa Records digital download, May 10, 2011)

The Frank Zappa AAAFNRAAAAAM Birthday Bundle 21.Dec.2011 (Zappa Records digital download, December 21, 2011)

The Frank Zappa AAAFNRAA Birthday Bundle 21.12.2014 (Zappa Records digital download, December 21, 2014)

Beat the Boots Series (RHINO)

Beat the Boots (July 1991)

As an Am
The Ark
Freaks & Motherfu#@%!*
Unmitigated Audacity
Anyway the Wind Blows
'Tis the Season to Be Jelly
Saarbrucken 1978
Piquantique

Beat the Boots 2

Disconnected Synapses
Tengo Na Minchia Tanta
Electric Aunt Jemima
At the Circus
Swiss Cheese/Fire!
Our Man in Nirvana
Conceptual Continuity

Beat the Boots III (January 2009, digital downloads only)

A six-disc set containing selected bootleg tracks from *Apocrypha*, *Pigs & Repugnant*, *Son of Pigs & Repugnant*, *Big Mother Is Watching You*, *Randomonium*, and *Zut Alors*.

Films and Videos

200 Motels (October 1971)
Baby Snakes (December 1979)
Dub Room Special (October 1982)
Does Humor Belong in Music? (January 1985)
Video from Hell (January 1987)
Uncle Meat (January 1988)
True Story of 200 Motels (January 1989)
The Amazing Mr. Bickford (May 1989)
The Torture Never Stops (1982/2008)

The Singles

"How Could I Be Such a Fool?" b/w "Help I'm a Rock, 3rd Movement: It Can't Happen Here" (Verve, June 29, 1966)

"Trouble Every Day" b/w "Who Are the Brain Police?" (Verve, November 14, 1966)

"Why Don't You Do Me Right" b/w "Beg Leg Mama" (Verve, April 10, 1967)

"Lonely Little Girl b/w "Mother People" (Verve, November 20, 1967)

"My Guitar" b/w "Dog Breath" (Bizarre/Reprise, September 1, 1969)

"WPLJ" b/w "My Guitar" (Bizarre/Reprise, February 23, 1970)

"Tell Me You Love Me" b/w "Will You Go All the Way for the USA?" (Bizarre/ Reprise, November 9, 1970)

"Tears Begin to Fall" b/w "Junier Mintz Boogie" (Bizarre/Reprise, October 20, 1971)

"Magic Fingers" b/w "Daddy, Daddy, Daddy" (United Artists, November 8, 1971)

"Cletus Awreetus-Awrightus" b/w "Eat That Question" (Bizarre/Reprise, November 6, 1972)

"I'm the Slime" b/w "Montana" (DiscReet, October 29, 1971)

"Don't Eat the Yellow Snow" b/w "Cosmik Debris" (DiscReet, October 7, 1974)

"Find Her Finer" b/w "Zoot Allures" (Warner Bros., November 29, 1976)

"Disco Boy" b/w "Ms. Pinky" (Warner Bros., March 7, 1977)

"Dancin' Fool" b/w "Baby Snakes" (Zappa April 2, 1979)

"Dancin' Fool (12-inch Extended Mix)" (Zappa, April 23, 1979)

"Joe's Garage" b/w "Central Scrutinizer" (Zappa, October 29, 1979)

"I Don't Wanna Get Drafted" b/w "Ancient Armaments" (Zappa, April 28, 1980)

"Goblin Girl" b/w "Pink Napkins" (Barking Pumpkin, October 26, 1981)

"Valley Girl" b/w "You Are What You Is" (Barking Pumpkin, July 5, 1982)

True Glove EP: "Be in My Video" / "He's So Gay" / "Won Ton On" (EMI France, October 12, 1974)

"I Don't Wanna Get Drafted" b/w "Ancient Armaments" (Zappa reissue, April 19, 1985)

"Peaches En Regalia" / "I'm Not Satisfied" / "Lucille Has Messed Up My Mind" (Rykodisc, November 13, 1987)

"Sexual Harassment in the Workplace" / "Watermelon in Easter Hay" (Rykodisc, April 1988)

"Zomby Woof" / "You Didn' Try to Call Me" (Rykodisc, April 1988)

"Montana (Whipping Floss)" / "Cheepnis" (Rykodisc, May 1988)

"Stairway to Heaven" / "Bolero" (Zappa, February 25, 1991)

Selected Bibliography

As I state in the introduction, the sources of information on Frank Zappa are many. This selected bibliography contains the sources I went to most often and the ones I trust as being most accurate.

Books

Barnes, Mike. *Captain Beefheart: The Biography.* London, England: Omnibus Press, 2010 (revised).

Butcher, Pauline. *Freak Out! My Life with Frank Zappa.* London, England: Plexus Books, 2011.

Courrier, Kevin. *Dangerous Kitchen: The Subversive World of Zappa.* Toronto, Canada: ECW Press, 2002.

Courrier, Kevin. *Trout Mask Replica.* 33&1/3 Series. New York: Continuum, 2007.

Greenaway, Andrew. *Zappa the Hard Way.* Bedford, England: Wymer Publishing, 2010.

Ives, Charles. *Essays Before a Sonata.* The Knickerbocker Press 1920; Dover Publications Ltd., 1962 (reissue).

Kaylan, Howard, with Jeff Tamarkin. *Shell Shocked: My Life with the Turtles, Flo & Eddie, and Frank Zappa, etc . . .* Montclair, New Jersey: Backbeat Books, 2013.

Komara, Edward, with Scott Parker. *ZaFTIG: The Zappa Family Trust (Compact Disc) Issues Guide.* Waterbury, Connecticut: SPB Publishing, 2015.

Lewisohn, Mark. *Tune In: The Beatles, All These Years, Vol. 1.* New York: Crown Architype, 2013.

Lowe, Kelly Fisher. *The Words and Music of Frank Zappa.* Lincoln, Nebraska: Bison Books, 2007.

Menuhin, Yehudi, and Davis, Curtis W. *The Music of Man.* New York: Methuen, 1979.

Miles, Barry. *Frank Zappa.* London, England: Atlantic Books, 2004.

Russo, Greg. *Cosmik Debris: The Collected History and Improvisations of Frank Zappa*. Floral Park, New York: Crossfire Publications, 2006.

Salzman, Eric. *Twentieth-Century Music: An Introduction*. (Second Edition) Englewood Cliffs, New Jersey: Prentice-Hall, 1974.

Slaven, Neil. *Electric Don Quixote: The Story of Frank Zappa*. London, England: Omnibus Press, 1997.

Watson, Ben. *Frank Zappa: The Negative Dialectic of Poodle Play*. New York: St. Martin's Griffin Press, 1996.

Watson, Ben. *Frank Zappa: The Complete Guide to His Music*. London, England: Omnibus Press, 2011.

Young, Jordan R. *Spike Jones off the Record: The Man who Murdered Music*. Beverly Hills, California: Past Times Publishing, 1994.

Zappa, Frank, with Peter Occhiogrosso. *The Real Frank Zappa Book*. New York: Poseidon Press, 1989.

Zappa, Patrice Candy. *My Brother Was a Mother: A Zappa Family Album*. Los Angeles, California: California Classics Books, 2003.

Articles

Barnes, Mike. "The Torture Never Stops." *PROG* magazine issue #57, July 2015.

Menn, Don (editor). "Zappa!" From the publishers of *Keyboard* and *Guitar Player*. San Francisco, California, 1992.

Pena, Carlos E. Book Review for *Frank Zappa and the And* (Ashgate 2013) ASRC Journal, Volume 45, #1, Spring 2014.

Thompson, Dave. "Frank Zappa: The Controversy and Touring Hell of 1970–71." *Goldmine*, 2002.

Web Sites

www.afka.net

www.angelfire.com/freak2/arfz/equipment.html

www.brucebickford.com

www.globalia.net/donlope/fz/index.html

www.groundguitar.com

www.lukpac.org

www.united-mutations.com

wiki.killuglyradio.com

en.wikipedia.org
en.wikiquote.org/wiki/Frank_Zappa
www.zappa.com
www.zappasgear.com
www.zappanale.de/en/
www.zappateers.com

Radio

Coulter, Phil. *I Am All the Day and the Night: The Music of Frank Zappa*. Toronto, Canada: CBC Radio, 2008. Three-part series.
Primetime with Ralph Benmurgui. Toronto, Canada: CBC Radio, Dec. 16, 1988.
Pure Radio Kaos, with Bobby Marquis, Ottawa, Canada: CKCU-FM. Interviews with Pauline Butcher, Bobby Zappa, Bob Harris, and Nigey Lennon.

Television (via YouTube)

CNN Crossfire, 1986
The Steve Allen Show, 1963
The Dick Cavett Show, 1982
The Late Show (BBC2) with Matthew Collings, 1993
The Mike Douglas Show, 1976
The Yellow Shark (Germany), 1992

Documentaries

The Mothers of Invention (Prism Films, 2005)
The Freak Out List (Chrome Dreams, 2009)

Index

Abbey Road, 86
Absolutely Free (album), 18, 34, 35, 40, 63, 100, 153, 200, 238, 239, 247, 272, 277
"Absolutely Free," 127
Abnuceals Emuukha Electric Symphony Orchestra, 123, 168, 230
AC/DC, 156
Adelaide Tonight, 216
"Adventures of Greggery Peccary, The," 92, 131
Ahead of Their Time, 119, 200, 241, 249, 250, 252, 279
Ahoy, the, 196
Alice Cooper, 47, 64, 65, 174, 217, 292
Allman Brothers, the, 215
"All I Want for Christmas Is My Two Front Teeth," 90
All Music Guide, 269
"All You Need Is Love," 87, 128
All You Need Is Love (TV series), 209
Alta Loma, California, 6
Alte Oper, 123
Altham, Keith, 21
Altschul, Mike, 41, 140, 230
Amazing Mr. Bickford, The, 217, 282
"America Drinks and Goes Home," 59, 271
American Society of University Composers, 17
"Amnesia Vivace," 18
Amos and Andy, 131
Andronis, Harry, 138
"Andy," 108, 156
"Angel in My Life," 21
Animals, the, 77

Antelope Valley, 3
Antelope Valley Junior College, 4, 6
Antelope Valley Union High School, 3
Anti-Defamation League (B'Nai B'rith), 113, 155
Any Way the Wind Blows, 109, 237, 238
Apostrophe ('), 48, 112, 151, 157, 183, 217, 236, 238, 239, 240, 242, 243, 248, 253, 263, 277
Apprenticeship of Duddy Kravitz, The, 198
"Approximate," 116, 184
Arf Society, 272
Askin, Ali, 138
Altenhaus, Phyllis, 216
Athens, Ohio, 35
Atlantic Records, 52, 54
Atlas missile, 3
Auger, Brian, 174
"Auld Lang Syne," 185
Avant-Garde, the, 11, 83, 109
Aynsley Dunbar Retaliation, the, 41

Baby Snakes (video), 213, 215, 217, 234, 238, 239, 245, 258, 280, 282
Bad Doberan, Germany, xiii, 271
Baker, Ginger, 193
Baker, Susan, 224
Ballard, Hank, and the Midnighters, 21
Ballets Russes, 14, 125
Baltimore, Maryland, xiii, 1–2, 223
BAM, 57, 74
Bancroft Library, 145
Band, the, 133
Banned from Utopia, 240, 245, 246, 247, 269
Barclay, Michael, 176

Barking Pumpkin, 69, 81, 270
Barking Pumpkin Digital
    Gratification Consort, 144
Barnes, Mike, 48–50, 255
Barney's Version, 199
Barrow, Arthur, xi, 119, 149, 182, 187,
    191, 230, 240, 246
Bartok, Bela, 23, 120, 192
Basement Tapes, The, 133
Bears, the, 233
Beat Instrumental, 84, 179
Beat the Boots, 135, 136, 249, 250, 281
Beat the Boots 2, 99, 136
Beat the Boots III, 86, 136
Beatles, the, 25, 27–28, 35, 63, 64, 78,
    83–87, 94, 95, 110, 126, 128,
    193, 199, 203, 205, 209, 285
Beatles Anthology, The, 87
Beats, 78
Bedford-Stuyvesant, 24
Beethoven, 142, 199
Belcher, Lorraine, 8
Belew, Adrian, xiii, 88, 118, 181, 186,
    213, 231–233, 258
Belmont University, 251
"Beltway Bandits, The," 146
Belvin, Jesse, 21
Bennett, Max, 233
Berkeley School of Music, 34
Berg, Alban, 14
Bergamo, John, 233
Berkman, Harold, 67
Berry, Chuck, 161, 175
Berry, Richard, 123
Bessman, Jim, 151
*Best Band You Never Heard in Your Life,
    The*, 24, 110, 116, 173, 197, 240,
    245, 278
Bethel, New York, 178
Bettini, Gianni (Inventor), 133
Bikel, Theodore, 205, 208
Bickford, Bruce, 211, 213, 215, 217, 220
Big Pink, 133
"Big Swifty," 42

Billboard, 37, 38, 65, 69, 71, 85, 95,
    103, 109, 118, 149, 151, 208
Billboard Hot 100, 24, 94, 95, 114, 154
"Billie Jean," 88
"Billy the Mountain," 97–98, 120, 201
Birds of Fire, 175
Bird on a Wire (film), 209
Bitches Brew, 42
Bizarre Records, 63, 250
Black, Jimmy Carl, 17, 25–27, 33–34,
    36–37, 149, 205, 234, 241, 246,
    267, 268
"Black and Blue Danube Waltz," 93
Blackouts, the, 4, 250
"Black Napkins," 40, 164, 220
"Black Page, The," 184, 213, 233, 234,
    237, 253
Blackwood, Nina, 214
Blake, Peter, 84
Blast magazine, 75
"Blessed Relief," 43, 270
Bley, Carla, 34
Block, Martin, 91
Blonde on Blonde, 35, 87, 108
Blood, Sweat and Tears, 34
Bluejeans & Moonbeams, 48
Blue Whale (band), 239
Blues, 11, 21, 42, 108, 158, 161, 236,
    239
Bogus Pomp, 268–269
Bogdanas, Konstantinas, xiii
Bongo Fury, 44–49, 77, 104, 120, 137,
    151, 234, 236, 238, 240, 255,
    256, 260, 277
Bonner, Gary, 95
Boone, Pat, 5, 54
Bootlegs, 86, 99, 133–136
"Bossa Nova Pervertamento," 93
Boston Chamber Orchestra, 19
Boston Globe Jazz Festival, 179
Boston Symphony Orchestra, 14, 19
Boulez, Pierre, 74, 123, 144, 217
Bowie, David, 35, 233
"Boy Wonder I Love You," 243

Bozzio, Terry, 118, 123, 183–184, 213, 234, 238, 261
Braden, Tom, 221
Brandstein, Eve, 75
Brandt, Eddie, 90
Bread for Heads Festival, 178
"Break Time," 137
Brecker, Michael, 236
Brecker, Randy, 236
Briggs, David, 65
Broadside (club), 26
Broadway the Hard Way, 24, 88, 92, 101–102, 110, 177, 190, 197, 228, 240, 245, 278
Brock, Napoleon Murphy, 116, 156, 211, 236, 261, 269, 272
Brown, Clarence "Gatemouth," 5, 21
"Brown Shoes Don't Make It," 153, 270, 272
Brown, T. B., 135
Bruce, Denny, 33
Bruce, Jack, 193
Bruce, Lenny, 64, 132
Bruford, Bill, 244
Bruner, Wally, 211
Buckley, Tim, 65, 67, 174
Buddy Miles Express, the, 174
Buffalo (album), 103, 118, 230, 237, 242, 257, 279
Buffalo Beat (newspaper), 269
Buffalo, New York, 80, 119, 174,
Buffalo Philharmonic Orchestra, 269
Buffalo Springfield, 34
Buff, Paul, 6–8, 137, 281
Buffett, Jimmy, 175
Burnt Weeny Sandwich, 18, 37, 93, 169– 170, 203, 238, 239, 241–243, 247, 252, 277
Butcher, Pauline, 38, 51, 62, 79, 85–86, 153–154, 204, 273, 287
Butler, Anya, 52
"Bwana Dik," 208
Byers, Bill, 41
Byrds, the, 28, 30, 94

Cable News Network (CNN), 220, 224, 226, 287
Cage, John, 35, 175, 270
Cadillacs, the, 21
California Institute of Arts, 234
"Can I Come Over Tonight," 23
Canby, Vincent, 208
Canned Heat, 34, 174
Capitol/EMI, 67–68, 84
Captain Beefheart, 5, 44–50, 65, 104–105, 109, 151, 172, 241, 250, 255, 260, 285
Captain Beefheart and the Magic Band, 35, 44–45, 48, 243, 252
Captain Beefheart vs. The Grunt People, 7
Captain Glasspack and his Magic Mufflers, 27
Carey, Tim, 219
Carlson, Van, 138
Carman, Paul, 164, 190, 237
Carnegie Hall, 98, 244, 248, 255, 279
Carter, Jimmy, 69, 103,
Cash, Johnny, 116
Castaway's Choice, 23
"Catholic Girls," 111, 153, 156
Cats (musical), 209
Cavett, Dick, 76
CBC Radio, 183, 187, 287
CBC Weekend, 58
CBS Symphony Orchestra, 18
"Central Park in the Dark," 16–17
Cerveris, Don, 4
Cesak, Vaclav, xiii
Chaffee Junior College, 6
"Chana in De Bushwop," 55
Cheka, Mark, 27, 62
Chepesiuk, Ron, 77, 88
"Chloe," 93
Cherry, Don, 174
Chicago Transit Authority, 174
Cholmondeley, Andre, 269
"Chunga's Revenge," 119
Chunga's Revenge (album), 97, 208, 233, 238, 239, 243, 244, 255, 277

Cincinnati College Conservatory of Music, 35
Circular, 67, 199
Circus Raves, 180
"City of Tiny Lites," 120, 231
City Slickers, the (Spike Jones), 90–92
Civilization Phaze III, 20, 125, 128, 202, 239, 240, 250, 279
CJOH-TV, 179
CKCU-FM, 4, 188, 212, 287
Clapton, Eric, 193
Claremont, California, 3, 6
"Cletus Awreetus-Awrightus," 43, 282
Cleveland, Ohio, 34
"Clonemeister," 35, 187, 191, 230, 231
Closing Time, 176
Coasters, the, 21
Coates, Albert, 19
"Cocaine Decisions," 59, 192
"Cocktails for Two," 92–93
Cohen, Herb, 27, 30–31, 33, 35, 37–38, 45, 49, 61–67, 96, 175, 250
Cohen, Scott, 180
Colaiuta, Vinnie, 237
"Conceptual Continuity," 93, 198–201, 270, 276
Columbus Dispatch, the, 86
Collinge, John, 262
Collins, Phil, 251
Collins, Ray, 7, 26–27, 33, 37, 128, 204, 238, 241
Coltrane, John, 19, 40
Compact Video, 215
Complete Works of Edgard Varese, Volume 1, 11–12
Connolly, Billy, 102
Convair, 3
"Concentration Moon," 127
Contempo 70 Festival, 96, 204
Corbett, John, 39
Corbijn, Anton, 50
Corsair, 23
Cosmo Alley, 62

Coulter, Phil, 183, 187–188, 287
Couric, Katie, 222
Courrier, Kevin, xi, 29, 46, 65, 131, 150, 155, 255, 273, 285
Cream (band), 193
Cream: Farewell Concert, 205
Creem Magazine, 64
"Crew Slut," 153–154, 156, 158
Crickets, the, 25
Crislu, Spencer, 86
Crosby, Bing, 91
Crosby, Stills and Nash, 178
Crossfire (CNN), 220, 224, 287
"Crucified on Technology" (artwork), 170
Cruising with Ruben & the Jets, 10, 101, 114, 149, 200, 238, 239, 241, 252, 277
CSI:NY, 55
Cucamonga, California, 6, 26, 137
Cuccurullo, Warren, 183, 188, 217, 238
Culver City, California, 211
Curtis Institute of Music, 18, 185, 230, 246

Dali, Salvador, 207
Daily Report, 8
Dallas, Karl, 74
Dalton, Kathy, 67
"Damp Ankles," 147
Dance Me This, 18, 20, 106, 124–125, 253, 280
Dancer in Wartime, A, 209
Danforth, Senator John, 226
Dangerous Kitchen, The, 29, 131, 150, 155, 273, 285
Darley, Dick, 211
"Darling Nikki," 224
Dave Brubeck Quartet, the, 179
Davis, Miles, 39, 42
"D.C. Boogie," 43
"Dead Girls of London," 69

Debussy, Claude, 12
Debutante Daisy, 101, 156, 158
Deep Creek, 248
Delaney & Bonnie, 242
Dells, the, 5
"Density 21.5," 12
"Dental Hygiene Dilemma," 207
Denver, John, 226
"Der Fuehrer's Face," 91–92
"Desérts," 13
Devores, Courtney, 264
Dial Records, 14
"Dickie's Such an Asshole," 196, 245
Diliberto, John, 145
"Dinah-Moe Humm," 107, 156–157
Dinner Music for People Who Aren't Very
    Hungry, 93
"Dio Fa," 128
Dion, 175
"Directly from My Heart to You," 128,
    243
Derek and the Dominoes, 242
Desert Island Discs, 23
"Dirty Love," xiv, 100
"Dirty Water," 37
Disco Music, 11, 29, 76
Disney Studios, 55
Dmochowski, Alex. See Erroneous, 41
Do It Now Foundation, 58
Does Humor Belong in Music (album),
    54, 278
Does Humor Belong in Music (video),
    163, 215, 247, 251, 256, 258,
    282
Does Humor Belong in Classical Music?,
    270
"Dog Breath, in the Year of the
    Plague," 200
"Dog Breath Variations," 200, 213
Don & Dewey, 21
Dondorf, Dave, 138
Doo-Wop, 11, 21, 101, 109, 114, 128
Douglas, Mike, 15, 64, 213, 220

Downbeat magazine, 39–40, 73, 185,
    266
Dr. Hook, 175
Driscoll, Julie, 174
Dub Room Special!, 215, 239, 240, 245,
    279, 282
"Duet for Violin and Garbage
    Disposal," 93
Duke, George, 41, 43, 93, 98, 116, 140,
    211, 238, 248
"Duke of Orchestral Prunes," 131
"Duke of Prunes," 100, 123, 168
"Dumb All Over," 150, 215
Dunbar, Aynsley, 41, 93, 98, 204–205,
    239
Duran, Tony, 267
Dylan, Bob, 29, 35, 83, 87–88, 94, 108,
    133–134, 247, 275

Easy Action (Alice Cooper album), 65
"Eat That Question," 43, 282
Ebert, Roger, 208
Echo Park, 6
Ed Palermo Big Band, 267
Edgewood, Maryland, 2
Edinboro, Pennsylvania, 117
Edison Records (bootleg label), 140
Einstein, Albert, 201
El Cajon, California, 3
Electric Don Quixote, 3, 29, 87, 96, 164,
    275, 286
Electric Flag, the, 174
Electronic Musician, 145
Ellis, Don, 230, 238, 243, 248
Ensemble Ambrosius, 270
Ensemble Modern, 18, 122, 270, 292
"Envelopes," 185
Epstein, Brian, 28
Erroneous, 41
Ertegun, Ahmet, 52, 54
Essays Before a Sonata, 17, 285
Estrada, Roy, 25–27, 33, 36–38, 149, 239
Evans, Bill, 39, 43

"Eve of Destruction," 87
Everything Is Healing Nicely, 126, 279
Exclaim!, 176

Factory (band), 34
Falwell, Jerry, 104
"Family Room," 4
Fantasy Faire and Music Festival, 178
Farren, Mick, 105
"Farther O'Blivion," 43
Federal Bureau of Investigation, 1
Federal Communications
    Commission, 155
Ferguson, Janet, 42, 205
Fernbacher, Joseph, 174
Fielder, Jim, 34
Fillmore East, 98, 179
Fillmore West, 179
Finer Moments, 241, 244, 248, 250, 252,
    255, 280
Fisher Lowe, Kelly, 100, 103, 111, 155,
    275
Firesign Theatre, 132
Fischer, Wild Man, 47
"Five Movements for String Quartet,
    Op. 5," 14
"Flakes," 87
Fleetwood Mac, 175, 193
Flint, Michigan, 34
Flo and Eddie, 42, 93, 95, 97–100, 120,
    204, 207, 229, 238, 239, 244,
    248, 250, 255
Florida Symphony Orchestra, 268
"Flower Punk," 127
Foghat, 175
Foo, Richard, 135
For Mother's Sake (book), 234
Ford, Mary, 171
Forte, Dan, 1, 3, 155
Four Deuces, the, 170, 242
Fowler, Bruce, 190, 196, 240, 246
Fowler, Tom, 116, 175, 188, 211, 240,
    247, 267, 269

Fowler, Walt, 164, 190, 240, 267
Fowler, William, 240
Frampton, Peter, 113–114
Francesco Zappa, 145, 200, 278
Frank Zappa (book by Barry Miles),
    63, 275
*Frank Zappa Meets the Mothers of
    Prevention*, 227, 228, 278
Franzoni, Karl, 30
Fraternity of Man, 34
Freaks, 29–30, 78
Freak Out!, 23, 28–30, 35, 38, 40, 43, 46,
    63, 79, 83, 87, 92, 106, 108–109,
    123, 138, 150, 152, 199, 223,
    238, 239, 243, 247, 277
Freak Out! My Life with Frank Zappa, 38,
    51, 62, 86, 153, 273, 285
Fred Zeppelin, 53, 261
French, John, 46, 255
French Tobacco Company, 1
Fritts, Edward, 225
"Frogs with Dirty Little Lips," 55
Fugs, the, 151, 174, 224

Gans, Geoff, 135–136
GarageBand (software program), 143
Gardner, Bunk, 34, 36–37, 65, 241,
    249, 250, 267
Gardner, Buzz, 37, 65, 241
Gardner, Donald, 90
Garfunkel, Art, 174
Gangel, Jamie, 222
Garner, Mousie (Sir Frederick Gas),
    93
Garrick Theatre, 34
Gehr, Richard, 161
Genesis (band), 251
George, Lowell, 37–38, 170, 239, 241
Genoa, Italy, 197
Geronimo Black (band), 241
Gillard, Roddie, 268
Gimme Shelter (movie), 203
Go with What You Know, 54

Gleason, Ralph J., 64
Glickman, Zach, 66
Goldthwait, Bobcat, 54
Good Times, 81
Gordon, Jim, 140, 242
Gore, Al, 224, 226
Gore, Tipper, 224, 226
Gordon, Alan, 95
Gordon, Jim, 140, 242
Gortikov, Stanley, 225
Goossens, Eugene, 1941
Graham, Bill, 179
Grammy Award, 54, 136, 147, 263
Grand Wazoo, The, 41, 43, 66, 100, 140,
     150, 230, 238, 239, 249, 277
Grandmothers, the, 234, 239, 241,
     249, 250, 267–268, 272
Granz, Norman, 62
Grateful Dead, 29, 78
Greasy Love Songs, 115, 247, 250, 279
Great White Wonder, 133
Greenaway, Andrew, 193–194, 274
Gritter, Headley, 74
Grove's *Dictionary of Music*, 145
"G-Spot Tornado," 147, 215
GTOs, the, 64, 273
Guanerra, Charles (Buzz Gardner), 37
Guanerra, John Leon (Bunk
     Gardner), 34
Guardian, the, 208
Guerin, John, 233
Guess Who, the, 174
Guitar (album), 114, 161, 163, 166–167,
     237, 238, 253, 256, 257, 258,
     278
Guitar Player magazine, 20, 77, 165,
     167–168
Guitar Slim (Eddie Jones), 21–23
Guitar World, 73
Gulfport, Mississippi, 252
"Gumbo Variations, The," 109, 150,
     233
Guy, Buddy, 23

Haden, Charlie, 34
Hague, The, 145
Haight-Ashbury, 60
Harkleroad, Bill, 46
Hammersmith Odeon, 118, 231, 245,
     258, 279
Hansen, Barry, 199
"Happy Together," 95, 244
Hard Day's Night, A (movie), 203, 205
Harris, Bob (trumpet), 242
Harris, Bob (vocalist), 106, 188, 242,
     287
Harpo, Slim, 23
Harris, Sugar Cane, 86, 97, 128, 171
Harrison, George, 242
"Harry You're a Beast," 153
Hart College of Music, 246
Hartford Courant, 245
Havens, Richie, 174
Havin' a Bad Day, 54, 261
Have I Offended Someone?, 151, 154, 224,
     244, 279
Hawking, Stephen, 200
Haworth, Jan, 84
Hayes, Isaac, 271
Hayward, Richie, 38
Head (movie), 203
"Heavenly Bank Account," 104
"Hello, My Baby," 17
The Helsinki Concert, 116, 151, 245, 253
Helsinki, Finland, 108, 116, 270
Hendrix, Jimi, 84, 85, 161, 167,
     178–179
The Hendrix Strat, 167
"Here Lies Love," 241
"Hermitage," 123
Herrmann, Bernard, 18
Hit Parader magazine, 186
Hite, Bob, 34
Hilton, Paris, 55
Hippies, 29, 78, 83, 126, 180
*History and Collective Improvisations of the
     Mothers of Invention, The*, 128

Hitline magazine, 87
HOARS (*Home Owners Association Regency Supreme*), 55
Holiday, Billie, 39
Holland, Marvin, 24
Hollie, Jeff, 181
Hollies, the, 28
Holly, Buddy, 25
Hollywood, California, 6, 32, 79, 117, 184, 218
"Homeward Bound," 174
Hopkins, Jerry, 28
Hörterer, Stefan, 234
Hot Rats, 37–38, 42, 93, 109–110, 150, 171, 233, 242, 243, 252, 255, 277
House Resolution 2911 (H. R. 2911), 226–227
Howarth, Elgar, 205, 207–208
Hower, Pam, 224
"How High the Moon," 171
Howlin' Wolf, 23, 40
Hudson, Garth, 133–134
Humble Pie, 175
Hummingbird Centre, Toronto, 264
Hunt, Ray, 26
Humphrey, Ralph, 243
Hurvitz, Sandy, 64

"I'm the Slime," 103, 217, 282
"I Don't Wanna Get Drafted," 69, 103, 283
"I Was a Teen-Age Malt Shop," 140
Idyllwild Arts Academy, 237
"Igor's Boogie," 170
"Igor's Boogie, Phase One," 170
"Illinois Enema Bandit, The," 131, 274
Imaginary Diseases, 43, 140, 240, 242, 248, 255, 279
Imperial Records, 21
In a Metal Mood, No More Mr. Nice Guy, 54
In a Silent Way, 42
"Inca Roads," 107, 213, 220, 231, 238, 245

Infidels, 87
Ingber, Elliot, 34, 229, 243
"Intégrales," 12
Internationale Essener Songtage, 179
Inventionis Mater, 270
"Ionisation," 12–13, 19
Is New Music Relevant in an Industrial Society?, 17
Italy, 1, 12, 34, 130, 197, 270
"It Ain't Necessarily the Saint James Infirmary," 114, 161
"It Just Might Be a One Shot Deal," 42
"It Must Be a Camel," 172
iTunes, 5, 12, 70–71, 82, 207, 227, 241
Ives, Charles, 11, 16–19, 23, 90
Ives, George, 16

J. Geils Band, the, 175
Jackie and the Starlites, 170
Jackson, Michael, 83, 88–89, 101
Jackson 5, 88
Jacobs, Johnny, 218
Jazz, 11, 19, 39–43, 46, 92, 114, 131, 140, 147, 171, 179, 188, 192, 233, 236, 240, 247, 248, 251, 256, 257, 258, 266, 270
Jazz from Hell, 131, 146, 150, 278
Jazz & Pop, 10, 77
Jazz in Transition, 40
Jazz Messengers, the, 40
Jobson, Eddie, 243–244
Joe's Corsage, 115, 238, 240, 279
Joe's Domage, 42, 140, 239, 279
Joe's Garage, 61, 69, 110–111, 151, 156, 165, 234, 237, 238, 247, 256, 257, 258, 277, 282
Joe's Garage, Acts II & III, 69, 278
Joe's Xmasage, 140, 279
Johnson, Lyndon, 84
Jones, Elvin, 34
Jones, Spike, 11, 13, 43, 80, 90, 92–93, 98, 100–101, 141, 214
"Jesus thinks You're a Jerk," 228
Jewels, the, 11, 21

"Jewish Princess," 113, 153, 155, 158
"Junier Mintz Boogie," 282
Just Another Band from L.A., 93, 97–98,
    120, 200, 239, 244, 248, 255, 277

Kaylan, Howard, 57, 94–97, 99, 120,
    204, 229, 244, 255
KCET-TV, 211, 213
KCRW (radio Santa Monica), 23
Keneally, Mike, 191, 193–195, 245
Kent, Nick, 47
Kenton, Stan, 230, 233
KFWB radio, Los Angeles, 29
Khovalyq, Kaigal-ool, 128
Kidson, Mike, 268
King Crimson, 233
King Lear, 112, 263
King, Mike, 71
"King Kong," 40, 129, 182, 194, 270
*King Kong: Jean-Luc Ponty Plays the
    Music of Frank Zappa*, 248
Knopfler, Mark, 87
Kobalt Music Group, 71
Kofsky, Frank, 30, 77
Komanoff, Ruth, 129, 252
Komara, Edward, 150, 152, 274
Kong's Revenge, 270
Koop, C. Everett, 102–103
Kooper, Al, 45
Koppel, Ted, 226
Koussevitzky, Serge, 19
Kottke, Leo, 175
KPFA-FM, 204
KQED-TV, San Francisco, 203
KROQ-FM, Pasadena, 68, 80, 130
Kuular, Anatolii, 125
Kunc, Richard (Dick), 35, 46, 252
Kutz, Wolfhard, 271–272
Kyser, Kay, 220

Lalala Human Steps, 123
"La Machine" (synclavier), 145
La Mesa, California, 11
Lambert, Kit, 52

Lamoureux, Francois, 261
Lamoureux, Pierre, 261
Lancaster, California, 3–4, 40, 98,
    203, 250, 256
Larry King Live, 226
Läther, 67–68, 80, 130–131, 140, 151,
    236, 239, 240, 242, 243, 244,
    248, 250, 257, 279
Laurel Canyon, California, 10, 37, 64,
    138, 211, 249
The League of Women's Voters, 190
"Legacy of a Cultural Guerilla"
    (*Downbeat* essay), 39
Leigh, Nigel, 28
Lennon, John, 25, 86, 94, 98, 209, 242
Lennon, Nigey, 102, 287
Lester, Richard, 203
Let It Rock, 24
"Let's Move to Cleveland," 258, 268
Lewisohn, Mark, 25
*Lexicon of Musical Invective: Critical
    Assaults on Composers Since
    Beethoven's Time*, 19
Library of Congress, 145
Lick My Decals Off, Baby, 48
Lickert, Martin, 205
Life, 9
"Like a Rolling Stone," 87
Linz, Austria, 196
Little Criminals, 83
Little Feat, 38, 67, 239, 241
"The Little House I Used to Live In,"
    18, 171
Little Richard, 5–6, 61, 243
Lloyd, Charles, 174
Loder, Kurt, 3
Lofton, John, 221
London, England, 42, 52, 81, 118, 119,
    141, 167, 200, 202, 205, 216
London Symphony Orchestra, Vol. 1 & 2,
    81, 125, 278
Long Beach, California, 90
Look, 11
Loose Connection, 182

Los Angeles, California, 3, 6, 9, 20, 21, 25, 29, 30, 32, 38, 41, 50, 52, 55, 62, 64, 74, 94, 98, 118, 123, 126, 138, 143, 168, 181, 183, 186, 191, 223, 233, 264
Los Angeles College of Music, 243
Los Angeles Free Press, 134
Los Angeles Philharmonic Orchestra, 134
Lost Episodes, The, 4, 9, 86, 97, 103, 138, 151, 152, 239, 240, 243, 248, 252, 257, 279
"Louie Louie," 123, 24
"Louisiana Hooker with Herpes," 86
"Lucy in the Sky with Diamonds," 86
Lunn, Doug, 256
Lumpy Gravy, 38, 109, 127, 230, 239, 241, 243, 277
LSD, 45, 60, 74, 243
Lynne, Gillian, 209

"Magdalena," 120
"Magic Fingers," 208, 282
"Magical Mystery Tour," 208
Mahavishnu Orchestra, the, 175, 249
Make a Jazz Noise Here, 18, 24, 110, 116, 120, 164, 197, 240, 245, 246, 256, 278
Malone, Tom, 140
"Managua," 213
Manor, Wayne, 228
Mann, Ed, 88, 118, 182, 190–191, 194, 196, 213, 214, 233, 245, 246, 269
Mann, Herbie, 34
The Man from Utopia, 59, 192, 237, 239, 242, 278
Mapleson, Lionel, 133
Marin County College, 192
Mars, Tommy, 103, 118, 182, 192, 213, 214, 246, 269
Martian Love Secrets, 69
Martin, Bobby (Robert), 18, 120, 182, 185, 190, 214, 230, 245, 246

Marquez, Sal, 41–42, 140
Marquis, Bobby, 4, 9, 102, 153, 188, 189, 212, 287
Maryland State Legislature, 216
Masters, the, 137
McCartney, Paul, 84, 86, 94, 193, 275
McCowan, Tom, 268
McGettrick, Kurt, 190, 194
McGuinn, Roger, 30
McGuire, Barry, 29, 87
McKillop, Keith, 3
McLaughlin, John, 175
McNally, John, 23
Meader, Dean, 133
Medium Cool, 216
"The Meek Shall Inherit Nothing," 104
Melody Maker, 74
Menuhin, a Family Portrait, 209
Mercury Records, 67, 130
MGM/Verve, 27, 35, 62
M.I. Magazine, 75
Miami Pop Festival, 167, 179
Miami Vice, TV series, 58
"Mice," 3
Mike Douglas Show, The, 64, 213, 220
Miles, Barry, 2, 8, 26, 30, 34, 63, 179, 275
Milkowski, Bill, 73, 81
Miller, Mike, 256
Milwaukee, Wisconsin, 164, 244
Mingus, Charles, 11, 39, 40, 43
Missing Persons (band), 236, 238
Mission Bay High School, 3
Mitchell, Joni, 17, 233, 237
Monday Conference (TV show), 220
"Mo 'n Herb's Vacation," 192
Monkees, the, 78, 203
Monster, 23
Monstrous Memoirs of a Mighty McFearless, The, 55
"Montana," 100, 107, 125, 151, 257, 282, 283
Montgomery, Wes, 161

Monterey, California, 3
Monteux, Pierre, 14
Montreal, Quebec, 37, 123, 179, 180, 199
Moore, Robert, 220
Moral Majority, 104, 228
Morgan, Fred, 90
Mothers of Invention, the (MOI), 7,
  17, 18, 23, 24, 25, 28, 30–31,
  32, 34, 36–40, 42, 45–46, 52,
  58, 61, 63–65, 75, 78–80, 84,
  92–93, 96, 99–100, 109–110,
  115, 119, 126, 128, 134, 138,
  141, 151, 167, 170, 174–175,
  178–179, 181, 191, 203–204,
  210, 216, 220, 223, 233, 234,
  238, 239, 241, 243, 244, 247,
  249, 250, 252, 267, 273, 280,
  287
"Mr. Tambourine Man," 30, 94
"Muffin Man, The," 49, 137
Muffin Men, the, 268, 272
Mull, Martin, 175
Mundi, Billy, 34–35, 204, 247
"Murder by Numbers," 24, 110, 177
Muroc Air Force Base (Edwards), 3
Musician Magazine, 1, 167
Music Business Journal, 71
MTV, 55, 214
My Brother Was a Mother, 2, 10, 286
"My Guitar Wants to Kill Your Mama,"
  128
"My Mother Is a Space Cadet," 54, 261
Mystery Disc, 4, 7, 152, 240, 241, 243,
  249, 279

Nagano, Kent, 81, 125–126
Naked Angels (movie), 250
Nassau Coliseum, 195
National Association of Broadcasters
  (NAB), 225
Negative Dialectics of Poodle Play, The
  (book), 58, 61, 78, 145, 154,
  209, 263, 276
Neon Park (Martin Muller), 128

Nevius, Sally, 224
New England Digital Corporation,
  143
Newman, Janet, 23
Newman, Randy, 83
New Music Express (NME), 21, 105,
  228
Newport All-Stars, the, 179
Newport Jazz Festival, 179
New York, 9, 10, 12, 21, 28, 34, 50, 52,
  71, 86, 91, 98, 163, 170, 174,
  178, 179, 188, 213, 215, 218,
  245, 246, 249, 251, 256, 269
New York Metropolitan Opera, 133
New York Public Library, 133
"Night School," 146
Nightline, 226
Nightwatch, 226
Nile Running Greeting Card Co., 6
"Nine Types of Industrial Pollution,"
  129
"Norwegian Jim," 86
"Norwegian Wood," 86
Novak, Robert, 221–222
Nugent, Ted (the Amboy Dukes), 67
Nuggets, 60

Ocker, David, 145
"Octandre," 12, 23, 24, 115
Odd Life of Timothy Green, The, 55
Offerall, Lucy, 205
O'Hearn, Patrick, 118, 202, 213, 247
"Oh No," 34, 85, 127, 128, 187
Oh No! Not Jazz!!, 100, 266
"Ol' 55," 176
Olsun, Rick, 268
One Shot Deal, 123, 243, 245, 248, 257,
  258, 279
One Size Fits All, 8, 43, 107–108, 116,
  156, 236, 238, 240, 245, 251,
  253, 264, 277
Opa-Locka, Florida, 2
"Opening Night at Studio Z," 7
Opus I Trios (Francesco Zappa), 145

Opus IV Sonatas (Francesco Zappa), 145
"Orange Colored Sky," 243
Orange County, 25
Orchestral Favorites, 68, 69, 123, 130, 140, 168, 230, 233, 234, 248, 268, 277
Original Sound (studios), 138, 281
"Orion," 20
Osaka, Japan, 164
Otis, Johnny, 11, 21, 28, 243
Ottawa, Ontario, 179,
Out to Lunch (Eric Dolphy album), 131
Outlaw, Jerry, 268,
"Outside Now," 61, 110–111
Over-Nite Sensation, xiv, 48, 66, 100, 103, 107, 151, 183, 211, 217, 238, 240, 243, 248, 253, 277
"Overture to a Holiday in Berlin," 170–171

Page, Jimmy, 116
PAL Studio, 6, 137–138
Palais des Sports, 147,
Palladium, the, 80, 213, 246
Palermo, Ed, 100, 266–267
Palermo, Sicily, 80, 187
Palmer, Tony, 55, 205, 207, 209, 216
Panter, Gary, 68
Parents Music Resource Center (PMRC), 224–227
Paris Chamber Orchestra, 14
Paris, France, 12, 14, 18
Parker, Charlie, 5, 40, 233
Parker, Howard, 167
Parker, Scott, 148–150, 274
Parks, Van Dyke, 33
Parlato, Dave, 123, 140, 248
Pasut, Alex, 268
Patterson, Brenda, 67
Paul, Les, 171
Paulekas, Vito, 30
Pauley Pavilion (UCLA), 96–97, 120, 204

Payne, Bill, 38
"Peaches En Regalia," 40, 54, 109, 150, 172, 263, 266, 283
Peacock, Gary, 247
Penguins, the, 21, 114
"Penis Dimension," 208
Pennati, Andrea, 270
Pepsi, 88
Pierrot Lunaire, 208
The Perfect Stranger, 123, 144–145, 148, 152, 200, 217, 278
Perrino, Joe, and the Mellow Tones, 165
Petit Wazoo, 43, 112, 140, 175, 240, 248
Petulant Frenzy, 272
Phantom of the Opera, The (musical), 209
Philip Jones Brass Ensemble, 209
Picker, David, 204
Pinewood Studio, 204–205
Playground Psychotics, 98, 239, 244, 248, 249, 255, 279
Pledge This!, 55
"Po-Jama People," 156
Pojama People (band), 269
Polygram, 68–69
Pomona, California, 26
Pons, Jim, 248
"Porn Wars," 227
"Pound for a Brown on a Bus, A," 4
Pacific Grove, 3
Pandora, 5
Philadelphia, Pennsylvania, 18, 100, 175, 185, 220, 230, 246
Phillips, Earl, 26
Philly '76, 244, 257, 279
Pickett, Wilson, 25
"Planet of the Baritone Women," 110, 280
Playboy, 73, 75, 87, 103
PledgeMusic, 54
Ponty, Jean-Luc, 172, 248
"Poofter's Froth Wyoming Plans Ahead," 104–105

Pratt Library, xiii
"Prelude to the Afternoon of a
    Sexually Aroused Gas Mask,"
    93, 128
Persuasions, the, 175
Prentis, Simon, 138
Preston, Don, 34, 36–37, 42, 45, 128,
    179, 182, 204–205, 216, 229,
    239, 241, 249, 250, 267, 269
Prince, 224
Prism Films, 34, 37, 287
Pro Arte Quartet, 14
PROG (magazine), 44
Pro Tools (software), 169
Project/Object, 198
Progression, 262
"Promiscuous," 102–103
"Punky's Whips," 234
Pursuit of Happiness, The (film), 209
"Pygmy Twylyte," 59

Quaudiophiliac, 239, 240, 245, 248,
    258, 279

RAM (Rock Australia Magazine), 74
Ramblers, the, 165
Rainbow Theatre (London), 41,
    99–100
Raumberger, Gabrielle, 145
RCA-Victor, 92
Read Magazine, 73
Reagan, Ronald, 86, 102–104, 190,
    215–216, 226
Real Frank Zappa Book, The, 2, 26, 73,
    89, 261, 276
Rebennack, Mac (Dr. John), 33
Recording Industry Association of
    America (RIAA), 225
Reed, Jimmy, 26
Religious Right, the, 83, 101, 104, 110,
    131, 228
Relix, 80, 140, 161, 169
Rembrandt, 199
Repercussion Unit, the, 233

"Republicans," 162-163
Return of the Son Of (ZPZ album), 120
"Return of the Son of Monster
    Magnet, The," 93, 109
*Return of the Son of Shut Up 'N Play Yer
    Guitar*, 162, 248, 278
"Revised Music for Guitar & Low-
    Budget Orchestra," 131
Revere, Paul, and the Raiders, 28
Rhino Records, 70, 135–136, 267, 281
Rhinoceros (band), 247
"Rhymin' Man," 110
rhythm 'n' blues (R&B), 5, 21, 43, 44,
    77, 109, 115, 140, 165, 178, 181,
    185, 233, 234, 236, 241, 250
Rice, Bob, 54
Richards, Emil, 123
Richler, Mordecai, 198–199
Rite of Spring, The, 14, 23
Road Tapes, Venue #1, 115, 241, 250,
    252, 280
Robb, David, 185
Robertson, Pat, 86, 104
Robertson, Robbie, 134
Rock, George, 90
RockHEAD, 180
Roddy, Joseph, 11
"Roland's Big Event/Strat Vindaloo,"
    126
Rolling Stone, 28, 65, 78, 161
Rolling Stones, the, 78, 99, 178, 203
"Rollo," 123
Romani, Pierpaolo, 270
Rosanne (TV Show), 55
Rose, Charlie, 226
Rosen, Steve, 168
Rosing, Vladimir, 18
Rossini, Gioacchino, 92
Roxy by Proxy, 118, 239, 240, 243, 280
Roxy & Elsewhere, 10, 48, 59, 117, 166,
    183, 236, 238, 240, 243, 249,
    250, 251, 253, 263
Roxy Music, 244
Royal Festival Hall, 210

Royal Philharmonic Orchestra, 122, 205, 210
Royce Hall (UCLA), 123, 168
"Rubber Shirt," 173
Rundgren, Todd, 54, 247
Run Home Slow, 4, 6
Russo, Greg, 67, 135, 275
Rykodisc, 69–71, 81, 149–152, 251, 274

Safe as Milk, 45
"St. Alphonso's Pancake Breakfast," 183
"St. Etienne," 131, 147
St. Urbain's Horseman, 199
Salonen, Esa-Pekka, 55, 209–210
San Anselmo, California, 192
San Bernardino, California, 3, 7, 26
"San Ber'dino," 8
Sanders, Ed, 151, 154, 224
San Diego, California, 3
San Fernando Valley, 53
Satie, Erik, 12
Schenkel, Cal, 41, 63, 84–85, 108, 136, 156, 170, 200–201, 204, 207, 249–250
Schoenberg, Arnold, 14, 23, 76, 208
Sgt. Pepper's Lonely Hearts Club Band, 35–36, 63, 83–84, 126, 199
SCRIPT (software program), 143
Secret Garden, The (musical), 209
SeaTac, Washington, 217
Seattle, Washington, 211, 217
"Set Up Two Glasses, Joe," 105
"Shaft," 271
Shankar, L., 69, 126
Shankar, Ravi, 178
Shannon, Joyce, 6
"Sharleena," 86, 97, 261
Shay, Gary, 88
Sheik Yerbouti, 69, 88, 113–114, 118, 155, 158, 172, 202, 231, 234, 236, 246, 258, 277
Shell Shocked: My Life with the Turtles, Flo & Eddie, Frank Zappa, etc . . . (book), 57, 94, 229, 244

Sherman, Kay, 6, 218
Sherwood, James "Motorhead," 34, 36–37, 204, 250
Ship Arriving Too Late to Save a Drowning Witch, 239, 242, 246, 247, 256, 278
"Short People," 83
Shut Up 'N Play Yer Guitar, 81, 162, 237, 238, 239, 242, 244, 248, 258, 278
Shut Up 'N Play Yer Guitar Some More, 162, 278
Sicily, 1, 80, 187
Silver, Horace, 40
Simon & Garfunkel, 174–175
Simon, Paul, 174
Simmons, Jeff, 93, 98, 204, 250
"Sinister Footwear," 24, 182
"Six Bagatelles for String Quartet, Op. 9," 14, 23
"Sixteen Tons," 137
Slaven, Neil, 3, 29, 38, 87, 96, 164, 275
Sleep Dirt, 68–69, 123, 130, 140, 234, 236, 238, 240, 242, 247, 248, 251, 253, 277
"Sleeping in a Jar," 4
Sloatman, Gail, 51
Slonimsky, Nicolas, 18–20
Smithtown, New York, 90
"Smoke on the Water," 54, 99, 136
Snider, Dee, 226
Snyder, Michael, 57
Snyder, Tom, 128
"Sofa," 156
Solomon, Jon, 265
"Son of the Monster Magnet," 40
"Song to the Siren," 65,
Songwriter Connection, 88
"Sound of Silence, The," 175
Southern Pacific Railroad, 90
Soul Giants, the, 7–8, 25–27, 234, 238, 239
Sovetov, Vladimir, 10
"Space Guitar," 22
Spain, 161, 197

Spanner Jazz Punks, 272
Spectrum, The, 174
Sporthalle, 196
Spaniels, the, 21
"Stairway to Heaven," 116, 237, 283
Stamp, Chris, 52
Standells, the, 37
Starr, Ringo, 86, 205
Starsailor, 65
Steely Dan, 175, 242, 263
Steve Allen Show, The, 218, 287
"Stevie's Spanking," 253
Sting, 24, 110, 177, 237
Stix, John, 73
Stockhausen, Karlheinz, 35
"Stolen Moments," 23–24, 110
Stone, Bob, 54, 251
Straight Record Label, 38, 45, 47, 62,
     64–65, 67, 250, 255
Strictly Commercial, 70, 151, 280
"Strictly Genteel," 123, 126
Strauss, Johann, 92
Stravinsky, Igor, 5, 11, 14–15, 18, 23–24,
     115, 120–121, 125, 142, 170
"Strawberry Fields Forever," 84, 86
String Quartet N14, Op. 131
     (Beethoven), 199
Stuart, Alice, 33
Studebacher Hoch, 98, 120
Studio Tan, 68, 92, 123, 130, 140, 230,
     233, 234, 238, 240, 244, 248,
     251, 253, 277
Studio Z, 6–7, 26, 138–140, 143, 151,
     218–219
"Subterranean Homesick Blues," 87
Sun Ra, 40
Surfmen, the, 26
Sutcliffe, Stuart, 25
Sydney, Australia, 220, 272
"Symphony of Living," 4
"Symphony Op. 21" (Webern), 14–15, 23
Synclavier, 18, 123, 125, 131, 138,
     143–146, 148, 169, 215–216,
     222, 227, 253

Synclavier II DMS, 143
Swaggart, Jimmy, 86
Sweden, 103
Swenson, John, 73

Taj Mahal, 175
Tampa Bay, Florida, 268
Tank C, 8
Taylor, Cecil, 40, 43, 131
Taylor, Livingston, 175
"Texas Medley," 86
"Texas Motel," 86
Thanks to Frank, 188
Them or Us (album), 55, 200, 236, 238,
     239, 242, 247, 261, 278
Them or Us (book), 200–201
"Theme from Burnt Weeny
     Sandwich," 170
Thesaurus of Scales and Melodic Patterns,
     19–20
Thicke, Alan, 77
Thing-Fish, 23, 131–132, 227, 234, 236,
     239, 242, 256, 257, 278
"Things That I Used to Do, The," 22
Three Stooges, The, 91
Thome, Joel, 245
Thompson, Barbara, 159
Thompson, Chester, 116, 211, 251
"Three Places in New England," 19
Thriller, 88
Thunes, Scott, 54–55, 190–193,
     195–197, 209, 214, 251
"Three Hours Past Midnight," 23
Tinsel Town Rebellion, 80–81, 118,
     237–238, 242, 248, 253, 256,
     258, 278
T'Mershi Duween (fanzine), 125, 175,
     191, 231, 268
Today Show, 222
Token of His Extreme, A, 211, 213, 217,
     220, 236, 239, 240, 251, 280
Top Score Singers, 205
Tornadoes, the, 137

Toronto, Ontario, xi, xiii, xiv, 148, 158–159, 175, 263–264
Torreano, Bradley, 269
"Torture Never Stops, The," 8, 88, 151
Touch Me There, 69
"Tour de Frank" (ZPZ), 261
Trance-Fusion, 162, 240, 245, 257, 258, 279
Transition Records, 40
Travers, Joe, 43, 70, 115, 139–140, 142, 152, 172, 217, 274
Trenner, Donn, 218
Trieste, Italy, 34
Tripp, Art, 17, 35–37, 48, 129, 248, 252
Trotter, John Scott, 91
True Story of Frank Zappa's 200 Motels, The, 216
Trout Mask Replica, 44–48, 65, 241, 250, 255
"Trouble Every Day," 29, 109, 223, 282
Tune In, 25
Turin, Italy, 12
Turner, Ted, 220
Turtles, the, 93–97, 99, 120, 204, 244, 248, 255
200 Motels, 55, 86, 97–98, 122, 134–135, 141, 203, 205, 207–211

Ugly Radio Rebellion, 258
U.K. (band), 244
UMRK, 70–71, 137–139, 141–142, 144, 151–152
"Unanswered Question, The," 16
Under the Same Moon (book), 242
Unified Field Theory (UFT), 201
United Artists, 204–205, 208
Uniondale, New York, 195
"Uncle Frankie Show, The," 140
Uncle Meat (album), 63, 128, 150, 238, 239, 241, 247, 249, 252, 277
Uncle Meat (film), 10, 120, 203, 205, 216, 242, 282
Underwood, Ian, 34, 36–38, 55, 64–65, 93, 98, 129, 170–171, 181, 191, 204, 209, 252

Underwood, Ruth, 116, 124, 187, 211, 245, 253
Unicorn, The, 62
United Mutations, xi, 30, 79
US Senate Committee on Commerce, Science, and Transportation Hearing, 226
US Constitution, 8, 60, 79, 224
Utility Muffin Research Kitchen (UMRK), 70–71, 137–139, 141–142, 144, 151–152

Vai, Steve, 119, 151, 158, 169, 191–192, 214, 217, 237, 242, 245, 253, 254, 261
"Valarie," 170–171
"Valley Girl," 53, 100, 153–154, 283
Van Halen, 54
Van Halen, Eddie, 260
Van Nuys, California, 10, 251
Van Vliet, Don, 5, 7, 44–45, 48, 50, 250, 255
Vards, the, 54
Varèse, Edgard, 5, 11–13, 15, 18–20, 23, 115, 116, 121, 123, 126, 128, 270
"Variations on America," 16
Vaulternative Records, 70
Vee-Jay Records, 26
Velours, the, 23–24
Vengerova, Isabelle, 18
Venice Biennale, 271
Ventures, the, 26, 94
Vestine, Henry, 34
Via Zamatta, 263
Vienna, Austria, 14
Vienna University, 14
Video from Hell, 215, 282
Vilnius, Lithuania, xiii
Viscounts, the, 26
Volman, Mark, 94–99, 120, 204, 229, 244, 255
Volpacchio, Florindo, 75

Wackerman, Chad, 54, 149, 188, 190, 194, 196, 214, 246, 256
Waits, Tom, 175–176
Waka Jawaka, 41–43, 100, 140, 230, 238–239, 249, 277
Walker, T-Bone, 21
Walley, Denny, 48, 256, 269
Ward, Burt, 243
Warner Bros. Records, 31, 63–64, 66–68, 80, 123, 130, 135, 152, 213, 249
"Watermelon in Easter Hay," 164, 283
Watson, Ben, 8, 58, 61, 78, 87, 145, 154, 209, 263
Watson, Johnny "Guitar," 5, 11, 21, 23, 40, 124, 165
Watts, Ernie, 41, 248
"Watts Riot," 29
Watts, California, 239
Weasels Ripped My Flesh, 37–38, 85, 93, 128, 238, 239, 241, 242, 243, 247, 252, 277
Webern, Anton, 14–15, 18, 23, 121, 126
Wein, George, 179
Weingarten, Christopher, 140
We're Only in It for the Money, 34–36, 63, 84, 126, 216, 234, 239, 241, 247, 250, 277
Wexler, Haskell, 216
"Washington Post," 17
What's My Line?, 211
"What's the Name of Your Group?," 210
"While You Were Art II," 146
"Whipping Post," 54
Who, the, 52, 99, 178, 205
"Who Needs the Peace Corps?," 126
Whisky a Go Go, the, 32–33, 62
White, Ray, 181, 189, 214, 247, 257, 269
"White Christmas," 91
"Why Is the Doctor Barking?," 266
"Why Don't You Like Me?," 88
Wichita, Kansas, 25

Wikipedia, 200
Wilber, Jason, 186
Wilkins, Thomas, 268
Willis, Ike, 86, 103, 110–111, 181, 189, 190, 194, 196, 215, 240, 257, 268–269
Willis, Jim, Sgt., 7
"Willie the Pimp," 109–110, 172, 233, 255
Wilson, Donald Roller, 145–146, 200
Wilson, Tom, 33, 39–40, 63, 87
Wing, Albert, 164, 190, 194, 247
WNEW, 91
Wolf, Peter, 118, 213, 258
Woodstock Festival, 37,
Woodstock, New York, 133, 178–180
The Words and Music of Frank Zappa, 100, 103, 111, 155
World-Wide Symphony Orchestra, 14
World War II, 5, 91
"WPLJ," 170, 282
"Wyatt Earp Makes Me Burp," 93

Xenochrony, 202

Yale, 16, 34
The Yellow Shark, 18, 122, 270, 279
"Yo Mama," 202
You Are What You Is, 55, 132, 150, 242, 256, 278
"You Are What You Is," 119, 216, 230–231, 283
You Can't Do That on Stage Anymore, Vol. 2, 116, 278
You Can't Do That on Stage Anymore, Vol. 3, 55, 278
You Can't Do That on Stage Anymore, Vol. 5, 17, 141, 238, 242, 247, 278
Youngbloods, the, 174
Young, Jesse Colin, 175
"Your Mouth," 42
YouTube, 4–5, 82, 134, 139, 163, 164, 165, 204, 218, 222, 271
Yvega, Todd, 125, 138

Z (Band), 139
Z3, the, 245
Zarubica, Pamela (Pam Z.), 51, 64
Zappa! (magazine), 20, 77
Zappa, Ahmet, 52, 54–55, 70–71, 260
Zappa, Carl, 10
Zappa, Diva, 52–53, 55, 209–210, 260
Zappa, Dweezil, xiii, 52–54, 68, 70,
    130, 139, 161, 164–165, 167,
    177, 217, 236, 257, 260–265
Zappa Family Trust, 55, 70–71, 152,
    210, 260, 268, 277
Zappa, Francis, 1–2, 6
Zappa, Francesco (composer), 145,
    201
Zappa, Gail (née Sloatman), 51–52,
    56, 70, 71, 85, 139–140, 142,
    145, 152, 217
Zappa in New York, 53, 67, 86, 130, 140,
    233, 234, 236, 244, 245, 247,
    253, 257, 277

Zappa, Moon Unit, 20, 52–54, 64, 100,
    155, 217, 260
Zappa, Patrice "Candy," 1–2, 9
Zappa Plays Zappa, xiii, 54, 120,
    165, 236, 255, 257, 260–261,
    263–264
Zappa, Robert (Bobby) 2, 4, 9
Zappa, Rose Marie (née Colimore),
    1–2, 9
Zappa the Hard Way, 193, 197, 274
Zappa Wiki Jawaka (website), 200
Zappanale festival, 10, 251, 271–272
Zappa's Universe, 245
Zappaween, 269
Zavod, Allan, 258–259
Zearott, Michael, 123
Zig Zag, 27
"Zomby Woof," 100, 107, 270, 283
Zoot Allures, 8, 31, 67, 163–164, 234,
    236, 239, 240, 248, 253, 277
Zuck, Barbara, 86

THE FAQ SERIES

AC/DC FAQ
by Susan Masino
Backbeat Books
9781480394506.................$24.99

Armageddon Films FAQ
by Dale Sherman
Applause Books
9781617131196.........................$24.99

Lucille Ball FAQ
*by James Sheridan
and Barry Monush*
Applause Books
9781617740824.........................$19.99

Baseball FAQ
by Tom DeMichael
Backbeat Books
9781617136061.........................$24.99

The Beach Boys FAQ
by Jon Stebbins
Backbeat Books
9780879309879 ....$22.99

The Beat Generation FAQ
by Rich Weidman
Backbeat Books
9781617136016 ....$19.99

Black Sabbath FAQ
by Martin Popoff
Backbeat Books
9780879309572...................$19.99

Johnny Cash FAQ
by C. Eric Banister
Backbeat Books
9781480385405.................$24.99

A Chorus Line FAQ
by Tom Rowan
Applause Books
9781480367548 ....$19.99

Eric Clapton FAQ
by David Bowling
Backbeat Books
9781617134548 ....$22.99

Doctor Who FAQ
by Dave Thompson
Applause Books
9781557838544....................$22.99

The Doors FAQ
by Rich Weidman
Backbeat Books
978161713017-5........ $24.99

Dracula FAQ
by Bruce Scivally
Backbeat Books
9781617136009 ....$19.99

The Eagles FAQ
by Andrew Vaughan
Backbeat Books
9781480385412....................$24.99

Fab Four FAQ
*by Stuart Shea and
Robert Rodriguez*
Hal Leonard Books
9781423421382....................$19.99

Fab Four FAQ 2.0
by Robert Rodriguez
Backbeat Books
9780879309688...................$19.99

Film Noir FAQ
by David J. Hogan
Applause Books
9781557838551....................$22.99

Football FAQ
by Dave Thompson
Backbeat Books
9781495007484 ....$24.99

The Grateful Dead FAQ
by Tony Sclafani
Backbeat Books
9781617130861...................... $24.99

Haunted America FAQ
by Dave Thompson
Backbeat Books
9781480392625......................$19.99

Jimi Hendrix FAQ
by Gary J. Jucha
Backbeat Books
9781617130953.......................$22.99

Horror Films FAQ
by John Kenneth Muir
Applause Books
9781557839503 ....$22.99

Michael Jackson FAQ
by Kit O'Toole
Backbeat Books
9781480371064 ....$19.99

James Bond FAQ
by Tom DeMichael
Applause Books
9781557838568....................$22.99

Stephen King Films FAQ
by Scott Von Doviak
Applause Books
9781480355514 .... $24.99

KISS FAQ
by Dale Sherman
Backbeat Books
9781617130915.......................$24.99

Led Zeppelin FAQ
by George Case
Backbeat Books
9781617130250 ....$22.99

M.A.S.H. FAQ
by Dale Sherman
Applause Books
9781480355897......................$19.99

Modern Sci-Fi Films FAQ
by Tom DeMichael
Applause Books
9781480350618 ....$24.99

Morrissey FAQ
by D. McKinney
Backbeat Books
9781480394483..................$24.99

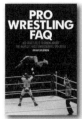    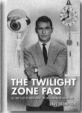 

Nirvana FAQ
by John D. Luerssen
Backbeat Books
9781617134500......................$24.99

Pink Floyd FAQ
by Stuart Shea
Backbeat Books
9780879309503......................$19.99

Elvis Films FAQ
by Paul Simpson
Applause Books
9781557838582......................$24.99

Elvis Music FAQ
by Mike Eder
Backbeat Books
9781617130496......................$24.99

Pearl Jam FAQ
*by Bernard M. Corbett and
Thomas Edward Harkins*
Backbeat Books
9781617136122........................$19.99

Prog Rock FAQ
by Will Romano
Backbeat Books
9781617135873......................$24.99

Pro Wrestling FAQ
by Brian Solomon
Backbeat Books
9781617135996......................$29.99

**The Rocky Horror
Picture Show FAQ**
by Dave Thompson
Applause Books
9781495007477......................$19.99

Rush FAQ
by Max Mobley
Backbeat Books
9781617134517........................$19.99

Saturday Night Live FAQ
by Stephen Tropiano
Applause Books
9781557839510......................$24.99

Seinfeld FAQ
by Nicholas Nigro
Applause Books
9781557838575......................$24.99

Sherlock Holmes FAQ
by Dave Thompson
Applause Books
9781480331495......................$24.99

The Smiths FAQ
by John D. Luerssen
Backbeat Books
9781480394490......................$24.99

Soccer FAQ
by Dave Thompson
Backbeat Books
9781617135989......................$24.99

The Sound of Music FAQ
by Barry Monush
Applause Books
9781480360433......................$27.99

South Park FAQ
by Dave Thompson
Applause Books
9781480350649......................$24.99

Bruce Springsteen FAQ
by John D. Luerssen
Backbeat Books
9781617130939......................$22.99

Star Trek FAQ
(Unofficial and Unauthorized)
by Mark Clark
Applause Books
9781557837929......................$19.99

Star Trek FAQ 2.0
(Unofficial and Unauthorized)
by Mark Clark
Applause Books
9781557837936......................$22.99

Star Wars FAQ
by Mark Clark
Applause Books
978480360181......................$24.99

Quentin Tarantino FAQ
by Dale Sherman
Applause Books
9781480355880......................$24.99

Three Stooges FAQ
by David J. Hogan
Applause Books
9781557837882......................$22.99

TV Finales FAQ
*by Stephen Tropiano and
Holly Van Buren*
Applause Books
9781480391444......................$19.99

The Twilight Zone FAQ
by Dave Thompson
Applause Books
9781480396180......................$19.99

Twin Peaks FAQ
*by David Bushman and
Arthur Smith*
Applause Books
9781495015861......................$19.99

The Who FAQ
by Mike Segretto
Backbeat Books
9781480361034......................$24.99

The Wizard of Oz FAQ
by David J. Hogan
Applause Books
9781480350625......................$24.99

The X-Files FAQ
by John Kenneth Muir
Applause Books
9781480369740......................$24.99

Neil Young FAQ
by Glen Boyd
Backbeat Books
9781617130373......................$19.99

Frank Zappa FAQ
by John Corcelli
Backbeat Books
9781617136030......................$19.99

HAL•LEONARD®
PERFORMING ARTS
PUBLISHING GROUP

FAQ.halleonardbooks.com

0316